THE BLACK RIVER
CHRONICLES
THE URSVAAL EXCHANGE

David Tallerman

DIGITAL FICTION
PUBLISHING CORP

DEDICATION

This one's for Flick, with thanks for the
never-ending Disney marathon.

Raoul appears in chapter seven. Look for
the burning dead guy.

Introduction

We've all been there.

You're still high from the adrenaline rush of having competed in your first role-playing campaign, having taken your Character[1] from a set of dice rolls on a piece of paper through to them becoming a fully-rounded person in their own right. You're buzzing from having slain the dragon / the wizard / the extra-planar entity and stolen your foe's treasure, experience points have been dished out like Halloween candy, and then you level up…and promptly fall at the first hurdle.

Your sword skills aren't what you thought they were, those spells you learned when you were starting out really won't cut the mustard anymore, and you feel like more of a noob than you did when you set out on your first adventure[2].

Welcome to Level Two.

This is the situation the heroes of *The Black River Chronicles* find themselves in within the opening chapter of this, the second book in the series. David Tallerman reintroduces us to Arein the dwarfish wizard, Hule the barbarian fighter, Tia the dun-elf rogue, and Durren Flintrand the ranger-in-training and the party's would-be leader—not forgetting the adorable Pootle—with all the skill of a consummate master storyteller.

We've all been all of them, at one time or another. The wizard afraid of her own abilities, unwilling to give in to her

---

[1] The capital 'C' is important.

[2] If you've never taken part in a role-playing game before (a) why the hell not? (b) join a role-playing group immediately and sign up for your first RPG session (c) replace the above analogy with a promotion at work; it pretty much amounts to the same thing, but with less magical axes and gribbly monsters. (The world of work, I mean.)

burgeoning powers lest she lose control. The taciturn warrior, whose reticence other people mistake for ignorance. The prickly rogue, impatient of others and with her own secret agenda. And the ranger, the victim of the high expectations placed upon him, none more so than by himself–under so much pressure to succeed, not wanting to let the mask of composed discipline slip for a second.

Through these disparate individuals, Tallerman takes us inside the world of the Black River Academy of Swordcraft and Spellcraft, but we don't remain there for long. The shadow of the events related in the first volume looms large over those in this second tale, and just as we and the gang are settling back into the old routine, Durren and the rest are dispatched to another school of student adventurers as part of an exchange.

And so they find themselves at the grim and dour Shadow Mountain Academy, appropriately enough, in the province of Ursvaal[3], with Durren in particular feeling like he's starting from Level One again. It's not so much a fish out of water story, as a koi carp plucked from its ornamental oriental pond and dropped into the ocean[4] story, and from there things only go from bad to worse.

But then, if they didn't, how could our heroes prove themselves to be just that?

Jonathan Green
London, November 2017

---

[3] Think Transylvania squared.
[4] An ocean full of sharks.

Chapter 1

So far, Durren thought—as he dodged to avoid a wad of saliva that splashed with a hiss against the trunk of the tree beside him—level two was turning out to be an awful lot like level one.

"Watch out for their spit!" he yelled to no-one in particular. "It burns."

"We wouldn't *have* to watch out if someone hadn't picked a campsite near a swamp," snapped back Tia.

Durren withdrew a hasty pace. The thing before him was monstrous: its slit eyes were yellow and bulbous, its mouth was a gash almost too wide for its head, its pale throat beat with a hypnotic pulse, and its skin was a crust of mottled purple. Nevertheless, despite the fact that what he was looking at was big as a large dog, he knew that the creature was basically a toad. And he was struggling to feel really intimidated by a giant toad.

Then the monster opened its mouth—the sight of that gaping cavity was almost paralyzing—and Durren barely had a moment to react as its tongue flicked out. He threw himself left, and the cord of pink flesh whipped past his ear, speckling him with stinging dribbles of saliva.

All right, he admitted to himself, *that was intimidating.*

Durren just kept to his feet. Nevertheless, he managed to free his bow from his shoulder and nock an arrow to the string, almost in the same smooth motion. That done, he spared a glance to make sure the others were all intact.

Hule was over to his right, and the big fighter already had his sword in hand. His expression was dour, though; he didn't look half as pleased as he normally did at the prospect of putting the weapon to use.

Arein was close to Hule, and the dwarfish wizard was conspicuously not casting any spells. Durren had hoped she was finally getting over her resistance to using magic, but apparently not today.

Tia, meanwhile, was to his left, the black of her cloak camouflaging her amid the shade of the trees. That she was still here at all surprised him; her first instinct as a rogue tended to be to vanish and attend to matters on her own.

All three of them were retreating towards the center of the clearing where they'd made their fire and raised their two tents, and Durren did the same—if only to get out of range of that hideous tongue. He dared one more glance, this time seeking their observer: the leathery, one-eyed entity that Arein, for reasons that made sense solely to her, had chosen to name Pootle. He spotted the little orb hovering near the treetops, staring down at them with grave attention.

In theory, someone back at the academy was watching them via the spell attuned to Pootle, and in theory they'd send help if the situation should grow too dangerous. But the five of them had been in some exceedingly dangerous situations before now and help had been conspicuous by its absence, so Durren wasn't holding his breath.

After a half-dozen steps, there was nowhere left to retreat to. Durren could feel the canvas of the nearest tent pressing against his ankle. He didn't like the idea of killing these dumb beasts, which were only being hostile because they knew no better. *Do no harm unless harm be done* was one of the Black River Academy's many cryptic mantras, and they'd been taught from the outset that their weapons were a final recourse, to be used when options such as talking and running were thoroughly exhausted.

Well, they were surrounded on all sides, so they wouldn't be running, and while Durren was no expert on giant toads, he was confident that their unusual properties didn't extend to making conversation.

Then the choice was out of his hands. As though with one mind, the toads were advancing from the shade of the clearing's outer edge. They moved in flabby hops that made their entire bodies quiver and covered a distance Durren could hardly believe. The one that had picked him out closed half the gap between them in a single leap. Barely had it touched the ground before it was in the air again and sailing towards him, its cavernous maw stretched wide.

Durren threw himself lengthwise and loosed his arrow. He heard the slap of the toad's landing, but didn't get to see whether his shot had flown true until he rolled back to his feet. The toad had come to rest on the nearer tent, the one that was his and Hule's. Its impact had collapsed the canvas wall, tearing the guy ropes loose. Durren's arrow had entered through the creature's throat and exited above its right eye; he could see where the metal head jutted, dripping violet ichor. Sprawled with arms and legs protruding, the toad's body practically covered the deflated tent.

Durren's first thought was, *Now where am I meant to sleep?* His second was the realization that the animal was dead and that he had killed it.

To his right, Hule was hacking at a cluster of three toads, all of which were managing to dodge aside with startling agility. Arein was waving her staff in the face of another, which seemed to Durren a singular waste of the most powerful tool at their disposal.

He considered telling her so, but by then a second toad had him in its goggle-eyed sights; he was alerted by a sizzle and a wet splatter, which he recognized for the sound of acid saliva striking the surviving tent. The culprit was glaring at him, in as much as an oversized amphibian was capable of glaring. Its mouth hung open, ready to unleash more spit or perhaps to unfurl its bullwhip tongue.

Durren cursed beneath his breath. Their actual quest had gone so smoothly—too smoothly, it seemed now. They'd been sent to sweep and clear some old mine workings supposedly infested with goblins, but they'd soon realized that the goblins had departed long ago, leaving only foulness and clutter to testify to their residence. Nevertheless, they'd explored from top to bottom, and Hule had insisted on drawing a map, even though Tia was adamant that the mining company would certainly have more accurate maps of their own.

But reaching level two, they'd been told, meant new challenges, and one of those was that they could no longer simply have Pootle transport them back to the academy once their quest was complete. Now they were to camp the night in the wilderness and travel the next day to a given extraction point.

All of which should have been straightforward—except that barely had they raised their tents and set a fire when the toads had found them.

Nearby, Arein yelped. Durren's initial impulse was to run and help her; the moment's distraction was enough that, when the toad spat again, he almost failed to duck aside in time. Immediately it seized upon the opportunity to hop closer—so that its mouth was suddenly right in front of him, like a fleshy passage into some awful netherworld. Durren's shock sent the arrow he loosed wide, grazing the creature's warty head and leaving a streak of violet, but otherwise merely making the beast angrier than it already was.

There was something unreasonably menacing about an enraged giant toad. Though Durren knew he should grasp for another arrow or for his short sword, he chose instead to stumble backward, until a wash of heat alerted him to the fact that there was nowhere left to go—not with their campfire directly behind him. To right and left he was conscious of the others fighting, and instinct assured him that they too were being driven back. Hemmed in and encircled, they'd be in serious trouble.

Durren expected the toad to press its advantage; one good hop and it would be on him. Rather, it shifted sideways, keeping the same distance, its springy limbs unsuited to such careful maneuvering. Durren wouldn't have known where to begin in reading toad physiognomy, yet something in the way its eyes flickered told him it was troubled. Maybe his arrow had deterred the purple monstrosity after all, or maybe—

"Fire!" Durren cried. Realizing that word alone wasn't

useful, he added, "They don't like the fire...that's why they're not coming any closer."

With his free hand, he snatched a brand from the flames, choosing a branch that blazed fiercely at one end and was untouched at the other. Still, the heat was intense. Durren ignored the discomfort and, not daring to give too much consideration to what he was about to do, charged towards the nearby toad. He bellowed incoherently—did toads even have ears?—and flailed with his improvised weapon, drawing stripes of fire across the air.

For a second he thought that he was wrong and that he was charging straight into the toad's yawning mouth: no animal, he felt, should be able to open its jaw so wide. Then the toad let out a raucous trill and took a rapid rearwards hop. Somehow it managed to flop around in midair, and its second bound carried it beyond the edge of the clearing, this time heading in the right direction.

By then Durren's torch was beginning to waver, and the licking flames threatened his fingers. He threw the brand after the retreating toad, wrapped his hand in his sleeve, and dashed back to the fire to claim another. He saw that both Hule and Tia had followed his example, and Arein had belatedly recalled that she was capable of casting spells: a ball of flickering orange burned about the tip of her outstretched staff.

Durren snatched up a second branch, but by that time there was really no need. Hule and Tia had both managed to dissuade their respective foes, and Arein was having even more success. The toads evidently weren't at all happy with this being not a great deal taller than themselves who could conjure fire out of thin air. Everywhere they were backing off or turning and fleeing, accompanied by a chorus of panicked croaking.

Seconds later and the battle was over. Nothing was to be seen of the toads except for a few scattered bodies and the desolation they'd left in their wake. Durren and Hule's tent might be ruined, and Arein and Tia's had three holes in its flank, seared by acid spittle; it wouldn't be offering much in the way of shelter if the gray skies overhead should unleash their burden of rain.

"Is everyone all right?" Durren asked.

Remembering how Arein had cried out, he realized that a gash had been burned in her left sleeve and that the red of singed skin was visible through the tear. Like the tent, she had evidently fallen foul of the toads' spit. Thankfully, the burn appeared slight, and Hule already had his water flask in one hand and a roll of bandage in the other. The fighter himself was unscathed, though his boots and trousers were filthy with mud; the ground of the clearing had been churned up by feet both humanoid and toad.

Durren looked to Tia, content in the knowledge that out of all of them she was certain to have escaped harm: uncommon dexterity was only one of the traits that made her wholly unsuited to being a mere level two student. Sure enough, she wasn't even out of breath. At that moment, having plucked a throwing knife from between the bulging eyes of a dead toad, she was wiping off the violet gunk that passed for their blood in the long grass.

Tia slipped the knife back into the bandolier she wore inside her cloak. "They won't stay away for long," she said. "We need to get packed up and away from here." She turned on Durren then, and her dark gray skin was darker still for the frown she wore. "And I don't care whether you're the ranger; I'm choosing where we spend the night."

"Look," Durren said, "this wasn't my fault. I mean, it *was* my fault, but it could have happened to anyone."

Tia's pale eyes were bright amid the shadows of her hood. "Oh…really?"

Her tone sent a shiver through Durren's spine, but he wasn't willing to back down. "They just—you know—wandered here. Sometimes monsters do that. I mean, wherever you camp there's always a chance of that happening."

Tia's glare somehow intensified. "Durren, this wasn't some random encounter. This happened because you picked the wrong campsite. Now are you going to stand here arguing, or are you actually going to be some help?"

He gave up. She was right. If he concentrated, he could catch the acrid odor of unclean water that should have alerted him; there was a swamp nearby, and even a brand-new first level student should have the brains to appreciate that where there was a swamp there would be something unpleasant making its home. The fact was, the tiredness of a long day trudging through the mines had made him sloppy, as the stench of goblin refuse had muted his sense of smell.

He knew he should apologize. He would have done but for Tia's manner. He wasn't the only person who'd ever made a mistake, and her inability to be pleasant or even basically well-mannered hardly counted as good teamwork. Worse, he suspected she had let him go wrong to make a point; if she'd known the spot was no good, why couldn't she simply have told him so? Her attitude was just as much a liability to their party as his own act of carelessness.

Well, maybe not *just* as much. Still, he had no intention of saying sorry until she did. Except that Tia never would—Durren wasn't persuaded that dun-elves understood the concept—and that meant the rest of the expedition was likely to be awkward at best.

With a sigh, he plodded over to make a start on the task of hauling the toad he'd killed off the remains of his and Hule's tent. This had already been a long day, and he had a hunch that he might not have seen the worst of it yet. Bloodthirsty giant amphibians were one thing, but he'd rather face those than Tia's bad temper.

To be on the safe side, they each took a brand from the fire to safeguard their retreat. However, they saw no further sign of their adversaries. Likely they were all back beneath the waters of the swamp, nursing their wounds and plotting a ghastly revenge upon the next travelers who happened by. They'd certainly seemed a lot more malicious than Durren had ever given toads credit for being.

Tia kept them walking for an hour, even though everyone was weary and footsore. While Arein never complained, Durren could tell from the way she winced with each step that the burn on her arm was bothering her. He wondered about suggesting that they just pick the next decent spot, but he knew exactly what Tia's reply would be, and he wasn't ready for another confrontation.

Instead, he found his attention drifting to Hule. The big fighter was uncommonly glum, when generally he could be relied on to retain his good humor whatever the circumstances.

Durren sidled over. "What's wrong?" he asked. "I'd have thought you'd have been glad of a good scrap."

Hule grimaced. His mouth opened and closed; he appeared to be struggling to find the words he was after. Of course, Hule had spent much of the last few months pretending to be the monosyllabic barbarian warrior that a stranger might easily take him for, and even now he had a tendency to slip back into that persona whenever his concentration lapsed.

Eventually he said, all in one burst, "Do you ever doubt that you've chosen the right class?"

That was the last response Durren had expected, and it was his turn to struggle for an answer. "Not really," he tried. "I mean, I suppose the question never crossed my mind. Ever since my father let me learn archery when I was little, I felt as though that was the thing I was best at. So when I heard there was a way to use it and learn lots of other skills too, and then travel around and help people…what I mean is, from the first time I heard that there were rangers out there, I wanted to be one."

He understood too late that his answer was precisely the opposite of what Hule had needed to hear; his downturned countenance was a sure giveaway.

"Look," Durren said, "I don't see the problem. What's wrong with being a fighter?"

If anything, Hule's expression sank further. "What's right with it? Rogues are sneaky. Wizards get to cast spells. You've got your bow and arrows. Fighters just fight."

"You *like* fighting," Durren pointed out. Better that than indignantly explaining how much more there was to being a ranger than having a bow and arrows.

"Not against toads. Fighting toads is stupid."

"Not when the toads are as big as sheep and intent on eating you."

Hule's only reply was a shrug that said that, in his eyes, there could be no conflict against the forces of toad-kind that wasn't inherently idiotic.

Durren gave up. Perhaps Hule was going through some sort of existential crisis, or perhaps this was the particular form his tiredness was taking; either way, Durren could think of no argument to persuade him.

Fortunately, Tia called a halt not long after that. She'd been scouting a little way ahead, and now she reappeared—in that particularly annoying way she had, where one minute she was nowhere to be seen and the next she was directly in front of you—and said, "Follow me."

There was no denying that the site she'd chosen was in every way better than Durren's attempt. The ground rose above the general level of the forest, the trees around were sparser, and an outcrop of stone broke through the grass, perfect to provide them with a little shade. He could even hear the tinkle of water; investigating, he discovered a spring feeding into a sliver of stream on the far side of the rock.

Durren was glad of that. Not only had he emptied his drinking flask during the unexpected march, but his clothes were all spattered with violet blood, and the stuff was beginning to smell. However, the sun was already low upon the horizon, and he'd hardly begun the job of cleaning himself before Tia was demanding coldly that he join Hule in rigging their tents.

Luckily, none of the ropes had broken under the toad's weight, and so they had a single undamaged tent at least. He and Hule quickly agreed that the two of them would take the one with the three holes burned in its side, which they'd patched as well as they could in what daylight remained.

Arein was sat by the fire rebandaging her arm, and being Arein, her first reaction was to protest. "You're just doing that because you're boys and we're girls. Tia and I are every bit as capable of being rained on as you are."

"But you're the one who's hurt," Hule responded. "So you sleep in the good tent, and that's the end of the discussion."

Arein gave him a shy smile. "In that case," she said, "thank you. That's very kind."

She was obviously having difficulty with the strip of fresh bandage she'd half-managed to wrap around her bicep. With a grunt, Hule knelt to take over, and this time Arein made no protest.

Durren sat down on the other side of her, glad of the fire's warmth. "Where's Tia?" he asked.

"Gone to get us something to eat," Arein said—and flinched, as Hule pulled the bandage tight and knotted its ends. "Do you think it'll scar?" she asked him.

Hule shook his head. "In a week you'll never know it was there."

"Oh." Arein sounded disappointed.

Tia was soon back, carrying three plump rush hens. As she set about preparing them with deft flicks of her knife, her eyes roved over the campsite—and Durren had no doubt that she was inspecting his and Hule's efforts in putting up and repairing the two tents. Well, let her; they'd done the best job they could with what they had to hand, and he'd been fastidious in testing the wind and finding the ideal spot.

He felt better for a dinner of roasted rush hen. He hadn't been aware of how hungry he'd become until he'd smelled the greasy odor of cooking flesh. No-one said much over the course of their meal, but perhaps that was only because the others, too, were preoccupied with filling empty stomachs.

By the time he'd finished, the last of Durren's anger had subsided. There was no getting the better of Tia, especially not when she was basically in the right. So it was that, when after she'd eaten she stood up and paced into the darkness, he decided to hurry after. He found her sat beside the stream, washing her hands and cloak in the flow. Her night vision was remarkable; Durren could never have located the spring without a light and had nearly twisted his ankle twice on the broken ground.

He cleared his throat, so that Tia wouldn't think he was sneaking up on her. Sneaking up on a rogue was never a good idea.

"I know you're there," she said. "What do you want?"

Durren had intended a hasty apology, but the moment he began speaking he realized he felt genuinely guilty for his foolishness—and before he could stop them, the words were gushing out. "Look, you're right. I made a stupid mistake. Because I was tired, I ignored half the things we've been taught about where and where not to camp. I should have made a proper check of the perimeter, I didn't, and I put us all in danger."

Finally, he ran out of words. That was the most earnest apology he'd ever made, and Tia couldn't help but be moved. Surely now she would say sorry in return and they could go back to normal.

Yet her voice, from out of the blackness, was stony. "I know," was all she said.

They set out early the next morning; there was an unspoken agreement that they'd already had more than enough of this quest.

Tia's hunt for a satisfactory campsite had diverted them quite a distance from their former route, and it took Durren some time first to find his bearings and then to plot a suitable course. If he was honest with himself, he knew Tia would have done a quicker job; just because the way she regarded herself as superior at virtually everything was annoying, that didn't make it less true. But navigation was a ranger's task, and he was determined to make up for the previous day's blunder. Anyway, he had his own experience to consider. How was he meant to learn if he kept deferring his role to a girl who seemed to have been born with knowledge of every useful subject?

He made a point of being alert and careful, and refused to save time by taking risky shortcuts. They were deep in wilderness country, far from any except the most far-flung of human habitations, and there was a significant chance they'd run into a threat as bad as or worse than the giant toads. Durren had been half right in what he'd said yesterday: wild beasts did tend to wander, often driven by growling bellies, and this far from civilization you always had to be on your guard.

Though once they glimpsed some old tracks in the dirt that likely had belonged to goblins, and on another occasion they heard the distant snarls of large beasts, the morning passed without incident—and a little before noon, Durren decided that he'd successfully brought them to their objective. To be certain, he rechecked the map against the landscape ahead of him. Yes, there were the distant hills, rising to a low peak at their middle, and there was the lake, kidney-shaped and with its broad edge facing in their direction. He was sure that the rise they stood on was the spot represented by the X marked on their chart.

"This is it," he declared.

Tia came up beside him, contemplated the map, glanced across the scenery, and gave an almost imperceptible nod.

That was all the corroboration Durren needed. "Pootle,"

he called, "we're ready to go."

He had long since stopped wondering how the small creature, essentially a sentient ball with a single, disproportionately huge eye, could possibly know when it was being spoken to. Certainly, he wasn't surprised when the observer bobbed to float at the center of their group.

As soon as it had settled, Tia spoke the phrase that invoked their transport spell—"Homily, paradigm, lucent"—and almost immediately the air began to thicken and shift. Durren should have been used to the effect, but as the scene before him started to dissolve in lurid streaks, he still had to fight the urge to clamp shut his eyes.

Then the view steadied, stone walls congealed out of the cascading colors, and he felt the solidity of tiles under his feet.

Durren breathed a sigh of relief. They were back at Black River.

Chapter 2

Since they were just returned from questing, the four of them were exempt from lectures and training for the remainder of the day.

Having said a few brief words to Hieronymus, the wizard in charge of transportation—who, as always, seemed profoundly disinterested in the details of their adventure—they trooped together into the passage. From there, Durren, Hule, and Tia walked with Arein to the infirmary. Though she insisted her wound was already half healed, Tia explained pointedly that toad venom could be infectious, and that she'd be no use to them as a wizard if she had to have her left arm amputated.

They found the infirmary comparatively quiet. The rough-and-tumble existence of the academy and the inherent risks of questing invariably led to a steady rate of cuts, bruises, and broken limbs—even if Black River's tutors prided themselves on the fact that, in recent years anyway, all of their students at least managed to survive their studies.

The head physician was otherwise occupied, and they were left with one of her assistants. His first question was, "Who was responsible for this bandage?"

Hule frowned. "I was."

The assistant physician nodded. "Not bad," he said, "not bad at all." Nevertheless, he wasted no time in cutting the strip of cloth off with a pair of scissors. To Arein, he added, "Giant toad spit, you said? Not pleasant, but you'll live."

With one hand, he ushered her towards a portion of the room partitioned by red linen curtains. With the other, he waved the rest of them away.

"You can visit her this evening if you like. Until then, rest and quiet are the best medicine."

After he'd parted from Hule and Tia, and once he'd changed into fresh clothes that didn't bear the lilac stains and rank odor of toad blood, Durren wondered what to do with the rest of his day.

He would almost have been glad of a lecture to occupy him. He thought about practicing archery alone, but a group of level five students were training at the range set out in the academy's expansive yard, so instead he stood and watched. Durren knew without pride that he was unusually good with a bow, yet any one of that assembly could have given him a run for his money; the targets had been moved so far back that it was barely possible to differentiate the painted circles, and still not one student failed to land their shot.

They all looked so mature—even though some of them might be a mere couple of years older than Durren himself— and so confident. After a while, Durren began to find the spectacle intimidating. Would he ever possess such easy assurance? Would there really come a day when he'd leave through Black River's gates for a final time, a certified ranger, ready for whatever threats the outside world could throw at him?

The truth was that, when they'd been promoted to level two, he'd expected everything to change—or if not everything then at least *something*. Yet it was remarkable how, in only a couple of weeks, his life at Black River had settled into its old patterns.

For a few days he'd felt like a celebrity. First he had been the student who'd been expelled and soon after un-expelled— a circumstance that, to the best of his knowledge, was unique in the academy's long history. Then, before that notoriety could be forgotten, word had got around that his party had been involved in the ruckus that had devastated the storeroom and left the storesmaster in the head physician's care.

No-one knew the reality, and Durren was sworn to secrecy. He could tell nobody that Storesmaster Lyruke Cullglass had been replaced by a shapeshifter and held captive in ruins far out in the forest, or that he, Hule, Arein, and Tia had been the ones to unmask that shapeshifter and help capture it. And such was life at Black River that it hadn't taken long for new excitements to capture everyone's attention: rumors of a dragon from a party sent into the Borderlands, another party uncovering ancient treasures in the dungeons beneath an abandoned fortress, and the usual gossip about the private lives of tutors, and who planned to assassinate whom in the capital this year.

Durren had been glad when people stopped staring and whispering whenever he went by. However, he'd hoped that the four of them had been changed by the experiences they'd been through together, and there he'd found himself disappointed.

Tia was the most noticeable example: ever since they'd defeated the false Cullglass, she'd been drifting back into her old habits, which basically meant doing things her own way and seeming to find the rest of them unbearably irritating. But Hule was also out of sorts, and Arein still refused to use her magic to her full ability, afraid of the terrible responsibilities that came with such power. All in all, Durren couldn't help feeling they were a level two party in name only—and hadn't he proved that yesterday, when his beginner's blunder had put every one of them at risk?

He wandered over to the library, thinking he'd return to a hefty textbook on bowyery he'd been studying. But despite his tiredness from a torturous night's sleep and the day's walking, he was full of nervous energy. As the words began to run and tumble in front of his eyes, he gave up and stomped to the rangers' dormitory. There he came across another student who'd returned from a quest today, Arlo Mainbrow, and talked him into practicing knife fighting with the rubber-bladed weapons kept handy for the purpose.

At last Arlo declared he'd had enough—they were both of them drenched with sweat by then—and Durren realized he'd succeeded in burning off his excess vitality. Once he'd cleaned himself up, he returned to the library and managed to settle to his studies this time. He read until the fourth bell of the day rang, when he remembered he'd meant to visit Arein.

He found her in good spirits. She was sitting up in bed, and her eyes lit when she saw him. "Hello, Durren!"

"Hello," he said. "You look better." It was true; the color was fully returned to her freckled cheeks.

"I'm fine," she told him. "They've said I should stay until morning, just to be certain there's no infection. Apparently, in one in a hundred cases, giant toad venom can make your limbs turn black and bloat to twice their size, so they want to be absolutely sure that's not going to happen." She couldn't have sounded less concerned by the prospect.

"I'm sorry I got you hurt," Durren said.

"Oh!" She appeared genuinely shocked. "It wasn't your fault."

"Tia seems convinced it was." A thought occurred to him. "Has she been to visit you?"

Arein shook her head, and then brushed aside the curls of auburn hair that had tumbled across her face. "Hule came by," she said. "And look, don't worry too much about whatever Tia's said. I don't know why she's so on edge, but I doubt it has anything to do with you."

Durren felt oddly reassured by that; at any rate, he was glad he wasn't the only one who'd noticed that Tia was behaving strangely. "All right," he agreed. "Well, take care of yourself, Arein…and if that arm starts swelling, call for a physician."

Arein smiled. "See you, Durren. And I'm sure we'll do better on our next quest."

Durren didn't join in the conversation over dinner, which mostly revolved around a party that had barely escaped from a run-in with a cave troll they'd inadvertently woken out of hibernation. His mind was still on what Arein had said. Strange that it hadn't occurred to him to wonder why Tia was acting the way she was; he'd focused solely on how her behavior had affected him.

As he mopped the last gravy from his plate with a chunk of bread, he decided that perhaps he'd get the chance to make his selfishness up to her the next time they were sent out together—or perhaps Tia would do what she generally did and deal with her problems in her own way. Anyhow, there was no point in worrying just now.

Back in the dormitory and in a more sociable mood, Durren joined the continuing discussion about the cave troll—the encounter had been exaggerated out of all proportion by that time—until the last bell of the day rang. Then he went to bed, as a couple of the other students snuffed out the lanterns they'd been relying on for illumination.

Durren pulled off his boots, slipped out of his shirt and trousers, lay back—and winced. A hard lump was digging into his head behind his left ear. Rummaging with one hand, he eventually realized that an object had been stuffed inside his pillow through a ragged seam: when he managed to tease it out, he decided by touch alone that he was holding a cylinder of toughened leather. Further investigation revealed that one end could be unscrewed, so he did. Of course, there was the possibility that the cylinder contained poisonous spiders or something equally unpleasant; but he had a feeling he knew how it had arrived inside his pillow, and if the person responsible had wanted him dead, this was scarcely the method they'd choose.

Sure enough, the cylinder's only content turned out to be a strip of pale cloth. Once he'd unrolled it, Durren could see dark marks that were most likely writing. There wasn't sufficient light to read by; the sky outside the narrow windows was overcast and starless. Resignedly, he pulled on his overclothes and boots, tiptoed the length of the dormitory, and slipped out the door. No-one would report him for ignoring curfew; he wasn't the first ranger to do so and wouldn't be the last. Regardless, it didn't do to draw attention when you were breaking rules.

Durren crept through the passages until he found one

where a torch still burned. There, he again examined the note. Written in large, delicately shaped letters, the message read simply MEET ME IN THE HERB GARDEN STRAIGHT AWAY.

Durren rolled up the strip of cloth and slid it back inside the cylinder. There was little question that Tia was the note's author, and he knew the garden she was referring to: he had once nearly punched Hule there, for betraying the secret that had led to Durren's temporary expulsion.

He thought about going back to bed, even as he acknowledged that he wouldn't. He felt at the same time intrigued and irritated, but he didn't doubt which emotion would win out. Still, he dithered for a full minute before deciding, and then only began to move because he'd remembered he'd get into trouble if anyone happened by.

Navigating the academy at night was no easy matter, and Durren's sense of direction was less than spectacular. He was almost ready to give up when he recognized the familiar, low door. Easing it open, he noticed that someone had gone to the bother of greasing the hinges since last he'd been here, and groaned inwardly. If he hadn't already been sure of who was waiting for him, that meticulous pre-planning would have confirmed his suspicions.

However, all he could see in the herb garden—which had been laid out in one of the many cramped courtyards that filled the academy's rambling interior—was the impression of a figure, somewhat darker than their surroundings. Durren threw the leather cylinder their way and, though his aim was off and the courtyard was well-nigh pitch black, they caught it deftly.

"You took your time." Tia's voice was eerie and disconnected amid the gloom.

"I'd have been here a lot sooner if you'd just asked to talk to me like any normal person," Durren said.

"Then everyone would have known," she pointed out, in a tone that implied he was being stupid and might want to contemplate stopping. "I needed to talk to you in private."

Yet having said that, Tia didn't continue. Amid the cool night air and the tension rising from her, Durren was conscious of the beating of his heart. He counted, *one, two, three*—before she added, "I know I've been…preoccupied."

If preoccupied means argumentative, bossy, and generally unbearable to be around, Durren thought, *then yes, that's the word for what you've been.*

But he had more sense than to say that. Because, to his astonishment, Tia was evidently trying in her own way to make things right between them—which meant he was on delicate ground. "I'm sure you have your reasons," he said finally, pleased to have arrived at an answer she couldn't possibly be offended by.

So he was disappointed when her only reply was a slight nod—enough to tell him that, yes, she had reasons, though she certainly wouldn't be sharing them.

Suddenly Durren felt impatient. He was past ready for sleep, and he had no desire to stay awake just to have cryptic conversations with Tia. If she truly wanted to say sorry, why couldn't she do so like anyone else?

"Well," he said, "if that's everything…" Without waiting for an answer, he turned away.

Fingers closed upon his sleeve. "Durren." Tia's voice was small in the darkness. "I apologize for how I spoke to you yesterday. It was…unprofessional of me. I mean, as a member of our party."

Durren didn't turn back, but secretly he was both glad and surprised. By Tia's standards, that was practically begging for forgiveness. "It's fine. Like I said, you were right. I got sloppy."

Her intake of breath told him there was more she wanted to say—though again the words were slow in coming. "The thing is, I need your help."

Oh—so *that* was it. He should have known Tia wouldn't have gone to this much effort simply to apologize.

"There's something I have to do," she went on, "and I can't manage alone."

He had been preparing to politely refuse—politely because he didn't want to get back on her bad side, but refuse because he really did want to go to bed, and he didn't altogether like that he'd been manipulated. Yet nothing could have caught his attention more than those words coming from Tia: *I can't manage alone.* If someone had asked him a minute ago what the last phrase he ever expected her to say was, that sentence would have been a likely candidate. Despite himself, Durren was intrigued.

He turned. She was standing quite close, at the bottom of the three stairs that led down to the garden path. "Tell me what," he said, "and I'll think about it."

She gave a barely perceptible shrug. "I can't. You'll just have to trust me."

Durren considered. "Is the reason you can't tell me because it's dangerous? Or because I'm likely to get into trouble? Or both?"

"I can't tell you that either."

He sighed. Tia was Tia, and he'd long since reconciled to the fact that being friends with her meant accepting her on her own terms, which in turn meant never having the faintest idea what was going on in her mind. And the truth was that he did trust her—at least, enough to believe she wouldn't do anything to get him killed or expelled, if only because either would inconvenience her by leaving their party short a member.

"So this is dangerous and likely to get me into trouble, you won't tell me what's going on or why you need me, and you expect me to come along anyway—is that about the size of it?"

Anyone else would probably have debated. Tia simply said, "Yes."

"Fine. But can we not be up all night? I'd like to get *some* sleep."

The silhouette that was Tia pointed to a patch of deep shade beside the shallow flight of stairs. "You'll need those."

Durren bent to look. "That's my bow. And my pack." For the first time he felt real trepidation: what could she want him to do that he'd need a bow for? "I'm not going to hurt anyone," he said.

"You won't need to." She brushed past him.

Durren quickly scooped up his bow, slipped his pack onto his shoulders, and hurried after her.

He wished she'd sounded more certain.

Durren had known the academy had its basements. Until today he'd never imagined the existence of a subbasement.

Tia had produced a phosphor lamp from under her cloak. He'd never seen one before, but he'd heard of them, and of how their light was produced by a unique moss that grew in rare spots deep beneath the ground. That was all well and good, except that the pale bluish glow the little lantern gave off was distinctly creepy; what it illuminated appeared slightly unreal and what it didn't became utterly black.

The subbasements were distinctly creepy too, full of claustrophobic passageways and the distant sounds of scurrying feet and dripping water, and the combination wasn't doing Durren's nerves a bit of good. He tried to remind himself that he'd once faced down a charging unicorn; but that had been by daylight, and if he was honest, *faced down* had effectively meant *run away from*. So maybe bravery wasn't among his strongest points after all.

They'd been walking for a long time by then, and Durren had lost count of how many twists and turns Tia had navigated them through; the ancient passages were beginning to blur into one. His attention only roused again as they passed a row of evenly spaced doors. All of them were closed, but what Durren found strange was the grilles in each at about head height.

As understanding dawned, he stopped abruptly. "Oh, no. No way, Tia."

Her response was to press a finger to her lips.

"No way," he repeated, though more quietly. "Tia, these are cells, aren't they? I'm not going any further. Whatever this is, you'll have to do it on your own—or better yet, don't do it at all."

Her scowl told him what she thought of that. Then her expression softened fractionally. "If I could manage on my own, don't you think I would?"

"That still leaves the second option."

"Durren, you know me well enough to know I wouldn't be taking risks like this if I didn't have to."

He pondered that. On the one hand, just because she'd broken the rules with good reason in the past, that didn't persuade him her motives were equally benign now. On the other, of them all, Tia had been most instrumental in discovering the shapeshifter; she'd investigated alone and taken chances the rest of them would never have dared, and thanks to that they'd rooted out one of the greatest perils the academy had ever faced.

He supposed he had no choice but to believe in her. And as she set off again and he followed, he only wished that he *did*. The fact was, believing in someone who behaved suspiciously and wouldn't trust you in return was far from easy.

At the next junction, Tia reached within her cloak. With the arrow that she drew out, she pointed to a patch of wavering amber light ahead. In a whisper she said, "I need you to shoot this just above the torch on the corner."

As he took the arrow, Durren felt a faint tremble in his fingers, which ran like lightning up his arm. "It's enchanted," he whispered back. "Where did you get this?"

"I bought it. Can you make the shot or not?"

"Of course I can," he told her irritably. In truth, what she was asking of him was relatively simple. "What will it do?"

"Hit the spot and you'll find out."

Well, he thought, *I've come this far.* Durren nocked the arrow to his bowstring; it was fractionally heavier than a regular arrow, and he took a moment to compensate. Then he aimed and loosed.

He hadn't known what to expect. At any rate, he'd never have predicted what happened next. In the instant its head struck the wall, the entire arrow dissolved and splashed impossibly across the stone. The torch managed one last flicker, before it died with an audible hiss.

An arrow enchanted with some kind of transmogrification spell, prepared so that on impact its substance would turn to water; Durren dared not imagine how much such an object would have cost, assuming Tia had told the truth in claiming to have bought it. But that was the least of his worries—for, as the torch had extinguished, he'd heard from around the corner what he felt sure was a grunt of consternation.

"Someone's there," he muttered.

Tia's dismissive nod said that obviously someone was there, and why would she be wasting exorbitantly expensive enchanted arrows putting out torches if there wasn't? "All I need you to do is to cause a distraction."

"A distraction?"

"Pull your hood up."

Reluctantly, Durren did as instructed.

"And be ready to hold your breath," she said.

Then she'd put her hand to the small of his back and shoved, and before Durren knew what he was doing, his feet had carried him beyond the corner.

The part of the corridor where he stumbled to a halt lay in deep darkness thanks to the extinguished torch. Ahead, though, a second torch burned, and by its light he could see clearly the metal gate that ended the passage and the guard who stood in front it.

The academy didn't employ many guards. Most duties that would have required them could be handed off to students, who were largely as capable and more eager to please. This one was undeniably not a student. He was old enough for there to be flecks of gray in his beard, and his face was that of a man who had fought more than his share of fights, some of them including sharp objects. He wore leather armor and a sword hung from his hip; Durren didn't doubt he'd be willing to use it, even if that meant having to explain away a dead ranger at some later point.

"Ah…hello," Durren said.

"You're not supposed to be down here," the guard told him, redundantly. But those were only the words that came out of his mouth: the meaning clear behind them was, *If you think for one instant you're coming past me, you'll be leaving in a lot of small, wet pieces.*

Durren was aware of a tremor of motion to his right. When his eyes darted to the shadows, there was nothing to be seen.

The guard had followed his gaze. Durren remembered his orders from Tia; so far he was doing the precise opposite of providing a distraction. He took a couple of steps nearer, careful to stop before he entered the light from the next wall torch. Even then, he couldn't help noticing that the guard's hand was already on the hilt of his sword.

"The thing is," Durren started, "I'm a new student, I arrived here last week, and I'm afraid I must have got lost, because I was studying in the main library and I fell asleep, and when I woke up there was nobody around, so I started back to my dormitory—I mean, that was where I meant to be going—only there were some stairs downward, and I thought, maybe you have to go down first and come up somewhere else, but—"

The next words died on his lips, as again Durren's eyes caught the slightest of movements, just as his ears detected the tiniest chink of breaking glass—before the guard's head was engulfed in a cloud of sickly green vapor. He gurgled some incoherent complaint, managed to draw his sword halfway, and then slumped into Tia's waiting arms.

Tia lowered the unconscious guard until he was sprawled against the wall, not without some difficulty, for he was a good head taller than she was. It didn't occur to Durren to try and help until after she'd finished.

Tia glanced at him. "I needed to get close," she said, as though by way of explanation.

"You needed to get close so you could *knock an academy guard unconscious*," Durren croaked at her, each syllable a struggle. He felt that describing what she'd done would somehow make the deed more real.

"I couldn't get past him otherwise." Her voice remained perfectly, worryingly calm. "Look, he didn't see your face, he definitely didn't see mine, and we're not going to be around when he wakes up. So you've nothing to worry about."

"But why do this at all?" Durren wished he could make her understand how preposterously misjudged her actions were.

"Because I asked Borgnin to let me come down here and he wouldn't, and because there's something I have to know, and because after tomorrow there won't be another chance."

"You *asked* the Head Tutor? Then he's going to guess exactly who did this."

"He'll guess. He can't prove anything. Now can we get on? The more time we waste, the more likely we are to get caught."

In fact, Durren would probably have left then if he'd imagined for one moment he could find his way back without Tia and her lantern. Instead, he watched, stupefied, as she crouched to check the guard's body, her hands dancing deftly over his still form.

Cursing, she stood and paced to the end of the corridor. The metal gate that blocked their way spanned from floor to ceiling, and obviously she'd hoped to find a key, rather than having to rely on the lockpicks that Durren saw glinting in her hand.

Selfishly, Durren found himself hoping that the lock was beyond her, and she did indeed seem to be deeply absorbed in concentration. Meanwhile, his eyes flitted between her and the motionless guard, who was now wheezing softly. He actually looked quite content, as though he were having a particularly pleasant dream, which was galling given Durren's own feeling that at some point he'd been plunged into a nightmare—one sure to end in the expulsion he'd already so narrowly avoided once.

He heard a soft but definite click. Tia drew on the gate and the bars swung inward, with a creak of unoiled hinges that made Durren suspect that this portion of the academy hadn't been used regularly in a very long time.

Beyond, another passage met theirs at a right angle. Only as he followed Tia through the archway could Durren see what lay beyond. At the end of a short length of corridor was a circular room, and in the center stood a square cage. Rather than bars, its walls consisted of a lattice of metal, the gaps not much bigger than coins. At first he could see no entrance. Then he spotted the hatch in the top: from inside there would be no reaching it without a ladder. In short, what he was looking at resembled a pen intended for a savage animal rather than a cell for any human being.

Yet the shape that huddled in one corner, dark beneath the harsh light from Tia's lamp, certainly appeared human. At the sound of their footsteps, its head flicked up, and Durren shivered with a sense of its gaze upon him.

Tia drew nearer. Durren wanted to tell her to stop. He wanted to say, *Don't you know what that is?* But the words died before ever leaving his throat.

The dark shape stared up at them. In the blue-white glow of Tia's lamp, its features were more formless than ever, like a sketch of a face drawn by a lazy artist. Its eyes were mere holes, its mouth a crease in flawlessly smooth flesh.

That mouth curved up now, into what might by the loosest of standards be considered a smile.

"So it's you two," the shapeshifter said. "I wondered if I'd see you again."

Chapter 3

Durren didn't like how close Tia had got to the cage. He didn't like that she was talking to the shapeshifter. He didn't like that he couldn't hear what she was saying, but he knew he wouldn't have been any happier if he *could* hear. The fact was, there wasn't anything to be liked about this situation.

He wanted to remind her of what she was talking to: a creature that not long ago had tried to murder them, having sent them on false quests just to gather magical treasures for itself, while the man whose face it imitated was imprisoned in the most horrible conditions. And Durren couldn't help noticing the irony: their first conversation with the real Lyruke Cullglass had been before such a cell as this, deep in the ancient ruins where the shapeshifter had held him captive.

There was nothing comforting about irony. There was nothing comforting about cages either, not when you were dealing with monsters out of half-vanished history that wielded powerful magic and could change their very physical forms.

Tia knelt almost touching the mesh of metal, her lamp on the flagstones at her side, and the shapeshifter crouched in front of her, its face not far from hers. What if it should decide to make its fingers into blades sufficiently long and slender to fit through those holes? Did even Tia have the reflexes to dodge such an attack? And why was the thing behaving so docilely, anyway? What was it telling her? Or—the question that troubled Durren more—what might Tia be telling it?

After a while, Durren found that he could bear watching the two no longer. He retreated to the barred gate and scrutinized the sleeping guard. Was it his imagination or did the man already appear to be stirring? No, Durren was certain his chin was nodding against his breast. His eyelids quivered, and he mumbled meaninglessly. Then he sank back, snuffling.

Durren wasn't persuaded he'd be out for much longer. Suddenly he knew with cold conviction that this had gone on long enough: whatever Tia's business with the shapeshifter, he wasn't about to wait here until this guard woke and saw them.

He darted back towards the cage. For the first time, Tia was raising her voice, but Durren caught just the end of the sentence, and the words "...*must* know where."

Durren didn't hear the shapeshifter's response, or much care. "We've got to go!" he snapped, clasping the arm of Tia's cloak.

"In a minute." She tried to shake herself free.

Durren refused to release her. Rather, he hauled. "Not in a minute. Right now."

He'd half expected her to hit him, and was startled when this time she didn't resist. Yet her expression was so anguished in that moment that he actually felt guilty. Only a faint mumbling from around the corner gave him the determination to keep going. Together, they turned into the main passageway.

The guard was awake.

At least, he was partly awake. Though he was knuckling his eyes and yawning, his scarred face hadn't quite lost its air of contentment.

Durren realized that he was stood staring when Tia yanked on his sleeve and snarled, "Come on!"

Now their positions were reversed, as she dragged him towards the pool of gloom around the extinguished torch. He leapt over the guard's legs, even as the man began to struggle to his feet.

"Hey!" the guard bellowed groggily. "Stop right there."

Durren didn't stop. He probably couldn't have if he'd wanted to, such was Tia's grip on his wrist. She had already shut the door of her lantern, and before them was deep darkness. He opened his mouth, meaning to explain that he couldn't see; instead, he jolted into a wall and had the breath slapped from his lungs.

Tia didn't allow him to pause. She released his sleeve but clutched his hand, and then she was dragging him once more. The faint, reflected light from the torch above the guard's station was gone, and they really were in absolute obscurity. Yet Tia wasn't slowing and, because her grasp was vicelike upon his fingers, neither was Durren.

From behind them came the guard's voice, simultaneously muzzy with sleep and harsh with anger: "You're just making this worse!"

Durren wasn't convinced. He fervently hoped that things were as bad as they could be. There came a crash and a grunt; at least he wasn't the only one having difficulty. In his haste, the guard hadn't thought to snatch the remaining torch down from the wall, and he too was running blind.

Tia dashed on, turning left and right, then right again, always through darkness. Even her eyesight wasn't up to so impossible a task, for twice she grazed against walls with a gasp, and Durren had no choice except to graze them with her. Behind, he could hear the guard's blundering footsteps. He'd sensibly given up shouting and was devoting his attention to staying on their trail.

But Tia's combination of extraordinary night vision and risk-taking had gained them a sizable lead. When eventually the blackness softened to a leaden gray and Durren glanced behind them, he couldn't see the guard.

"There are stairs ahead," Tia muttered, barely in time to stop Durren stumbling over them.

At the summit was more light. Narrow grates in the ceiling let in the faintest glow, which after the profound dark of below seemed nearly bright. Tia pressed on without hesitation, through another turning and another, and by the time they reached the top of a second flight of steps, Durren could no longer hear the guard's faltering pursuit.

Still Tia kept going. If she appeared to be choosing her route at random, Durren knew her better than that. He suspected she had the entire vast layout of Black River committed to memory. When she finally came to a halt, it was in an enclosed garden not much different to the one they'd met in earlier that night, this a small orchard devoted to miniature fruit trees.

A long while passed before Durren had even half of his breath back. His ribs ached, not only from the running but from his numerous encounters with the stone walls. Leaning with his back to a tree, his nostrils were filled with the sour tang of unripe fruit.

After a minute, Tia, who seemed hardly out of breath and had been hovering near the doorway they'd entered by, announced, "All right...we've lost him."

Durren had largely recovered by then, though the pain of his bruises was sure to stay with him for days. They were one of the many reasons for the fury bubbling within him. He couldn't have contained that anger, and he didn't try.

"I can't believe you did that! I mean, even knowing you, I actually can't believe you did something so dangerous and wrong. And if I could, I wouldn't believe you'd be selfish enough to drag me into it after all that's happened."

"He shouldn't have woken up so quickly," Tia said. She actually sounded faintly penitent. "I must have diluted the dosage too much."

"Do you really think that's the point? Whether or not the guard you knocked out woke up too soon?"

She sighed. "I'm just saying. Things didn't exactly go as planned."

"But the part where you used me to help you break into the academy's deepest cells and then drugged a guard, so you could talk to the monster that tried to kill us and our friends—*that* was all in your plan?"

"Yes." This time Tia's tone was defiant.

"And you still won't tell me what this is about?"

"Trust me, it's better you don't know."

"That's the thing," he said. "I *can't* trust you."

Tia didn't reply at once. Durren had never had much luck with reading her face, and in the dark he could barely make out her features—but for an instant, had she looked hurt? "Then—I'm sorry. I needed help, and you seemed the best person to ask. I made a mistake."

"Yes. You did." Brushing past her towards the doorway, he growled over his shoulder, "Just don't ever ask me for anything again."

And he'd stormed halfway down the passage before he realized he had no idea how to get back to his dormitory.

Half an hour of anxious wandering later, Durren at last slipped into bed.

However, he scarcely slept that night. When he did, it was to find the shapeshifter waiting for him in weird and mercurial nightmares: At first it was inside its cage, leering in the ghastly light of Tia's phosphor lamp; then it was impersonating Lyruke Cullglass, though Durren could see through the disguise, and became increasingly afraid with each moment the creature refused to abandon its pretense. His dreams grew yet more sinister and muddled: the shapeshifter was Tia, pretending to be his friend only to deceive him in the end. The shapeshifter was Arein, her timid smile melting into a lipless grin. The shapeshifter was Head Tutor Borgnin and was running Black River for its own wicked ends.

Durren woke cold with sweat and with a stifled cry lodged in his throat, determined not even to try and get back to sleep. He lay until the first chill daylight slid through the windows, and tumbled from his bed as the wake-up bells chimed. Dragging on his boots and trousers, he noticed that both were thick with dirt and dust; he quickly scrubbed the worst of the incriminating marks away. He told himself he was acting guiltily, but no-one was paying him any attention. If there was a time to get away with odd behavior in the rangers' dormitory, it was at the crack of dawn.

Checking the schedule after a breakfast of gray and lumpy oatmeal, Durren saw that his first lesson of the day was a lecture, and hurried to the designated room. Under other circumstances he'd have been glad for the return to normality. As it was, he spent every instant expecting to be dragged out, by Borgnin or the head ranger Eldra Atrepis, or even by the guard from last night. He couldn't concentrate, and could make no sense of the presentation. It didn't help that the subject was celestial navigation and that the tutor had covered the windows in black cloth so that the images cast by the modified lantern he used could be better seen; sitting in darkness brought back too-vivid memories of their flight through the academy's hidden levels.

Fortunately, Durren's next lesson was in the courtyard, and the daylight and open air began to dispel a little of his tiredness and disquiet. He assured himself that if the guard had identified him and Tia then he'd know by now. But thinking of Tia brought another doubt: he wondered if he'd been too hard on her. Hadn't she practically said that she'd come to him because there was nobody else she could rely on? There was no chance she'd put her faith in him again, and probably he would never find out what she was up to.

It wasn't long before worries of Tia and of the previous night were pushed from his mind by a more immediate concern. His group were practicing with wooden swords in the arena normally reserved for the fighters when the disturbance began. Suddenly there was a great deal of noise from around the main gates—which, as Durren glanced that way, began to creak open.

That was unusual in itself: generally, visitors arrived by the smaller side door, and the only time carts entered was when supplies were brought in the early hours. The parade of riders that marched through the open gates were definitely not bringing supplies, and the large wagon of dark wood and black metal that followed wasn't carrying them; the vehicle looked as though it been designed to withstand a fireball flung at close range.

Durren recognized the crest on the door, a clenched hand picked out in gilt upon a black-rimmed circle of red, before he thought to wonder at the elaborate armor the riders wore. He had heard plentiful stories of the Brazen Fist, the royal order that was part official state army, part police force to the capital, and part mercenary regiment at the hire of anyone with coin to spend and a cause at least not actively immoral. They were both legendary and notorious; tales of their heroics were spoken freely, while other, less respectful rumors were reserved for whispering in private.

Yet to Durren, these men and women certainly looked like heroes. Their burnished armor, of the brown-gold shade that gave the order half of its name, shone with reflected sunlight; their faces were hard without being callous, not those of people who fought merely for the sake of fighting.

"I heard they're collecting a prisoner," one of the girls, Fayla Ludinker, declared in a whisper loud enough that nobody could miss it. Her father was someone or other in the capital, and she seemed always to have gossip that no-one else did.

"A prisoner?" another student asked puzzledly. The academy's usual practice was to hand wrongdoers over to whatever local authority would take them.

"Yes! Do you remember—" Then Fayla caught Durren's eyes on her and dropped her voice, to a level where only the small group clustered about her could hear.

Durren understood, both what she was saying and why the Brazen Fist were here. Indeed, he surely possessed more of the facts than Fayla Ludinker herself. She would be reminding her audience of the incident, not so long ago, when the stores had been partially demolished; she would further hint that, whoever the true perpetrator, they'd been cooling their heels ever since in the academy's dungeons.

How she got her information Durren neither knew nor cared. All that mattered to him was that the Brazen Fist were here for the shapeshifter: Borgnin had made the creature their problem, and now they were readying to transport it, for punishment, interrogation, or perhaps even for execution. Whatever the case, the wretched monstrosity would be far away by tomorrow, and he would never have to stare into its blank and awful face again.

As the riders spread across the courtyard, the tutor in charge hastily ordered everyone indoors; evidently he'd decided that what was about to happen wasn't suitable for the eyes of students. He marched towards one of the academy's numerous entrances, which took them in the wrong direction for the rangers' classrooms but had the advantage of not crossing paths with the expedition from the Fist, who already had their armored carriage drawn up almost to the main doorway.

There was some muted grumbling among the other students, who clearly had wanted to stay and watch what was taking place, whether it was a prisoner transfer, as Fayla Ludinker had claimed, or some event even more exciting. Durren, who knew the truth, felt only relieved. He had no desire to see the shapeshifter being carted out; that it was leaving was quite enough.

His relief lasted until he arrived at his third lecture of the day, late in the afternoon—whereupon he found Eldra Atrepis waiting for him. She looked sterner than she normally did, which was saying something.

"Durren Flintrand, you're wanted immediately in Head Tutor Borgnin's office," she told him.

That Atrepis had merely ordered him and not actually escorted him Durren interpreted as a good sign. If he was known to have been involved with the events of last night, he would hardly be getting off so lightly. Conversely, if he wasn't being summoned to Borgnin's office over Tia's nocturnal excursion then why was he? His imagination could offer no possibilities.

Rounding the final corner, he was faintly relieved to see Hule, Arein, and Tia. Arein and Hule were sat on the bench beside the door, while Tia was a couple of paces away, stood with her back to them. She turned at the sound of Durren's approach, but said nothing.

At least Arein was looking better. Durren noticed that the burned tear in her sleeve had been mended, and thankfully by someone with more skill at darning than she; the seam was barely visible. Seeing him, she jumped to her feet. "Hello, Durren."

"Hello, Arein," Durren said. "Hello, Hule." He'd meant to greet Tia too, but by then she'd looked away again, and he found that he couldn't bring himself to.

Instead, since they were all here, he knocked. From within, Borgnin's stentorian voice rumbled, "Enter."

Durren opened the door and they trooped inside.

Borgnin was behind his desk; Durren had come to suspect that he spent the vast proportion of his life there. His office was much the same as Durren remembered: not exactly untidy but definitely busy, with scrolls and books crammed into drawers and upon shelves, and with little in the way of ornamentation to announce that the man in front of them was head of a moderately prestigious academy.

Though there were chairs, Borgnin gave no indication that the four of them should sit in them, so Durren resigned himself to standing. He attempted to read Borgnin's expression and failed. The Head Tutor was inscrutable.

"I have unfortunate news to share," Borgnin said.

That was unexpected—and not exactly a reason to relax. If unfortunate news might be better than expulsion for attacking a staff member, it was still, by definition, not good.

"You may be aware," Borgnin continued, "that earlier today a detachment of troops from the Brazen Fist visited the academy. You may even have guessed that they were here to remove the shapeshifter the four of you were so instrumental in capturing. They also insisted, against my own arguments, in taking with them the magical items the creature had been gathering, including the object known as the Petrified Egg." He sighed. "That was a grave mistake."

He picked up a scroll and toyed with it, without apparently reading it. Durren caught enough of a glimpse to note that the missive was brief and had been written with a carelessness that implied haste. And was that smudge of brown near the bottom a bloodstain?

Durren couldn't be sure, and Borgnin was already rerolling the scroll and returning it to its place on his desk. "What you won't have heard," he said, "because only I have been told, is that the shapeshifter was rescued from the custody of the Brazen Fist in the forest outside Olgen."

Durren thought of the warriors he'd seen, those unconquerable-looking men and women in their shining armor. Before he could stop the words, he'd murmured, "That's impossible."

Borgnin's gaze was inquiring.

"I mean…it would have taken an army," Durren tried.

"Obviously the Brazen Fist imagined so. In fact, according to their report, they were assailed by a single antagonist—though on the question of *what* that adversary was, they remain unclear. The sole detail they seem certain of is that the beast was flying."

Durren was unable to repress a shudder.

"By all accounts," Borgnin went on, "the thing attacked them from the air. Three of their number were killed and many were wounded; their wagon was, in their own words, torn into so much firewood. Once the cage within was open, their prisoner joined the fray, and from that point onwards they were lost. So, unfortunately, were the objects they were transporting—meaning that not only is the shapeshifter at liberty, it possesses the treasures it went to such lengths to gather."

The shudder came again, stronger this time, so that Durren had to clench his fists to make sure his reaction didn't show. He thought of the Petrified Egg, which the shapeshifter had used its borrowed face to trick them into stealing. He'd seen a little of the Egg's power, and that had been enough to make him fearful. He didn't like to consider what such an artifact might be capable of in the wrong hands—as it most assuredly was now.

Borgnin cleared his throat. "That's one of the matters I wanted to inform you of. Since you were involved in its capture, it stands to reason the shapeshifter may pursue revenge against you. I wish to assure you that I and this academy will take every reasonable measure to ensure your safety."

Until then, Borgin's scrutiny had been unfocused, as though he were concentrating on all four of them at once. Now his eyes roved visibly along the line they'd formed, and was it Durren's imagination, or did they hover for a fraction of an instant longer on him?

"However," Borgnin said, "there's another concern you should be aware of: an assault on a member of our guard staff that occurred in the subbasements last night."

The breath Durren had been about to draw stalled halfway to his lips, and he was convinced his heart had stopped beating. For all he knew, even the blood in his veins had ceased to flow.

"The intruders' purpose, it would appear, was to contact the shapeshifter. The guard in question did not get a good view of the perpetrators; nevertheless, he believed they may well have been students. From what he saw of their clothing, his best conjecture was that they were a ranger and a rogue."

Durren stared hard at the floor. If he'd had to guess where Borgnin was looking, he would have said without a shadow of a doubt that the Head Tutor's attention was on Tia—Tia who had specifically requested that she be allowed to speak with the shapeshifter, Tia who had the skills required to knock out a guard without him glimpsing her face, and Tia who had a ranger to hand, a ranger who was enough of an idiot to be dragged into her schemes.

Borgnin's voice was more stern than ever as he said, "It's no great leap to suppose that these two events may be connected. It's equally plausible that whoever met with the shapeshifter last night acted today to aid its escape. Perhaps, at this moment, Black River harbors another threat within its walls."

Why doesn't he just accuse us? Durren wondered. He'd long since realized that Borgnin liked to play his hand close to his chest, but this was ridiculous. Could he be tormenting them on purpose, or waiting for one of them to blurt a confession? Durren might even have done so, had there been a drop of spittle left in his mouth to lubricate the words.

No, that wasn't true. Annoyed as he was with her, he wouldn't betray Tia, and certainly not without knowing what she was up to. Nor would she ever give herself away; she'd be as icily calm as ever. If Borgnin should accuse her, she probably had an escape plan already figured out. In his mind's eye, Durren watched Tia hurl a smoke bomb at the Head Tutor's feet and leap out of the window—and despite the tension in the air, he had to stifle a smile.

Somehow, that flight of fancy restored his courage. He dared to look up—to find that Borgnin's attention was on neither him nor Tia. Rather, he was once again occupied with one of the scrolls arranged haphazardly upon his desk. This was more formal and in better condition than the last. Durren could see the wax seal, broken neatly, but could make no sense of the design, which involved two jagged, mirrored shapes that joined at the middle.

"There's one last matter," Borgnin said. "Something only indirectly related to today's news."

This time, Borgnin turned the relevant scroll to face them, as if as evidence, though the handwriting was so crabbed that Durren couldn't have hoped to read it from a distance.

"I recently received a proposal from a fellow head tutor, Murta Krieg of the Shadow Mountain Academy in the province of Ursvaal to be precise, querying whether Black River might be interested in a student exchange, in hopes of broadening our mutual perspectives."

Durren had dimly heard of Ursvaal. He recalled that the country was somewhere to the north and east. Yet the name had specific, and negative, connotations for him, and he wracked his brain to remember why. Then the memory came back: a servant in his father's household named Elikith who'd been from there and had mentioned the place often. Or rather, she'd never actually discussed her homeland, only sworn by it: the winter's days were never cold, they were as cold as Ursvaal; the night wasn't dark but as dark as Ursvaal. And those had been her more polite references.

Belatedly it occurred to Durren to wonder why Borgnin should be telling them this—and his heart began to sink. *Oh no,* he thought, *you wouldn't. You can't...*

But he knew before Borgnin opened his mouth that he could, and would, and was about to.

"Given the circumstances," the Head Tutor said, "and given the potential risks you face, I've made my decision. I've agreed to take Head Tutor Krieg up on her offer, and told her that the four of you shall be the students Black River sends to Shadow Mountain."

Chapter 4

"Maybe he's punishing us," Durren proposed.

The four of them had stayed together after leaving Borgnin's office and had wandered without direction, in a kind of shared stupor, until finally they'd come to an empty lecture hall. The embossed design above the door suggested that the room belonged to the wizards, but no-one was likely to be attending lectures at this hour.

Arein looked at him questioningly. "You mean because of yesterday's quest? I don't think we did *that* badly."

Durren tried to catch Tia's eye, only to find that she was gazing resolutely ahead. "No," he said, "I guess that's true."

"I feel as though I'm being sent home," Hule complained gruffly.

"Oh, that's right," Durren remembered, "Ursvaal is close to the Borderlands."

Hule's scowl deepened. "You know, there are people who regard that as an offensive term. The country is called

Durkhaan."

Durren was sure he'd heard Hule himself refer to the region of his birth as the Borderlands on more than one occasion, but he decided to let that go. "What's so bad about being near to home?" he asked instead. "Maybe you'll get a chance to hop across and see your family."

"I came here," Hule said, "so that I don't *have* to see my family."

There was no real bite in the words. Hule had often spoken critically of his people, who he'd implied were too preoccupied with hitting each other and not enough with basic social niceties like talking; yet there had always been a hint of obvious affection in even his most damning comments.

"I'll be a lot nearer to home as well," Arein said quietly.

In her case, Durren really couldn't judge whether she deemed that to be good or bad news, and he decided against asking. From her tone, he suspected she hadn't made up her mind herself.

"Anyway," he said, "I expect it's not as though we'll be wandering off to visit relatives. We'll be students there, won't we? Just like we are here."

"Perhaps not *just* like," Hule responded.

"What's that supposed to mean?"

"It means, Ursvaal is…strange. Strange things happen there. They do things strangely."

"That doesn't exactly tell us much, Hule," Durren pointed out.

The big fighter shrugged. "What is there to tell?" he said, which Durren took for an admission that he didn't know anything besides the sort of vague rumors folk everywhere liked to invent about their neighbors.

"They have some strange ideas regarding magic," Arein put in.

There's that word again, Durren thought. "How so?"

"The way I heard it," she said, with obvious discomfort, "they sort of *worship* the unbalance."

From Arein, Durren had learned that the unbalance was the source of all magic, a fissure in the very fundament of reality and one that was being constantly eroded, pouring into the world intangible debris that could be harnessed and worked into spells. He knew too that responsible wizards—which these days meant all except the hopelessly evil ones—used certain practices to repair the damage they did. Magic was far from being wholly beneficent, and uncontrolled it tended to have effects that nobody desired; the shapeshifters were one example, but there were no end of others.

He could imagine, then, how someone could make the leap from maintaining the unbalance with rituals of meditation to an outlook that resembled worship. Though that might be odd, it didn't strike him as actually harmful.

Maybe the question was on his face, for Arein said, a touch defensively, "I don't agree, that's all. The unbalance is a force of nature. No-one made it; it doesn't do what it does deliberately. It's just there, like a forest or a river. You don't worship a river because it waters your crops or a forest because it gives you firewood."

Probably some people do, Durren nearly said, but he felt he was beginning to understand what bothered Arein so—and that this boiled down to a matter of professional pride. In her eyes, superstition had no place in wizardry.

"I suppose we're just going to have to make the best of this," he said. "I don't think Borgnin will take no for an answer."

"How do you feel about leaving for Ursvaal, Tia?" Arein asked suddenly.

Tia, who'd been standing apart, looked uncomfortable to be made the center of attention. "I don't have an opinion either way," she replied.

Yet for an instant, her face had claimed differently. Durren had failed to read her brief glimmer of an expression, except to say that it seemed to him she *did* have an opinion on Ursvaal, and one based on more than neighborly gossip or contention over the unbalance.

The possibility both intrigued and concerned him. Or maybe what troubled him was only the sense that there was more going on here, something Borgnin was keeping from them and that perhaps Tia had knowledge of too. After all, wasn't this an unlikely coincidence? The shapeshifter escaped from custody and Borgnin just happened to have an invite waiting for four students to a far-distant rival academy?

"It could be that this Shadow Mountain place won't be so different," Durren suggested, trying to cheer himself up more than the others.

The look Hule gave him said he had little confidence in that theory.

"At least we'll all be together," Arein added. "As long as we're a party, I'm sure we can deal with practically anything."

But she, too, sounded more hopeful than certain. And though a week ago Durren might have agreed with her, he wasn't convinced he did now. He'd always known, without ever fully realizing, how much they relied on Tia and her unofficial leadership. If she was following her own agenda, where would that leave them? Back with the sort of half-baked teamwork and slapdash adventuring that had characterized their earliest quests, no doubt.

Durren said none of that. Clearly Arein was doing her best to disguise her own misgivings, and he wasn't selfish enough to worry her further to no good purpose. "You're right," he agreed. "The party that caught a unicorn and defeated a shapeshifter can handle a little Ursvaalian strangeness."

Durren had one more lecture that day, on the dubious subject of edible fungi. He allowed his mind to wander, regardless of the tutor's assurances that many a student had been undone by mistaking orange spots for red splotches or frilled goosecap for gray witchnose.

The truth was that he had grown fond of Black River; he'd come to consider the place as home, albeit an eccentric, dangerous, incessantly demanding home. Certainly he was more settled here than he ever had been back in Luntharbor with his father, being prepared for a life of selfish comfort and grubbing after gold. Black River was where he belonged—yet now, for reasons he didn't fully grasp, he had no choice except to go elsewhere and start over again.

As he trudged out of the lecture, Durren recalled that Borgnin had assured them the transfer was only temporary: for a term, he'd said. But terms were an ill-defined concept at Black River, and seemed to vary according to class, level, and the temperaments of tutors. Maybe they were being sent away for a month and maybe for a year. Though Durren told himself that the latter was unlikely, he couldn't escape the conviction that it would be a long time before he wandered these corridors again.

He wished he could have talked to somebody. It occurred to him that he should probably say goodbye to his acquaintances among the rangers, but the day wore on, and opportunity after opportunity went by, and still he didn't. By the time they sat down for dinner, he understood why: explaining to someone else that he was leaving would make it real and irrevocable.

Durren didn't expect to sleep, but he did, and did so dreamlessly. One night under leaking canvas and another broken by nightmares was enough to ensure that. He woke with the first bell, and scrambled from beneath the blanket. So here it was: the day he left Black River.

He hadn't much preparing to do. A perk of reaching level two was that you were allowed to keep your pack at the end of your bunk and were responsible for the stocking of your own provisions, so he already had everything organized. In any case, his possessions were scanty—really, not much more than a couple of changes of clothes, those being all he'd managed to smuggle out when he'd left home.

As he swung his heavier-than-usual rucksack onto his shoulders, one of the other ranger students sidled up. It was Arlo Mainbrow, Durren saw, who was perhaps the closest he had to a friend among his classmates.

"Off on another quest so soon?" Mainbrow asked.

"Um…not exactly."

"Oh?"

"Actually, we're being sent on an exchange. To the Shadow Mountain Academy in Ursvaal."

"Oh," Mainbrow repeated. He took a moment to digest this news—and grinned. "Sounds like fun."

Of all the possibilities, Durren hadn't contemplated that one. But something in Mainbrow's reaction was infectious, and he found himself smiling back. "Maybe it will be. See you around, Arlo."

Halfway to the transportation chamber, Durren ran into Hule. The fighter was wearing the hangdog expression that seemed to have become a fixture on his face these days. Thinking to cheer him up, Durren spoke before he'd given his words due consideration.

"You know," he said, "this is a good thing for you, isn't it? I mean, going away like this. It's a fresh start. You can stop pretending to…what I mean is, you can stop behaving as if…"

The look Hule gave him made Durren wish his tongue had shriveled inside his head. "I can stop pretending to be stupid?"

Durren winced. "I wasn't going to put it exactly that way—but yes. You can behave however you want at Shadow Mountain. And by the time you get back, no-one's going to remember how you used to be. They'll assume your horizons have broadened or something."

Hule had slowed down. All his concentration was on his own feet. "What if I really am stupid?" he said. "What if I just thought I was pretending?"

"You're no stupider than any other fighter I've met," Durren told him—and yet again regretted his own tactlessness.

Sure enough, Hule only appeared more crestfallen. "That's right. If I was at all smart, I'd be a rogue or a wizard or a ranger." He glanced sidelong at Durren. "Well, maybe not a ranger."

Durren couldn't help but laugh. "Perhaps you just need to be a different kind of fighter. A smarter kind."

"Perhaps," Hule agreed. He didn't sound convinced.

By then they'd reached the passage where the transportation chamber was. Arein and Tia were approaching from the opposite direction, Tia marching ahead and Arein hurrying meekly behind; two of her steps were needed to match a single one of Tia's strides.

Durren had vaguely envisioned that Borgnin might come to see them off, though he couldn't have explained why. Nor could he account for the disappointment he felt at the Head Tutor's absence. *Just because we happened to foil a plot to infiltrate and plunder the academy*, he told himself, *that doesn't make us special.*

Arein knocked, a mumbled response came from inside, and the four of them entered. Old Hieronymus was waiting in his chair. Pootle rested in his lap, and the wizard was scratching the observer's head with one yellowed fingernail—attention the observer seemed to be enjoying, in so far as a disembodied eyeball could express enjoyment. Seeing them, Pootle zipped into the air and floated over, bobbing in a fashion that Durren had come to interpret as its idea of a greeting.

"Hello, Pootle," Arein cooed. "Have you missed us?"

The observer's weaving grew briefly more frantic, which Durren took for a yes. Then it rose to its preferred spot at the center of their group.

Hieronymus was regarding them with his usual impatience. "So. Ursvaal, is it?"

Arein nodded. "We're going to be gone for quite a while," she said timidly. "And on behalf of all of us, I wanted to thank you for the many occasions you've helped us by...you know...transporting us to places and back."

Hieronymus scowled at her. "Quite a while, you say?"

"Maybe months."

He humphed into his beard, and pointed. "Take care of the little one," he said.

For a moment Durren thought that Hieronymus was referring to Arein herself, and that he was being particularly impolite; dwarves had been known to start fights over less.

Then he realized that, rather, the wizard's gnarled finger was indicating Pootle.

"We will," Arein agreed. "We have to; he's one of our party."

This time, the noise Hieronymus made was more of a snort, and implied that he didn't think highly of treating magical eyeball creatures as if they were persons. However, the twinkle in his own eye suggested otherwise.

"Well," he declared, "let's be off with you."

Hieronymus began to chant, in a low rumble from which Durren could pick out only the occasional gibberish syllable. The spell seemed to go on for longer than usual, perhaps because their destination was so much farther away. He was almost growing bored by the time the familiar sensation crept upon him: the sense that the world was all of a sudden being picked apart at its seams.

The gray of the walls ran and smudged like butter left on a hot windowsill, and Durren fell—without actually falling. He knew they'd arrived from the rush of bitter cold and the drizzle that lashed his face. Nothing he saw, though, was significantly less gray than the stone of Hieronymus's chamber; not the grass under his feet nor the wiry bushes that peppered the rising slopes beyond. He'd never encountered a place so colorless in his life.

Wherever they were, it wasn't inside the Shadow Mountain Academy. Durren had known to expect that much: by custom, using transportation spells to move people into anywhere occupied by other people was held to be the height of bad manners. Probably the practice had once been widespread, and everyone had grown heartily sick of visitors materializing from thin air. Nevertheless, in this case Durren wished the rules could have been relaxed. Appearing outside the academy felt ridiculous, as if they were pretending they'd walked all the way from Black River.

He looked around. Ursvaal was roughly what he'd been expecting—though expectation didn't make the sight more palatable. They'd arrived high up, on a hillside that was part of a range that descended behind them into a long valley, one of a number of long valleys Durren could see in that direction. They were all more or less the same: patterned with dense patches of forest, the green nearly black in the bleached light, and with the occasional drab patch of water reflecting drabber skies. Of civilization there were few signs, and certainly nothing resembled a city; only a couple of the shy clusters of buildings would even deserve the description of town. Generally he felt he was looking at villages and farmsteads, dispersed to make the best of what little the landscape had to offer.

That was the prospect behind. In front was Shadow Mountain. They were some distance away, on the verge of a rough track that wound up the hillside, yet still the academy was unmistakable. It struck Durren that, when he'd envisaged Shadow Mountain, he had basically been picturing Black River with the odd cosmetic change. And there were undeniable similarities: both were ancient and chaotic and had evidently been modified, decade by decade, according to the changing demands of the day.

But the one major difference outweighed any alikeness: Shadow Mountain was a fortress. That crucial detail informed every aspect of its design, from the battlements and arrow slits of the walls to the way no portion reached beyond four stories, and all was squat and square and ugly. If Black River was defensible, in places it was also frivolous, with features that could only be regarded as showing off. Shadow Mountain did not show off. What Shadow Mountain did was loom.

And had the academy not been doing a fine job of looming all by itself, the fact that, true to its name, it lay in the shadow of a mountain—a particularly large, imposing, and quite sinister trinity of peaks—would have sufficed. Wondering who'd think that the dank and dismal foot of a mountain was the ideal place to build an educational establishment, the one conclusion Durren could come to was, "the kind of person who liked wasting lamp oil."

Tia had already begun walking, Arein fell in after her, and Durren hurried to catch them up, almost in the same moment that Hule did. Whether due to inaccuracy on Hieronymus's part or bloody-mindedness, they really had arrived a long way away, and the slope was steep. Durren was soon out of breath, and sweating despite the cold. When a sprinkling of snow began to fall, he was glad of the chill touch on his brow.

The closer they drew, the more formidable and inhospitable the academy seemed. Then they crested a rise and its entrance, previously hidden by the lie of the land, finally came into view. As with Black River, there was a large main gate and a smaller side door. The notable difference was that in this case the main gate was reinforced with beams of iron and looked as though it had been intended to withstand a lengthy siege. Also, the two guards very much gave the impression of being real guards, the kind who anticipated violence and were well-prepared to deal with it. They eyed the approaching party distrustfully, as if four youths dressed for adventuring might be the prelude to a full-scale assault.

Tia stopped a good few paces away, maybe noticing, as Durren had, how the guards were readying their pikes. "Four students on exchange from Black River Academy," she said, as though such things happened all the time.

The guards' expressions offered no clue as to whether they were expected. One of the two leaned his pike upon the gates and entered by the smaller door; his companion leveled his weapon and glowered, as if daring them to approach even one more step. A minute later and the first guard was back. When he waved towards the door, the four of them hurried forward in single file, and both guards watched warily as they passed through.

The brief darkness of the gatehouse lessened only slightly when Durren stepped out on the other side: he had never dreamed a space could be so dusky in broad daylight. Between the mountain, the walls, and the building itself, every element conspired to leave the cobbled expanse in front of them sunk in gloom.

Shadow Mountain's courtyard was a great deal smaller than Black River's. Indeed, the entire academy was smaller, unless perhaps its interior penetrated the rock behind. At any rate, while there were signs that students practiced here—a small fenced arena, battered straw dummies, targets propped against one wall—Durren couldn't imagine four classes all training together in these confines. Doing so would have been a recipe for disaster.

Tia had come to a halt, and the rest of them followed her example. Durren's feeling was that the guards should have told them where they were expected to go or what they were meant to do; since they hadn't, he was glad at least that Tia hadn't already abandoned them to explore on her own.

He appraised the building before him, as best he could in the dim light. The academy was largely what he'd expected from outside the walls: grim and oppressive, and built as though its architect had expected an attack by ogres at any moment. Durren made out three entrances, but the main one was clearly the archway directly ahead. Above the door was a symbol he recognized, embossed upon a stone shield half as large as the opening itself. It was the same design he'd noticed on the seal of the scroll on Borgnin's desk.

Now he could make more sense of it. A third element had been lost when Borgnin had snapped the wax: between the top crooked line that presumably represented the mountain and the inverted crooked line that Durren took to be its shadow was a third, like a fissure separating one from the other. At first he couldn't guess its meaning. Then he remembered what Arein had said about Ursvaal's attitude towards the unbalance. Might that be what the toothed division represented?

His theorizing came to an abrupt halt when he realized a figure was approaching through the open archway. She paced quite near and stopped with a click of heels on cobbles, her hands on her hips. Durren couldn't resist the conviction that he was expected to bow, or perhaps salute.

He took the woman who confronted them to be Murta Krieg. She definitely had the look of someone who'd have a name like Murta Krieg. She was, he assumed, a wizard: she had the flowing robe and the staff almost as tall as she was. But wizards were prone to flamboyance, at Black River anyway, whereas Krieg's robe was a charcoal shade better suited to a rogue and her staff a plain length of dark wood that might have been plucked from a dead tree, with only the faded sigils burned into its edge to betray it as more than it appeared to be.

Krieg's face was of a piece with her outfit. She had hard features: hard cheekbones, a hard forehead, and even a hard nose, which Durren had never considered possible until then. Her lips were thin and pale, and her eyes were narrowed, as though with suspicion. He could tell that her graying hair had once been black as a raven's wing, for her brows still were, and they accentuated her fierceness.

"You're the students from Black River," she said. The utterance clearly should have been a question but wasn't phrased as one, and Durren had no idea whether she expected an answer—until Krieg barked, "*Well?*"

"We are," Tia said.

Krieg nodded. "Let me see if I have this right. You are the rogue, Tia Locke. The wizard is Areinelimus Ironheart Thundertree."

"Mostly people call me Arein," Arein replied sheepishly.

The look Krieg gave her said that she could expect to be called Areinelimus and to like it. And as she turned her eyes on Durren, her expression grew yet more withering.

"Durren Flintrand, yes? The ranger who was expelled and then wasn't."

"That was a misunderstanding," Durren managed to mumble through his shock.

"I find that unlikely. I've met Head Tutor Borgnin and, whatever his failings, he didn't strike me as a man prone to misunderstandings."

Durren had no answer to that, except for a small choking sound that he couldn't quite suppress—and Krieg's attention had already moved on.

"Last but conceivably not least, the fighter…Hole Tremick?"

"Hule," Hule corrected, with a slight grimace.

"Yes? Well." Krieg's tone said that she didn't necessarily

trust Hule with the details of his own name. "Head Tutor Borgnin had filled me in on some of your past endeavors, and in particular the unfortunate business that preceded your advancement to level two. He's spoken highly of the four of you, though with several caveats, which I see no reason to delve into now."

Durren's first thought was that he didn't like the sound of that, and he had to remind himself that so far he hadn't liked a single word that had come out of Krieg's mouth. Still, *caveats* seemed particularly disheartening; had Borgnin really conveyed all of their past failures and indiscretions? Her attitude suggested so.

Krieg looked them up and down once again, and her gaze was, if anything, more scornful than before.

"Understand this," she said, "you will be given no special treatment. The standards of Shadow Mountain are not those of Black River. We will require your best, and for your best to become a great deal better. Remember these facts and perhaps there's some hope of success for your time here."

Chapter 5

Durren expected Krieg to introduce them, then, to whoever would be acting as their mentor at Shadow Mountain—or at least to introduce them to *someone*. Instead, she said, "I'll leave the four of you to settle in. Keep out of areas where you're not meant to be."

By the time he'd established that this was all the initiation they could hope for, she was marching off in the direction from which she'd arrived. Durren had just long enough to consider calling after her—maybe to ask how they were meant to identify these prohibited areas—before she was gone.

Why had Krieg invited them here only to behave as though their presence was an almost intolerable inconvenience? Again he wondered if this was Borgnin's idea of a punishment; might he have warned Krieg of his suspicions regarding their prison break-in? On the other hand—and this was the most positive scenario Durren could think of—perhaps the last minutes had been nothing more than an introductory ritual, and Krieg talked to all of her new students this way.

"I'm going to have a look around," Tia said.

Durren nearly contradicted her. *Look around*, for Tia, most likely meant, *stick my nose into those places we've just been told not to enter.* Then he thought that possibly he should ask if he could go with her—she was sure to do a quicker job of getting to know their new home than he would—but she was already walking away.

He watched her vanish through the archway, and sighed. They'd been here precisely five minutes and things were going terribly.

"I'd better see about getting Pootle reoriented," Arein said. The observer had settled to hover above her shoulder.

Durren, who had no idea what she was meant, merely nodded. When she was gone, there remained only he and Hule. "What about you?" Durren asked. "Do you have any plans?"

Hule gave a laconic shrug. "There must be a dormitory for fighters. I suppose I'll ask for directions and start there."

Durren was surprised; that was actually a sound proposal. He still tended to forget that Hule wasn't as dim-witted as his appearance, and frequently his behavior, suggested.

"Mind if I come with you?" he said. "I mean, not to the dormitory, but to find someone who'll give us directions?"

Hule shrugged once more. "Why not?" And he began to lope towards the entrance.

Maybe, Durren thought, *I need to learn to think more like Hule.* The idea made him shudder. Nevertheless, the fighter seemed only mildly put out by their transfer to Shadow Mountain, or Krieg's icy reception, or the fact that no-one was inclined to offer them the most basic information. Left to his own devices, Durren feared that he might have simply waited in the yard until someone came along to tell him what to do; he'd changed a great deal since the day he'd begun his ranger training, but unlearning the habits of a lifetime was hard, and his old existence in Luntharbor hadn't exactly encouraged initiative.

The interior of Shadow Mountain was much like the yard: cramped, dismal, and unwelcoming. The walls were largely bare, and where they were decorated with tapestries or carvings, they were gloomy tapestries and gloomy carvings. Durren began to wonder how anything got done here. Didn't they spend their days sunk in despair?

He and Hule had been exploring for five minutes before they found anyone, through passages so undifferentiated that, for all Durren knew, they'd been walking in circles the whole time. Since the pair they nearly bumped into were wearing robes and carrying staffs, Durren assumed they were wizardry students. However, their robes were an identical pale gray shade that, like Krieg's, struck him as not very wizardly. Fortunately, they were capable of providing rudimentary directions, even if they eyed Hule and Durren with distrust and were quick to hurry away.

"Well," Durren said, "I guess I'll see you around." *At least, I will if anybody ever pays us enough attention to actually send us on a quest.* "Good luck."

"Sure." Hule trudged off, his rucksack snared casually over one shoulder.

Durren made his way to the dormitory with a couple of wrong turns along the way, only to find the room empty. He chose a bed that looked as if it hadn't been slept in for a while and dumped his backpack there. If he was wrong, no doubt someone would be quick to let him know.

After deliberating, he picked up his bow and removed the few coins he had stashed from the pocket of his pack. Leaving valuables untended here might not be the wisest of decisions, and anyway, he felt naked without his bow: now more than ever, he needed the solid reminder it provided of who and what he was.

He gave himself a minute and then stalked back out. On the way down the stairs into what he understood to be the main portion of the rangers' wing, he steeled himself: this first day was bound to be wearisome and humiliating, but there wasn't a thing he could do except get on with it.

So he set himself the task of talking to everyone he could find, making no effort to hide his ignorance and trying not to be offended when the responses he received were rude, or patronizing, or mere stony silence. Nor did he bother to wonder when no-one seemed the least bit interested in who he was or where he'd come from.

Most of those he spoke to had a definite accent: their w's sounded like v's and their a's like u's, and all in all he had to pay careful attention to understand even a word they said. He quickly concluded that the majority of students at Shadow Mountain were from Ursvaal itself, or at farthest from its neighboring countries; the prospect of someone coming from anywhere as distant as far-southern Luntharbor was perhaps too much for their imaginations.

By late afternoon, Durren felt he'd grasped the basics. He knew which sections of the building he'd be spending his time in and which rooms tended to be allocated to lower-level students. He'd seen where the schedules for lectures and training could be found. He'd attempted to reach the library but had got lost; thankfully he'd had more luck with the dining hall, and in the short term he could survive more easily without the former than the latter.

Lastly, he worked up the courage to track down the class head for the rangers and introduce himself. Except that matters were a little more complicated than that, because, strictly speaking, there was no head of rangers—since, as Durren had discovered to his tremendous shock, there were no rangers.

The one possibility about Shadow Mountain that had never crossed Durren's mind was that classes would be different. He'd regarded the four classes as being basically a constant of the universe, and the revelation that someone could change them simply because they wanted to had shaken him badly. But such was the case, and he would have to deal with it. The fact was, he was no longer a ranger. Now he was a bard, whatever that meant.

The office of the head of rangers—of bards, Durren corrected himself—was on the third floor, at the end of a particularly long corridor. He found it by the badge carved above the door, which he'd noticed elsewhere nearby and had been unable to make any sense of: the design looked something like a pear with an unusually long, squared stem. He'd wondered if it might represent some unusual Ursvaalian variety of bow; but the more he thought, the surer he became that what was portrayed there was no weapon.

He hesitated outside the door. All he'd managed to ascertain was that the Head Bard was named Reille Crovek, and there was only one way he was going to find out more. He knocked.

The voice that answered, "Yes?" was both reedy and airy, like a breeze blowing over the edge of a lake.

Durren took that *yes* to mean he should enter. The voice

had already confused his expectations; the ranger tutors at Black River tended to be rugged, hardy folk, and that was certainly true of their head.

Reille Crovek, on the other hand...

Well, he'd evidently spent a lot of time outdoors; despite the Ursvaalian climate, his skin was tanned to a nut-brown shade. Ruggedness, however, was another matter. Crovek's unruly gray hair hung past his shoulders, and the green robe he was attired in, embroidered around the V-shaped collar with motifs of silhouetted trees and birds, looked more like something a particularly ostentatious wizard might wear. Also, and most dismaying to Durren, there wasn't a bow to be seen anywhere in the room. Eldra Atrepis kept hers ready for use at a moment's notice.

Crovek was perched on one side of his desk, rather than sitting in the broad-armed chair behind. He inspected his visitor with mild puzzlement, which Durren supposed was better than the unveiled suspicion he'd encountered from everyone else. "And you are?"

"I'm Durren Flintrand. A level two ranger from Black River, here with my party on a student exchange."

"Ah." Crovek digested this. "Yes, Head Tutor Krieg...told me you would be arriving."

In that slight pause, Durren could have sworn Crovek had substituted *told* for another word—and he strongly suspected that word had been *warned*.

But Crovek's mind had already moved on. "I trust you've come prepared? Where is it?"

Taken aback, Durren presented his bow, though it had never been less than clearly visible.

Crovek's brow furrowed. "What? Not that! Don't tell me

you don't have one? Well, perhaps it's too much to expect. Not every academy has the same standards as Shadow Mountain."

He jumped to his feet and hurried to a cabinet in the corner, jerked the doors open and rummaged inside. The object he plucked out he dropped into Durren's hands—and Durren was so startled that he nearly fumbled it.

"What's this?" he asked stupidly. He recognized the basic shape from the design on the shield above Crovek's door. The rotund body and slender neck were of polished wood and the strings of some wiry substance he feared was catgut. A padded leather strap hung from its longest edge. Durren handled the thing with wariness, as if it might bite.

Crovek stood over him. "You really don't know?"

Durren shook his head.

"What exactly have they been teaching you at this so-called Black River Academy?"

"Oh…the usual? Archery, knife work, orienteering, sword fighting, things like that."

Crovek looked mortified. "No wonder the world's in such a state, when the most vital skills are neglected."

Durren, who felt that the skills he'd listed were the definition of vital for a ranger, had no idea what to say—and so said nothing.

Having taken a moment to gather his thoughts, Crovek cleared his throat. "A bard's role," he said, "is to be the heart and the soul of his party. This function is every bit as important as his capacity to shoot an arrow or wield a sword. A bard must be ready at all times to raise his companions' spirits, with a tale or with a song."

"With…a *song*?"

"Precisely. And since only barbarians sing unaccompanied,

he must be able to play an instrument." Crovek motioned to the article in Durren's hands. "In this case, the lute."

Durren stared at the unwieldy wooden pear. "But...I don't know how."

Crovek nodded glumly. "No, I suppose you wouldn't. You've a great deal of catching up to do; most of those we take have at least a little music in their blood. That can't be helped. I'm sure you'll try your best."

"I will," Durren agreed. All he could think was how unfair it was that he was relegated to being a beginner again—and because of something that, as far as he was concerned, had no part of being a ranger.

Grin and bear it, he told himself, *this isn't forever.* Yet he had no doubt now: their presence here was a punishment devised by Borgnin. Maybe his ploy was that, sooner or later, Durren or Tia would crack under the pressure and confess. Maybe if they didn't, this torment would go on forever.

Durren tried to imagine himself graduating as a level five bard, and the vision was profoundly depressing. He'd already decided that, compared to the rangers of Black River, bards were a poor substitute—and the fact that they seemed to believe the opposite only made matters worse.

"Perhaps you should devote the rest of the day to practicing?" Crovek advised.

"I'll do that," Durren lied.

By the time evening arrived, Durren found himself clinging to whatever similarities he could find. He was glad that there was a dining hall and that the classes ate together, as at Black River, and he was even glad that the food was bland and brown and probably terribly nutritious, just like the fare he was used to.

No-one made any effort to talk to him, or indeed to disguise that they were conspicuously *not* talking to him, and Durren had had enough of making an effort by then. The atmosphere in the hall was gloomy—he realized how much he was coming to associate that word with Shadow Mountain— and the conversations were muted. He'd never thought of Black River as being lively; compared with here, it was like a sailors' tavern just before kicking out time.

Nonetheless, there *were* conversations, and Durren listened in as well as he could, though he suspected that a part of the reason the nearest participants were keeping their voices low was precisely because of his presence. He was most of the way through his flavorless dinner when the discussion began to grow more heated; two students were practically arguing, though still at a muted volume. Durren had been starting to lose interest, but that changed when he caught one single, pronounced word...

Monster.

Leaning forward over his bowl, Durren heard the next exchange distinctly:

"Look, nobody's claimed to have seen it in weeks. Maybe it was never real in the first place."

"My uncle saw it last harvest time. Are you calling my uncle a liar?"

"Of course I'm not. All right, maybe it flew away for good."

"And maybe it didn't."

Was it possible they were talking about the same flying monster that had attacked the Brazen Fist convoy? Or another of the same species, whatever that might be? But perhaps the likeliest explanation was that they were discussing a different creature altogether. Durren was sure Ursvaal had more than its share of horrors, and it followed that some of them would have wings.

Finishing his dinner, he wandered back to the dormitory, taking care to remember the route he'd learned earlier. No-one seemed to mind about the bed he'd claimed, so Durren sat down there. He considered the lute Crovek had given him, which he'd carried around ever since; on impulse, he strummed the strings. The discordant note that rose from his fingers was louder than he'd expected. When he looked up, all eyes in the long room were turned his way. Flushing with embarrassment, Durren quickly stilled the leathery cords with the flat of his hand.

He hung the lute from the end of his bed; a glance around had told him that was where the other students stored theirs. Then, despite the fact that no-one else was yet doing so, he took off his boots and overclothes, crawled under the blanket, and closed his eyes.

He'd had more than enough of Shadow Mountain for one day.

The next week was every bit as difficult as Durren had been expecting. In many ways, his life had been reset: here he was for all intents and purposes a level one student again, with everything to learn and no friends to help him.

He had to remind himself that, regardless of how he felt, nothing could take away what he'd learned over the last months. He might effectively be a level one bard at Shadow Mountain, but he was a level two ranger at home, and that must count for something.

With no reason to hold back, he did his absolute best at

archery. There was some comfort in having the finest aim of anyone in his group, but not as much as he'd have expected—because nobody seemed particularly impressed, not even the tutor. It was as though they simply didn't understand how significant skill with a bow was to their trade of choice.

In other martial disciplines, as at Black River, Durren was more middling. He could hold his own against the better students with a knife or a short sword; unarmed he fared less well. These Ursvaalians were big for the most part, and his opponents were more like Black River's fighters than the lightly-built rangers.

On the academic side, he did adequately in all subjects bar one. Durren soon decided that he could practice until the stars fell from the sky and he still wouldn't be any good at playing the lute. He was trying his hardest—at least he assured himself he was—but music had never been a field he'd felt the slightest affinity with. He enjoyed listening to it well enough, and recognized the pleasant distraction it offered. To actually play was another matter. His fingers refused to understand the timing required; tunes fell apart the instant they entered his mind. The idea of reading music was as alien as that of reading wizards' runes, as though the tiny symbols represented a language he wasn't meant to know.

Durren tried to persuade himself that his inaptitude didn't matter—and couldn't. To his tutors, and even to his fellow students, he surmised that it mattered a great deal. He had begun to think that his competence with the instrument Reille Crovek had forced upon him might be the single biggest bar to his making friends from among the other bards. After a week, he was still being treated with the precise same degree of distrust he'd experienced on the first day. As much as he strived to be friendly, nothing he said or did cracked their reserve.

In desperation, Durren sought to distract himself by learning as much about Shadow Mountain as he could. He imagined that would be what Tia would be doing right now, and hers was as good an example to follow as any. He was particularly interested in the variations between classes—for he'd quickly discovered that rangers weren't the only ones to have been reinterpreted. At first he'd assumed the changes were essentially meaningless, just new names for the same old roles, but the more he observed, the more he doubted that was true.

Wizards were called clerics, a term he'd come across on occasions in Luntharbor and which made a certain sense. From what he'd managed to gather, they focused on different types of spells to those practiced at Black River, which tended to favor either practical manipulation or the inflicting of damage. Durren didn't know how spells were made, but he supposed that enough had been concocted for specialization to be both sensible and necessary. So clerics, on the whole, he could accept—though he wasn't convinced Arein would feel the same way.

Rogues were even simpler: known as scouts, they were otherwise largely identical, apart perhaps from a greater emphasis on staying on the right side of the law. Durren had noted before how Black River taught a great many skills with the potential to be abused by the unscrupulous; the tutors of Shadow Mountain had apparently given such questions a little more thought. Even so, Durren wasn't persuaded that the distinction was as meaningful as they believed: scouts still dressed in black and favored the shadows and gave the impression that one wrong word might find you at the bottom of the nearest lake. Rogues, he decided, were rogues the world over, whatever you chose to call them.

Fighters were more complicated, and less easy for Durren to make sense of purely by observation. At Black River, their mission was as straightforward as could be, and entirely summed up in their name. They were merely intended to be good at fighting, in as many ways and with as many implements as possible, in the assumption that they'd always be first into and last out of any fray. Here, they were called paladins, and the discrepancies seemed mostly to revolve around how they were expected to behave: that required lots of bowing and gesticulating and general ceremony. Hule had been looking for a change, and perhaps he'd found it—though whether this was what he'd sought was another question.

Aside from the classes themselves, the similarities between Shadow Mountain and Black River probably outweighed the differences: at the end of the day, the place was still an academy, its goal to train young people to be worthy of careers in their chosen specialties. Yet for Durren there *was* a crucial contrast— one of atmosphere and of attitude, one he could barely put his finger on but felt in every moment. It wasn't only the unfriendliness he was encountering or the subtle deviations in rules; it ran deeper. By the end of that initial week, he'd come to accept that he would never feel at home here.

He longed for a quest. A quest would mean getting out into the wider world—even if that was just elsewhere in Ursvaal— and it would mean seeing the others again. He'd been missing Arein, Hule, and Tia more each day, and had often considered tracking one of them down. He might have, had he not worried he'd embarrass them by doing so; maybe they'd settled in by now and he was the only one struggling to find his place.

Then, on the seventh day after his arrival at Shadow

Mountain, Durren overheard a conversation that raised his hopes of finally seeing some action—while at the same time making him wonder if he should be so eager after all.

They were meant to be watching a practice bout in the yard's small arena, but neither of the students involved was particularly capable, and as they devoted their energies to circling and avoiding each other, a few low conversations began to spring up among their supposed audience. With effort, Durren could discern two students muttering behind him over the scuffling of feet on the weathered boards.

"Did you hear? What they're saying happened in Gruilick?"

"What? No. I've an aunt in Gruilick."

"You should hope to the unbalance she's all right."

"Why? Will you just tell me?"

"They're saying"—the first student dropped his voice further—"that the dead walked through the streets."

"What do you mean? Walked where?"

"No-one knows. They got up from their graves, and then they were gone."

"That doesn't make any sense."

"Still, it happened. And I heard it wasn't only Gruilick either."

At that point, one of the duelists at long last made a move, slipping within her opponent's lax guard and striking a glancing blow upon his shoulder—at which the tutor called the fight won, with transparent relief.

Durren wished he could have heard more of the conversation; but by evening there were others in a similar vein, and everyone was too excited to worry much over whether he might be listening. All of the stories were basically the same, though the places varied, and sometimes there were embellishments: more than once he heard fresh mention of the flying monster that had been spoken of on the first night. Inevitably, a variety of explanations were being touted; if most assumed that someone or something was abusing magic, there were darker and more outlandish theories as well, and a few melodramatic students were already half-convinced that the end of the world was near.

Nevertheless, the basics were consistent: from around Ursvaal were coming accounts of the dead rising from their graves and lurching into the night. The consensus seemed to be that they weren't going out of their way to inflict harm, but also that they weren't shy about doing so should anyone get in their way. There was no indication that they recognized the living or remembered their past lives.

The mood was electric all through the remainder of the evening, and Durren wasn't surprised when students began disappearing off the next day, presumably sent questing at short notice. However, morning gave way to afternoon and still he had heard nothing—though his third lecture was practically empty.

Just as he was starting to despair, a messenger came to the door and spoke briefly with the tutor. The tutor turned to his diminished group and announced, "Kurzo, Larrowbless, Gullifen, report to your respective mentors. Be quick!"

Durren found that he was holding his breath. He only dared to exhale when the tutor turned his way.

"And Durren Flintrand…you're to go and see Head Tutor Krieg."

Chapter 6

Durren had to ask directions to Krieg's office, and still he nearly got lost. Not for the first time, he was glad that Shadow Mountain was a good deal smaller than Black River. He wasn't the least surprised to find the others waiting in the corridor outside; nor did the way that Tia was scowling at him change the rush of gladness he felt to see the three of them.

"Hello, everyone," he called.

Arein returned his greeting, Hule nodded, and Tia merely sighed impatiently. By the time he'd reached them, she had already knocked on Krieg's door and was turning the heavy iron handle in response to the summons from within.

Krieg was on her feet, and dressed much as when they'd first encountered her, if not identically. The room around her was barren as a cell: there was little in there but a desk and a chair, and no ornamentation except an embossed seal on the wall above, showing the academy's arms and the symbols of each class. A large sheet of parchment unfurled on the desk was blocked from Durren's view by Krieg herself.

"Thank you for coming," she said. "I'd hoped to give the four of you longer to settle in before I sent you beyond the safety of our walls. Regrettably, the academy faces something of an unusual crisis, and I'd be irresponsible to leave even partially trained students sitting around when they might be helping the folk of Ursvaal."

Durren suspected that in fact she'd been hoping not to send them on any quests at all, and maybe to forget about their presence entirely. He knew he should keep his mouth shut, but he'd been through a lot this last week, and Krieg's manner was an annoyance too far. "Is this to do with the reports of the dead rising?" he asked.

"So you've heard." Krieg's tone suggested that, merely by keeping his ears open, Durren had overstepped a boundary. "Yes—an irregular occurrence, to say the least, assuming the stories we've heard prove true. As yet we've no definite confirmation, merely rumors and a great many desecrated graves. While necromantic magic isn't unheard of, it's certainly uncommon, especially here in Ursvaal."

To Durren's mind, if dead people were going to get up and walk then Ursvaal was precisely the place they'd do so, but he had enough restraint left not to say that to Krieg. He'd already concluded that the Ursvaalians judged themselves to be special, no doubt because of their worshipful attitude towards the unbalance. He could see how the fact of someone practicing the darkest, most illicit of all magics within their borders might not be well-received.

Stepping aside, Krieg motioned to the document spread across her desk. Durren saw that it was a map, with the terrain picked out in grays and greens, and what he took to be settlements in dark blue. He noticed the academy's sigil towards the upper right-hand corner, and that several needles laced with red thread had been driven into the paper. There were seven of them and they formed a clear, if wavering, line.

"The pins," Krieg said, "represent reported incidents. They are, of course, not wholly reliable. Some may be the result of growing hysteria, now that word has got around, and we've reason to suppose there may have been desecrations we're yet to hear of. Regardless, I feel we have enough information to estimate where further defilements are liable to occur—if indeed this rash of crimes isn't already over.

"We'll be detaching parties to a number of towns and villages along this path"—she continued the line of the pins with the scrape of a fingernail—"in the hope of intercepting the culprit, or even confirming that there *is* a culprit. Given your relative inexperience, I've picked out for you a spot unlikely to see trouble."

Durren clenched his fists behind his back. He wanted badly to point out that they were the match of any level two students at Shadow Mountain; exactly how many of them had ever defeated a shapeshifter or caught a unicorn? But he sensed Krieg was purposefully baiting them in the hope of just such an outburst.

"Your quest will take you to a village named Furtz," she clarified. "Though they've reported no sightings, they do have an unusually large graveyard. You are to spend the night there. In the unlikely event that anything should happen, your objective is principally to make careful note of the direction in which the dead are traveling. Also, I hope I need not tell you that protection of the local populace is paramount. You'll set out as soon as you've gathered your equipment."

Krieg glanced around them. "Well? Questions?"

Durren, preoccupied with the notion of spending the night in a graveyard in the middle of nowhere, had no questions. Neither did anyone else. So, with that, Krieg bid them farewell—or rather, turned her attention to her map and waited silently for them to leave—and they each went to pick up their packs and gear.

They reconvened outside the transportation chamber, one of the scattering of places at Shadow Mountain that Durren had successfully memorized the location of. Pootle was hovering behind Arein's shoulder, and somersaulted in midair at the sight of the rest of them; Durren wondered if she'd been keeping the little observer with her all this while.

Within, the room was not unlike Hieronymus's chamber. There was the same sunken central area, reached via shallow steps and differentiated here with an intricate mosaic design of the academy's crest. And sat opposite the entrance was a wizard, or at least a cleric: his beard was graying rather than white and trimmed just past his chin, and overall he looked a good few years younger than Hieronymus, but he gave the impression of being every bit as disinterested by their presence.

"You have your own observer, eh?" the cleric noted. "Is it correctly oriented?"

"I saw to it myself," Arein confirmed.

"Right. Good. And…Furtz, is it? Hurry up, get yourselves ready."

The four of them hastily descended to the depression at the center of the room, Pootle taking care to keep close. The cleric, who Durren realized hadn't even shared his name, had already begun his incantation. He was quicker about it than Hieronymus, snapping out syllables as though he had far more important things he'd rather be doing.

For the first time, Durren was glad when the scene around him began to dissolve: stomach-turning as the effect might be, it meant he was to get some much-needed relief from the dreary monotony of Shadow Mountain.

He should have known better. The view that congealed from the hallucinatory smears of color was every bit as dreary and monotonous in its own way. The late afternoon sky was an unbroken expanse of gray that promised rain at any moment; what he could see of the surrounding landscape was painted in the soberest greens and browns.

Then there was Furtz itself. Durren didn't know what the requirements were in Ursvaal for calling somewhere a village, but he could hardly believe that Furtz met them. They'd arrived in a square, distinguished by a sort of monument, which was really only a menhir with a crooked line carved into its face that Durren took to represent the unbalance. Round about were clustered perhaps ten houses, and Durren counted as many more beside the road that wound off in either direction. All were of a single story, built of stone, and roofed with what appeared to be turf. They had small doors and smaller windows; smoke crawled from narrow chimneys, as though eager to escape.

"Should we introduce ourselves?" he wondered.

Krieg had implied that they were to continue here until morning. Unless they all stayed up throughout the night, that would mean persuading the locals to lodge them and keeping a lookout in shifts. At any rate, this was sure to go a good deal more smoothly with their support.

Tia had apparently gone through the same thought process and arrived at the same conclusion, for she was heading for the nearest doorway. She rapped three times on the crude planks, which quivered beneath her fist.

There followed a lengthy pause. Durren expected Tia to knock again, but she only waited patiently. Finally there came a scuffling from the other side, and the door swung inward.

The old man who'd opened it was so stooped as to be almost bent double. What hair remained to him was a snowy white, which was more than could be said for the stubs of teeth left in his mouth. He was supporting himself with one hand on the doorpost, and since his head only came to the level of Tia's chest, he had to crick his neck to meet her gaze.

"We're here from Shadow Mountain," Tia said.

The old man squinted. "Oh?"

"On a quest," she explained.

He shook his head. "No need for that."

"We hope not," Tia agreed. "There have been strange reports from nearby, so we've been sent just in case."

"No need at all," the old man muttered, as though he hadn't heard a word she'd said. Then he slammed the rickety door in her face.

"I guess we won't be staying there tonight," Durren observed.

"Should we try somewhere else?" Arein asked.

"Maybe he's the village idiot," Hule proposed.

But Tia was already walking away. Each house was cut off from its neighbors by low ditches, and had a scrap of garden to the rear. Between two such plots, a raised path ran out of the village, and that was evidently her target.

Annoyed that Tia was once again taking control without discussion, Durren made a point of not hurrying to follow. "Perhaps we should scout around and get a sense of the place," he suggested. "We don't really need to worry until the sun starts going down."

The reports that had reached Shadow Mountain had been predictably panicky and vague; but there had been common factors, and one was that all the incidents had happened by darkness. It was for that reason that many of the occurrences had gone unnoticed for a day or even longer.

Following Tia and the path, Durren saw that the village was surrounded on three sides by trackless moors, a blanket of purple heather rising and sinking with the unevenness of the land. Where there were patches of green, they were of a sickly shade that, to Durren's mind, represented boggy ground. Only a few strewn clusters of warped thorn trees rose to any height.

They hadn't gone far before the path dipped. Ahead was a broad depression in the earth, which seemed shallow and yet sufficed to cut off Durren's view of the village behind.

This was the spot the folk of Furtz had chosen to house their dead.

In fact, the graveyard was probably larger than the village itself, and certainly older. The marker stones resembled miniature versions of the menhir in the village square, and all bore the same lightning slash design. There was an overwhelming air of isolation, though they were barely a minute's walk from the village proper.

Trying to count the graves, Durren found that to do so with any accuracy was impossible. Many had long since crumbled to mere nubs, or were less even than that, just slight hillocks in the grass. How many bodies lay beneath their feet, he wondered? And an icy shudder tickled his spine. The notion of corpses suddenly digging themselves out of the earth had been bad enough when pictured from the security of Shadow Mountain, but his eagerness for a quest had helped distract him. Currently his imagination was proving a lot more active on the subject.

"What do we do now?" Durren asked.

Arein looked abashed. "I was worried we might miss dinner. So I brought some bread and cheese."

Durren nearly laughed at her single-mindedness; but in truth he was glad of Arein's foresight. He'd forgotten to pack any rations beside the barely edible hard biscuit that had been at the bottom of his rucksack for longer than he could remember.

"Good thinking," he said.

Arein picked out a spot on the bank that formed the graveyard's edge, and Durren and Hule sat with her. After a minute, Tia—who had been slowly circumnavigating the entire cemetery—came to join them.

"Everything seems normal," she announced.

Durren felt he could have established that much just by looking: this place had an air of having sat undisturbed for centuries. Oh, presumably someone would need to be buried every so often, and likely the occasional local came down here to remember their lost loved ones. But essentially the graveyard was a world of its own, ignored by the passage of time.

Arein handed around bread and cheese—she'd brought a startling quantity—and the four of them sat munching their simple dinner. After a while, Durren noticed that Arein was staring at him. When he caught her eye, she pointed and asked, "What's that?"

"Oh." Durren had contemplated leaving his lute behind, and at the last had decided he'd better not. "I'm supposed to be learning to play it. Apparently that's a thing rangers do here. Actually, I'm coming to suspect they consider it more important than being able to shoot a bow."

"You should try being a wizard," Arein said. "All they talk about is the unbalance this and the unbalance that. It's like they think it's making magic on purpose and might stop if they offend it."

Durren had never heard Arein sound angry, and she didn't precisely now, but there was no end of frustration in her voice. "What about you, Tia?" he asked quickly. "How does being a scout compare with being a rogue?"

She glanced at him. "I'm *still* a rogue."

Durren didn't clarify his question. He realized she'd understood perfectly well and that her reply was just the truth as she saw it.

"Hule, how are you getting on?" he said. "What's being a paladin like?"

Hule's expression implied that he was genuinely pondering. But, seconds later, his only conclusion was, "I'm not sure yet."

With that, the discussion dried up. Durren could remember how much he'd been looking forward to seeing the others, and now that they were back together they were all caught up in their own thoughts. Then again, the ancient graveyard wasn't exactly conducive to conversation: something about the weighty stillness in the air made every word feel like an act of sacrilege.

Durren finished his bread and cheese. Regardless of if they were talking, he was glad to be with his friends. He didn't even care that Tia was fully returned to her old self. She had already resumed her patrol, though what she expected to find he couldn't guess. She'd taken to working her way through the graveyard in a zigzag path, sometimes bending over a patch of ground or running her fingers over the lichen-encrusted face of a headstone. Occasionally she'd stop and stare beyond the perimeter. She was evidently on edge, and maybe that was the sole reason for her watchfulness.

Durren wrapped himself tighter in his cloak. The day was cold, as all days in Ursvaal seemed to be; despite the sheltered spot, the wind managed to whip around him. Feeling his lute jab into his back, he adjusted the strap, and wondered about attempting to pick out a tune he'd been introduced to the day before: a simple, plaintive piece he had been surprised to find he'd taken a liking to. But if he did, he would embarrass himself; no matter whether he enjoyed the music, his fingers still refused to be in the right places at the right times.

So he concentrated on keeping warm instead. After a while, he couldn't help noticing that the sun was beginning to set. Its bloody orb was visible where the clouds had fractured in the west, painting the sky in stripes of ochre and pink. Every shadow had grown long and deeply black, and given how most of the objects casting shadows were headstones, the effect was particularly sinister.

"Are we really going to wait here all night?" Durren asked.

"I've brought a lantern," Tia replied, as though that somehow answered his question. There again, perhaps it did: her tone suggested she was quite ready to stand guard until dawn if need be.

"Why don't we take shifts?" he proffered. "Two of us could get some sleep and we'll swap in the early hours. We could agree on some kind of a signal, in case anything happens." *Which it won't*, he assured himself. Hadn't Krieg made a point of how she'd picked the safest location for them?

Then Durren noticed Arein. She'd climbed the bank at the graveyard's edge and was gazing into the distance. Just as he was wondering what had her so entranced, she said, "A spell."

Durren wandered over and followed her eyeline. "What?"

"Someone used a spell." She pointed. "Over there."

He thought he could make out the tip of a tower in the direction she'd indicated. Maybe there was another village or even a town. "Is that strange?" he asked. Only, he already knew what her response would be; wizards were hardly so common that you'd expect to find another one all the way out here. "Does it mean students from Shadow Mountain?" he tried.

Arein nodded. "Most probably."

"We should take a look," Tia said.

"Hold on! No. That's exactly what we shouldn't do." In that moment, Durren felt he could see the future with perfect clarity: Tia would insist that they ignore Krieg's orders, and when they returned, Krieg would ensure that they never set foot outside the academy's walls again.

"I think they're in trouble," Arein murmured. More clearly she added, "That was a powerful spell. No-one would use magic like that without good reason."

"We're supposed to stay here."

But the more Durren thought, the less convinced he was that Arein and Tia were wrong. Krieg had said they were to see if anything out of the ordinary occurred, not that they were to specifically watch over this one village. Even if she had, that still didn't mean doing so was the correct course. It was apparent that she intended to give them as few opportunities to show their worth as possible, and Durren had no desire to remain a level two bard at Shadow Mountain for the rest of his life. So maybe now was the time to start bending the rules a little.

"Are you sure, Arein?" he asked. "If we leave and tomorrow morning this place is full of empty holes, Krieg's not going to be impressed."

"I'm as sure as I can be," Arein confirmed, and there was determination in her voice.

"All right, fine. How do we get there? If something's really happening then it's likely to be over by the time we arrive."

"I saw a cart," Hule said. "In one of the yards. We'll borrow that." And before anyone could query the idea, he'd set off back towards the village at a run.

Hule was right: a cart rested on a strip of dirt beside one of the houses, and was just about big enough to accommodate the four of them.

Hule was already hammering on the nearest door. As Durren caught up, it was opened by a woman of middle years, wearing a scrappy shawl over a sack-like gown and an expression the precise opposite of welcoming.

"We're here from Shadow Mountain," Hule blurted out. "We need to borrow your cart. It's an emergency."

The woman had given the impression that she was ready to chase them off her property, but plainly something in the seriousness of Hule's tone had reached her. "Then I suppose you'll need the horse harnessed," she said. "I'll get my husband."

A minute later and husband and wife were persuading a tired-looking mare into place in front of the cart; from the horse's perspective, being expected to work at night was evidently an insult without precedent. She appeared to comprehend, too, that the four of them were responsible: she kept baring her teeth and eyeing them murderously.

The preparations seemed to take forever, though only a minute or two could have passed. Hule's excitement and Arein's eagerness were infectious; despite the fact that common sense assured him they were hurrying towards danger, or at best risking a fall further into Krieg's bad books, Durren felt as if sparks rushed through his blood.

At last the woman finished whatever she was doing with the harness and announced, "You take good care, do you hear me? One scratch on that cart, one bruise on our old Bess, and we'll be sending the bill to that Shadow Mountain of yours."

Durren would have liked to point out that, while they might temporarily be students there, Shadow Mountain was in no way *theirs*. And at the same time he wondered how the pair would possibly know that their cart had sustained a scratch when the vehicle looked ready to fall apart at the slightest nudge.

"I'll drive," Hule declared, and had jumped onto the seat and grasped the reins before anyone could challenge him.

Tia took the place beside him, which left Durren no option but to climb into the back. Arein clambered on hands and knees to join him—and with a whoop and a crack of the reins, Hule was off.

As they broke from the edge of the village, Durren decided that Hule must have extensive experience with horse-drawn vehicles—and that those vehicles had likely been chariots. For that was how he seemed determined to drive the cart. He obviously didn't appreciate that the contraption wasn't designed for fast cornering, or that a carthorse wasn't bred for running. Durren would have protested, except that they really were in a hurry—and all his attention was devoted to clinging on for dear life.

Partly because the sun was sinking and partly because the highway rose and fell in broad sweeps, but mostly because he was bouncing up and down so much, Durren couldn't gain much of a view ahead. Nevertheless, as they crested a rise, he glimpsed buildings on the near horizon. Most were diminutive and squat, as those in Furtz, while a handful showed more architectural ambition. The town remained some distance away, enough so that he was impressed Arein had been able to recognize a spell being cast. What must the world be like viewed through her eyes? He wanted to ask her if she still saw any traces of magic, but if he tried then Hule's driving was sure to rattle the teeth from his head.

In fairness, the fighter couldn't exactly be described as a *bad* driver. Now that he was familiar with the cart, his confidence was growing: Durren was certain they were picking up speed. And as they passed a junction, the road, previously little more than a track, improved dramatically; suddenly there were cobbles beneath them. Hule was clearly pleased, but to Durren an unyielding surface meant only that their progress became even more bone-jolting.

At least the last leg was brief. The road widened further, and they began to pass the first houses straggling on the outskirts. Soon the dwellings grew densely packed. By comparison to Furtz, the place seemed massive. And had Durren doubted Arein, the number of men and women in the streets, gazing around in alarm or arguing in anxious voices, would have dismissed any last uncertainty.

Though Hule finally slowed—it would have impossible not to without running someone over—Durren still felt that they were navigating the narrow thoroughfares at vastly too great a speed. Maybe people assumed they must be in such haste because they'd come to help, or maybe they guessed that the four of them were from the academy; whatever the case, a few pointed directions as the cart clattered by.

Abruptly, Hule was drawing on the reins and bellowing at

their poor horse to stop. They'd come out at a low hill, the flanks of which rose unevenly towards a building at the summit. Durren could see what he took for torches burning up there, scant pinpricks of light amid the descending darkness. That building must be the one he'd seen from all the way in Furtz: the tower that rose from its far end marked the highest point of the entire town.

And the town had one thing in common with Furtz: its graveyard was disproportionate to the space devoted to the living. There were more of the stone markers, in uncountable numbers, along with small structures Durren took for mausoleums, and all told the site was very much like a village in itself, so much did it sprawl across the expanse of the hillside.

Having brought the cart to a halt, Hule jumped down to the road that surrounded the edge of the cemetery. Durren could hear the horse's labored panting. He slid to the ground too, and reached to help Arein. Only when she was standing beside him did he dare to turn and face the scene that confronted them.

He had half persuaded himself that, whatever might be going on, they would arrive too late to witness anything except its aftermath. He'd been wrong.

The sun was almost vanished, largely hidden by the hill itself and more violently red than ever. There was no other color in the sky, just that bloody smear below somber blue-black unmarred by cloud or star. By the ghastly light, Durren failed to make sense of what he was seeing; his eyes reported a great many dark shapes bobbing like froth upon swamp water.

Then he understood.

Those shapes were figures: a multitude squirming like insects revealed by the turning of a rock. Their movements were jerky and erratic, as though they'd forgotten how bodies were meant to work. Durren didn't need the smells of rot, preservative herbs, and turned earth to tell him that they were every one of them dead.

At first he could see nothing but walking corpses. The sight filled him with a numbing fear such as he'd never known: there was a unique terror in acknowledging that the things before him, so repulsive and mechanical in their motions, had once been people, with friends and families and lives of their own. They had been inhabitants of this town, they'd died and been buried—and now they walked again.

Just as he'd convinced himself that no-one could be alive amid that horde, that if anyone had been they'd long since succumbed, he saw the other students.

The four were huddled together, not far from the summit, an island at the center of the sea of uprooted dead. They were fighting; the weariness of their resistance said that they had been fighting for a good while. And even a single glance told Durren that they weren't winning.

Chapter 7

"We have to reach them," Tia cried, pointing.

Durren agreed, and at the same time had no idea how they were meant to do so. The dead were everywhere, pressed close as bricks in a wall.

Yet so far they'd offered no direct threat. Their attention was focused on the group near the summit; those around the four students were attacking, while the remainder milled back and forth and stared that way, as if distracted in the middle of some important task that had slipped their putrefied minds.

Though Tia had a blade in her hand, for once she looked hesitant. Durren guessed she had arrived at the same conclusion he had: if they tried to penetrate that crowd and were turned upon, not only would they be no help to those they'd come to rescue, they wouldn't last long themselves.

Durren turned back to the barrier of shambling dead. The sight made his stomach threaten to melt. He'd seen bodies before, at the funerals of family friends or when some unfortunate beggar had failed to survive a harsh winter's night, but there had always been a reassuring distance between him and them.

Now, the mingled smells of the grave choked his nostrils. He couldn't tear his gaze from the multitude of ashen faces, sometimes rotted or withered, frequently eyeless, occasionally even noseless or lipless, and all wearing the same expression— or rather, the same lack of expression. That was worst, the fact that there could be no seeing those faces and pretending they were alive. They were like puppets made from the cast-off bodies of people, and that comprehension made Durren's skin want to crawl off and bury itself.

At least they didn't need to worry about restraint. The townspeople might not be happy to hear that the remains of their loved ones had been hacked up, but he was sure they'd get over it; better that than wondering forever where those loved ones had wandered off to. And if moderation wasn't a concern, their first move seemed obvious.

"Why don't you try a spell?" Durren suggested, turning to Arein.

Arein held her staff ready, but her uncertainty was clear. "I don't know any spells that work against dead people."

Durren thought back to their encounter with the toads. "How about fire? Fire works on virtually everything."

Her frown said she wasn't convinced. Nevertheless, Arein began to mutter and to gesticulate. Durren found he was holding his breath, positive that at any moment the dead would turn their way. Yet they didn't. Those close by continued to mill aimlessly, and the fight near the summit raged on—though Durren couldn't believe the Shadow Mountain students would hold out much longer.

Light flared, painfully bright in the mounting gloom. Durren raised his free hand to protect his eyes from the crackling sphere balanced precariously at the tip of Arein's staff. Then, with a flick of her wrists and a small cry, Arein sent the fireball whooshing towards the horde.

There came a soft *wumph*, resembling the flap of a great bird's wing. Arein's fire had split and splashed like hot oil, spattering the ground with pools of flame and spreading across eight or nine of the nearest dead. Their ages underground had left them dry as dust; where scraps of decayed clothing or of burial shrouds hung, they caught like old paper.

So we have one effective weapon, Durren told himself with relief. *As long as Arein can keep casting those, we have a chance.*

But he was wrong—and his suggestion had been very wrong indeed.

The dead remained ablaze. They were also still standing and still moving. In fact, they didn't seem aware that they were on fire, except in as much as their interest was now diverted away from the hilltop and towards Arein. What Durren saw too late was that setting the dead alight didn't stop them. It just meant that not only were they facing animated corpses, they were facing animated corpses that blazed like fresh candles.

"Oh no…" Arein's voice was strangled.

Almost before he knew what he was doing, Durren had an arrow nocked. He chose for his target the nearest of the burning dead, which was lumbering with patient steps in Arein's direction.

"Aim for its head," Tia instructed, from beside his elbow. "Even if it's not alive, it still needs a brain."

Durren did as instructed, forcing himself not to flinch as he loosed his arrow—though there was something peculiarly wrong-feeling about shooting at a walking cadaver. At such a range, he couldn't possibly have missed, and the arrow entered through one hollowed eye socket, precisely where he'd been aiming.

The corpse staggered. It tilted its head, as if attempting to stare at the fletching that protruded from its own blazing face. Then it looked back at them, with rotten teeth gritted, and took another step.

Durren heard a noise that was nearly but not quite an intelligible word, a sort of breathless "Wuh." He realized it had come from his own mouth. Horror had frozen his every muscle. Fire didn't work. Arrows didn't work, not even arrows to the head. So what would? Perhaps nothing. And all they'd accomplished was to attract attention, not only of those who blazed with Arein's magically concocted flames but of others nearby as well.

"We'll just have to force our way through," Tia declared, raising her voice over the crackle of the conflagration.

The shock of her words sufficed to break Durren's paralysis. "*What?*"

"Maybe we can't stop them, but they're slow and we're not. And there are plenty of gaps if you look for them. Hule, you'll lead; clear us a path. Durren, back Hule up. Arein, you and I take the rear. That staff of yours is still a heavy length of wood, so it's good for something. Whatever happens, we keep moving. Is everyone ready?"

Durren was far from ready. Yet he couldn't deny that Tia was right: as usual, she was level-headed enough to weigh their options and pick the one that stood a slender chance of success. Nevertheless, the prospect of entering that lifeless swarm made his knees weak. He knew that if he let himself consider, he'd freeze up again, and there was no time—not only because the others might set off without him but because he could feel the heat rising off the enkindled dead.

Quickly he slung his bow and drew his short sword. Hule already had his own, substantially larger blade in his hand. His expression was grim, as befitted someone who'd just been tasked with charting a course amid a thicket of lumbering corpses. Arein looked petrified, but she was staying near to Tia and had her staff leveled. Tia herself had a long knife clasped in each fist.

"Here goes nothing," Hule muttered. He allowed the barest moment for anyone to contradict him, and then he was off.

Durren saw that the fighter had seized on a breach in the throng. As Tia had said, there were ways through; for all that the dead were a multitude, they weren't everywhere. However, they were also in constant motion. An opening in their ranks might be plugged an instant later. The task she'd set Hule was a desperate one, especially given the distance they had to cover. At this angle, the hill seemed indomitable as the highest mountain.

Then again, Hule was quite capable of making his own path. As the route he'd picked began to narrow, he lashed out, using the flat of his sword rather than the blade. The result was surely less than the fighter had hoped for, and less than he'd have achieved against a living foe. But though the withered form he'd targeted merely staggered aside, that was enough.

Duren followed his example, swiping at a gaunt wrist that flailed too close for comfort. The result was unexpected: he hadn't readied for the jolt that shot up his own arm. He was used to opponents that at least tried to flinch away, whereas it was evident that the dead were as untroubled by being struck as they were by arrows and fire.

Durren resolved to use his sword only when he absolutely had to. With each step they took, it was becoming more and more apparent that the dead responded solely to direct stimulus, such as a blow from a sword or a group of students charging into their midst: then they'd clutch with wizened hands and snap toothless jaws. Probably they were only assaulting those higher on the hill because they'd been provoked into doing so. Whatever their motive for relinquishing the comfort of their graves, it didn't appear to involve confronting the living.

That was certainly an advantage, but not really much of one. Though Hule had also grasped that hitting the dead was best reserved for emergencies, still there were so many of them that passing through their midst without inciting them was nigh impossible. Worse, once their awareness had been drawn, it wasn't easily shaken. As much as the four of them were making steady progress, Durren was conscious that at the same time they were leading more adversaries towards their beleaguered comrades.

Nevertheless, they were almost halfway there now, and Hule was growing confident in his role as leader: he was making less effort to fight and choosing his steps more carefully, reading the flow of the crowd, identifying gaps before they opened. And somehow the students fighting near the hilltop hadn't abandoned their resistance; maybe the sight of approaching relief had been enough to keep them on their feet.

As Durren thought that, the ground gave way beneath his own.

He was buried past his knees in cloying, dark earth. His fear was strangling. He'd dropped his short sword; he began to scrabble frantically for it. Only as his fingers clenched around the hilt and he scuffed his knuckles on rough stone did he understand what had happened. He'd stumbled into one of the recently evacuated graves.

The realization should have amplified his fear. Instead, it calmed him ever so slightly. A hole was just a hole, even if a corpse had once lain there. Yet he was conscious, too, that the smallest delay might be the end of them—for already the dead were clustering, and he was in no position to fend them off. Durren nearly let go of his sword again, but the prospect of being defenseless made his fingers tighten at the last.

Rather, he scrabbled for the grave marker with his free hand, striving to gain enough purchase to haul himself loose. The surface was too rounded. He wasn't sure that even with both hands together he'd have more luck, and to every other side was crumbling dirt.

Fingers closed about his. For a moment, Durren was convinced that it was one of the dead, readying to drag him beneath the earth. Then he registered that the hand was warm, the grip strong, and nearby someone was yelling words that finally penetrated his terrified brain.

"Come on, idiot!"

He looked up into Tia's face—and saw how his three companions had gathered to protect him. Hule was waving his sword wildly, using the blade's significant reach to maintain a circle of space around them. Arein was jabbing and shoving with her staff, relying on her lack of stature and proportionate stability to make herself a bulwark.

Her courage, and the fact that the three of them had put themselves at such risk on his behalf, gave Durren determination. With a roar, he put all his strength into his legs, as Tia hauled upon his arm—and in a shower of soil, he flopped to land at her feet. He hadn't an instant to catch his breath before Tia had yanked him upright and shoved him forward, and then the four of them were off again, Hule once more taking the lead.

This time, Durren paid a great deal more heed to his footing—though watching his own feet while dodging corpses while keeping track of Hule in front of him was no easy task. As they grew closer, he saw that the other party had managed to hoist themselves onto the flat roof of a mausoleum. Only two of the four, the paladin and the cleric, were still standing. They fought with all their remaining might to shield their fallen companions, despite the hopeless odds. Their expressions revealed that they'd long since discovered what Durren and the others had—that the dead could be briefly deterred but not stopped.

"Look!" he heard Arein gasp.

Absorbed by the fight ahead, Durren couldn't tell at first what she regarded as so important. Then he glanced to his right and understood. He remembered he'd seen the glimmers of torches from below, clustered around the building on the summit. Now he recognized that those flambeaux had been in the hands of men and women, presumably trying to preserve their sacred place.

Which was all well and good, except that somehow one of them had set alight the temple itself; likely a torch had been knocked from a careless hand and landed in the long grass growing in the shadow of the walls. Whatever the case, the fire had taken hold with shocking swiftness, especially given the wretched Ursvaalian climate. Already a flickering sheet of yellow had consumed half the nearest wall.

Yet another problem—albeit not one they could do

anything about. And in the longer term, the blaze might even prove to their advantage, as a distraction for the dead.

At least they were almost at the other students, with a mere few paces and a dozen ambling cadavers between them. "Hurry!" Hule bellowed—though how he had the breath left Durren had no idea, for his own was practically spent.

All the same, when Hule charged he stayed close, disregarding the lacerating pain in his side. Hule was once more laying about with his sword, but this time his goal was clear: he wasn't aiming to harm the dead, only to draw their attention from the besieged group on the mausoleum.

Durren could barely imagine how they'd lasted this long. Their stubborn resistance had stirred the dead to unprecedented violence: some of them had actually armed themselves, plucking lengths of board from broken coffins to use as bludgeons, and one or two even had rusted swords and maces that must have been buried alongside them. If they wielded those clumsily, like children playing at fighting, that scarcely made much difference; a weapon was still a weapon, and the dead were strong, for all their decades or centuries in the grave.

As Durren watched, and as Hule hacked his way across the last distance, the paladin went down. A wound to her left leg had already rooted her in place; as a plank shattered against her calf, the last strength went out of her. Without so much as a murmur of complaint, she crumpled. Her broadsword slid from her fingers, to clatter on the plinth below.

The cleric's eyes went wide. Then he began to twist at the air with the fingers of his free hand. There was rage in his face. Abruptly he gestured with the tip of his staff, and a thrashing corpse sailed into the air and flew halfway down the hillside.

The cleric sagged. Dramatic as his retribution had been, he'd clearly overreached himself. All his staff was good for now was support; without it, he'd probably have toppled off the rooftop altogether.

By contrast, Hule seemed indefatigable. He was choosing targets with an uncharacteristic degree of strategy, hacking and clubbing and shoving with a view not to winning an unwinnable fight but to creating space. Durren followed his example. His arms ached so much that he was barely able to lift his sword, yet whenever one of the dead came near he found new vigor. Nothing could have been more motivating than their proximity, and the anticipation of lifeless hands clamping upon him.

Arein and Tia had also caught up and joined the fray. Tia had renounced her knives and was relying solely on her nimbleness. As Durren watched, she tripped a cadaver with the swipe of a leg and, catching another by its outstretched arm, flipped it neatly over her shoulder. Arein, meanwhile, was working a spell with one hand while using her staff as a club with the other, a combination that undoubtedly taxed her beyond measure.

Just as Durren had decided her ambidexterity was doomed to failure, the tip of her staff illuminated a harsh purple. At first he thought the spell had done nothing. Then he noticed how the group of dead before her had slowed; they clawed and snapped at the air with puzzled lethargy, as though glue had been poured over them. Concentrating, Durren could discern a mesh of faint violet strands wrapped about them like a net. Arein had stumbled on a spell that worked: if it didn't stop the dead, at least it rendered them temporarily harmless.

But Arein looked drained, too much so to do the same again, and four walking corpses incapacitated was a drop in the ocean. Nor would the spell last forever; even powerful incantations had a duration of mere minutes. No, they couldn't rely on magic to save them—and they couldn't defend themselves for long.

Durren darted a glance upwards, confirming what he'd already suspected: there was no more room on top of the mausoleum. Of the three bodies slumped behind the cleric, only the paladin was still moving; she was kicking feebly at the nearest dead. The other two appeared to be unconscious—or Durren hoped that was all they were.

"Come on," Hule addressed the cleric, "we need to get out of here."

The cleric's head jerked, as if he'd been rudely woken from a deep sleep. "These abominations have to be stopped," he gasped, though how he had the strength left in him was anyone's guess. His robe was torn and ragged and he was bleeding from an ugly gash on his shoulder; the end of his staff was decorated with scraps of desiccated flesh.

Hule took a step back towards Durren. "When I give the word," the fighter muttered, "you grab his legs and I'll take his arms."

Durren wanted to protest. Except that maybe Hule was right; if they stayed here, they'd fare no better than these four had. Then again, nor could they carry off the cleric and all the wounded together, and the prospect of leaving anyone behind was inconceivable. Durren had a hunch that they might be safe with no-one nearby to antagonize the dead, but he was hardly sure enough to risk the lives of others on his conjecture.

At any rate, he doubted their opponents would give them time to struggle among themselves. Seeing allies join their foes had roused the horde to even greater hostility. Then there were the fresh arrivals they could soon expect, those they'd aggravated on their way up. One thing Durren knew for certain was that the dead weren't going to stop: they'd never grow weary or decide they'd sustained sufficient injuries for one day. Perhaps all they wanted was peace from these meddlesome students, but they'd pursue that goal with tireless determination, and sooner or later they were bound to triumph.

Durren staggered. In concentrating on a corpse that was clutching for his face, he'd failed to notice another that had edged into the gap between him and Hule. Trying to fend off both, he almost slipped; the ground here was churned from the long fight. Fortunately, the mausoleum was there to keep him from falling; unfortunately, the cold stone knocked the breath right out of him.

Something seized his ankle, and a scream bubbled in his throat. Durren didn't want to look, yet he had no choice; the grip was tightening. At his feet, one of the dead was crawling. Having secured a hold, it was straining with its free hand and craning its neck, ready to gnaw with the stumps of blackened teeth. Durren noted with distant repulsion that its legs had been severed at the knees, either during the fight or perhaps before its owner had ever been interred.

Durren swung his sword, and was both relieved and revolted when the blade sliced cleanly through the cadaverous wrist, leaving the hand still clasped about his ankle. He kicked, and his boot connected with a hideous crunch; the force of the blow was enough to tumble the corpse onto its back, but Durren was almost more pleased to realize he'd dislodged that withered hand.

By then, though, the first two were upon him, groping at his cloak and hair—dragging him down. Durren swiped blindly and missed. He swung again and felt an impact. The clutching fingers were no less persistent. He wanted to cry out, to Hule or to Tia, and knew neither of them would reach him in time. While they must be nearby, while he could hear the thuds of their blows and their harsh breathing, he couldn't see them. To left and right were his decayed antagonists; at his back was the mausoleum. There was no way out.

From somewhere far off there came a piercing whistle. Terrible as the cry of a nocturnal hunting bird, it chilled Durren to the marrow of his bones. He wanted badly to know where that sound had come from. Instinct told him the knowledge was important. Yet so long as he was fighting for his life and for the lives of others, he wasn't about to tear his attention from the dead.

But the dead weren't moving. All the fight had gone out of them. They were precisely as still as corpses should be, and only the fact that there were standing transfixed betrayed them as in any way out of the ordinary.

Leaning around the corner of the mausoleum, Durren followed the line of their gaze, behind him and upwards. He found his eyes drawn towards the rooftop of the blazing building, and to the flat pinnacle of its tower.

There, a figure squatted.

What he saw was just a black shape—until, with a clap of crushed air audible even from where they were, it spread its wings. Then he was looking at something not unlike a bat, if a bat was larger than a man, with humanoid arms and legs and a wingspan wide as any creature to have ever haunted a night sky.

This must be the monster he'd heard discussed, the one so frequently sighted around Ursvaal. Durren felt that he was staring at a nightmare given form, an effect amplified by the flames that licked from below it. Moreover, he was nauseatingly sure that here was the one who'd summoned the dead from their graves.

The creature beat its great ebon wings. Smoke whirled in horrid curlicues; the flames roared and spread, like a reflection etched in fire. As Durren watched, the fiend leaped into the air and, caught by the updrafts of the burning building, soared skywards.

It swooped towards them, dreadful wings spread wide, and Durren readied for its attack—even as he knew there was no possible way they could defend themselves.

Chapter 8

For a moment that seemed to last forever, all Durren could see was the black shape falling towards him. With the burning building behind, it was nothing except a silhouette. Its wings were vast and leathery, and he could hear each ponderous flap. Its legs ended in claws like knives, and he saw long fingers too, displaying similarly savage points. What he couldn't see was its face, leaving his imagination to sketch in gleaming ruby eyes and dripping fangs.

Even if Durren's courage held, to fight with the stubby blade in his hand would be as futile as trying to shovel a lake dry. Then he remembered his bow, and a small portion of his mind wondered at what a well-placed arrow might accomplish; to the monster's head, say, or to the tendon joining shoulder and wing.

The idea seemed fanciful, like a children's story he was telling himself. He could no more have taken his bow from his shoulder and nocked an arrow than he could have casually turned away from the descending creature. In fact, he wasn't certain he'd even persuade his muscles to let him dive out of the way, which he felt increasingly would be his one slim hope of survival.

Yet before the horror had drawn near, it began to rise once more, and reeled to the left, beginning a half circle that flung it over their heads with a *whump* of torn air. Its course carried it beyond the graveyard and low above the town. As it shrank from sight, Durren again heard the shriek of a whistle, fainter this time but still piercing.

He noticed something else, too. Upon one of the bordering roofs, beneath where the winged creature had passed, lurked a second obscure shape. He struggled to be sure when the only light was the sun's last carmine glow and the fierce flicker of the burning temple. However, he felt reasonably confident that he was looking at a figure, this of merely human height.

He pointed. "I think there's another one."

The only person who paid him any attention was Tia. As she followed his outstretched finger, the figure vanished, springing lithely into the darkness.

Tia twitched, as though a shiver had run through her from head to toes. Her mouth opened, but no sound came out. Then she caught herself. "I'm going after them," she said.

"What?" Durren couldn't believe he'd heard her correctly. "No, you're not."

"Are you going to stop me?"

He nearly said, *If I have to.* He knew that was just the anger talking, compounded by the adrenaline of the last few minutes, and that he couldn't if he tried. He hauled down a deep breath and told her, "I'm not. The fact that you're a member of this party and that you know better than to go running off right now *is*. We've wounded to look after; we have a lot of frightened people and a building on fire. Are you telling me you'd turn your back on all that?"

He'd never seen such fury in her eyes. And there was something more too, something he couldn't explain—a sort of frenzied desperation. He was positive she'd ignore him and go anyway, and maybe would even strike him down to do so if she imagined he'd get in her way.

Instead, the fury vanished, leaving only the urgent need. Then that too was gone, and Tia's eyes revealed nothing. "Fine," she said.

Durren couldn't keep in a sigh of relief. Facing bat-monsters and animate cadavers was a minor concern compared to the prospect of having to defend himself against Tia. And with a start he realized that, in the heat of the moment, he'd somehow managed to forget that they were surrounded on all sides by the dead.

But where *were* the dead?

"They're leaving." Arein sounded disbelieving. Yet she was right.

The evacuation, having apparently started on the edge of the cemetery beyond which the winged creature had vanished, was spreading like a wave—and had swept as far as where they were. All Durren could see of their former opponents was their retreating backs. Even those in no state to do so, like the corpse with the severed legs, were making their best efforts to descend the hillside.

"We need to go after them," the cleric said, and already he was clambering down from the mausoleum. "We have to stop them." But when he reached the ground, he gasped, and barely caught himself by driving his staff into the churned earth.

"You're not following anyone," Tia told him. "And neither are we. Helping the wounded takes priority."

"That and the fire," Durren added. The entire temple roof was alight now, and the flames were spreading to the far side of the building. Sparks rose in geysers and drifted upon the wind. All it would take would be for burning debris to find its way to a rooftop below and the entire town might soon be ablaze.

Still, the cleric looked unconvinced. His eyes were fixed on the retreating crowd of dead, the head of which was constricting to navigate the streets below. Durren could only imagine the thoughts of those who gaped from windows and doors as a small army of corpses—some of them perhaps even familiar—trooped by.

Hule put a hand on the cleric's arm. "Let them be someone else's problem," he said. "We've enough of our own to deal with."

"But—the quest…"

Conceivably he was in shock. While the cleric was the least wounded of the four, there was a good quantity of blood on his robe, and his stare was hollow.

"Look," Durren said, "they're leaving a trail a blind man could follow. So just settle down, all right? What's your name?"

The cleric considered him warily. His skin was as dark as Tia's, though a walnut brown rather than her dun-elf gray. His eyes, despite the half-darkness, were visibly a piercing shade of green, and his black hair was a mass of short coils. Given that he spoke with a hint of the accent common to the lands about the Middlesea, Durren guessed that wherever he was from was closer to Durren's own part of the world than to Ursvaal—and wondered how the cleric had ended up here. Shadow Mountain didn't appear much inclined towards recruiting from outside the nation's borders.

At any rate, he seemed finally to have concluded that Durren's question wasn't some sort of trap. "I'm Cailliper," he said. "Cailliper Ancrux."

"That's a mouthful," Arein told him, evidently unaware of the irony of anyone with a name like Areinelimus Ironheart Thundertree expressing an opinion on the subject.

"Then call me Caille," the cleric offered grudgingly.

"Caille." She smiled. "I'm Arein. That's Durren, that's Hule…and there's Tia."

Caille's nod suggested that making friends was of no real interest. Having been forced to stop, he was calming down quickly, but that in turn was draining whatever vestiges of strength were keeping him upright. "My party…" he began, and raised a wavering finger towards the mausoleum.

Tia was a step ahead of him. Having already hoisted herself onto the roof, she was hunting within her backpack. She drew out a lantern, the same one she'd used during her and Durren's expedition into the bowels of Black River. Its blue-white glow was less reassuring than ever in the midst of a graveyard that had just vomited up its every inhabitant.

"We should try and get help," Durren proposed.

"Help should come to us." Arein pointed.

Durren saw that she was indicating Pootle. Through everything that had happened, he'd forgotten that the little observer was dutifully watching. And to his shock, he realized Pootle had acquired a twin: his heart skipped when the second eyeball bobbed from behind a headstone. But of course the other party would have their own observer, and both should have been transmitting back to Shadow Mountain all this while.

So somebody must have seen. Maybe they'd decided that

dropping more students into the middle of a horde of belligerent corpses would only place additional lives at risk, but now that the immediate crisis was over, Arein's faith was well placed.

"In the meantime," Tia said, "we need to get the wounded down. We can't do anything for them like this."

Durren had attended enough lectures on field surgery to know that you were generally better off moving injured people as little as possible. In this instance, though, Tia was right: there wasn't room on top of the mausoleum to administer proper treatment.

They lowered Caille's party one by one, taking the utmost care, with Durren and Hule doing most of the work and Tia coordinating from above. Arein, whose stature disqualified her from the task, and Caille, who could barely keep himself upright, were assigned by unspoken agreement to helping the injured once they were safely on the ground.

Durren was relieved to discover that all three were still alive. The paladin, lifted down first, was weak but conscious; Arein set to cleaning the wound in her leg, which was unmistakably deep. The scout had taken a blow to the head, and half his face was purple with bruising; at least his breathing was steady, and surely that was a good sign. Their bard was in the worst condition: dark patches of blood spread from four separate spots, and she was making a hoarse wheezing sound.

Even so, they managed to bring her down, and with that done, Durren and Hule concentrated on making her comfortable. When Durren slipped off his cloak and rolled it to tuck beneath her head, she mumbled wordlessly and stirred ever so slightly, then lolled back with a groan.

Beside them, Arein was crouched over the scout, with

Caille kneeling beside her.

"Do you know any healing spells?" he asked.

"A simple one," Arein answered sheepishly. "Well, it's more of a pick-me-up really."

"It's worth a try," Caille opined.

Dutifully, Arein began her spell, clutching her staff with one hand and motioning with the other, muttering all the while under her breath. But she'd barely pronounced a dozen syllables before the cleric snapped, "That's not how you talk to the unbalance!"

Arein's glare was equally fierce. "I'm not talking to the unbalance. I'm casting a spell."

"Disrespectfully."

"Who cares, so long as it does what it's supposed to?"

"It won't, not half as well as it could. You'll do more harm than good by being insulting."

"That might be true if I was ordering a drink in a tavern. Since I'm reciting a formula to help focus stray magical energy, I don't see how—"

"Stop it." Tia was standing between them, her hands on her hips, her expression implacable. "These three need your help. Work separately if you can't work together."

Arein's mouth opened and closed. She looked both mortified and ready to keep arguing. Then, quietly, she said, "You're right." She stood up, went over to the prostrate paladin and knelt once more, this time with her back firmly to Caille.

Meanwhile, the cleric's expression was thunderous, and only became more so when Arein started up her spell again. But he obviously had sense enough to appreciate that whatever help she provided his friends was better than nothing—and that arguing with Tia would be seriously misjudged. Putting his hand out, he began a spell of his own. Durren found that he recognized how differently the cleric mouthed the words. What he'd said was true, so far as it went; where Arein demanded, Caille entreated.

Without Durren's noticing, Tia had moved to look down at him and Hule. "You two aren't helping here," she said. "I'll take over. See what you can do about that fire."

She made a valid point. Durren was nearing the limits of his medical knowledge; at most, he and Hule could probably manage a competent job of bandaging up the scout between them. Durren couldn't say for certain that Tia's experience extended beyond that, but since she was Tia, the chances were good.

However, he didn't altogether like the thought of leaving her. He wished he could have faith that she'd do what she'd said and wouldn't go chasing off after any shadowy figures. Unfortunately, wishing didn't make it true. The fact was, he was having a harder time trusting her than ever.

There was nothing he could do. His one option would have been to warn Arein, and she was deep in concentration; the stress of using yet more magic after her previous exertions showed clearly in her face. He would just have to hope that Tia had seen the error of her earlier impetuousness.

Hule had already set off towards the blazing building, and Durren hurried to catch up. The graveyard was almost eerier without the dead swarming upon its slopes. They'd left behind the signs of their passage: scuffed earth, tumbled headstones, and a general air of devastation. Strangely, picking his way among empty graves made Durren more aware of his own mortality than fighting against animated corpses had done. The sight seemed to imply that not only was death inevitable, it also wasn't that important in the grand scheme of things. Death was rotting away in a hole in the ground—and if you were lucky, getting to stay that way.

He pushed such morbid thoughts aside. Surely the correct message to take from the evening's events was that the four of them were lucky to be alive, and that Caille and his party were even luckier. What mattered now was ensuring the night didn't end in tragedy.

By the time he and Hule were halfway to the burning building, it was apparent that there was no point in approaching nearer. The locals had fled, presumably once they'd realized that not only had they failed to protect their precious temple, they'd actually been the cause of its destruction. There were no bodies to be seen. Nor was anyone yet trying to put the fire out; perhaps they were unwilling to assume that the dead wouldn't return.

Durren and Hule skirted the building, not able to get close for the heat. On the far side, the fire had barely taken hold, likely because a bitter wind blew from that direction. Durren could see the houses spread out below, and that there remained a great many people in the streets. The parade of dead, though, had vanished, swallowed by the darkness. Durren wondered if what he'd told Caille was true; would they really be able to pick up their trail later? Or rather, would someone else be able to? For he suspected they'd already deviated further from their quest than Krieg would tolerate.

He pointed. "It looks as if there's a gathering." He'd spied a small square not far from the road that encircled the cemetery.

As they drew near, Durren saw that the square was more like a courtyard, with a covered well at its center: the townsfolk had managed to accumulate a few buckets and were filling them one by one, to the accompaniment of a great deal of bickering and conflicting instructions.

As Hule and Durren reached the edge of the group, their presence began to be noticed. A large man in a none too clean apron squared up to them. "What's this?" he asked gruffly.

"We're from Shadow Mountain," Hule said. "And if you don't hurry with those buckets, one burning building will be the least of your worries."

The man appeared eager to contradict this stranger who was abruptly telling him his business—but Hule had already brushed past. He kept going until he was almost at the well, then cleared his throat loudly and faced the assembly.

"You need more water and more people," he declared. "And you need them both now."

"Where are we meant to get more water from?" one woman wondered angrily.

"This is the only well in town?"

"No, of course not, but—"

"Who's in charge here?" Hule cut her off.

"We're just trying to help. Nobody's in charge."

"Then you can be. Somebody ought to be knocking on doors. Who do you suggest?"

"Well…I suppose Berth and her sons could do that." Her eyes were on a bossy-looking woman with three gangly boys of various ages clustered around her skirts.

Hule turned to the woman named Berth. "Good. You should probably split up. Tell everyone you find to gather here until we're better organized." He turned back to the first woman. "Now, how about those other wells?"

Bare minutes later and the chaos had been replaced by fragile order. Hule had arranged the gathered townsfolk into four work parties, and a bucket chain was taking form, one that splintered off in three directions to link with wells deeper in the town. Rather than staying to supervise, Hule was among the first to take a bucket, and Durren emulated his example.

Halfway up the slope, as they were picking a path between disturbed graves, Durren leaned closer to the fighter—careful not to slosh his precious cargo—and muttered, "Are you all right, Hule?"

Hule looked faintly puzzled. "I'm fine."

"Only, I've never seen you act like that before."

Hule's perplexity turned into a frown. "Someone had to," was all he said.

By the time they'd returned to the summit of the hill, more lanterns were burning around the spot where Arein, Tia, and the others were. Durren could see a number of person-shaped silhouettes hurrying back and forth. At least two more parties had come to their aid, and he wouldn't have been surprised if a tutor or two had joined them. Minor casualties might be an accepted hazard of academy life, but three severely wounded members from a party of four was a catastrophe, and one Shadow Mountain would treat with the utmost seriousness.

Then again, that was assuming Caille's group were the only ones to have met with danger. That winged monstrosity was still out there, and so were its army of the formerly interred. Who could say what other horrors this night had seen, or what might be occurring elsewhere in Ursvaal?

Remembering their encounter with the bat-creature, Durren found himself trying to espy Tia. He was half-convinced that she'd have abandoned her charges to take off after the mysterious figure she'd been so preoccupied with. Who or what could they have been—or, perhaps more importantly, who or what did Tia think they were? *Sooner or later,* he told himself, *you're going to have to confront her about this*—and the prospect made him shiver despite the nearby heat.

"Do we stay and keep helping?" he wondered aloud.

"I'm staying," Hule responded gruffly.

Durren sighed. The fighter was right. As much as they were likely to get into even deeper trouble, helping people was high on the list of reasons he'd become a ranger, and he wasn't about to stop just because Krieg might disapprove.

The first wave of buckets didn't achieve much, but the chain was gaining traction, and more were on their way. At the same time, new arrivals struggled up from below, until soon they had a half circle of bodies spaced around the most violently burning portion of the temple.

Hule had already made clear to everyone that their goal wasn't to save anything; this place was lost, and what mattered was containing the damage. So it was that, once they'd begun to make progress, he sent orders to the base of the hill for axes and hammers to be brought. As much as the locals wouldn't like it, they would have to knock their sacred building down before it burned down.

Soon after that and the destruction was in full swing: a mob of burly men and women set to tearing down the few portions the fire had yet to reach, while the bucket chain steadily encroached upon the burning sections, chasing dancing flames as if they were the living beings they resembled. By then, the townsfolk were functioning like clockwork, with brimming buckets arriving in a steady stream and empty ones departing by the same route.

Durren had lost track of how many pails had passed through his hands when he glanced up and saw Tia striding towards them. She looked as weary as he felt.

"We've done what we can here," she said. "The wounded are stable, so we're heading back to Shadow Mountain. Arein says Pootle won't transport us unless we're all there."

Durren half expected Hule to argue. Instead, the fighter gazed around him, at the string of people and buckets that linked the now significantly less on fire building with the town below. With a small nod of approval, he said, "Fine."

But before he left, he tapped the nearest man on the elbow and muttered to him briefly.

"What was that about?" Durren asked. "They can manage without you, you know. I've never seen a better-organized bucket chain."

"Not that," Hule said. "The cart, remember? Somebody needs to make sure it gets back to Furtz."

Durren had entirely forgotten the cart, along with the poor horse. Far more surprising was that, out of everyone, Hule had remembered. What was going on with this hardly recognizable new version of the fighter? He certainly seemed a considerable improvement. Or maybe it was only that, thanks to his efforts at persuading them of his own stupidity, they'd all been underestimating Hule for a long while now.

When they reached the mausoleum, they found a third party of students milling about. Tia explained under her breath that they were on guard duty in case the dead should return, and that yet another party had set out to follow their trail. In the meantime, the injured were still being cared for by Arein and Caille, who appeared to have at least temporarily set aside their differences in opinion. Though the scout and bard remained unconscious, the paladin was sitting up, and her wan features had regained a dash of color.

Seeing that Tia was back with Hule and Durren, Caille glanced skyward and called, "Observer!"

One of the two eyeballs hovering over the scene plummeted to float in front of him. Arein stumbled tiredly to her feet and retreated to a safe distance.

"Goodbye," Caille said.

He spoke a few short syllables to his observer. The air surrounding him swam and smeared; for an instant Durren couldn't have said just what or where he was looking at, and had to avert his eyes until his head stopped spinning. When he raised them, Caille and his party were gone.

They tarried a minute. Then Tia picked up her lantern and said, "Our turn." Pootle swooped to join them without needing to be asked, as if in competition with its counterpart.

Durren stared one last time about the cemetery. Ahead, the fire was well on its way to being extinguished, though the townsfolk still had many hours of grueling work before them; unlucky for them that today should be the rare day when the Ursvaalian skies chose not to deliver rain. Elsewhere, empty graves gaped, waiting patiently for their former inhabitants. But Durren presumed they were gone for good—leaving behind them such questions as how, and where, and most of all why.

"Homily, paradigm, lucent," Arein murmured.

And around them, the graveyard began to melt.

Chapter 9

There was no comfort in being back at Shadow Mountain.

In those moments of transit, as reality dripped and sloshed around him, Durren had unconsciously expected to return to Black River—and even as the walls came into focus, a part of him anticipated Hieronymus's transport chamber. Only as he felt solid stone beneath his feet did memory complete the gaps in his tired mind: Black River was the past, as distant now as his father's home in Luntharbor.

He'd barely stepped from the pit in the center of the room when exhaustion caught up with him. The last hours were a blur. But even if he could scarcely remember the details of their bone-shaking cart journey, the battle up the hillside, their hopeless-seeming stand against the assailing dead, or the struggle to douse the burning temple, his body recalled every instant. He ached from head to toe.

Durren glanced down at himself. His clothes were black with soot. He drew fingers across his cheek, and they came back black too. He could hardly imagine what he must look like. Then he saw Hule and realized he didn't have to imagine. The fighter resembled a scarecrow that someone had set on fire and extinguished. Only his eyes showed white through the filth that caked him.

Durren wondered if he'd be able to find hot water at this late hour. The prospect made him almost dizzy with longing. Yes, he'd find hot water somehow and scrub himself clean, maybe salve his bruises, and after that he'd stumble to the dormitory and collapse into—

"We should go and make sure Caille and the others are all right," Arein said.

After the heated words they'd exchanged, Durren was surprised that Arein would much care what happened to the haughty cleric. Then again, likely she was more worried about their mutual patients. Arein looked as anxious as Durren had ever seen her; surely the possibility that there was an injury she'd failed to spot or a wound she'd mistreated must be what weighed so heavily.

It seemed unfair that such responsibility had been thrust upon her when she'd never claimed to be any kind of healer. Yet hadn't they all been forced to adopt new roles tonight? And he could almost hear Adocine Borgnin's voice, explaining how the ability to adapt to the unpredictable was at the heart of being an adventurer, regardless of class. If Borgnin were really here, he'd no doubt be commending them—which made it even more unfair that instead they would have Krieg to deal with, and that her response was certain to be less favorable.

Durren didn't, however, expect to run into her immediately—so that when they arrived at the infirmary to find her standing outside the door, he felt wholly unprepared. He might have proposed they beat a hasty retreat and come back later, were it not obvious that Krieg had seen them.

She waited until the four of them were before her. Then she said, her voice colder than the night outside, "I trust your visit to Furtz was uneventful?"

Durren's first impulse was to make a stammering explanation of how they had not, in fact, spent the last few hours in Furtz. But it was clear that Krieg was toying with them, and in any case, Tia had already stepped forward to elect herself as spokesperson.

"Head Tutor," she said, "soon after we arrived in Furtz, Arein saw that a powerful spell was being cast nearby. Concerned that other students might be in jeopardy, we collectively decided that our most responsible course was to investigate. As it turned out, our concerns were warranted: we discovered that another party were in grave danger and intervened in time to come to their aid."

Throughout, Tia's features were impassive. She could not have spoken the words more mechanically. And Krieg's reaction was the same: her face was perfectly still.

"I'm grateful to you for aiding my students," she said. (Durren couldn't help noting her implication that the four of them were *not* her students.) "Nevertheless, I fear your education at Black River, and the different approach of my counterpart there, has misled you as to what your roles entail. You're not here to act on your own initiative. You're here to follow the quests you're given, to their letter."

"I understand," Tia replied. She sounded remarkably calm, far calmer than Durren himself felt. He was caught between indignation and fatigue, and rather than canceling each other out, the two together were making his thoughts and his heartbeat race.

There were a dozen things he wanted to tell Krieg—not least that, were it not for them, Caille and his party would undoubtedly be dead by now. But not only was he aware that saying any one of them would probably be the end of his time at either Shadow Mountain or Black River, he simply couldn't summon the energy. So Krieg wanted to berate them for obeying their own judgment over her orders; what did that matter? He knew they'd made the right choice. And he felt certain Krieg knew too, even if she wasn't willing to admit the truth.

"Well," she said, "I assume you've come to look in on those you assisted. I'll bid you a good night." And with that, she stalked away down the passage, her dark cloak wrapped tightly about her.

"What's her problem?" Hule muttered beneath his breath.

Durren had no answer for him. It seemed Krieg disliked them all the more for having done something noteworthy and saving the lives of four fellow students in the process.

"I think she may just be worried," Arein said.

Trust her to see the best in someone. Yet she might have a point. Durren could only guess at what had been happening here at Shadow Mountain while they and so many others had been out in the field, or what difficult decisions had been made as the scale of the crisis became apparent. Unsympathetic as he found Krieg, he was willing to believe that she'd have struggled over the decision to hold off a rescue attempt for her beleaguered students. And maybe it rankled, too, that the four people she apparently liked least within her academy's walls had been the ones to accomplish what she couldn't.

Inside, the infirmary was surprisingly quiet; Durren had

half expected to find the room full to brimming. Perhaps, after all, they and Caille's party had been the only ones to encounter the risen dead. Caille was sitting at the bedside of a heavily bandaged someone who Durren finally recognized as the bard girl, her head nearly invisible amid strips of white.

Caille looked even more haggard than before. Durren suspected he intended to stay here all night, or until he passed out and someone carried him away—and he knew that, if he were ever placed in these circumstances, he'd do exactly the same. Indeed, seeing the cleric like this was a stark reminder that, in a curious and hard-to-define way, Arein, Tia, and Hule were closer to him than mere friends could ever be.

"How are they?" Arein asked.

The cleric nodded wearily. "Not bad, they tell me. Likely to live, at any rate." His expression, already solemn, somehow grew more so. "I realized when I returned that I'd never thanked you. So, thank you."

"You're welcome," Arein told him. "We're just glad we got to you in time."

Caille exhaled a great sigh. "None of us had the faintest idea what we were getting into. We were standing there, talking...Loria was telling stupid jokes, the way she always does. And there came a noise, like nothing I'd heard. Earth moving, stones rattling. But it was coming from every direction at once. At first I thought it was an earthquake. I looked down, and at my feet was a grave, and out of the grave a hand was reaching up. All I could do was watch."

He sagged in his chair and balled a fist under his chin, as though trying to stop himself from sliding to the floor. Caille sounded as if he were talking only for his own benefit as he continued, "Then, after everything we went through, to see the winged monster…to discover it was real. I don't think I'd ever truly believed the stories. And *then* to find out there were not one but two…"

"What do you mean?" Hule asked. "Two what?"

The cleric started. "Didn't you notice? There was another creature, waiting on the rooftops below. It vanished at the same time the first flew away."

Durren flinched inwardly. For reasons he couldn't quite explain, he'd been hoping no-one except he and Tia had seen that mysterious second figure.

"I don't know what you think you saw," Tia snarled, "but just because someone else was there, that doesn't mean they were on the monster's side."

Oh yes, Durren recalled, *that was why.* Until he'd had an opportunity to discuss what they'd witnessed and Tia's inexplicable reaction with her in private, he'd intended to keep the matter a secret.

Meanwhile, Caille was glaring with a mixture of puzzlement and resentment. "I don't know what you saw either," he growled. "There were two creatures on two rooftops, and one followed after the other. That's what I'll tell anyone who asks."

Durren glanced back to Tia, and it was all he could do not to gasp. Whatever else Tia might be, she was always calm—but she certainly wasn't calm now. She was, in fact, shaking; her hands, where they were clenched within the sleeves of her cloak, were visibly vibrating.

She's going to go for Caille, Durren thought. *She's going to start a fight with an injured Shadow Mountain student over—what? Whether one creature was in league with another? What's going on here?* He wanted badly to put a steadying hand on Tia's arm, and didn't. To do so would have been like grasping a coiled snake.

In any case, the chance had passed. Tia had fixed her gaze upon Caille. Her hands were no longer shaking; her composure was perfect once more. "You're an idiot," she told him, "and it's no wonder you nearly got your whole party killed." With that, she turned and marched from the room.

There was a long moment of choked silence—as if, in leaving, Tia had sucked all the air with her. Arein was first to break it. "I'm so sorry," she said to Caille. She sounded as shocked as Durren felt. "She isn't normally like that. I mean, maybe she *is* normally like that. Just not to people other than us."

"I think you should go," Caille said. "I'm supposed to make sure the others get peace and quiet."

"We'll check in on you again," Arein suggested.

But this time, Caille said nothing.

Arein looked as though she'd have liked to stay and keep trying to mollify the furious cleric. Yet when Durren told her, "Come on," and started towards the door, she followed. Hule trooped after as well, with obvious relief.

The three of them got as far as the passage outside before Arein came to a halt. "We need to talk. All four—or, well, all three of us." She dropped her voice. "We should meet somewhere. Tonight. After last bell."

Durren stifled a groan. He was half ready to contend that they wait until tomorrow; he dearly wanted to. However, the same urgency in Arein's voice that made him eager to put off hearing whatever she wished to say also made him appreciate that she must be every bit as tired as he was, if not more so. She wouldn't be proposing this without good reason.

"Fine," he conceded. "But where?"

"There's a lecture room in the paladins' wing that's not

being used," Hule said. "A mock fight got out of hand and part of the floor caved in."

"That sounds…better than nothing," Durren agreed hesitantly.

So Hule gave him and Arein directions. Fortunately, the room was also on the very edge of the region given over to the paladins, meaning they weren't likely to run into anyone who might pose unwelcome questions.

"Should I try and persuade Tia to meet us too?" Arein asked.

"Maybe we need to leave her alone for a little while," Durren said. "Sooner or later we're going to have to find out what she's so worked up about. Just—perhaps not tonight."

Arein nodded, and somehow gave the impression of being at once relieved and disappointed in herself. Her expression said that she felt they were letting their friend down, and Durren suspected she was right. Only, he was right too; none of them were currently in any condition to unravel Tia's state of mind.

They separated with brief goodbyes, and Durren drifted in the direction of the bards' wing, unsure of what to do with the intervening time. The hour couldn't be as late as his aching body and his throbbing head insisted; how long had passed since the sun had set? In all probability it was sometime after the penultimate bell, the one to announce the end of dinner.

Thinking that word, *dinner*, almost decided his next step. While generally the rules were strict about missing meals in the dining hall, exceptions were made for those who'd been out questing, and he imagined that went doubly for circumstances like tonight's: he was confident that explaining how he'd battled for his life against rampaging corpses should buy him a few scraps.

Yet, though he was hungry indeed, he didn't actually have any desire to eat. Really, he had no idea what he *did* want to do. He still felt shaken by Tia's outburst; he was worried about her, and he was annoyed to be worried. Why couldn't she just discuss her problems the way anyone else would? He wondered if he should track her down himself, and if that would go some way towards settling his restless mood. But he wasn't certain he had the courage, and in any case, the advice he'd given Arein was probably sensible. Tia needed space to calm down, and perhaps to admit that she'd been in the wrong, if such a thing was possible.

Durren knew he was telling himself what he wanted to hear. Regardless, doing so was enough to free his thoughts from the subject of Tia and return them to the question of his own wracked body. He remembered his plan to wash off the soot he was plastered with, and decided that should be his priority; he was dismayed to notice how he'd left dark smudges where he'd leaned against the wall.

As it turned out, the only water he could find was icily cold. Though he was shivering from head to toe by the time he'd finished, he at least felt more awake, and his appetite was fully restored. In fresh clothes, he hurried down to the kitchens and explained his reasons for missing dinner. No-one was especially sympathetic—he expected they routinely heard such stories— but one of the kitchen staff did spoon leftovers into a bowl and offer him a table in a corner. Durren wolfed his belated meal down and watched the bustle around him from the corner of his eye. Something about the hectic atmosphere of the kitchen took him back to his father's house in Luntharbor, and for maybe the first time since he'd left, he found that he was genuinely homesick.

Fortunately, at that point, the clamor of bells made the air tremble: the last chimes of the night. Durren hastily finished his dinner, thanked the woman who'd fed him, and dashed off.

As always, he was glad Shadow Mountain wasn't so huge or so labyrinthine as Black River. He located the lecture hall Hule had given directions to without much trouble; it helped that there was a parchment pinned outside that read, in broad strokes, "KEEP OUT! DANGER!" Pushing through the heavy oak door, Durren discovered Arein and Hule already in there waiting—and favoring the near end of the room because, as Hule had warned, a portion of the floor was currently a gaping cavity.

Arein had taken a seat on the row of benches farthest from the hole, while Hule stood nearby, chewing idly at the nails of one hand. Both of them were in a considerably better state than when Durren had last seen them. Hule, in particular, had also cleaned himself up and now no longer looked as though he'd been dragged backward through a bonfire.

"So what did you want to talk about, Arein?" Durren asked, as he eased the door closed behind him.

Assuming she intended to return to the subject of Tia, he'd been comforting himself with the likelihood that all she would need would be a little reassurance that they'd confront their ill-tempered rogue in a day or two. Therefore he was disheartened when Arein said, "I've been wondering about that winged creature."

"I overheard some students claiming it was a vampire," Hule said. "Everyone knows vampires are just children's stories," he added scornfully.

Durren wondered how the fighter could be so dismissive

given some of the sights they'd seen with their own eyes; doubtless there were those who regarded unicorns to be the stuff of fantasy as well.

"From what I've heard," Arein said, "the general theory seems to be that it's a lich…that is, a sorcerer who's given themself over to dark magic so wholly that they're not entirely alive anymore. But I'm not sure liches are real either. I always thought they were just a cautionary tale to keep people from experimenting with the worst sort of spells: 'Don't try and cheat death or you'll turn into a lich', that sort of thing."

That struck Durren as a sensible enough moral. "If it wasn't a vampire and it's not a lich," he wondered, "what *was* it?"

Arein looked contemplative. "You know that, back at Black River, I did a lot of research into shapeshifters."

Durren nodded. Arein, as the closest they had to an expert on all things magical, had set herself the task of comprehending the threat they'd faced. Until now, though, she'd never raised the topic—perhaps recognizing that none of them wanted to think too hard about what they'd been through.

"The problem with studying shapeshifters," she said, "is that it's so long since anyone saw one. And even before they were wiped out, there were never very many. On top of that, it's not as if people ever got to ask them questions; they were too busy doing their best to slaughter them. All that's left to work off is rumors and myths and guesses."

"We appreciate that," Durren said, wondering where this diversion was leading. "Still, surely some sources are more reliable than others?"

"Of course," Arein agreed. "But it's actually one of the stranger theories I've been pondering."

"Go on," Hule encouraged. "Anything could be useful."

"That's what I thought too. What I mean is, there were once so many contradictory ideas about shapeshifters that the more eccentric ones tend to be dismissed these days. For example, there was a scholar named Studderbliss who was absolutely obsessed with them: he wrote this huge book called *A History in Changes*. His contemporaries said he was mad; he insisted all the way through that shapeshifters had never meant any harm and that the way they'd been slaughtered was a dreadful crime."

"Arein," Durren said, "this is interesting, but..."

"Oh—yes. The point is, one of his ideas was that sometimes shapeshifters would get sort of—stuck. If they tended to keep using the same forms, or the same kinds of forms, eventually that would be all they could do. Studderbliss viewed it as a natural advantage they'd developed, like how we specialize to get better at our particular classes. So for example, maybe our shapeshifter had been pretending to be people for a long time. That meant that while it was very good at mimicking a person, if it had tried to be a wolf or a tree—"

"They could pretend to be trees?" asked Hule, aghast.

"Oh, I doubt it. I really don't know. Look, it was just an example! The point is, if Studderbliss was correct then our shapeshifter was what you might call a person-shapeshifter."

"I suppose that makes sense," Durren decided. "I don't altogether see what it has to do with tonight, though."

"Because," Arein said, her tone abruptly serious, "what if there was such a thing as a monster-shapeshifter? One that wasn't remotely interested in imitating people? One that had spent all its time being as frightening as possible?"

Perhaps it was the way she spoke those last words, but Durren couldn't fend off the shiver that trickled down the nape of his neck.

"That's what you think we saw?" Hule asked. "Another shapeshifter? One that would rather scare people than hide?"

"The whole history of Ursvaal is full of monster sightings," Arein said. "What if those were actually the same monster? It's only an idea; all the same, it explains a lot."

The more Durren wished she was wrong, the more he realized that she'd convinced him. And suddenly he was certain of something else as well, a possibility that had been lurking in the back of his mind for a long while now. "If you're right," he said, "we should assume that the shapeshifter here is also the flying creature that rescued our shapeshifter from the Brazen Fist. It's too great a coincidence otherwise." A further thought occurred to him. "That would explain the gap in the local sightings too, wouldn't it? Their monster really had taken a holiday."

"Yes," Arein agreed, "that would be my guess."

"But that means we're dealing with two shapeshifters in Ursvaal. I don't think we can keep this to ourselves, Arein. This needs to be something Krieg hears about."

She considered him steadily. "Isn't there one problem, though?"

She was right, of course. When you were dealing with shapeshifters, there was always at least one problem with no easy answer: who did you trust?

"I get what you're saying," Durren told her. "Even so, the odds of them managing to infiltrate the academy, let alone to replace the Head Tutor, are tiny—aren't they? Whatever our opinion of the teachers here, they're not idiots. They'd work out pretty quickly if Krieg had been substituted."

"You're assuming there are only two of them," Arein said

softly.

"Just wait," Hule cut in. "Not so long ago you were telling us that everybody thought shapeshifters were extinct. Then you say there might be not one but two of them left. And now there may be even more. What's going on here? Either shapeshifters were wiped out or they weren't."

"Then they *weren't*." Arein's voice held an uncharacteristic edge of annoyance. "How am I supposed to know? This is ancient history; everyone believed there were no more shapeshifters. Obviously there *were* survivors—so maybe they've been hiding all this while. Maybe they've been planning. The one we fought claimed to have been alive for centuries. If that was true, who can imagine what they could be up to?"

Durren dearly wished he could unhear those final words. The last thing he wanted to do tonight was lie awake wondering what horrifying conspiracies shapeshifters were concocting at that moment. Nor did he much want to worry over the possibility that there might be two or five or fifty of them out there in Ursvaal, and that no one would uncover their existence unless they chose to reveal themselves—by which time it was sure to be too late.

"So what do we do?" he asked. "I mean, if we're not going to talk to Krieg, where does that leave us?"

Arein's brow furrowed. "I think our one choice is to wait and see what happens. And, you know, keep a close eye on things—and people. Perhaps we can trust Krieg after all. This isn't Black River; we can't just go off on our own, can we?"

That observation stirred yet another concern in Durren's mind. "Is that what Tia's been doing? Is that why she's been acting strangely since we arrived?" *Or rather, since before that*, Durren thought. "Should we be trying to find out what she's learned?"

Arein blinked nervously behind her thick glasses. "We could," she said hesitantly. "Only, don't you think maybe we ought to have some faith in her? Anyway, if she is investigating on her own, we can't stop her. And she'll include us when she needs us."

Durren wondered if now was his chance to share the details of the mission Tia had roped him into in the depths of Black River. Once more he concluded that he couldn't. Absurd as it seemed, and as frustrated as he was with her, he couldn't shake the feeling that he'd already let Tia down, and that to involve Hule and Arein after she'd deliberately excluded them would be a betrayal of her trust too far.

Instead he said, "I suppose you're right," and feigned a yawn that quickly became genuine. "Well then, we'll follow your plan, Arein. We'll keep our eyes and ears open for evidence that the creature we saw is really a shapeshifter, or that our shapeshifter has ended up here in Ursvaal. If one of us discovers something, let's find a way to meet again. In the meantime, all we can do is hope for the best."

But Arein's words still rang in his thoughts—and behind them was the memory of that sinister winged shape swooping down upon them, and those moments when he'd felt certain it would pluck him from the ground or rend him to pieces with its razor claws.

If that flying nightmare truly was a shapeshifter, with all the innate magical ability and cruel intelligence that meant, they were going to need a great deal more than positive thinking to protect them.

Chapter 10

Over the next few days, both Durren's worries about Tia and the fears regarding shapeshifters that Arein had planted in his mind began to recede a little.

It helped that, as far as questing went, life had quieted down at Shadow Mountain. Not that Durren was convinced Krieg would allow his own party out again after what had happened; still, he'd certainly have noticed had there been anything close to the mass deployment of that night. Though stories continued to arrive of overturned graveyards and batlike shadows glimpsed high above the treetops, the academy could hardly send students chasing around the countryside based on such meager and outdated information.

At any rate, the impression Durren got was that, even out in Ursvaal, things had calmed a great deal since the night of their quest. Maybe whatever threat lurked there had been intimidated by the attention it had drawn; maybe it was biding its time and quietly putting the complex parts of a wider plan into motion. Either way, the result was that Shadow Mountain had largely returned to what passed as normal.

One significant puzzle remained: that of where the army of corpses they'd encountered had vanished to. It turned out that the dead were better at hiding than anyone would have given them credit for. No doubt part of the reason was that they were unhindered by factors that would have slowed a similarly sized force of the living. They didn't need to eat, or sleep, or even to breathe.

Theories abounded that they'd disguised their trail by wandering through lakes, or that they lay hidden beneath the surface of one of the countless swamps that patterned the dismal landscape. If the general feeling was that they'd been moving towards the center of the country, nearer to the vast tract of forest known as the Dolorwood, more specific details had proved frustratingly absent. Tracks petered out or disappeared abruptly. The prints of decayed feet arrived at riverbanks and failed to continue on the far side. Absurd as it seemed, the dead had been wandering Ursvaal and no-one could say with any certainty where they'd gone.

That was obviously worrying; but since there wasn't anything Durren could do, he saw no sense in dwelling on the matter. As for Tia, after a day had gone by he'd persuaded himself that the opportunity was passed: there'd be little point left in interrogating her over her outburst towards Caille. Though he felt both guilty and cowardly, the truth was that Tia wasn't only someone who wouldn't ask for help, she was someone who'd refuse it until she had no alternative. Durren couldn't conceive a scenario in which she would give him straight answers. So he put off the problem, knowing that was exactly what he was doing.

Perhaps if he'd run into her, or into Arein or Hule, then things would have been different. But Durren saw nothing of them, not so much as a glimpse across the courtyard or in the dining hall. And in the meantime, there was no shortage of matters to divert his attention. Word of their adventure had got around quickly, and particularly of the fact that they'd come to the last-minute rescue of another party. Surely because of that, the attitude of the other bards had thawed perceptibly. If that wasn't to say they were suddenly being friendly, at least they were no longer actively hostile, and that small change alone was a relief.

As such, Durren found that he was hating being a bard a good deal less than before. Of course he'd never be convinced that Shadow Mountain didn't have thoroughly wrong-headed notions about his class of choice. But for the first time he was able to relax and to give himself over to his studies. He made a greater effort to talk to his fellow students, and occasionally they even made the effort to respond.

More than anything, he attempted to take his lute-playing seriously. He could pick out a simple tune now; that was definite progress. He could play "O'er All, the Stars" and "The Shepherd's Lay" and "Cease Your Weeping, Fickle Wench" from start to end and barely drop a note. But those were peasant ditties and nursery rhymes, the sort of songs the Ursvaalian students had likely been playing since they were small themselves. Whenever Durren tackled a more complicated piece—"Dance of the Moonflies", for instance, or "My Lady's Rose"—his mind and fingers refused to coordinate. He just couldn't feel the music, not in the way the others seemed to. He felt as if he were striving to translate from a language he wouldn't ever understand and could only memorize by ear.

Still, he tried. And perhaps that he was seen to be trying was another reason his fellow bards were starting to look more favorably on him: no longer was he the outsider who disdained their habits and traditions. Durren found them to be a great deal more serious than the scholars of Black River, both about their training and in general; it was as if the grim climate of Ursvaal had penetrated their blood and bones. There was little of the joking or telling of wild stories he was accustomed to, and much after-hours practicing and debate of technique. When quests were discussed, it was generally with an eye to what could have been done better, rather than to boastfully describing successes.

On that front, Durren kept quiet. His one quest had been an unmitigated failure from the formal perspective of Shadow Mountain. On other topics, though, he seized every opportunity to join in, if only to contribute a word or two. He was also learning quickly to laugh at his own inadequacies, especially when it came to the instrument Reille Crovek had forced upon him. And increasingly the other bards would laugh with him rather than at him, or even offer tips as to where he'd gone wrong.

Part of him was glad to be fitting in. Another part warned him not to get too comfortable. *This isn't home*, he cautioned himself. *Sooner or later—and hopefully sooner—you'll be heading back to Black River.*

At that point, the first part would remind him that probably, after all, he was going to be here for a very long time indeed. Possibly their presence was a sentence that Borgnin had no intention of ever repealing. And maybe Durren would do well to accept that his future lay at Shadow Mountain.

Five days after their last excursion and Durren had almost given up hope of ever receiving another quest. They'd been at the academy for two weeks and still not even been appointed a mentor. For all that his day-to-day existence had improved, he'd have been deluding himself to imagine he was the equal of other students at Shadow Mountain. In Krieg's eyes, he, Arein, Hule, and Tia were a resource to be called on only in the direst of emergencies.

Then the summons came—and under familiar circumstances. Again, a great many parties were being sent out at once, though on this occasion Durren hadn't heard talk of any crisis to warrant so massive a deployment. Nevertheless, by afternoon his class was nearly empty, and he sat with a curious tingling in his belly, one that might have been hope or trepidation. If they weren't assigned a quest now, it was safe to assume Krieg was punishing them and likely would continue to do so forever. If they were, that meant something dreadful was going on, of the same order of magnitude as a graveyard spitting up its dead. Wishing for a quest felt too much like wishing for disaster.

He had just about persuaded himself that being left behind was ultimately for the best when a messenger arrived—and this time, the messenger was Hule.

"Can I borrow Durren Flintrand?" he asked the tutor, in a bellow that drew every remaining eye in the room. "We're to report to the Head Tutor's office."

Durren felt more embarrassed than he could quite justify. Out in the corridor, he asked peevishly, "What are you doing here? Why did Krieg send you?"

Hule shrugged, without slowing. "She didn't, my tutor did.

I was told to find you and go to Krieg's office, so that's what I'm doing."

Durren suspected the unusual summons was a sign that something was seriously amiss out there in Ursvaal—or at best an indication that Krieg wouldn't waste any opportunity to show the contempt with which she regarded her four transfer students. Nonetheless, his annoyance was brief, for by then his attention had fixed upon another detail.

"Hule…what's that?"

Hule glanced away almost bashfully. "What's what?"

"That. On your jerkin."

"Oh." Hule cleared his throat. "I thought I should make an effort, that's all."

He'd certainly done that. To be precise, what Hule had done was to sew a strip of gold cloth onto his black jerkin, one cut in the lightning bolt design that represented the unbalance. The stitching was amateurish but careful; Durren had no doubt Hule had done the work himself. The overall effect was striking and more than a little preposterous.

"So you're taking all this seriously? I mean, being a paladin, studying at Shadow Mountain?"

Was Hule blushing? "They have some interesting ideas. Here it's not just about hitting things. It's about—you know— *how* you hit them. And why. And what kind of a person you are when you're doing the hitting."

Just then, they turned a corner and saw Arein and Tia hurrying towards them. "Oh, hello!" called Arein, and Tia gave a barely perceptible nod. Clearly Krieg wasn't willing to squander the time of anyone on her staff when she could simply have the four of them gather each other.

As a group, they trudged in silence the last distance to her office. There they knocked on the door and were greeted with a curt, "Enter."

Inside, Durren was taken aback to see the cleric, Caille, standing stiff as a board in front of Krieg's desk, as though he were a soldier readying for an inspection.

Krieg, sat before them, left a moment for her surprise to sink in. "As the five of you have already met, I trust there's no need for introductions?"

"Hello, Caille," Arein said brightly, and the rest of them murmured acknowledgments. Caille, in return, only stood awkwardly. Now he looked to Durren more like a convict awaiting his sentencing.

He didn't have long to wait. "Since Cailliper's usual companions aren't in any shape to be questing," Krieg said, "and since the five of you have experience of working together, it's my decision that he'll be temporarily joining your party. I trust no-one has any objections?"

To judge solely by the expressions on faces, both Tia and Caille had a great many objections, and Arein didn't appear entirely pleased. But no-one was about to say anything, especially not when it seemed Krieg was practically daring them to.

"Good. Obviously this means that you'll have an advantage most parties lack. However, I'm willing to consider Cailliper's presence a compensation for your lack of local knowledge, so it won't count against your experience."

To Durren's mind, having two magic users who couldn't even agree on how magic was to be used was no advantage at all. He refrained from pointing that out. Caille and Arein's conflict would have to be just one more problem to be managed.

"Now," Krieg continued, "to business." Her gaze fixed on Durren. "I recall that you have an ear for rumors: doubtless you'll have heard that we've had significant difficulty in ascertaining what's happened to the dead who've risen in recent days. This is perturbing; without knowing where they're going, we can hazard no guess as to why they've been summoned. Unfortunately, that leaves us in the position of chasing up information that normally would pass beneath our notice. One such instance is a report from a village named Gurlveig. In all likelihood, investigating will be a waste of time and resources. Nevertheless, I've agreed to do so."

Only, Durren thought, *because you have four students whose time you don't mind wasting, plus one more who's no use to anyone until the rest of his party are back on their feet.*

"Let us be clear," Krieg said, "you're to follow your quest and only follow your quest. In the event of unforeseen trouble—or even of *foreseen* trouble—you're to return to the academy, whereupon more seasoned students will be dispatched. Certainly if you should come across either the reanimated dead or the winged creature, you're to avoid conflict as much as is reasonably possible."

With that, Krieg began to explain what their mission would entail—and sure enough, it sounded like the fool's errand she evidently judged it to be. By the end, Durren had a definite sense of what had been going on in Ursvaal since their last expedition: how tales of the resurrected dead had spread from village to village, how frightened folk stared into the night, how every strange incident was accounted for with the least rational of explanations. A sheep went missing and not wolves but a winged monster was blamed; that silhouette moving in the twilight wasn't a bush caught by the wind but a walking corpse.

And a great many of those reports had been finding their way to the desk of Head Tutor Murta Krieg, who had then to sift the plausible from the ridiculous, the likely leads from the dead ends. No wonder her temper was foul.

"I trust you'll make the best of this opportunity," she concluded, "limited though it may prove to be. I shall expect you to behave with the decorum and civility required of all students at Shadow Mountain—and please do try not to get distracted."

The five of them left together; no-one seemed willing to be the first to break away. The collective mood was bleak. Finally they had another quest, and it was patently a waste of effort, granted to them only because somebody had to do it. Out of all of them, perhaps Caille's countenance was the most dour: suddenly, through no fault of his own, he'd found himself assigned to the least respectable party at Shadow Mountain.

Arein was the one to break the silence. "I don't understand," she murmured. "If she didn't want us here, why would Krieg ask Borgnin to exchange students with her?"

Caille came to a halt so suddenly that Hule, just behind, nearly tripped over him. "Wait," he said, "is that what you think?"

Arein stopped also. "Is *what* what I think?"

"That you're here because our head tutor contacted your head tutor?"

"That's what happened," Arein agreed, clearly put out by the cleric's condescending tone.

"No, it isn't. Everyone knows Krieg was virtually blackmailed into taking you; students from outside Ursvaal aren't encouraged. I should know, I'd never have been allowed to enter Shadow Mountain except for the fact that my father was Ursvaalian."

"What reason would Borgnin have to lie to us?" Arein answered hotly. "You've got it all wrong. Just because almost everybody else is intolerant, that doesn't mean Krieg has to be too. Maybe that's exactly why she wanted to do an exchange, to let some fresh ideas into this place."

Only, Arein sounded less sure with each word, and by the end was barely disguising the doubt in her voice. She must have realized that any theory that relied on Krieg's open-mindedness was doomed to failure.

She frowned. "I don't see why Borgnin would make something like that up."

"Unless…" Hule started.

When he failed to continue, Tia prompted, "Unless?"

"Well, unless Borgnin wanted us to be here, and he didn't want us to know that he wanted us to be here."

"Hule," Tia said, "Every time I start to imagine you've begun to talk some sense—"

"No," Durren cut her off, "maybe he's right. We're just a group of level two students. Borgnin could hardly say, 'I need someone to go spy on an academy in another country and you four are the ones I've picked.' But if he knew the shapeshifter was headed to Ursvaal, who better to send than us?"

Too late did it occur to Durren that he should be saying none of this with Caille standing before them—and only then did he register the way the cleric was looking at him.

"Um…" Durren began, desperately seeking some words with which to extricate himself.

"You just said *shapeshifter.*" Caille's tone was so carefully neutral that they might have been discussing the perpetually dismal weather.

"What I meant was—"

"I don't care what you meant. What you said was, 'he knew the shapeshifter was headed to Ursvaal.'"

"I think we should tell him," Hule declared nonchalantly. "He's one of us now."

"Temporarily," Tia pointed out. "And we've no reason to trust him." That she was unshaken by what Durren had inadvertently disclosed was all the proof he needed that she'd reached the same conclusion.

"I'm right here, you know." Caille's temper was evidently beginning to fray. "And the way I see it, you have two choices. Either you explain what's going on, or I head straight back to Krieg's office and repeat everything you've just said. I'd rather you choose the first option; I don't exactly like the thought of informing on fellow students. Still, I will if I have to."

"We should tell him," Arein decided. "I mean, it would be rude not to."

"You should," Caille agreed. He sounded no less impatient.

"If we do," Durren said, "it has to be a secret between the five of us. You'll understand why afterward, but I need your word beforehand."

"That's ridiculous. You want me to promise to keep quiet, and you tell me I'll understand why after you've told me the thing you won't tell me until I agree."

"That's about the size of it. And look, we *did* save your life, not to mention the lives of your entire party. Maybe you owe us a little trust?"

Caille's expression only darkened; probably the fact of being rescued not just by other students but by students from a rival academy had been rankling these last few days. "Promise me something in return. I need to be certain that by keeping this secret of yours I won't be putting Shadow Mountain in any danger."

Durren hesitated. How could he answer honestly? There was every chance that by staying silent about what they suspected they were putting the academy at risk. Then again, speaking up was as likely to have the same effect.

Fortunately, Arein was more quick-witted. "We're doing what we think is best for everybody," she assured Caille. "We wouldn't deliberately jeopardize Shadow Mountain or anyone here. Is that enough?"

Caille didn't look convinced. "I suppose it will have to be."

"All right," Durren said. And he began to narrate the story of their first term at Black River: of how they'd discovered that their mentor was a shapeshifter who was holding the real Lyruke Cullglass captive, and of how, ultimately, they'd confronted and managed to subdue it.

As he ran out of breath, Arein took over, filling in the details of her suspicions regarding the winged creature and relating how a similar monster had rescued their shapeshifter from the custody of the Brazen Fist. To conclude, she returned to the difficult topic of why they'd kept this to themselves.

"So you see, the problem is that there's always the chance they could be just about anyone. Which makes it awfully hard to know who you can trust."

"Yet," Caille said, "you're asking me to trust you."

"Well clearly *we're* not shapeshifters," Hule said, as though it really were the most obvious thing imaginable.

But Durren found his gaze seeking Tia, and was shocked by his own reaction. Was he this ready to doubt his friend? After all, nothing Tia had done had been the least bit out of character.

Except for how she attacked a guard just so she could break into the dungeons and talk to the creature that tricked and nearly killed us.

He pushed the misgiving from his mind. Once he began thinking that way there'd be no end; he might as well assume he was surrounded by enemies. For the first time he truly comprehended why shapeshifters had been so hated: not only were they powerful and perhaps immortal, they made you paranoid. How much worse must that have been when there were hundreds or even thousands of them? The idea that they'd been systematically wiped out was horrifying; the possibility of coexisting with them was unimaginable.

"Krieg *has* been acting strangely since the four of you arrived," Caille said, breaking upon Durren's thoughts. "Everyone put it down to her being annoyed with Borgnin for dumping you on her. And probably that's the reason." He hesitated, and a shadow passed across his face. "I understand why you're asking me not to share this. And I'll keep my promise—unless doing so puts lives at risk."

"That's all we ask," Arein assured him.

Ten minutes later and, having hurriedly gone their separate ways to collect their gear, the five of them were once more together outside the transportation chamber. Within, Caille greeted the wizard with a polite, "Good afternoon, Gallowpall."

The wizard, Gallowpall apparently, only sniffed and considered him indifferently. He waited until they'd tramped down into the central depression and said, "Gurlveig, is it?" When no-one answered immediately, he tutted to himself.

A second later and he'd begun to chant and to gesticulate. This time the spell took longer, though Gallowpall still rattled off the syllables as if each was an inconvenience. Perhaps that meant their destination was farther away.

But eventually the familiar impression began to take hold, a sense that the air itself was about to turn inside-out. *Here we go*, Durren thought, as the walls dripped and frothed like custard. *Now all we can do is hope this quest isn't the waste of time it sounds to be.*

Chapter 11

Durren was coming to realize that one village in Ursvaal looked like any other, and that they all had certain qualities in common: they were glum, squalid places populated by glum, squalid people.

Even accepting that, Gurlveig was a particularly miserable spot. In fact, he remembered Furtz as being somewhat homely by comparison. Gurlveig was both larger and more desolate. Despite the high winds that roared among the unpaved streets, the buildings were set far apart, as if spurning each other's company. They were arranged haphazardly and built of dark stone crusted with moss and flaking yellow lichen. The village had an air of ancientness; but out here, exposed to the harsh elements, perhaps that effect could be accomplished in a mere matter of years.

Arein had drawn Pootle from one of her cavernous pockets, and the little observer was flitting about, disappearing for moments at a time and returning almost faster than the eye could follow. It seemed entranced by their surroundings, though Durren could see nothing anywhere that qualified as remotely interesting. There again, if Pootle had been living in Arein's pocket, the poor creature might simply be glad to be out in the open.

"What do we do now?" Hule wondered. He was standing in the middle of the street, hands on hips, craning his neck.

"I don't know," Durren replied. Krieg had neglected to mention who they were meant to speak to.

"Come on," Caille said. He'd already set out walking.

"Don't tell me you've been here before?" Durren asked.

"No," Caille called back, "I just know Ursvaal. There's one place to go for information in a village like this."

It would have been generous beyond measure to describe the building they'd come to as an inn. Even the dockside taverns in Luntharbor, notorious for their moral laxity, their watered-down wine, and for being held together only by the grime that permeated every brick and timber, had a touch of class that this establishment lacked. It was identical with the houses to left and right, except for being perhaps a shade larger and having above its door a broken plank into which had been burned the words, The Troll's Head. Durren supposed he should be thankful the amateur sign maker hadn't attempted an accompanying illustration.

Caille led the way inside. In one wall, a fire produced much smoke but little in the way of heat. In a corner, a makeshift bar had been constructed from barrels and more planks. A few locals sat stiff-backed upon stools, scowling at each other and sipping from clay tankards. What scant conversation there had been dried up instantly, as everyone turned to scrutinize the new arrivals.

"We're from Shadow Mountain," Caille said. "We heard you've been having some problems around these parts."

At first the sole response was a wave of scattered coughs and grunts, as though no-one was quite willing to confirm that they might be having anything so serious as problems. When somebody finally spoke up, it was the middle-aged man behind the bar, who had the arms of a blacksmith and the belly of a pregnant sow; his bulk was wrapped in an apron that conceivably had once been white.

"To be honest," he rumbled, "we didn't expect anyone would come. But with all of what's been going on, old Helvig contended that it might be irresponsible of us to keep silent. And then Barss Gurtlinger was heading down Lupreck way and said, what did one scroll matter for the extra weight it would be, and that decided the matter in the end."

Durren was confident of having understood at least one in every three words. It didn't help that the innkeeper had a tendency to slur and a particularly strong accent, or that the smoky atmosphere and prevailing reek of spirits was beginning to make his head spin.

"Now that we're here," he said, "maybe you could describe what's been happening. We were told something about missing persons?"

"Oh, no." The innkeeper looked mortified. "Not what you'd call missing. I suppose the phrase would be 'unexpectedly quiet'. It's the tannery down near the river, see."

Five minutes later and Durren was barely any the wiser. Krieg had given them the loosest possible account of the summons she'd received from Gurlveig; perhaps she hadn't deemed it worth wasting more breath on. And after listening to the innkeeper's story, accompanied by occasional interjections from those around the room, Durren was inclined to agree.

"Basically what you're saying," he tried, "is that it's unusual to have not heard from this tannery in so many days?"

The innkeeper scrunched his brows with a mixture of thought and perturbation. "I don't know about unusual, precisely."

Durren restrained a sigh. "But it's not *normal?*"

"No, no…not normal, and that's the truth. The fact is," the innkeeper volunteered, with a gravitas that promised his next words were certain to make everything clear, "they do have a weakness for the drink."

"Ah." In fairness, that did clarify a great deal. Then again, Durren guessed the same could be said for half the village, including the proprietor himself.

"Perhaps we should go and take a look?" Arein suggested. "I'm sure they're fine and this is all a misunderstanding. Only, you know, if they're *not…*"

The innkeeper took a dirty mug from beneath his improvised bar, and a dirty cloth from its crude surface, and began to wipe at the one with the other. "I suppose," he said, "that *would* be the thing to do."

Barely had they arrived back in the street and Durren suspected they were on the verge of an argument.

"I'm not proposing we steal horses," Tia was saying, "just that we should ask to borrow some and that, if the locals are unreasonable enough to refuse, we should borrow them anyway."

"Paladins don't steal," Hule told her flatly.

"I explained to you how it wouldn't be stealing."

"And I'm saying it would be and we're not doing it."

Hule really was getting strange notions into his head of late, Durren thought. Two weeks ago he would have been the first to agree with Tia.

"The rules of Shadow Mountain clearly prohibit any borrowing of property without permission," Caille put in. "Anyway, these people are better off not antagonized. Out here, the law tends to involve acting first and considering the consequences as little as possible."

"That's all well and good." Tia pointed upwards. "Except we're running out of daylight."

Durren followed her finger. Yet despite the many lectures on interpreting the weather he'd attended, he could make no sense of the ruffled blanket of gray that hung above them. It was undeniably gloomy, but gloomy in the manner of the moments preceding a storm; for all that those skies revealed, the time might have been noon or an hour before sunset.

Based on when they'd left Shadow Mountain, though, Tia was right: there couldn't be a great deal of day left, and now more than ever they didn't want to be stuck exploring in the dark. However, Hule and Caille were right too: any attempts to procure transportation were sure to get them in trouble, and trouble was something they already had enough of.

Durren could see a single solution. "We'll just have to hurry," he said.

The innkeeper's directions had been less than clear, but their options had been equally limited: only two roads ran out of the village. Gurlveig was nestled on the edge of foothills that gave way, in the distance, to low mountains; the route they'd picked quickly rose. Durren drew his cloak tighter around him.

Without the limited shelter of the surrounding houses, the wind was biting and damp, threatening rain at any moment.

They trudged in silence. Durren pondered sidling closer to Tia and trying to make conversation, but there was no missing how she'd deliberately separated herself by walking ahead. Plainly she didn't want company, and Durren was in no mood to be rebuffed. He couldn't keep from wondering how they had come to this. Not long ago, they'd been the heroes of Black River—even if almost no-one had actually known of their heroism. Now they were a laughingstock, sent on quests that barely warranted the name.

With each step they took, the scenery grew more hostile and lifeless. Aside from short grass, brittle heather, and a few thorny trees, nothing could hope to take hold here. A persistent drizzle began to fall; the wind drove the drops in sheets, so that soon Durren's clothes were thoroughly sodden. Then, just as he was telling himself their circumstances could get no worse, he caught the odor drifting upon the turbulent air. Quickly he shut his mouth. He wished he could have shut his nose as well. The smell was vile—though at least it confirmed they were heading the right way.

In Luntharbor, as in most towns and cities in what Durren regarded as the civilized portion of the lands, tanneries were kept well outside the boundaries and in the opposite direction of the prevailing wind. As such, Durren had been fortunate enough never to see or smell one. Luntharbor also had a tendency, in its poorest portions, to not keep its sewers clean or unblocked—so that the odors assailing his nostrils still weren't altogether unfamiliar. But even a clogged Luntharbor sewer lacked the ghastlier notes he was picking up here. A keen undertone of rotting meat made his worst memories almost tolerable by comparison.

Durren had assumed that being able to smell the tannery must signify they were close. The truth was that the stink was just carrying very far indeed—which meant he'd become more than familiar with it by the time they passed over the summit of a rise and saw the place spread out below.

From the way the innkeeper had talked, Durren had been expecting a single building. In fact, there was a main hall like a low-roofed barn, a number of sheds, and at a substantial distance, a half-dozen crude huts. All of this was perched amid landscape bleak and rugged even by the standards of Ursvaal. Beyond the tannery, a deep gully cut across the earth, with the solitary crossing a rope bridge that rocked visibly in the wind tearing down from the hills. Durren couldn't see into the depths, but he could hear the rush of white water as a constant barrage upon his eardrums. On the other side, nothing was visible except an expanse of greenery that stretched uninterrupted to the horizon, which Durren took to be the Dolorwood.

He almost said, *We all know this is a waste of effort, don't we?* What held the words back was a twisting in his gut that he could only call professional pride. Krieg might be happy to waste their time, and the locals of Gurlveig doubly so, but he was a ranger and that meant something, to him if to no-one else.

Instead, he pointed out a fact he'd been growing increasingly aware of as they descended: "It doesn't look as if anyone's around."

It was true, of course, that the workers might be inside. Yet what he was commenting on somehow went beyond that. The place had an air of abandonment that increased the nearer they drew.

Staring down the hill meant that the rain drove more vigorously into his mouth and eyes, and the stink of rot and worse crawled more freely into his nostrils, so Durren turned his notice to the track. All along there had been indications that this way was used regularly; the innkeeper had said the tannery folk visited the village about once a week, and the road's state corroborated that. Two shallow ruts had been carved by cartwheels, and the ragged grass verge had been trampled by frequent pedestrian traffic.

What caught his attention was that ahead the marks grew perceptibly heavier. More, the stripe of disturbed ground veered into the underbrush, and broken stems implied the passage of something large, though Durren saw no clue as to why carters might halt their overladen vehicles at this particular spot.

Before him, Caille had stopped to kneel down. "These are the tracks of feet," he said.

Durren bent to study the scuff marks. Caille was right. There were clear impressions, but so many that they'd blurred together. Nevertheless, on careful inspection he could just make out the indentation of a heel here or of toes there. And that detail was important, he realized: these were actual footprints, not boot prints.

There was only one explanation of why anyone with bare feet would have passed this way. Corpses torn from their graves had no need for shoes.

"The dead came through here," Durren said.

Caille nodded. "And continued down towards the camp. There must have been a hundred, maybe more."

Durren shuddered. Despite his own brush with the awakened dead, imagining what it must have been like to witness that grotesque parade descending was enough to rattle his nerves. Certainly they had their answer of why the tannery workers hadn't been seen in a while: no doubt they'd fled and never looked back.

Yet when at long last they arrived, there was no more trace of the dead than of the workers. A glance within the central building sufficed to confirm it empty of life, even the horrifying and artificial sort—and that glimpse was all Durren's suffering nasal cavities could tolerate. They tried a couple of the nearby structures too. One contained fresh skins, another a variety of tools, but neither was inhabited—and it was apparent by then that if anybody had been around, they would have come out to question these five nosy young trespassers.

"We need to know where everyone went," Arein said, though Durren had to take a moment to translate, because she'd pinched her nose between thumb and forefinger and was taking care to open her mouth as little as possible.

"Why don't we search around the outside and then work our way back inwards?" Durren proposed. That way, he told himself, at least they'd get a brief reprieve from this awful place.

Probably that was why the others readily agreed. They started with the living quarters, and sure enough, the clustered huts offered a degree of respite; the site had evidently been chosen because it was out of the wind, and therefore of the stink. There was still no ignoring the tannery's proximity, but Durren was grateful to find that his eyes had stopped watering.

Nevertheless, the tiny hamlet was as vacant as everywhere else. More, there were obvious signs that people had been there until recently and had vanished in a hurry. A fire pit was reduced to cold charcoal, and the pan suspended above contained a blackened mass so burned as to be unidentifiable. Bedding was rumpled, clothes were discarded, bowls of food were half-eaten and, in one hut, a flask of strong-smelling alcohol had been left to dribble its contents into the dirt.

That, to Durren's mind, was perhaps the surest sign. From what the innkeeper had told them, those who'd worked here weren't the sorts to waste good liquor. And in fairness, he had already decided that, if he ever found himself working in a tannery, his first step would be to drink the most potent spirits he could lay his hands on until his sense of smell refused to function.

Aside from that insight, he'd learned little. Though the evidence said the tannery workers had left hastily, he was only assuming they'd done so of their own volition. For that matter, even if they had, that wasn't to say they'd managed to get away safely. The ground was hard around the huts, just as it had been near the main building: combined with the increasingly heavy rain, there was no telling what route the dead had taken or which way the workers had gone.

The lack of definite answers was dispiriting. As Tia had warned, they were rapidly running out of daylight; even taking into account the foul weather, the sky was significantly darker. Likely they had an hour or less left, and Durren had no desire to be here when night fell.

Regardless, they could hardly stop now, and nor could the task be rushed. "Maybe we ought to split up?" he suggested. "We could break into two parties and head around camp in each direction, then meet up on the other side."

"I'll go east with Caille," Tia said, without waiting for a discussion. "The rest of you cut west towards the ravine."

Already Durren doubted his own proposal. Wouldn't they be safer staying together? But the choice was out of his hands.

"Fine," he agreed. "Shout at the first sign of trouble. And Pootle, let us know if you see anything out of the ordinary. Circle twice for danger."

The observer bobbed obligingly—and once they'd parted ways, was studious about whisking between their two groups, so swiftly that its motion became a blur. Durren found the small creature's presence reassuring; he knew from past experience that Pootle had exemplary night vision, and could be relied upon to do as it had been told.

There was little to see on their side of camp. The tannery had clearly been here for a great many years, and in that time most of the foliage had been removed or trampled, leaving the earth barren all the way to where the jagged scar of the ravine split the land.

"We should head for the bridge," Durren asserted. If there had been a mass exodus, either of the living or the dead, there was a good chance they'd have headed that way.

But when they arrived, the results were disappointing. As elsewhere, the combination of packed dirt and driving rain had left a blank slate, and there was no way to judge whether anyone had recently crossed the bridge itself. Yet as he knelt to look more closely at the point where the support beams penetrated the rocky ground, Durren couldn't escape the conviction that there should be *something* to see. He wasn't the best of trackers, certainly not Tia's equal; all the same, if a hundred or more bodies had passed this way, there would surely be some indication.

Gossip around Shadow Mountain had concluded that the corpse horde's objective lay within the vast tracts of the Dolorwood. Perhaps the gossip was wrong. For the first time, Durren thought to seriously wonder why anyone would reanimate a multitude of cadavers and send them traipsing across the countryside. He had been vaguely assuming the gathering was an army; but there had been few reports of violence, and those had all occurred, as with Caille and his party, only when someone forcibly got in the way of the dead. There was a mystery here, and Durren couldn't shake the uncomfortable feeling that he was missing vital clues.

From somewhere behind and to the right, he heard Tia's shout. Almost in the same instant, Pootle shot into view and whipped around rapidly in the air.

"Come on!" Durren yelled, already running.

He was glad to note that the observer was leading the way, at a pace he could just about keep up with. They skirted the central buildings. Ahead, the land sloped upwards in anticipation of the hills beyond; here the terrain was peppered with gnarled trees, their trunks all but black and their conical heads the darkest shade of green. Beneath, the shadows were clustered and pitchy. There was no sign of Tia or Caille.

"Tia?" Durren called. There came an answering shout from off to his left, though any words were muffled by the downpour. He could see a path now, snaking upwards, and he headed towards it, his gaze darting frantically. *I knew we shouldn't have split up*, he told himself, *I knew—*

"Where are you going?" Tia asked.

Durren skidded to a halt. Following Tia's voice, he saw her and Caille standing under a nearby tree—and that they both appeared puzzled at his dramatic arrival.

Durren took a moment to catch his breath. "I thought you were in trouble," he complained, as behind him, Arein and Hule stumbled to a stop.

Tia regarded him quizzically, as if to say, *Why would you ever think that?* "We found something."

"Oh." Durren glanced around to identify what she and Caille had discovered. He realized the particular tree they'd picked out was near to the path. But where that had been scrubbed clean by the rain, the spot where the two stood was sheltered by the foliage above—and there were clear imprints in the dirt.

"See here?" Tia moved her palm in a sweeping motion over the disrupted soil. "A lot of feet passed this way in a hurry. Notice how the path bends? They were cutting the corner. And these are boot prints, so it was the workers rather than the dead. Since there are no marks of bare feet, it doesn't look as if they were followed."

"They ran into the hills," Durren observed. "Or even kept going all the way to the mountains; I suppose there are caves up there where they thought they'd be safe."

"There are a lot of mines in Ursvaal," Caille agreed. "Probably there's one not too far away and they decided they'd be better off there. Then perhaps they got to drinking and telling stories; that happens a lot in Ursvaal too, especially out here."

"So they've gone, and we know they weren't harmed," Durren summarized. "Is there anything left for us to do? Maybe we should head back to Shadow Mountain and make our report."

He couldn't deny he was arguing at least in part because of the foul weather, the fouler smell, and the encroaching darkness. Nonetheless, he felt he made a good point. Yet, while Arein, Hule, and Caille all looked ready to be convinced, Tia's face was set in a manner he'd long since grown accustomed to.

"Something happened here," she said. "We were sent to

investigate, and that's what we should do."

"We *have* investigated," Durren pointed out. "What's left? Do you honestly want to follow that trail? There's no reason to imagine the workers are in any danger."

"We still have no idea where the dead went."

"Probably they crossed the bridge." But Durren failed to keep the uncertainty from his voice, and he could tell Tia had heard it. "Fine, I don't think they did either. Regardless, we've checked everywhere, and we can hardly go tramping into the wilderness at night."

"Krieg would consider that another strike against us," Tia admitted. "All right, let's have one last look at the main shed. That would have been where most of the workers were before they fled; there could be a clue we missed."

So they started back. All the while, Durren's eyes kept creeping towards the darkened sky. The clouds had split in places now, far away over the Dolorwood, but the one thing those glimpses of amber light revealed was that the sun was close to setting.

Outside the central building, they stopped together. No-one wanted to be first to insist they go inside and experience again that awful reek in its full force. Or so Durren assumed, anyway. Belatedly he noticed Caille's absorption, and how he held one hand outstretched, as though clutching for a prize just out of reach.

"There's a trace of magic," Caille said, his voice soft and distant. "I should have detected it earlier. It's faint—as if it's being masked somehow."

"I can't sense anything," Arein told him. Or rather, the words came out as "Gai Garnt Senk Knitting," because she once again had her fingers clamped upon her nose.

"That's because you're not listening to the unbalance," Caille scolded.

That was enough to make Arein release her nostrils. "Obviously I'm not listening to the unbalance! I wouldn't listen to a hammer while I was driving a nail in, either."

Caille rounded on her. "So you can't sense anything. You choose not to understand. You decide not to hear and you don't."

Arein grimaced. "I *decide* to be rational."

"That's what you call it? You just compared the most powerful force in existence with a common tool! As long as you think like that, you'll never be a true cleric—or any other kind of magic user."

Durren could see that neither of them was likely to let this go; Arein's cheeks were actually flushed with anger. "If you really have found something," he said quickly to Caille, "then we need you concentrating, not arguing. What is it and where?"

Caille scowled, and pointedly turned away from Arein. "I don't know. Let me try inside."

So they trooped through the broad entrance, the double doors of which had been left standing open, as though to better spread the stink from within. As bad as the smell had been from a distance, to stand close to the vats that filled the space in all directions was an experience Durren was wholly unprepared for.

He was familiar with the basic principles of tanning. The idea was to get every last scrap of rotting flesh and fur off hides so that they could be made useful—and that involved, at various stages and in various combinations, the use of salt, noxious chemicals, urine, dung water, and mashed-up animal brains. While he had no intention of examining the putrid stench any more than he had to, he had no doubt that if he did he could have picked out each of those ingredients.

He focused his attention on Caille, dearly hoping the cleric would be able to do what he needed to do quickly—or better, that he'd admit he'd made a mistake so they could get out of here.

Caille had shut his eyes. Like that, he glanced around the colossal room. Then he opened them once more. "A spell—or something similar to a spell. Certainly there's magic, but it's so diffuse as to be barely there. It feels…dormant. That's the best word I can think of."

Arein, meanwhile, now gave the impression of being perturbed more than cross. "He's right," she admitted grudgingly. "If I really concentrate, there *is* a trace of magic. But I can't place it either."

Durren sighed. "Then all we can do is search and hope we spot something out of the ordinary."

No-one disagreed, though nor did anyone look pleased. Without discussion, they spread out. Durren was already regretting his suggestion. What were they ever going to discover here? Even had there been clues, there was no longer light enough by which to find them. Aside from the open double doors, there were slits of windows in the remaining walls, but together they allowed in merely the faintest of dusky glows.

In a sense, that was a relief. Assuming he wasn't going to stumble upon any useful evidence—a hastily written note, perhaps, or a map showing where everyone had rushed off to— Durren would much prefer to see as little as possible. Between the low brick wells of the vats, brimming with fluids he didn't want to so much as consider, and the animal skins draped like morbid laundry, he might easily have mistaken the tannery for some ogre's den out of a ghoulish bedtime story.

He was approaching the middle of the room. To either side, the others had made similar progress—and no-one looked glad about the fact. Only Pootle, who was rushing back and forth above their heads, appeared unconcerned. There were definitely advantages to being a floating eyeball without nose or taste buds.

This is futile, Durren thought and nearly said. All that stopped him was the recollection that Tia had agreed to abandon their fool's errand after this. Still, he found that his feet had brought him to a halt, as the foulness of the air and the growing darkness and the charnel atmosphere momentarily overwhelmed him.

Stopping was worse. His head spun. He reached for support. All that was close by was the wall of the nearest pit. The bricks were slick beneath his hand, and he'd have dearly liked to pull away—but his dizziness was passing slowly.

Instead, he stared at the baneful bath within. The surface was dark as ink. Yet for an instant he'd been sure he'd caught a hint of movement, as if before him was a pond in which fish swam.

Of course, no fish could live in that rancid sludge. Only, there it was again: the shadow of motion, and bubbles popping with lazy splashes. Durren's next breath refused to come. A voice in his head assured him with infinite calm that nothing could possibly be alive in that vat. He leaned closer, though he hadn't intended to.

More bubbles rose. He heard each burst: they made a muted *plish*. A ripple started near the center and spread. Another began towards one edge and the two broke against each other. The surface trembled. Now Durren had no more doubt that he could see a shape moving. Something large was struggling to free itself.

But that's impossible, the serene mental voice said—just as a hand broke the dark liquid. No, a *skeletal* hand, one stripped of all bar a few gray tatters of flesh. Fingers of bare, yellowish bone twitched.

Then they clasped upon Durren's wrist.

Chapter 12

The calm voice in Durren's mind was still talking. Right now, it was commending him on having not screamed.

I can't scream, Durren told himself. *I'm too scared. I can't move at all.*

The skeletal hand didn't seem to understand what it had a hold of. It was pulling, but as though trying to draw itself free, not as if it meant to haul him into the vat. Possibly there should have been some comfort in that. There wasn't. After all, Durren would have much preferred that the hand's owner stayed just where they were.

No such luck. A skull followed, rising as a mound beneath the vile fluid, which sloshed aside to expose the ivory of bleached bone. Vacant eye sockets regarded Durren impassively. The hand tightened its grip. Lipless teeth parted, as if their owner desired to speak—and then clacked shut.

Next came bony shoulders and a second arm. The thing must have been lying curled in the vat, while the virulent substances within finished off the final processes of decay. As its ribs revealed themselves, Durren saw that a few gristly scraps of flesh still clung.

Someone cried out behind him. He thought the voice was Arein's.

Suddenly Durren's mind was working normally once more—as normally, at least, as could be hoped for when he was in the grip of a skeleton that was staring straight at him. Frantically he strived to free his short sword from its scabbard. The bony fingers clenched yet tighter, as though comprehending his intention. Tears started in the corners of Durren's eyes; the pain was awful.

Finally he fumbled his sword free. He swiped for the elbow. Wielding the weapon slantwise made him clumsy, and he missed the point he'd been aiming for. The edge of his blade clipped an ulna with a ghastly crunch. The bone didn't break, but the shock of the impact transmitted up Durren's own arm.

Now the skeleton was squeezing his wrist with determination. The torment was nearly unbearable. Durren had to make himself ignore it, so that he could angle his body for a more calculated blow. Readying his aim, he struggled against a sense of absurdity; nothing held these bones together, and he could even see the gaps between one and another.

This time, he managed to land a solid clout upon the spot he'd picked, right where upper arm and forearm met. His blade should have passed straight through; instead, it met resistance. But not enough: as Durren wrenched downward, some intangible connection gave way beneath his sword's edge.

Still the hand clung on. It hadn't so much as relaxed its grip. Durren hacked and hacked, though he was dangerously close to striking his own wrist. All the blows achieved was to make his muscles ache.

Only when the leering skull clacked its jaw in what he took for anger did a different approach occur to him: Durren swung for its head with his entire remaining strength. The blade struck with a crack. Teeth hurtled in every direction. The skeleton recoiled—and the hand, at last, released its hold, to slop into the foul blackness below.

Durren stumbled aside. A fleeting look told him his wrist was already bruised purple, and marked by the pressure of bony digits. At any rate, he could move his fingers, so there was no real damage. This would have been the worst of times to find himself reduced to one-handedness.

For, now that he had an opportunity to glance around, he saw that there were skeletons all about: one for each of the vats, and occasionally two or even three tangled together. Some were just beginning to rise from their fetid second graves; a few were almost out, and seeking to clamber onto the tiled floor.

Durren sought the others, and was relieved to see that none of them had been foolish enough to let themselves be caught as he had. Hule had his sword in hand, but was making no attempt to use it. Arein and Caille had both readied their staffs. Tia took longer to find: eventually he spotted her balanced with feline ease among the rafters that threaded the cavernous roof space.

She at least was safe for the moment. Unfortunately, her solution wouldn't work for the rest of them. Durren wasn't convinced that he, Hule, or Caille had the necessary agility to hoist themselves up, and there was absolutely no way Arein would be able to reach.

"We need to fight our way towards the entrance," he cried.

He was wasting breath on stating the obvious. They were

all already retreating in that direction. The problem was that the dead were everywhere, and there were too many in the way. Also, talking about fighting was well and good, but experience had taught him that doing so would be another matter entirely. Somehow, being diminished to mere animated bones had only made their opponents sturdier, and the weapons they had were ill-suited to defeating them. What they needed was heavier implements, ones designed for smashing rather than slicing, ones such as—

"Hule," Durren shouted, "can you get to that?" He pointed with his sword.

For once, the fighter was quick on the uptake. He'd seen what Durren had, a part of the space where a block of vats was midway through being rebuilt. The work had been temporarily put on hold, or perhaps the laborers had fled their task in terror; either way, they had left their tools propped against the partly crumbled basins.

Between Hule and them were the dead—and they didn't look inclined to let him have his way. Most were free of their vats now, and stood dripping loathsome fluids onto the filthy tiles. As Durren watched, the first took a tentative step, as if testing its newly simplified body. The clack of bony toes and heels was horrid.

Hule charged. Having surely seen the difficulty Durren had experienced, he shoved with the flat of his sword rather than slashing with its edge, and relied as much if not more upon his buckler. The first skeleton he made contact with staggered, slipped, and tumbled into the basin behind it with a massive splash. Hule kept going without a backward glance. The next two were close together, and he aimed for the gap between them, at the last flailing one way with his shield and the other with his sword.

These two managed to stand their ground, but by then Hule was through. A fourth he dodged past, though its fleshless fingers nearly snared his pack. Hule was picking up pace; even in such cramped confines, he was quite the runner. He barged into another skeleton, and Durren was certain he heard a distinct crack, as of a ribcage splintering.

By that time, Hule was within reach of his goal. He sheathed his sword, and in its place used both hands to clasp the massive hammer that was propped against one of the half-demolished vats. His first, experimental swing carried a nearby skeleton's head clean off its shoulders. Hule actually guffawed with delight as his foe teetered and crumpled.

Only then did Durren realize that, rather than watching Hule, he'd have been better looking out for himself. All of the dead were stirring now, as though they moved with one mind. Everywhere they were closing in.

Being stripped of their decaying flesh had robbed them of what vestiges of humanity remained. There was no imagining anymore that they'd once been people. Even the way they moved was different, as if they'd forgotten the subtleties of walking; they were like puppets, taking exaggerated steps and bending their limbs as little as possible. There again, Durren supposed that puppets were precisely what they'd become. In their new form, it was all the more clear that they followed the guidance of another intelligence. And before Durren tore his eyes from Hule, he saw with sinking horror that the skeleton the fighter had decapitated was back on its feet. Since they were without minds, being headless was no impediment.

Durren knew he didn't have Hule's bulk. There were skeletons behind and in front of him, and he doubted he had the might to jostle his way through as the fighter had. Already they were closing, empty eye sockets and gaping jaws revealing the blackness within hollow skulls.

There was one course left. Maybe he lacked Hule's raw strength, but that wasn't what being a ranger was about. Durren leaped onto the edge of the nearest basin. The bricks were slick with foulness, and for an instant he saw himself slipping into that stinking poison. Instead, he used his momentum and leaped again, landing at a stagger. As soon as he'd regained his balance he was up once more, onto the next vat, and being more careful this time.

He'd dimly hoped he'd be able to make it all the way to the entrance. But mindless though the dead were, they weren't altogether stupid; those ahead were clambering to block his escape. Durren was forced to change direction, knowing that doing so would lead him farther from safety.

Out of the corner of his eye he glimpsed Hule, and he at least was making headway: while the huge hammer might not be stopping the skeletons clustered about him, having limbs smashed and ribs pulverized was certainly disorienting them. Hule was stepping and swiping with steady determination, seemingly unwearying. If Durren could have got close to him, perhaps he'd have stood a chance. But the harder Hule fought, the more opponents lumbered into his orbit. Maybe they understood enough to know that isolating their enemies was crucial to overpowering them.

On that note, Arein and Caille appeared to have escaped serious attention so far, and despite their mutual antipathy, the two magic users had drawn near to each other. However, they remained cut off from everyone else—and the dead were no longer ignoring them. From the way they were gesticulating, the pair were evidently aware of the impending threat and readying to defend themselves. Whether they could do so in time was another question.

Since he was just as unable to reach them as he was Hule, the best Durren could do was ensure that nothing else did either. "Hey!" he bellowed. "Look this way, stinky dead people."

The words were barely out of his mouth before he grasped that shouting wasn't going to work. Skeletons, after all, didn't have ears. Not one bleached head turned his way, and now the dead were almost upon Arein and Caille.

Clearly a more direct approach was required. Durren sheathed his sword, unslung his bow, nocked an arrow and loosed. He'd chosen his target at random from those nearest the two magic users. The shot struck its skull, as he'd intended—and to his surprise, pierced the bone, perhaps weakened by centuries beneath the earth. Even with the shaft lodged there, point protruding from one side and fletching from the other, the skull's owner seemed at most mildly perturbed. Nevertheless, it turned his way, and that was all Durren had intended.

A neighboring skeleton stumbled. When it gazed empty-eyed at the rafters, there was a throwing knife lodged into one socket. Tia had recognized Durren's intent, or else had arrived at the same conclusion. Durren loosed a second arrow and a third, in quick succession. As they struck, he saw the glints of more of Tia's knives flickering through the semidarkness.

He considered a fourth shot, but by then he'd attracted more interest than he knew what to do with. Not only were the dead he'd avoided by his dash over the vats converging on him, those around Arein and Caille were lurching his way too. Returning the arrow to its quiver, Durren glanced desperately for an escape route—and found none. While he'd been causing a diversion, he'd made the mistake of being diverted himself. He was hemmed in on every side.

Thankfully, Arein chose that moment to complete her spell. Durren heard it before he saw it: a clap like thunder, doubly deafening for being so close. Then a bolt of lightning crackled halfway across the room. Where it struck the skeletons, sparks exploded and rained in showers, and each connection re-energized the bolt and extended its jagged path.

The effect was awesomely dramatic, making the dim expanse brighter than any summer's day, and replacing the stink of rot and filth with the odors of ozone and burned air. But it didn't stop the dead. Oh, a few had been knocked from their feet, and a couple had lost limbs; that wasn't enough to more than slow them. And Arein looked utterly exhausted. The spell had clearly stretched her capabilities to their limits.

If nothing else, she'd bought Caille time to finish his spell. As Durren watched, a ball of soft and green-tinged light shivered into existence at the tip of his staff and, having rapidly grown to be larger than the cleric's own head, suddenly shot off. Even moving at speed, there was something oddly restful about the orb, as though it was a window onto some more peaceful place. Just the sight of it restored Durren's courage.

Its effect on the dead was quite the opposite. The four that the ball struck directly were blown apart in a hail of charred bones, and those it merely passed were flung away as if by the slap of a tremendous hand. Whatever that sphere consisted of, whatever the cleric had summoned, it was the antithesis of the dark magics that gave the dead their shallow semblance of life.

Yet even that marvel had taken only a scattering from the fight. Those that had been knocked down were already fumbling back to their feet. And Caille, too, seemed temporarily spent; he was leaning on his staff to keep from falling. More, while he'd managed to create a route for himself and Arein, that helped nobody except the two of them. Hule was still managing well enough on his own, though his hammer blows were manifestly growing less fierce, and Tia remained safe in the roof space. Which meant that, right now, only Durren was in trouble.

He was in very bad trouble indeed. In as much as expressionless faces could signal intent, he felt the dead were angry. Probably they didn't like being smashed with hammers and blasted with magic. Doubtless they didn't appreciate arrows and knives flying their way. Perhaps, having seen that four of their intended victims stood a chance of escape, they were determined to focus on the one who didn't.

At any rate, there were a great many of them. They were like a wall—or rather, a fence of bones. The click of their approaching steps resembled the roll of a thousand dice. They stretched their arms, and gaunt fingers waved like twigs on a moonlit night.

Durren redrew his sword and struck. A few small bones pinged past him—he'd managed to shatter some knuckles—but the impact hurt him more than it did the dead. Hitting bone was akin to hitting stone; his arm was numbed to the elbow. Regardless, he swung again—and the clumsy blow wedged his sword between two ribs.

Fear nearly got the better of Durren. Kicking and yanking in a frenzy, he managed both to free his blade and to drive that one skeleton backward—but he was within reach of the others. Everywhere blanched claws plucked at him. Instinctively he crouched, and realized that doing so had made matters yet worse. Now not only were they all around him, the dead were above him too, and threatening to pile upon him.

Almost wild with panic, he hunted the slightest gap, anywhere he might squeeze through. And there was a spot: two skeletons blocked the way, but beyond lay clear space. He swung as well as he could, though the result was more of a swipe. Nonetheless, one of the two tottered aside, and that would have to do. Durren shoved forward as if he were on the starting line of a foot race—

And found that he couldn't move. Spindly fingers held him tight: bunched in his clothes, grasping his pack, and clutching at his hair. He tried to roll onto his back, so that at least he could hack with his sword. Even that was beyond him. Having snared their prey, the dead weren't about to let go. There was no way out.

"Keep down!" Tia shouted, from somewhere above him.

As if I have a choice...

For a second time, Durren heard a clap like thunder. This sound was subtly different from that of Arein's spell: more of an explosion, and very close. For an instant, he felt intense heat on the nape of his neck. At first he couldn't identify the bitter scent that permeated the smoke rolling across him. Then he remembered how he'd encountered the same odor once or twice on the docks of Luntharbor. It was the rare explosive powder that wizards, assassins, and street conjurers sometimes employed, which they called shock dust.

He climbed to his feet. No skeletal hands impeded him. Most, he saw, were no longer attached to wrists. The explosion had been tiny but intense, and, had he moved at the wrong moment, would likely have taken Durren's head off too.

Tia landed in front of him, dropping from the rafters above

with easy grace. Before he'd entirely registered her presence, she had hold of his free hand and was pulling.

He could tell she already had her path planned out. In no time they were through the barrier of dead that had hemmed Durren in. But there were still many between them and the exit. He decided he had no choice except to put his faith in Tia. He was half deaf from the explosion, his head was ringing, and he'd barely recovered from the horror of expecting to be torn apart by unliving fingers.

"You know," Tia snapped, "I was saving that for a special occasion."

Durren wasn't sure whether she meant that saving his life was such an occasion or that she was frustrated to have wasted a valuable resource, though he suspected the latter. Where was Tia getting these toys from? He'd heard of high-level rogues using shock dust for traps and diversions, but the costs were prohibitive. Knowing Tia, she was probably making them herself, despite the immense risks involved.

If that were the case, he wished she'd made a couple more. She dragged him left and right, both times avoiding the dead by the narrowest of margins. Durren couldn't tell if they were heading towards or away from the exit. Finally Tia released him—only to hop onto the surround of a vat. From there, she aimed a deft kick that sent a skeleton reeling backward. Then she leaped down and was off again, with Durren sticking doggedly to her heels.

At last he could see the way out. For all that night had nearly fallen, there was enough of a glow in the evening sky to mark the doorway as a rectangle of smudged blue-gray. There, too, were the others. Hule was still methodically swinging away with his hammer, while Arein and Caille made judicious use of their staffs, but mostly did their best to keep clear.

Despite their different routes, the five of them left the tannery almost as one. Hule was last out, having slowed his progress to cover them. Sweat was pouring down his face, and his jaw was set in a stoic grimace. Durren had no idea how he had the remaining strength to lift the huge hammer, let alone to wield it. As Hule saw that the rest of them were safe, he flung it away from him, and Durren watched as the tool sailed through one skeleton and another, to land with a crash amid a web of shattered tiles.

They'd made it. Not only that, they'd managed, more by luck than judgment, to complete their quest. Now they just had to get far enough away that Pootle could transport them back to Shadow Mountain. There they could report what they'd found, Krieg would send higher level students to put down this post-mortem uprising once and for all, and—

Durren heard the flap of great wings.

His heart sank. Even as he began to turn, he felt a crushing pressure of air, such that he had to bow to avoid being knocked to the ground. The noise was deafening and near—so near that he expected claws to lacerate his shoulders.

But the beating rhythm passed overhead, steady as a drum. Before them, a dark figure alighted. For a moment, those enormous wings hung fully outstretched—until, as the creature turned, it wrapped them about itself like a black cloak.

The earlier rain had relented to a fine drizzle, and Durren could see clearly. At close range, the fiend was more horrifying than at a distance. It resembled nothing more than a distorted compromise between human and bat, with the worst characteristics of the latter: in particular, its wings were like ragged leather sails, and fluttered with a queasy motion even when it was still.

Yet its features were not an animal's. There were deep-set eyes and a slit of a mouth; there was no nose, only two slender nostrils. And Durren knew with certainty that Arein's theory was the truth. What they faced was a shapeshifter that had no interest in hiding among men. Here was a monster that *liked* being a monster, and had found a form that satisfied it: one that let it fly, one with lethal claws on hands and feet, one with powerful muscles and prodigious height.

Here too was a danger far greater than the shapeshifter they'd fought back at Black River—a threat they couldn't hope to match. Nor did there seem much hope of talking to it. Would such a thing even be able to speak? There was intelligence in those eyes, but of an awful sort: the wiliness of a wolf, the hungry attention of a hawk, and the murderous determination of a big cat all together.

Their sole hope, then, was to get away. Maybe if they could reach the trees the monster wouldn't be able to pursue. Only, behind them, the dead were pouring from the doorway and forming up in ranks, exactly like an army presenting before its general. So in a way, the more restrained theories at Shadow Mountain had been right too: this creature was also a necromancer, for it had gained mastery over the reanimated dead.

Hule dragged his sword from its scabbard. The chime as it slid free was unduly loud. "Wish I'd kept that hammer," he grumbled to himself.

Beside him, Tia drew her own short sword. She did so soundlessly and said nothing. Meanwhile, to Durren's right, Arein leveled her staff and Caille planted his in the earth in front of him, as though afraid the spell he had in mind might be ferocious enough to tear it from his grasp.

After a split second's consideration, Durren sheathed his own sword and unslung his bow. If they were going to go down fighting, that was the weapon he wanted in his hands.

But there was no *if*. They couldn't beat the skeletons, and now they had to confront both them and a shapeshifter that lacked even the veneer of humanity to soften its monstrous nature.

Durren nocked an arrow and picked his shot. It might well be his last, and he intended to make it count.

Chapter 13

Durren never had the chance to loose his arrow.

What happened next was too quick for his senses to follow. There came a whirring sound, at once familiar and strange; almost in the same instant, the shapeshifter recoiled and unleashed a hissing cry.

Only as it reached to its shoulder and plucked out a delicate sliver of metal did Durren begin to understand. His initial thought was of Tia, but Tia was beside him, and he could see she hadn't thrown the knife; all else aside, she couldn't have hoped to catch the monster by surprise. Then it occurred to him to follow the shapeshifter's view—and he found himself staring at the roof of the tannery and towards the black-clad figure crouched at its edge, their right hand still upraised.

When the creature took off, the first slap of its wings nearly hurled Durren from his feet. It rose rapidly, flying almost straight up—though he had no doubt that soon it would plummet once more. And the figure upon the roof had clearly decided the same, for already they were running. In a moment they'd disappeared from sight.

"Come on!" Hule bellowed.

The dead had been spreading out all the while, encircling the five of them—but Hule had spotted a gap. Durren was about to follow when he realized Tia wasn't responding; that in fact she was perfectly motionless, her eyes locked on the shapeshifter as it readied to swoop.

Slipping his arrow back into its quiver, Durren caught Tia's arm and tugged. He might as well have tried to move a mountain by prodding it; she didn't as much as look at him. Potential futures flashed across his mind: one where she stood watching until the dead reached them, another in which she intervened in the fight about to break out on the rooftop. Neither ended well.

"Tia," he gasped, "you're going to get yourself killed! And me too, because I'm not leaving without you."

He meant it: he'd stay here and defend her to the best of his ability if that was the single choice she left him. He dearly hoped it wouldn't be. The wall of dead around them was closing, and soon not only would their escape route be blocked, but any prospect of rescue by Arein, Caille, and Hule would be lost.

Tia twitched. Her gaze met his. The expression she wore was so unlike her that Durren had no idea how to react: she looked scared, and at the same time imploring. He didn't know what she expected. Even if the two of them somehow made their way up to the roof, what could they possibly accomplish?

He hadn't time to think. Much more delay and any chance they had would be gone. Durren went for the first words that came to him, hoping they might mean something to her.

"Whoever that was," he said, "I'm sure they can take care of themself."

To his startlement, that achieved the effect he'd hoped for. Some of the worry vanished from Tia's face, to be replaced by her usual steeliness. Then she was off, in the direction the others had taken, and Durren was dashing to keep up. As he ran, he tried to make sense of what had just happened. So Tia had been right; the second figure wasn't in league with the shapeshifter. How could she have known? What was she not telling them? And surely the most important question—who were they?

Such concerns would have to wait. As he'd feared, the perimeter of dead had closed ranks. At least Hule, Arein, and Caille were safe beyond. More, they'd recognized the peril their remaining party members were in and were readying to clear a path. The problem was that all of them appeared to be on their very last legs, and there were a considerable number of skeletons in the way.

From somewhere beyond the tannery, a keening whistle split the air: two notes, subtly different, the second close upon the first. As one, the dead turned, skulls snapping round attentively—though again Durren couldn't help noticing that they had no conceivable means to hear.

Yet already they were responding. They seemed to have utterly forgotten him and Tia, and indeed all the antagonism of the last few minutes. Now they were in full retreat, moving in awkward unison towards the invisible point from which the whistle blasts had issued.

Their focus elsewhere, the dead were no longer making any effort to block his and Tia's escape. Tia picked a gap and they scurried through. Beyond, Durren saw that, rather than increasing the distance between themselves and the trooping skeletons, Hule and the others were staying near and observing their passage warily. He understood. Shadow Mountain's mission, if not the actual quest they'd been given, was to trace where the dead had gone and what their ultimate destination might be. They'd managed the first part, and here, perhaps, was an opportunity to accomplish the second.

Seeing that Tia and Durren were free, Hule beckoned. Then he set off at a lolloping run, keeping parallel to the marching dead, who were currently streaming around the tannery. Clearing the far corner, Durren saw that they were spread out over the barren ground beyond; the foremost were just reaching the bridge, which creaked protestingly beneath bony feet.

"I don't like this," Arein gasped. "What if they change their minds? Maybe we shouldn't be in the open."

She made a good argument. Durren had experienced more than enough brushes with death for one day, in every sense, and he doubted his waning strength would hold out if the skeletons abruptly changed course or if the winged shapeshifter should return.

"Look there," Caille said.

At the spot to which he pointed, a rough path approached the edge of the ravine. When they got closer, they could see that it joined a narrow ledge hugging the cliff face. Probably the tannery workers had taken this route to go fishing on the bank far below, or just to get a break from the stench.

Without discussion, the five descended, all the while glancing cautiously at the bridge and its passengers. A little way down, they found a rocky projection where the ledge broadened; behind, a dent in the cliff not quite worthy of being called a cave offered a degree of concealment. With the sun's only legacy a band of softer blue at the base of the sky, Durren felt confident they could hide from anything but a determined search.

He glanced once more towards the bridge. The dead did not move quickly. It would be a couple of minutes yet before the last of them was out of view. And still their attention remained focused entirely ahead, as though they somehow continued to hear those mournful whistle blasts.

From Durren's elbow, Arein said, "I have an idea. Do you think you'd be able to hit one of them with your bow?"

"Of course," Durren told her indignantly. They were well beneath the level of the bridge now, but the distance wasn't so great. Any half-decent ranger could have managed the shot.

"All right. Could you do it in such a way that the arrow would stay wedged? You'll only get a single try."

Admittedly, that was more difficult. Durren considered the possibilities and settled on one that stood at least a chance of working. "I think so."

"Good. Then give me an arrow."

He did as instructed. Hurriedly, Arein sat cross-legged, placed the arrow in her lap, and began to mumble, while her fingers wove the air. The spell was brief and sounded unusually simple to Durren's ears. By the time Arein brought her incantation to a close, it had also had no evident effect.

Nevertheless, she handed the arrow back. "It has to be firmly lodged," she said, "or else it's useless."

Durren refrained from pointing out that, as far as he could see, it was useless either way. Whatever her intention, he was intrigued by the challenge: now she was asking for something that would defeat the majority of Black River's rangers.

Don't overthink, he told himself. His fingers knew what to do, and a portion of his mind that he'd learned to trust had already calculated distance, angle, and wind speed and taken them into account. He'd picked his target, and that it was moving, that at any instant it would be out of range or obscured by the supports of the bridge, and that the last of the earlier rain still made the air hazy, just made the challenge more interesting.

He loosed. He couldn't hope to follow the arrow's passage, so he concentrated instead on his objective. He thought he heard, faintly, the chink of metal striking bone. Then the skeleton he'd picked out was absorbed by the pack, and he couldn't be certain he'd made the shot, let alone achieved the further goal that Arein had set him.

But no, there was his arrow, lodged diagonally through a ribcage, its tip protruding near a bony elbow. As long as that skeleton stayed in one piece, Durren's arrow wasn't going anywhere.

He breathed a sigh of relief. And only then did he realize that any more delay would have cost him his chance; the last of the dead were on the bridge, and in a few moments even they would be upon the far bank.

He looked round to see Arein beaming at him. "You did it!"

"Apparently."

"And now we have a way to track them."

"We have?"

"Obviously! What did you think I was doing?"

Durren just shrugged. Suddenly he felt very tired. After everything that had happened, such intense focus had taken more of a toll on him than he'd anticipated.

"I cast a small enchantment," Arein explained. "One with

a sufficiently unusual magical signature that I'll be able to trace it from a distance. Well, until the spell fades, anyway, which is likely to happen within about a day."

"So," Durren said, "all we need to do is wait until the dead are a safe way away. Then Pootle can take us back to Shadow Mountain and you can tell Krieg how to track that enchantment of yours."

"Ah." Arein looked uncomfortable. "You see, it doesn't exactly work that way."

"What doesn't?"

"Um…any of it. The thing is, I can't just describe a magical signature to someone. Caille and I have seen it, so we'd recognize it again. But given that the skeletons are basically magical creatures, and the shapeshifter certainly is, finding that arrow if you didn't know precisely what you were looking for would be like hunting for a needle in—well, a pile of much bigger needles."

"What you're saying," Durren clarified, "is that our choice is to keep following the dead or to head back to Shadow Mountain? We can't do both?"

Arein hung her head. "Maybe if I'd had more time I could have come up with something better."

Caille's expression was grave. "I don't like this. No offense, but being stuck in a party with you four is bad enough; I don't want to get into more trouble. I know that perhaps things worked differently at your old academy. At Shadow Mountain, rules are there to be obeyed. You don't just start inventing your own quests."

Hule scowled at him. "Funny…I've been told that being a paladin is about doing what's right, not what's easy. According to my tutors, that's why we're more than mere fighters." He ran a finger down his chest, and the golden bolt he'd sewn there. "And I was starting to believe that. I'd hate to find out it wasn't true."

"Also," Durren put in, "I seem to remember you once saying how the dead being brought back was an abomination. What's most important, stopping this or you not getting told off?"

Caille's frown deepened. "This isn't about me. It's about us being students, students who've been given strict instructions. You don't get to decide what the correct course is; that's Krieg's job. And she needs the information we've uncovered to make her decision."

Arein pointed at Pootle, where it hovered above them. "I'm sure that when we don't return she'll ask whoever's been watching what we've been up to; then she'll know as much as we do. If she really thinks we're doing the wrong thing, she can always send a party to bring us back."

Durren hadn't contemplated that possibility. Abruptly he wondered if Caille was right. Life had been starting to settle down for him at Shadow Mountain, and here he was, potentially throwing that progress away to go running off on another self-imposed quest.

Yet he knew in his heart that they had a chance that might never come again. Something terrible was going on, a plan that perhaps stretched across centuries, that could conceivably be the final gambit in the shapeshifters' ages-long conflict with the other races. And he understood then what truly terrified him: the shapeshifters weren't hiding anymore. Whatever that meant, he refused to believe it was good.

"Caille," he said, "I appreciate you not wanting to get into trouble. None of us do. But with all the resources at the academy's disposal, they still managed to lose track of the dead once. From what I've heard, the Dolorwood is vast; who's to say that, if they vanish now, they won't be lost forever? And what if this is the last opportunity anyone has to stop that monster?"

"Those are both big ifs," Caille replied. But he sounded less certain.

"Tia," Durren tried, "what do you think?"

She spared him only a glance. "I'm not going back," she said.

That didn't exactly help his case, though it didn't surprise him either. In fact, he kept expecting to turn round and find that she'd rushed off alone to hunt for the mysterious stranger who'd saved all their lives.

"Tell you what," Durren said, "why don't we give it an hour? We'll talk this through and see if we can't figure out what's going on. Maybe there's a solution we're missing, some way to track Arein's arrow that doesn't require us staying here, perhaps."

Caille only nodded. Durren felt a degree of sympathy for the cleric. He was right to resent having been thrust into this situation, and it struck Durren that this might be the very reason Krieg had attached him to their party: to provide a dissenting voice. He hoped Caille had the sense to see that she was more to blame for his predicament than they were.

The five of them trudged back up the path. At the top, Arein said, "There are the huts. We could shelter inside and even stay the night if we had to. I mean, I know it's a little creepy…and a lot smelly…but they're probably our best option."

"I agree," Hule told her. "We could sleep in shifts and set

out with the dawn."

"We haven't decided that we *are* staying," Durren pointed out, glancing towards Caille.

When the cleric didn't respond, Durren let his gaze drift on in the direction of the huts, which looked no more hospitable than when they'd searched them barely an hour before. He felt sure of just one thing. Whether they did as Arein and Hule had said or returned to Shadow Mountain, this was going to be a long and unpleasant night.

Minutes later, they'd finished making one of the huts about habitable. After a brief discussion, they'd shifted the tannery workers' possessions to another of the small shelters; with the space all but emptied, their comforts extended to bunks and a fire, though the former were doubtless unsanitary and the latter they didn't dare light for fear of drawing the shapeshifter's attention. As such, their only illumination was from Tia's lantern, propped on a shelf.

Beneath its eerie glow, Durren glanced around at the others. Hule was sat working methodically upon his sword with a whetstone he'd produced from his rucksack. Tia was standing in a corner, her concentration apparently consumed by the floor of hard-packed dirt. Caille stood in the opposite corner, his brows drawn in an intense frown that said he wanted nothing less than to be here, and was frustrated by the knowledge that, just possibly, here was where he ought to be. Lastly, Arein had sat on one of the bunks—it was high enough that her feet didn't quite touch the ground—and was fishing in her backpack.

"Why don't we have some dinner?" she suggested.

Personally, Durren was at once hungry and nauseated by the prospect of eating. Every time his stomach growled, there came an aftershock of queasiness at the notion of ingesting food with the tannery's stink still heavy on the air. Nevertheless, he suspected Arein's real goal was to bring the five of them together, and if he was correct then her idea was a good one.

"I suppose we'll have to rely on what we brought with us," he said. The only place they stood a chance of catching game would be within the Dolorwood, and he'd need an infinitely better reason than hunger to cross that rope bridge tonight.

"Actually," Arein replied, almost apologetically, "I found a few bits and pieces." She withdrew a cloth bag from her pack.

It turned out that Arein's attention had been largely centered on scavenging what edibles she could find from the other huts: she had a round of smoked cheese, a stick of dried meat, some bread that was narrowly on the right side of fresh, and some rather wizened apples. She'd also found tin plates, and now she set to dividing her haul into equal portions.

Durren had never felt more grateful for Arein's hearty dwarfish appetite. None of the food looked especially appetizing; really, he couldn't conceive how anything would in such circumstances. But it was certainly more appealing than the rations they'd been provided by Shadow Mountain, which exceeded even Black River's paltry fare for the degree to which they tasted like sawdust.

With no table, they sat on the ground around the lifeless fire. As Durren began to eat, he forgot rapidly about the smell and his own filthy state and even about animated skeletons and flying shapeshifters. Whatever his opinions on the matter, it appeared that food was precisely what his body had been waiting for. He was chasing the last scraps by the time he remembered that they were supposed to be deciding their course and interpreting the fresh information they'd acquired.

"What have we learned?" he wondered out loud. "There must be some sense we can make from all this. Why raise dead people and then go to so much trouble to turn them into skeletons? What can they do that they couldn't before?"

Arein looked meditative. "I was wondering that. I think maybe skeletons would be easier to control. They're…simpler, you know? They have less moving parts. In magic, that's important. I mean, I can barely imagine the sort of power that would be needed to manipulate that many at once, but it would undoubtedly be easier this way."

"Or maybe," Hule proposed, "the shapeshifter just thought that having a lot of skeletons around was less disgusting than having a lot of smelly rotting corpses."

"That might be a factor, too," Arein conceded. "But, for the sake of argument, let's assume my theory is right: that whatever the shapeshifter has in mind, it needs manual labor and numbers to make it work."

"Though not intelligence," Caille contributed. Durren couldn't escape the impression that his joining the conversation was an announcement of sorts: that, for the moment at least, he was willing to go along with them.

"No," Arein agreed, "not intelligence. All it's after is tools. And I suppose that makes sense, in a horrid kind of way. It's not as if shapeshifters can simply go out and recruit when they want a job doing."

"That's hardly an excuse for desecrating graves," Caille protested.

"I know that! All I'm saying is, just because they're using dead people like puppets, that doesn't mean what they're planning is *evil*, necessarily."

"Maybe that's true," Durren said quickly, before Caille had

a chance to reciprocate. "In a way, though, I think it's the wrong question. It's possible the shapeshifters don't intend any direct harm. There haven't been any fatalities so far, and whenever someone's been hurt it was because they actively interfered. On the other hand, we need to remember that we're dealing with what may well be the last members of a species that our own races tried hard to wipe out. Even if their goals aren't precisely hostile, they're not likely to be doing us any favors."

"Where does that leave us?" Hule complained. "We still don't know anything. Once again, all we have is theories and—"

Both his sentence and his concentration were broken, as abruptly Tia leaped to her feet. Durren had seen and heard nothing. Yet as he looked up and followed Tia's frantic gaze, he realized a figure stood outside the entrance, visible only as a shape in the darkness.

No, not just a figure—*the* figure. Unless there was more than one person wandering out here in the wilderness dressed in black from head to toe, he felt safe in assuming this stranger was the same one who'd intervened against the shapeshifter, and surely also the one they'd spied watching from the rooftops during their first encounter with the creature.

Tia took two rapid steps closer to the doorway. Durren had never seen her so startled or so defenseless: her face was wholly open and revealing, and what it admitted to was a mix of excitement, fear, astonishment, and joy, crashing together like lumps of ice in a thawing winter stream.

Meanwhile, the figure was perfectly unmoving. Their stillness in itself felt like a threat: there was the sure sense that they could react very quickly indeed if they wanted to. Then again, perhaps Durren was only registering the fact that they'd got this near without any of the five of them noticing.

As for Tia, she too stood motionless. Her lips trembled, as though she was attempting to say something. Overwhelmed by curiosity, Durren strained to hear. But when Tia finally spoke, she did so in her own tongue, simultaneously harsh and lilting, and all she said was a solitary word: "Gada."

Chapter 14

At first Durren took the word Tia had spoken for a name. Then it occurred to him that he'd heard it before: he'd picked up bits and pieces of many a language around the docks of Luntharbor, and Dun-elf was no exception. Now that he thought, the word really was familiar.

Only, his memory refused to comply—and in any case, he couldn't tear his attention from Tia. She had taken a third step towards the stranger, who hadn't moved in even the smallest degree.

Suddenly, Tia turned back. All emotion had been wiped from her face and she was at least partly her old self. "We need to do something about Pootle," she said. There was urgency in her voice.

"What do you mean, *do something?*" For her part, Arein sounded both nervous and protective.

"I mean, whoever's watching can't see her. We need to cover Pootle up. And is there any way to ensure another party can't transport to our location?"

Arein considered—even as Durren wondered how Tia had known to call the figure, who still hadn't revealed themself, *her*.

"I don't think they'd dare if they couldn't see where they'd arrive," Arein said. "But—"

"Please." There was genuine pleading in Tia's voice. "Will you just do it? I'll explain later, I promise, but it has to be now."

Arein nodded. "Pootle…did you understand that?" She held out her hand, as though she were offering food to a trained bird.

Pootle, however, didn't respond immediately. The observer zipped back and forth, in a fashion that perhaps was the closest it could come to expressing uncertainty.

"You know Tia's your friend," Arein said gently. "We're all in this party together, and I'm sure she wouldn't ask unless this was important."

Pootle bobbed once more—and then dipped to land smoothly in her palm. It blinked its huge eye at her almost sleepily.

Arein smiled. "That's right. Have a nap, and we'll wake you when we need you again." She slid the observer into one of her baggy pockets. "You're safe," she called towards the doorway.

The figure took a hesitant step forward. Their cloak was a lot like Tia's, even down to the color; the cut was near-identical, and the garment was equally concealing with the hood pulled forward. Perhaps realizing this, and how suspiciously they were behaving, the figure reached and drew the cloth back from their face.

The blue-white light from the lantern was weird and distorting: Durren took a moment to appreciate that their skin was actually the slate gray shade it appeared to be. *Just like Tia's,* he thought—and that countenance, too, said dun-elf. The woman's features were all angles, with no softness anywhere. Her eyes, beneath the flat illumination, were practically black.

They really do look alike. Not just similar, but—

At last Durren remembered what that word, *Gada*, meant, even as Tia said, "Everyone...this is Kyra Locke. My mother."

The silence that followed her announcement was so thick as to be strangling. Somehow, the very notion that Tia had parents seemed unaccountably strange—yet here Durren was, face-to-face with one of them, in the middle of nowhere and under the most extraordinary circumstances. There were simply no words appropriate for such a situation.

"Hello," said Arein. "It's nice to meet you."

All right, Durren corrected, *there were words perfectly suited for the occasion—and trust Arein to find them.*

"Hello," he mumbled, and Hule and Caille echoed the greeting.

"Why don't you sit down?" Arein offered. "Then we can treat that."

Wondering what she meant by *that*, Durren belatedly noticed how, all the while, Kyra Locke had been clasping one hand to her ribs within the folds of her cloak.

"I can manage," she said. But she did pace to the nearest bunk and sit—though with caution, as if she still wasn't quite convinced that she was safe among them.

What had happened to this woman, that she'd be so guarded around her own daughter and her friends? The answer came to Durren immediately and without prompting: *shapeshifters have happened.* And in that instant he felt he had one small part of this puzzle, even if he didn't know where or how the piece fit.

Tia remained near the doorway. She had turned mechanically as her mother brushed past and was watching her with glazed eyes. She seemed in shock, or else overcome with such a mix of emotions that none could reach the surface.

"They told us you were drevoi," she said.

Kyra met her gaze. "They were right."

Suddenly there was fury in Tia's voice: "And I was just supposed to accept that?"

"Wait," Durren blurted out. As Tia's head jerked round, he was already regretting opening his mouth. Nevertheless, he pressed on, "I know this is an important moment for you, but right now, whatever's going on, we're a part of it. So please can you use words we all understand? What does drevoi mean?"

"Drevoi means *vanished*," Tia retorted. "Only, it means lots of other things as well. You see, my people—at least our Shadow Council—like words that can cover plenty of eventualities, or even say nothing much at all. So drevoi can also mean dead. And banished. And *traitor*."

Kyra appeared unmoved by her daughter's outburst. "You misunderstood," she said. "Drevoi has one meaning above all others: not to ask questions."

"Oh, I understood! And I didn't ask anyone anything—not even Father. What could they have told me I didn't already know? That maybe you'd come back and maybe you wouldn't, and if you did, it might be in months or perhaps years. I didn't speak to anybody or tell them what I was thinking, because I knew there'd be no point. I just made a decision: that I'd find you, and that if you could vanish without a trace, I could too."

Kyra sighed. "You haven't changed in my absence, have you? Still stubborn and headstrong."

"I'm your daughter, aren't I?"

For an instant, Durren perceived the faintest ghost of a smile upon the older woman's lips. "It certainly seems so." Then any hint of amusement or sympathy was gone and she said, "Tia, I realize there may be much you wish to say to me. This isn't the time; we have more important matters to attend to." She winced. "Also, as your friend here observed, I'm not in the best of conditions."

Immediately Tia's manner softened, and some of her earlier hesitancy returned. "If you're hurt, let me bandage you."

"I can manage perfectly well myself." Kyra glanced at Arein. "But I could use some fresh water, if there's any available."

Arein bobbed her head and hurried out. A minute later she was back with a bucket, which she placed at Kyra's feet.

"I saw what you did earlier," Kyra told her, and her eyes flickered between Arein and Durren. "Am I correct in thinking you have a way to track that arrow you shot?"

Arein nodded. "It's enchanted, and I can follow its signature, as long as the dead don't get too far away. Going by how fast they were moving, I should be able to pick up the trail in the morning."

"Then we'll set off at dawn," Kyra said. Nothing in her tone suggested she recognized the possibility that anyone might have a differing opinion—as though, with those six words, she'd declared herself leader of their party. Yet Durren wasn't willing to argue, and a glance at the others convinced him that no-one else was either.

Anyway, Kyra seemed to have forgotten about all of them, even Tia. She'd removed her cloak and was teasing up the edge of the garment beneath. Durren only glimpsed the gash in her side before modesty averted his eyes, but that was enough to tell him that it was deep and that she'd likely lost a fair amount of blood.

He gulped. "Perhaps we ought to leave your mother to it, Tia. I mean, if she really doesn't need our help."

Hule and Caille were already halfway to the door. Arein hovered a moment, caught no doubt between wanting to be polite and wanting to be helpful. And Tia didn't respond at all until Durren put a hand on her arm.

"Let's give your mother some privacy," he said.

Tia shrugged his hand away. Still, she followed the others, and Durren followed her in turn.

Outside, Hule, Arein, and Caille were standing in a huddle at a distance from the hut, Arein shivering in the cold breeze. When Durren turned back, Tia had vanished. He could just discern her retreating form against the gloom.

His first thought was that he should leave her alone, as she clearly desired to be left alone. Yet hadn't he been doing a lot of that lately? Not challenging her, and maybe not listening to her either? He could barely imagine how hurt she must feel, having tracked down her mother only to be told in no uncertain terms that her interest was unwanted—but he *could* imagine, because he wasn't exactly a stranger to difficult parental relations.

Any chance would be gone if he kept debating with himself. Hastily he set off into the night after her, ignoring the curious glances Hule and Arein threw his way.

Initially he was sure he'd lost her. The sun had set, the moon was low and cloud-covered, and there was no finding Tia at the best of times, not when she didn't want to be found. Then he saw her, or rather a black outline he sincerely hoped was her. He hurried nearer.

She was standing close to the edge of the ravine, by the spot where the path descended. She didn't react to his approach, though Durren was making no effort to mask his footsteps. He was starting to wonder if she truly had failed to detect him when she said, without turning, "After all this. After everything."

Durren decided not to ask what she meant. He thought he knew. He'd heard what she'd said back in the hut, and already those few sentences had quadrupled the knowledge he had about her.

"Who is she?" he asked instead. "I mean, who is she that she would be—you know, that word you used? That she'd be made drevoi?"

Tia looked at him properly for the first time. Perhaps she was surprised that he'd managed a vaguely sensible question. "Have you heard of Sickle Moon?" she inquired in return.

Durren shook his head, though he felt a distant sense that he had, in an overheard dockside discussion or when he'd caught part of one his father's business conversations not intended for his ears.

"That's what the outside world calls them. In Sudra Syn they have a different name; like every dun-elf word, it has at least five meanings at once. The thing with my people is that we've never been good at minding our own business. Oh, we stay within our borders, and we make a big show of not caring what anybody else is doing; that's not the same as not interfering. Sickle Moon is one of our ways of interfering. Only, it doesn't officially exist, and if you asked the Shadow Council, they'd deny it."

Durren was so stunned by Tia's impromptu lesson in the secrets of her culture, which she'd never as much as alluded to in the past, that he almost forgot to respond. "And that's who your mother is? She works for this Sickle Moon?"

To his further astonishment, a smile danced across Tia's lips. "Of course not. There's no such thing."

"Ah. Right." He felt he was beginning to see where this was going. "If there was, though, I suppose rumors of shapeshifters might be the sort of subject they'd be interested in?"

"I suppose you'd be correct. They might even plant one of their agents as a teacher in an academy—if they had reason to think that a shapeshifter was operating nearby."

Now Durren really did understand, not just who Tia's mother was but so much of what had happened since he and Tia had first been thrust together. She'd come to Black River not to study to be a rogue, a trade she had a more than impressive grasp of; she'd come because she'd heard of a tutor who matched a description she'd long been hunting for.

By the time she'd arrived, her mother was nowhere to be found. So Tia had begun her own investigation, seeking any clue that would lead her in the right direction. And she had absorbed the rest of them into that investigation—which, by pure chance, had absorbed them in return, as the clues led back to their very own mentor.

Finding the shapeshifter, however, had not proved the same as finding Tia's mother. Probably, having failed to expose her target, she'd been reassigned or had decided herself to try elsewhere; could it be that she'd discovered tidings of an unidentifiable creature in Ursvaal and reached the same conclusion Arein had? At any rate, she'd come here, presumably even before Tia had enrolled at Black River.

That had left Tia with only one lead to her mother's whereabouts: the captive shapeshifter and the hope that it would have answers. Had it chosen to aid her, for its own indecipherable reasons? Had it let slip some reference to Ursvaal? And was that why she'd been unperturbed by their assignment, not to mention why she'd been acting strangely ever since?

Maybe half the details were wrong, but Durren felt that he had the basic outline. Tia had left home searching for her mother and, after many months, the trail had led to this place and this moment. Yet all she'd received in thanks was rejection and dismissal. It was hardly surprising that she'd come out here on her own—and Durren wondered if the better course would have been to leave her be. No doubt she had a lot to consider before she faced the woman waiting behind them once more.

Just as he was about to mumble an excuse and turn away, Tia said, "Durren, I'm sorry. I had no right to drag you into my problems the way I have. I had no right to expect any of you to help me." Her tone became abruptly bitter. "Especially not when it was all a wasted effort. I should have realized my mother didn't want to be found."

Durren briefly pondered putting a comforting arm around her shoulders, imagined her feline reflexes misinterpreting the gesture for an attack, and decided not to. "I don't think that's what's going on," he said.

"Oh?" There was a hint of aggression in her voice, but also genuine curiosity.

"No. I think that your mother is protecting you in the only way she can. If you had someone you were afraid for and wanted to keep safe, would you bring them on quests with you? Or would you want them to stay home, even if that meant you wouldn't see them?"

Tia made a small scoffing sound. "You don't know my

mother," she said.

"That's true. Is it possible you don't either? I mean, not as well as you believe you do. Or, look—this mission, this being drevoi, what would have happened if she'd said no?"

"She'd never have said no. No dun-elf ever would."

"All right. For the sake of argument—"

"Bad things," Tia said. "Yes, I take your point. She had no choice. And obviously she couldn't take her daughter with her." Amid the darkness, she sagged. "But she could have looked pleased to see me."

Then, without thinking, Durren put his fears aside and his hand upon her shoulder—and was grateful when he didn't find himself plunging into the abyss. "I know what it's like to have a parent who doesn't even care if you're there or not," he said. "That wasn't what I saw just now. To be honest, I think your mother's angry with you."

Beneath his palm, Tia's shoulder blades clenched. "What reason does she have to be angry?" She sounded almost plaintive; he suspected she already knew the answer he was about to give.

He gave it anyway. "Because she wanted you to be safe, back home in Sudra Syn, and instead you're here, in danger. She's saved our lives at least once, hasn't she? Probably she had to choose between doing that and what was right for her mission; probably she didn't want to have to reveal herself. And now she's wounded—"

"That's hardly my fault!"

"I know that. I'm sure your mother does too. Still, the fact is, she'd prefer not to have to worry about protecting you. Just like you wish she'd never gone away on this drevoi thing."

Tia sighed. "She's not 'on a drevoi thing.' She *is* drevoi. If I really had to translate it, and to get all its different meanings into one, the best term I can come up with would be 'outcast until further notice.' Do you understand?"

"I think I do." And Durren thought, too, that he comprehended why Tia had done what she'd done. To discover that her mother was on a secret and surely hazardous mission was bad enough. For that mission to be denied by those who'd issued it, who in turn belonged to an organization so clandestine as to effectively not exist, and for there to be no end in sight...

In short, he had a hunch that not knowing had been what compelled Tia at the last. She could bear with adversity and fear, but ignorance was her great weakness. While Durren had always regarded her as a dun-elf through and through, maybe the truth was that at heart she was ill-suited for life in Sudra Syn.

"We should head back," Tia said. "The others will be wondering where we've got to."

She slid away from his hand and started towards the huts. The night was sufficiently dark that Durren could barely distinguish the squat structures, and had to navigate primarily by smell: he could tell, if nothing else, in which direction the tannery lay. Tia, though, picked her path without hesitation, and soon he could see Arein, Hule, and Caille, huddled in the narrow slants of light that crept around the closed door.

Tia marched straight over and knocked. "Are you ready, Mother?" she asked. If she was calmer than before, she still spoke the words with an edge of uncertainty; maybe she was concerned that her mother would somehow have sneaked away once more.

But the door opened and Kyra, standing in the gap, beckoned them inside with a nod. She was again wearing her cloak, and any hint of vulnerability had vanished from her posture. She looked stern, and intimidating, and very much like her daughter.

"We'll be setting out early," she said. "You should get all the rest you can; tomorrow will be a long day."

If Durren was taken aback that she didn't propose posting a sentry, on consideration he decided that both she and Tia, even in sleep, would react more quickly than the rest of them could hope to. Besides, the dead were surely long gone, and if the winged shapeshifter had intended to return, it would have done so by now. As for more traditional predators, he refused to believe that any animal with a sense of smell would come near this place.

Luckily there were bunks enough for all of them, despite Kyra's unanticipated presence. Durren found himself beneath Hule, which was unfortunate, because from experience the fighter was prone to snoring like a hog. Then again, the small space didn't offer much in the way of privacy for any of them.

Rather than bother to undress, Durren merely slipped his boots and pack off and piled them at the head of the bed. He didn't at all trust the cleanliness of the ratty blanket and reasoned that the less of it that touched his skin the better. Nor was the bunk remotely comfortable. Of course, neither was his bed at Shadow Mountain, which in turn was harder and lumpier than his straw-stuffed mattress back at Black River; really, the last time he'd slept in actual comfort was the night before he'd left home.

Tonight it scarcely mattered. He didn't for one moment expect to sleep. In fact, the prospect was inconceivable: if he could somehow ignore the bruises that covered his flesh and the countless questions cavorting around his head, there would still remain the tannery's malignant odor to render any sort of rest impossible.

Yet, mercifully, sleep came. His head barely touched the pillow he'd made from his bundled cloak before he was out. And even more surprisingly, that sleep was both deep and unbroken, as though his mind had decided that the only reasonable response to the day's hardships was a retreat as far from consciousness as possible.

Durren woke, riddled with aches and staring into darkness, to find that someone was roughly shaking his shoulder. The room was pitch-black except for the faint bands of gray that fell through the gaps about the door. He recognized Tia, eventually, by her outline and the way her cloak masked the shape of her.

"Get up," she said. "We're heading out."

Chapter 15

By the time he had his boots on, Durren's eyes were beginning to adjust. The hut was far from well-made, and he saw now that light was penetrating not only around the badly sealed door but also via a multitude of cracks in the walls and roof. The more he looked, the more he found that no two planks quite aligned correctly.

Tia had moved on to Hule, who grunted and rolled away, until she practically dragged him from his bunk, at which point he stumbled upright with a groan of complaint. Meanwhile, Arein—no doubt disturbed by the noise the rest of them were making—had sat up and was blinking through tousled waves of reddish-brown hair, and Caille was clambering from his bunk on the upper tier.

Kyra, naturally, was already on her feet and perfectly composed. Her movements hid her wound well; only a slight stiffness betrayed her. Yet she couldn't disguise that, even by the standards of her raw-boned people, her face was gaunt, or that her eyes were dark-ringed and puffy with sleeplessness.

There was no suggestion that she meant for them to eat breakfast before setting off, and no-one had the courage to raise the topic. But Arein looked mortified, and Durren was startled by his own hunger. Somewhere in the night, he'd learned to cope a little with the stench from the tannery, and it no longer dominated his senses as it had yesterday. He'd have been glad even of the flavorless slop served up at Shadow Mountain; as it was, he'd have to make do with cold rations eaten while he walked.

Outside, the sky was just barely light; enough so that, with concentration, he could pick out the roof of the tannery. Durren wondered, for the first time in hours, about the missing workers, and when they might intend to return. Probably they should be told that they no longer had to fear skeletons marching through their camp or hiding in their tanning vats. He reminded himself that someone back at Shadow Mountain knew more or less what they did—at least until the moment when Arein had hidden Pootle. So perhaps it was safe to say they'd solved the mystery of the vanished tannery workers after all.

He doubted that would win them much favor in Krieg's eyes. He'd never heard of anyone purposefully hiding their observer so as to withhold information from their academy, but if anything was likely to be an expulsion-worthy offense then surely they'd found it.

With that, Durren's thoughts turned to Caille, who was walking just ahead. Of all of them, he'd had the least say in this, and he definitely had the least reason to be here. Really, there was a certain irony to the fact that they'd saved his life only to destroy his academic career. As the six of them paced towards the bridge, Durren sidled nearer and said, "How are you holding up?"

Caille seemed surprised by the question. "I'm fine."

"Okay. Good."

Comprehension dawned upon the cleric's face. "Oh—I understand. You're worried about me."

"Well," Durren admitted, "a little."

"You think I might have been planted by Krieg to keep an eye on you four troublemakers."

"What? No."

"I promise you," Caille said hotly, "I was as dismayed as you were to find out I'd be joining your party. And I may not agree with everything you've been doing, but I'm not planning to betray you. If Krieg asks, I'll have to tell her the truth, so the less I know the better."

"Caille," Durren replied, striving to keep his voice steady and soothing, "that's not what I meant at all. What I meant was, I'm worried about how we've dragged you into this mess. Nobody's been thinking you might betray us." *Well*, he corrected mentally, *maybe Tia has; she doesn't trust anyone.* "And look, for whatever it's worth, I'll do what I can to make Krieg see that we didn't leave you with much choice."

The cleric scowled. "Are you saying you could have forced me to come along with you?"

"No, of course not! I just meant that—"

Caille's glower turned into a grin. "Relax, I'm joking. Honestly, I went over this in my head last night, and I understand that you've all made the choices you believed were right. Hopefully they will be, but if not then I'm as to blame as anyone."

Durren was so relieved that he didn't know what to say.

Anyway, by that time they had come to the beginning of the rope bridge, and further conversation would have to wait. Because, as he regarded the expanse in front of him, Durren realized he was going to need to keep his mouth clamped firmly shut if he didn't want to embarrass himself.

He'd never been afraid of heights. Not being afraid was one thing and taking sensible precautions not to fall to your death was quite another. Here, the only sensible precaution would have been to find an alternative route—except, that might take them hours or days out of their way. And probably the bridge had been entirely safe before a hundred skeletons trooped across. Now, its span looked distinctly the worse for wear.

Perhaps the tannery workers had compromised between their occasional need to cross and their reluctance to do so by leaving the bridge to steadily deteriorate into a death trap. The ropes were old and weathered; a couple of planks were missing, a few were clearly damaged, and doubtless others would reveal their failings under a careless foot. Some attempts *had* been made to patch the most obvious damage, but they were half-hearted at best.

"I'm sure it's safer than it looks," Arein noted with forced cheer.

She was in the lead, followed by Hule, then Kyra and Caille, with Durren and Tia at the rear.

"Go slowly," Kyra said. "Spread out and test each step."

As though we'd need to be told that, Durren thought. Was she aware that they were level two adventurers? Did she have any idea of what they'd been through to reach this point? Maybe from her perspective they were nothing more than her daughter and her daughter's friends, a group of young people not much past being children. He hated to imagine how Tia must be feeling; not only was her mother not pleased to see her, she seemed wholly oblivious of her accomplishments.

Arein had already started upon the bridge. She might be the smallest of them, but that just meant her mass was concentrated lower to the ground. She was following Kyra's advice to the letter, not putting her full weight on any plank without a tentative initial step. As it became Durren's turn, he wondered if he wouldn't rather run across and take his chances; at least that way there'd be none of this dreadful tension. Waiting for Arein—and then Hule, and Kyra, and Caille—to move before he could, and taking care to ensure the gap between them never narrowed, was nearly intolerable.

When Arein hopped onto the far bank, Durren released a small gasp of relief. In that lapse of concentration, he found that his eyes had strayed, and that he was staring between a gap in the planks, down a great distance to where white water thrashed against jagged stubs of rock.

The post-dawn gloom had been a comfort so far, making detail indistinct. Now he felt that what he couldn't discern only left more for his imagination to complete. He could see, too, how old and worm-eaten the wood beneath his hovering right foot was. Thanks to the growing daylight, he could even make out clear tunnels through the plank where enterprising insects had burrowed.

"What are you waiting for?" Tia asked irritably, from close behind him.

Almost simultaneously, Arein's voice carried from the far bank: "Um, everyone…"

Durren tried to ignore them both. He managed to persuade his foot to pass on to the next plank, which looked sturdier. It creaked—and held.

"The thing is," Arein called, "this rope…"

What was she talking about? Durren took another step, and abruptly his body was his own again. All he had to do was keep his eyes forwards and press on and he'd be across in no time.

But as he glanced up, there was Arein, and Arein's expression was frantic. "It's awfully frayed," she continued, her voice rising in both pitch and volume with each word. "I don't know that it's going to hold much longer. So I really think you ought to hurry."

She didn't need to have said even that much. Beneath her words had been the groan of the straining rope and the sound of threads snapping, individually and in bunches. Each separated with a distinct *thwip*.

At the same time, Hule took a last, broad step and reached safe ground beside Arein. Caille wasn't far behind; three paces would be enough to cover the final distance. If they all hurried as Arein had said then just maybe—

"Everyone get down!"

Kyra's tone was incontestable. Though rationally he felt that stopping, let alone kneeling, was the worst course imaginable, nevertheless Durren did precisely that. Ahead of him, the others, even Arein, had done the same; only Kyra herself remained standing.

In her right hand she held a pendant of metal barely longer than her palm, and in her left was a length of fine cord. When she flung the pendant free, he realized why their ducking had been so imperative: in an instant she was whirling the leaf-shaped blade around her head. She swung it through six tight circles; below its insectile drone, Durren could still catch the pop and crack of ropes giving way. Then Kyra threw.

He didn't see the pendant strike its target, but he heard: a whirring followed immediately by the thud of metal embedding in wood. As she worked rapidly to tie her end of the cord to the rope rail beneath her hands, Durren understood what Kyra had done: by securing the other end about the post, she'd substituted her own temporary replacement for the damaged cable.

Alas, the crucial word was *temporary*. As if on cue, the rope gave a last, catastrophic shudder: he watched the length near Arein snap and flail into the gulf. The bridge creaked and tilted; only by clutching the surviving support did Durren keep his balance. All that held them up on the left side was what remained of the original rope patched with Kyra's cord—which looked awfully frail by comparison. It couldn't possibly take their weight and that of the bridge too.

"Now—go," Kyra demanded. She sounded absolutely calm, as though repairing collapsing bridges while she stood on them was an everyday task.

Caille didn't have to be told; he was already across. And Kyra was quick to take her own advice. Durren forced himself to mirror her precise steps, conscious that he and Tia needed to keep their distance or they'd all be done for. But to do anything except dash for safety was agonizing. Kyra's movements seemed almost leisurely, and he wanted to scream at her. Didn't she understand that at any instant the three of them would be cast towards that thrashing water and those jutting rocks?

That was just the fear trying to find a voice; he gritted his teeth to restrain it. And now Kyra was over, stepping easily from bridge to outcrop. Yet Durren was still a good five paces away, and he knew with sickening surety that he wasn't going to make it—which meant Tia wouldn't either. Even if the cord didn't fail them, the shock of the rope snapping had sent such a tremor through the nearest portion that the bridge was beginning to come apart. The question was not whether he could get to the other side in time but what would let him down first, the crumbling planks or Kyra's oh-so-impermanent solution.

The answer was the cord. He heard it break and felt it whip across his arm, and the pain was startling, like the most intense of burns. Now nothing held one side of the bridge up. The planks underfoot were giving way, their angle descending steeply. Durren darted forward regardless, hoping that the surface would last a little longer—certain it couldn't. He only needed to manage a couple more strides, and to do so was impossible.

In that moment, unexpectedly, he thought of Tia. Even if he somehow made it, she wouldn't. And before he fully comprehended what he was doing, Durren was glancing back, and—seeing she was right behind him—had reached for her hand. Their fingers entwined.

For no reason, he felt hopeful: two more steps and they'd be safe. He made the first; but the boards were halfway to vertical and already he was falling. He tried for the second, though the gap was too far and he was treading on thin air—

That held him. Incredibly, he was floating in space. His eyes found Arein, and registered the absorption that contorted her face. He knew what she must have done—just as he knew that her levitation spell lasted scarcely a second. And while he was supported, Tia wasn't; the sudden shock of her weight was dragging him over, and he grabbed in desperation for the surviving rope, or for anything.

What he grasped was Hule's outstretched hand. Caille in

turn was holding onto Hule, and as Durren found himself swung to safety, Kyra clasped her daughter's free hand. Before he could quite appreciate what had happened, all six of them were standing safely in a tight huddle, with the void a mere whisper away.

He nearly jumped out of his skin when the second rope broke. The sound came from directly beside his ear. Rather than watch the bridge's final demise, he took a couple of quick steps, distancing himself from the chasm once and for all. He felt better for noticing that the others followed his example, even Tia and Kyra.

The six of them took a minute to catch their breath. Only then did they turn, one by one, to look back at the devastation.

"Was this the creature's doing?" Caille wondered. "I mean, the way that rope was weakened?"

Kyra shook her head. "If it had wanted us dead, we would be. It doesn't need to set traps, especially not traps as ineffectual as that was."

To Durren's mind, the damaged bridge had come close to being very effectual indeed. Nevertheless, she was right; most likely this was a combination of bad luck and the fact that the bridge had been in no shape to withstand the passage of dozens of marching skeletons.

Like the rest of them, Hule was staring at the gap, and at the sad tail of broken planks that drooped down the far cliff of the ravine. "We won't be going back that way," he observed.

Durren let out a shaky laugh. "Would we have wanted to?"

Hule pulled a face. "No, of course not."

By the time the sun broke fully above the trees, they were well within the Dolorwood, and all of them had more or less regained their composure—though Durren's heart still raced whenever he remembered those last instants, as the planks tilted under his feet.

Already it was evident that they wouldn't have stood a chance of tracking the dead without Arein's trick with the arrow. The Dolorwood was extraordinarily dense almost from its edge, the foliage wrapping in such tangles that it seemed to deliberately bar their passage. To Durren's eyes, there weren't even the usual narrow animal trails he'd have expected; despite the occasional hoot or trill of birdsong from the canopy above, the forest felt lifeless.

Further, the skeletons had left next to nothing in the way of tracks. The rain that featured so significantly in the Ursvaalian climate barely penetrated beneath the trees, and the earth was hard and gritty. Every so often he'd notice what might be a clue to their passage, a snapped twig or a patch of crushed grass, but invariably the detail could be as easily explained in other ways.

No, his tracking skills would have been utterly defeated, and as much as the family Locke would surely have fared better, he was willing to believe that even they would have had to give up eventually. Anyway, the more attention he paid to Kyra, the more he suspected that she needed the greatest part of her concentration to stay upright. Whenever the ground became unduly difficult or she had to duck to avoid low branches, there was no mistaking how she winced and clutched her side.

Were it not for her wound, Durren had no doubt that she'd have pursued the dead all through the night. Certainly she'd never have involved her daughter in the chase, let alone anyone else. The five of them were here because they'd become the best chance Kyra had to succeed in her mission. Or rather, Arein was, and he, Hule, Tia, and Caille were allowed along only because Arein's presence dictated theirs.

Yet Arein was struggling the most. While walking in a straight line amid such impenetrable forest was a feat in itself, the rest of them could at least concentrate on looking where they were going. Arein might as well have been finding her way with one eye shut—or, perhaps, with both eyes focused on a place no-one except her could see. Hule was staying close and gently intervening whenever she seemed sure to collide with a bush or tree, but that was the most any of them could do.

It didn't help that, increasingly, the entire task of finding their way was falling to her. As the morning wore on, it became apparent that Caille had a far looser grasp on the enchantment's signature than she did. Try as he might, he could only pursue its trail for a few paces before stumbling into a trunk or tripping headlong. Durren could tell that the cleric was doing everything in his power to allow her brief respites, but more and more Arein was left bearing the responsibility alone.

Finally, well into the morning, she staggered to a halt. Despite the cool beneath the canopy, sweat was coursing down her brow and cheeks—and it was obvious that, for the moment, she couldn't go on. Durren half expected Kyra to scold her. Instead, the dun-elf woman wandered aside and stood staring in the direction they'd been traveling, as if solely through power of sight she might pick out their distant target.

Arein, meanwhile, had collapsed onto a fallen tree trunk. Though she appeared close to tears, all she did was snuffle deeply and set to wiping the sweat from her glasses with the hem of her cloak.

"I'd hoped Pootle would be able to help," she explained to no-one in particular. "But, you know…"

And she gently patted the pocket in which, presumably, she was still hiding the observer.

Caille sat beside her. "I'm sorry I'm not more use," he said earnestly.

Arein shook her head. "It's not your fault. There wasn't time to describe what I was doing; you only caught a glimpse of the enchantment."

"All the same." Caille clearly wasn't reassured.

Arein pulled her flask from her pack and took a long, noisy swig. "If you're worried, there's a way you could pay me back."

"Of course."

"That spell you used yesterday—the one that was so effective against the dead. Could you teach me it? Or maybe just the basics? I've never seen anything like that."

Caille looked even more uncomfortable than he already had. "I...don't think I could. The spell worked so well because the unbalance doesn't want its power to be abused. The magic was just following its natural inclination."

Arein sighed. "Caille, I know that's what you believe..."

Durren decided he had no desire to listen to the two resume their bickering on this topic. He turned away before the cleric could answer. He thought about talking to Hule or Tia; but he was footsore and weary himself, so instead he walked a short distance, found a stump to prop himself on, and rummaged in his pack for something to eat.

Something meant the hard biscuits Shadow Mountain favored so highly; they tasted like wood pulp and careful chewing was required to avoid breaking a tooth. Durren managed two and could bear no more. He washed the last flavorless dust from his mouth with a gulp from his flask—at which point Tia called, "Durren, we're moving!"

He spared a glance for Caille and Arein as he rejoined the group. Their faces failed to betray whether one of them had won this latest round in their ongoing dispute, or whether they'd simply argued to a stalemate.

As they set out again, Arein seemed more composed for her rest; or perhaps her task was growing easier the nearer they approached their target. At any rate, Durren's attention drifted increasingly to the forest itself. He knew that, as a ranger and now a bard, he was meant to feel at home in the wilderness; he'd lost track of the many lectures in which he'd been told to read the signs of nature and allow himself to experience his surroundings.

Here there was little to be read, and less he wanted to experience. Even deep in the Dolorwood, there was still only the barest sense of life. There must be birds above, and animals stalking the underbrush, and insects creeping among the fallen leaves. Yet it was as if every living thing was doing its best to disguise all trace of its presence.

More, the forest had a deep air of ancientness and—was it possible for trees to be sinister? Rather, it wasn't the trees themselves but an unshakeable impression that they were here for some purpose. After all, in a country like Ursvaal, where the climate was harsh and resources scarce, wasn't it strange that these vast tracts of woodland had been ignored for centuries? It was as though, at some point in the ancient past, an agreement had been reached that nobody had subsequently dared challenge: what was within the Dolorwood would stay there, and what lay without would not intrude.

Or maybe Durren was letting his fancy run riot, based on his vague expectations of what they would find. For by early afternoon, there could be no question that they were drawing close to their mysterious objective. Every so often Arein had been pausing to comment on their proximity, and her last observation had been, "Only a little farther."

The forest was opening up as well, becoming less oppressive: where before they'd walked in the equivalent of twilight, now they moved between patches of weak sun, and the canopy above was sparse enough for the ground to be frequently slushy with rainfall. Grass grew in a thick carpet, and there were even patches of flowers, though their colors were washed-out and somber: frosty blues and purples, and yellows and greens so pale as to be practically white.

The sound was what erased any doubt. It rose from ahead, faint at first but mounting steadily, revealing its details from amid a toneless cacophony. If Durren had had to guess, he'd have supposed that something was being built; he could pick out clear notes of stone striking stone and a general suggestion of many bodies moving with a single purpose.

Or—not bodies, precisely. He remembered what Arein had said, that the advantage of skeletons over corpses was that they were better suited to undemanding labor. Probably what he was hearing was the sounds of the dead, put to work after their days-long trek. And as much as Durren knew that the nightmarish images his mind threw up must be worse than the reality, they almost forced him to a standstill.

Though he persuaded himself to keep going, his unease refused to pass. Nor was it only the distant noises that unsettled him. For the first time since they'd entered the Dolorwood, he felt the sure sense that they weren't alone. He glanced around at the others. Arein and Caille were intent on the arrow's mystical signature, and Hule was as oblivious as ever. But was it Durren's imagination, or were both Kyra and Tia picking their steps with care and favoring the shadows?

Ahead was a wide strip of clearing, descending shallowly to where the forest resumed and riotous with verdure, like a meadow in miniature: the grass was ankle-high and filled with the same flowers he'd seen elsewhere, speckled pools of blue and yellow.

Durren found that, with no thought on his part, his eyes had sought out the far line of trees—and one particular spot, where two broad graywoods stood close together, casting the gap between into deep darkness.

He felt certain there'd been nothing to see a moment earlier. Now there was: a black figure, naked and glossy-skinned, its face as simple as a snake's and more expressionless.

Durren froze. He had heard no beat of giant wings, no disruption of the foliage above. And as he looked, he saw clearly that the creature was not the same one they'd confronted outside the tannery.

This wasn't the winged monster, though it was as familiar and more so. There should have been no identifying that blank countenance, and still, Durren was sure: in front of them was the shapeshifter they'd fought back at Black River.

Chapter 16

Kyra was first to react, and did so faster that Durren could follow. He hadn't registered that she'd moved, yet there was a knife in her hand that hadn't been there before, and she was halfway to closing the distance between her and the shapeshifter.

The shapeshifter's response was even quicker, and more unexpected. It blocked her with one forearm, the motion as swift and assured as if it were meeting her blade with the sturdiest of shields. But there was no shield, only its own ebon flesh.

It served just as well. Kyra's knife bounced away, and she recoiled with an audible gasp. Otherwise she seemed undeterred, and Durren understood then that she'd expected precisely such a result. She knew what she was dealing with.

Already she'd crouched lithely beneath the shapeshifter's guard and was striking at its exposed side. The result was identical, on both counts. Again her knife failed to draw blood and again Kyra simply kept moving, bobbing and weaving and lashing out. Durren thought he grasped her strategy: she believed the shapeshifter exerted itself to harden its skin, and that eventually a lapse in its concentration would offer the opening her blade sought.

"Back her up," Tia snapped, and at the same instant Durren caught a flicker of movement; only after he'd registered the metallic glint spiraling from the shapeshifter's shoulder did he understand that the motion had been a knife she had thrown.

The creature had effortlessly defended itself on two fronts. Could it do so on three, or four, or five? When they'd originally fought it, they'd failed to coordinate their attacks. Weren't they more capable now? Maybe this time they had a real chance. And even as the notion entered his mind, Durren was readying his bow and hunting a shot that wouldn't jeopardize either Tia or her mother, both of whom were darting about the creature like moths around a flame.

He was all set to loose when, with a roar, Hule dashed across his view, sword held high. Durren cursed and sidestepped—to find Caille in his way, staff upraised. Abruptly Durren realized that this wasn't going to work at all. He, Arein, Hule, and Tia had struggled to cooperate before, and here they were, trying to incorporate two new party members.

Taking a couple more quick sidesteps, he concentrated everything on picking a fresh shot—which, sure enough, was ruined as Hule swung a blow for the shapeshifter's head, one it ducked easily. The fighter, Tia, and Kyra were each slashing from different angles, yet still the creature seemed unconcerned by their efforts. It blocked with outstretched limbs or slid away, flowing as smoothly as water and suffering as little damage from its passage.

Only then did it occur to Durren that the shapeshifter had made no attempt to fight back. There had been plentiful opportunities to turn a parry into a blow, and that it carried no weapon was irrelevant. Its bare flesh was as good a club as it was a shield, and Durren had experienced the creature's extraordinary strength at first hand.

So it was that he was less surprised than he might have been—and less than Kyra, Hule, and Tia appeared to be—when, without warning, the shapeshifter sprang upwards, to land beyond their reach.

Tia and Kyra hesitated for just an instant before they turned to pursue. To Durren's eyes, mother and daughter had never looked more similar: whatever this Sickle Moon that Kyra belonged to might be, she was above all else a rogue, and there was no doubting where Tia had learned the foundation of her skills.

At the same time, Durren had never seen Tia so aggressive. Normally she was the one to hang back and strike from the shadows, or to conjure some novel solution that avoided fighting altogether. But having found her mother, she was evidently determined to keep her safe, even if that meant placing her own life on the line.

Yet the shapeshifter had no intention of letting Tia endanger herself. As the two drew close, and while Durren strived to track its movements with the tip of his arrow, it sprang once more into clear space. Landing deftly, the shapeshifter raised both hands and cried, in a voice deep and barren as the canyon they'd so narrowly managed to cross that morning, "Stop this!"

Its authority seemed irresistible. Durren wondered if some magic was being worked, for suddenly he found his fingers relaxing and his bowstring slack. But he was more surprised to see that Tia and her mother had also skidded to a halt.

"My name is Tulpek," the shapeshifter said. "And if I'd intended to harm you, I would have done so. I ask you, please, to calm yourselves."

"I don't care what your name is," Hule snarled. Slower on the uptake than Tia or Kyra, he was only just beginning to lope towards the shapeshifter's new position. "We beat you once and we'll beat you again."

The creature—Tulpek—considered him with head aslant. "You interrupted me, back at Black River. A delay is not a victory. Now here we are. You can't hurt me and I can certainly hurt you. Regardless, what do you lose by listening?"

Time, Durren thought, *we lose time*. This could be nothing more than an attempt to delay them. On the other hand, continuing their battle would have delayed them every bit as well, and the shapeshifter was right: even with Kyra on their side, they probably wouldn't have stood a chance.

"Hule," he said, "what's the harm in hearing what it has to say?"

Hule finally stopped, and glared his way. "What's the harm in listening to a monster that tried to kill us all as part of some evil plot against Black River? I don't know, let me think."

"No," Arein interjected, "I agree with Durren. We should at least listen; isn't that what we've been taught? To fight only when there's no alternative."

"I'm not convinced this is the kind of situation our tutors meant," Hule grumbled.

But Durren had already realized what Arein and Hule would soon enough: the decision wasn't theirs to make. For his gaze had shifted to Kyra, who remained closest to the shapeshifter and who still had a knife in her hand. If Kyra Locke decided that the correct course was to fight on then she would, and their options would be to support her or to watch her die in a duel she couldn't win alone.

For that reason, Durren felt relieved when she slid the knife within her cloak and said, "So talk."

Was it his imagination, or was there also relief in the way the shapeshifter ever so slightly relaxed? Despite its apparent confidence, it had been ready to fend off another assault. Again Durren wondered if making use of its armored skin taxed it, and if that meant it could potentially be exhausted to a degree where its defense would no longer function. Again he filed the question away for later examination—for Tulpek was speaking.

"I'm here to offer you a choice," it said. "Go home and live, or continue on your current path and die for nothing."

Though Kyra made no move, every detail of her posture said that she was prepared to attack at the smallest provocation—or maybe without any whatsoever. "You're here to threaten us," she translated.

Tulpek shook its head. Since it looked so inhuman, the gesture was stranger than it should have been, like a lizard imitating a person. "I make no threats. Why would I? You know I can defeat you."

Kyra's lips turned up in a faint smile that never reached anywhere near her eyes. "Do I?"

"Yes. I can smell the blood on you; I can taste it in the air. One blow to the right spot and you'd be a mewling heap on the ground. But come, this conversation is beneath us. Take my word; I've no interest in threats."

"Then what?" Arein interrupted.

"Exactly as I said. I wish to grant you an opportunity to

change this futile course you've set yourselves on. My companion would not show you such mercy. Apaek sees things…differently. She hasn't worn a human shape or impersonated a human mind in a very long while. Conversely, her memories of other ages remain undulled; she has no liking for your races. Yet even Apaek has spared your lives on occasions."

That much was true—to a point. The winged shapeshifter (Durren assumed that must be this Apaek that Tulpek referred to) could undoubtedly have stayed to exterminate them when they'd been cornered and down to their last strength on their first encounter. However, to Durren's mind, what Tulpek claimed as mercy might as easily have been a desire not to waste time on needless conflict. The same went for their meeting at the tannery; the second shapeshifter had had no qualms about wounding Kyra, and that it hadn't finished the job might mean only that it deemed her unworthy of the effort.

Something else occurred to Durren. He had always thought of Tulpek as *it*, but the shapeshifter had described its companion as *she*. While perhaps he had no reason to think so, Durren was sure now that Tulpek was in fact male. Oddly, that made him seem less an inexplicable horror and more like a person.

Then Durren noticed how Tulpek's attention had fallen on him. His eyes were hollows; they showed no hint of life or emotion. His face was a blank slate. Whatever glimmer of sympathy Durren had felt vanished in that instant. Just because there were males and females among the shapeshifters, that didn't mean they could be reasoned with, or that they weren't monsters.

Yet Tulpek's next words were not those of a monster. "You

were brave to come here. But despite what you may believe, you are still children." His blank eyes roved, from Durren to Tia to Arein to Hule. "Your lives should not be forfeit for no purpose. Would you persuade yourselves that I didn't spare you when we last fought? I'm not sentimental; trust me when I say that no being who'd watched the passage of centuries could hope to be. Nevertheless, I choose to think that lives have potential. I'd take no pleasure in snuffing yours out."

Durren had no answer. Even if he should accept that Tulpek meant what he said, where did that leave them? They could hardly walk away and disregard everything they'd seen. And they could hardly listen to this creature, who'd worked to undermine Black River from within, remorselessly deceiving and stealing and torturing to further its ends.

But Tulpek wasn't finished. "What we're doing is no danger to you," he said, "or to any of your kind. I understand that you resent the mistreatment of your dead. Yet all we did was take what you'd discarded and put it to fresh use. The crime, in perspective, is not so great. By tomorrow morning, the dead will walk no longer, and we will be gone—for good. No harm will befall anyone in the interim, not unless they should force our hands. Leave. Forget this place. Or the next time we meet, there'll be no forbearance."

With that, Tulpek sprang away once more. His leap carried him to the far edge of the clearing. In an instant, Kyra had started after, a knife again in her grasp. When she threw it, Durren's eyes weren't fast enough to register the slender blade's passage; he did see where it embedded itself nearly to the hilt in the trunk of a tree. He heard Kyra mutter a single word in her own tongue, and guessed he was better off not knowing its meaning.

She paced to the tree and levered the knife free. Then she checked the blade, tutted, and slid it back into its sheath. Durren thought she might pursue Tulpek. Instead, she turned and rejoined them.

"I hope," she said, "that none of you believed a word that thing said."

Durren was taken aback. He had expected distrust, but outright disbelief was another matter.

"Would we be so wrong to?" he asked, before he could stop himself.

"Not if you were wholly unfamiliar with their past and the crimes they committed."

Arein stepped forward. "I've studied quite a lot of the records from that time. From what I understand, bad things were done on both sides."

"And it's true that he could have killed us," Durren added. "I mean, I think that if we're honest we all know that: he could have and didn't. Doesn't that mean there's a chance the rest might be true? What does Tulpek accomplish by lying to us?"

"That's simple," Kyra said. "If only one of you managed to escape and to report this location back to your academy, the shapeshifters wouldn't be fending off five students, they'd be facing an army."

She was right, and perhaps Tulpek genuinely was afraid— not of them, of what they represented, the full brunt of Shadow Mountain brought to bear. Shapeshifters were extraordinarily tough, but history had proved them far from indestructible.

Still, Durren wasn't convinced. "We saw Tulpek because he let us. If he hadn't, he could easily have taken us by surprise. He must have disguised himself to get so close without our realizing; couldn't he have stayed that way and picked us off before we ever knew he was there? Anyway, all he really had to do was target Arein; without Pootle, we'd be stuck here, and Shadow Mountain would have no possible way to send reinforcements."

Kyra regarded him steadily. Her gaze was not much less cold than Tulpek's had been. "It sounds to me as though you want to believe. Are you scared to go on?"

Durren felt as if he was withering beneath her stare—and he tried to summon a scrap of anger with which to defend himself. "Obviously I'm scared! I'm scared for myself and my friends. I'm even scared for you. We fought that monster once and we almost died; there's no reason to think we'd do better against two of them together." He took a deep breath. "That doesn't mean I'm wrong. Surely we need to at least consider the possibility that the shapeshifters don't mean any harm?"

Without warning, Kyra took a step nearer to him—and for the first time, it struck Durren that of all the justifications he had for being afraid, perhaps this formidable dun-elf rogue was high among them. He'd trusted her because she was Tia's mother and because she'd given them little choice except to do so. Only now did it occur to him that she was also an agent for an organization so secret that it might as well not exist, and that he had no grounds to assume her agenda was remotely the same as theirs.

"My mission," she said, each word sharp as a barb, "is to find out what those creatures are planning and to stop it. What the five of you do is your own choice."

Durren's eyes automatically sought Tia. *But it's not*, he thought, *because your daughter is here and she isn't about to let you go off alone.* And sure enough, that was precisely what Tia's expression said: that she'd stick by her mother through whatever came, regardless even of whether it was right to do so. Durren suspected there would be no dissuading her, and he wasn't certain he'd be willing to try.

Then Kyra sighed, and abruptly she was simply a rather tired-looking woman and not a terrifying agent of some sinister dun-elf spy force. "That creature was correct about one thing; this isn't a fight for some first level students from a training academy."

"We're second level students," Tia observed acidly.

"Fine. As far as this conflict is concerned, those amount to exactly the same. You should go back, before you get in any more trouble."

Durren knew Tia would argue, and that she would keep arguing, just as it was clear that Kyra wouldn't be swayed by a word her daughter said. "We still don't know where the shapeshifters are or what we might be facing," he pointed out. "Shouldn't we wait until we have all the information and then decide what happens next?"

This time, no-one disagreed—though Durren felt keenly that he had merely delayed the inevitable. Nonetheless, he traipsed after Arein as she set off into the forest, again following the enchanted arrow's trail.

Not that they really needed her to. The noises were sufficient; the one difficulty was that they soon grew so loud, and echoed so peculiarly among the trees, that they gave the impression of issuing from every direction at once. Yet there came a point when even Arein stopped relying on magic and simply used her ears.

The forest remained thinner than before, and ahead the trees petered out altogether, in a long and curving line. The six of them approached with care, and with Kyra and Tia in the lead, both all but invisible now as they drifted from shadow to shadow. Durren settled for scampering to the cover of a row of low bushes upon the very border of the woodland. Moments later, Hule crouched to his left and Arein slid into the gap on his right.

What spread in front of them was a great and shallow-sided bowl carved in the earth. At its edges, the forest halted sharply—and again Durren had that sense of an ancient pact being maintained, as if in ages past the trees had been warned to trespass no further and ever since had kept their distance. Beyond their line, nothing except grass grew, and then patchily.

The slope descended towards the activity at the center: from above, the scene might have resembled a round eye, with that focus as a dark pupil. Durren first noticed the skeletons— because it was hard to pay attention to much else when there were that many skeletons moving about—and only afterward the building they surrounded. Or rather, the ruin, for whatever had once stood here had long since fallen and been left to the sort of decay that required eons to achieve.

There was no guessing what the structure had been. The sole clue was the amount of rubble, and that was scattered across so wide an area that even to say how tall the original design had been was impossible. For some reason, though, Durren's mind went to a tower, a great finger of black stone clawing the grim Ursvaal skies. Perhaps it was only that a tower would have allowed the occupants to gaze out over the expanse of the Dolorwood, whereas anything of lesser stature would have been hidden by the lowness of the land and the surrounding forest. There again, it was just as likely that hiding had been precisely the intention. After all, who would build in such a spot if they wanted to make their presence known?

It occurred to Durren then why there was both so much rubble and why the pattern of blocks reached almost to the perimeter of the clearing. He had noted the laboring dead without pausing to acknowledge what they were busy doing. All of them, he saw now, were either bearing blocks of stone—alone, in pairs, or in groups of three and four—or were marching back from the border towards the center to acquire a fresh load.

Were they rebuilding? No, the more he watched, the more he understood that they were in the business of demolition. They had already cleared a path through the wreckage of the upper tiers, those that had protruded above the ground. But there were subterranean levels also: Durren could see the entrance as a slab of darkness and that skeletons were mounting and descending the broad stairs there, in two orderly lines that made him think of marching ants.

What did it mean? What lay beneath that warranted summoning an army of the dead from graveyards all across Ursvaal, just to make of them a slave labor force to excavate this place? Durren decided that perhaps he was better off not speculating—if for no other reason than because each idea he came up with was more horrifying than the last.

"Oh! Look." Arein pointed.

Durren followed her finger, and had to clap a hand over his mouth not to laugh. Midway between the center and the edge of the clearing, a skeleton was in the midst of laying down the oblong block it bore upon its shoulder—and as it stood upright, he saw the arrow lodged through its ribcage.

Of course, anyone else could see that arrow too. Surely this was how Tulpek had known to expect them. Their plan might have worked, but it had hardly been discreet.

From behind, Durren heard the faint noise of voices, Kyra's first and then Tia's. However, with each exchange they were growing less faint and more heated. While he doubted the skeletons below would be able to hear anything, the prospect of an argument breaking out still made him nervous. Durren got to his feet and hurried towards the sounds of the discussion, to where Kyra and her daughter stood a little way in from the forest's border.

He failed to catch what Kyra said, but Tia's response was a barked, "No!" There was the distant threat of tears in her voice, like banks of thundercloud on the edge of a clear sky. "There must be over a hundred of those things, and that's before you reach the shapeshifters. If you go in there alone, you're going to die."

Kyra's face was somehow furious and calm at once. "Tia, I have been doing this for longer than you've been alive. You can't stop me, and you won't try. You'll show some respect."

Durren could see that Tia was shaking; only her hands and only very gently, yet because he knew her, he couldn't possibly have missed the detail. It was as if she was already grieving her mother's death, as if she'd seen it happen and was powerless to change that fate.

"I just found you," she said, and her voice was strangled.

Kyra's manner softened ever so slightly. "I'm proud that you did. One day you'll serve our people well. But right now, you have to accept that this is what I am." And she turned towards the forest's edge.

"Wait!"

All eyes looked to Caille, for he was the one who'd spoken. He seemed as surprised as anyone, and more so when Kyra actually hesitated.

"What if there was another way?" he asked.

Her tone was distrustful. "Go on."

"We could send support from Shadow Mountain in a matter of hours," Caille said. "I mean, enough to do this properly. You're not the only one who wants to stop whatever's going on down there. And with all respect, if you should fail then there may not be a second chance."

Kyra didn't look remotely persuaded. Durren suspected that, like her daughter, her preferred approach to any situation was to rely on the known quantity of her own skills and to not have to worry about being jeopardized by the weaknesses of others.

Or maybe there was more to this. How long had Kyra been on her mission? Months, certainly, judging by Tia's time at Black River—and he had no idea how long her daughter had taken to track her that far. But assume for the moment that Kyra had spent mere months of her life seeking a nebulous threat from the darkest annals of history, one that could hide anywhere and be anyone; assume she'd been hunting them alone for even a year, traveling the lands, following whispers and half-formed clues, chasing rumors, and always finding herself two steps behind.

Perhaps she liked this life—who could say? And perhaps she missed her family just as much as Tia had missed her. Maybe she'd yearned for an end to a quest that, for all she'd known, might have no end. Now, here was that conclusion in sight, one that would slip from her grasp as the others had if she failed to seize it in time.

"Could you give us until nightfall?" Durren proposed. "You can't hope to get inside before then, anyway."

He felt certain she'd refuse, if only because she was Tia's

mother and Tia had never been the easiest of people to convince.

So he was taken aback when Kyra agreed, "Till nightfall, no longer. And make sure your Head Tutor understands to bring her very best."

Durren hadn't realized how tense he was, partly on his own behalf but mostly on Tia's, until he heard those words. Before he could feel reassured, however, he hit upon yet another problem. How exactly were they meant to send anyone here? He doubted that simply describing the location would be enough.

Then he had an idea. "Is it possible," he asked Arein, "for Pootle to transport us without being transported itself? Could it stay to—well, to keep an eye out? And so that Shadow Mountain knows where to travel back to?"

Arein considered. "I don't see why not. Pootle doesn't transport us; it's just a medium, and a fixed point for the spell to be channeled to. All that would be needed would be for Pootle to move out of the spell's radius at the last instant. Whether it can be persuaded to, though? I don't know."

"Will you try?"

She nodded. "Only…" She looked towards Kyra.

The dun-elf woman understood. "Don't worry. I don't intend to be seen—not by your observer or by anything else."

"Of course." Arein's smile was timid. "Well, I suppose this is goodbye; it's been nice meeting you." She glanced deeper into the trees, and then towards the rest of them. "We can't travel from here. Pootle wouldn't allow it, not with danger so near."

Durren, Hule, and Caille said a hasty goodbye to Kyra, which she acknowledged with the barest nod. Tia, though, clearly wanted to say more. She was waiting close to her mother, hesitant as a callow apprentice about to ask his favorite housemaid to a dance. Durren might never get used to seeing her so anxious; this version of Tia, the one with emotions like those of normal people, was virtually a stranger to him.

"We should give her a minute," he suggested.

He, Arein, Hule, and Caille retreated a few steps and stood with their backs turned. But as it happened, whatever was said between Tia and her mother didn't even take a minute. Moments later, she was pacing past them.

Durren chose not to wonder at what had been discussed. There'd been enough drama with the family Locke for one day, and he could only hope that knowing her mother was safe for the time being would calm Tia's nerves.

They went a short way into the forest, and once she was positive Kyra was out of view, Arein drew Pootle from the ample depths of her pocket. She held the observer cupped in her hands while she whispered to it. Finally she said, "I think Pootle understands."

If the little creature was no worse for wear from its long interval in darkness, it nevertheless seemed overjoyed with its renewed freedom: it zipped towards the treetops, and then hurtled back to spiral about them, moving so fast that all Durren could see was a blur. After that, the observer flitted round them, hesitating before each face, as though making sure that everyone was present and unhurt. Only when it was satisfied did it rise to take up its favored position at their center.

Durren was still half expecting Tia to change her mind, to try and convince her mother to come with them or to let the five of them accompany her into the ruins. He realized he was watching her with trepidation—and that she'd noticed.

But her reaction was simply to mouth the words, "Homily,

paradigm, lucent."

Chapter 17

This time, Durren felt scant relief to be returning to Shadow Mountain. He was more than ready for a rest, and certainly eager for a wash and a good meal, but he had a suspicion that even such humble luxuries would be denied them in the immediate future. First there was the matter of explaining where they'd been and what they'd discovered, and there was no reason to assume Krieg would make for a sympathetic audience.

Still, he was glad when trees blurred into walls and little by little the cool of the forest gave way to musty airlessness, and more so when the nauseating effects of the spell began to diminish, so that he was seeing one view and not two smeared awkwardly across and through each other.

Then the spell was done and they were really, fully in the transportation chamber. Durren looked around—and froze. Of course he'd known that the wizard, Gallowpall, would be here, and while he hadn't anticipated finding Krieg waiting, he wasn't wholly surprised. But it would never have occurred to him to expect the six burly students she'd brought along with her.

A glance was enough to tell him that they were of level four or five: at least a couple of years older than Durren himself, and with a toughness to them that spoke of experience gained by dint of great effort. More, they were armed, despite the fact that students were forbidden from bearing weapons within the academy's walls except in the most specific of circumstances.

Only as he registered Krieg's expression did Durren comprehend that these armed students were here for them.

In case there was any doubt, Krieg said, her voice cold as an ice floe, "Stay precisely where you are. You're under arrest."

Durren knew that asking her why would be futile. He understood what crimes they'd committed in her eyes, and the list wasn't short. Their gravest offense, though, was surely hiding Pootle. And too late did he begin to see how that must look from Krieg's perspective. Whoever had been watching then via the observer, they'd have glimpsed a cloaked figure in the shadows—and nothing more. They'd had no way to know that figure was Tia's mother, and the knowledge would have meant little to them if they had. But there were worse possibilities Krieg could have arrived at, and one so dreadful that Durren couldn't believe he hadn't considered it before. What if she was aware of the shapeshifter threat? What if she thought that their mysterious visitor had been one of them?

So perhaps they weren't merely being arrested. Perhaps they were being quarantined, lest one among their number was other than they appeared to be. At the least, there was the chance Krieg viewed them as collaborators. Then again, if she'd known who they'd really been speaking to, would that be better? Or would they have been associating with a potentially hostile foreign power?

Just as Durren had decided this terrible situation couldn't hope to get much worse, Tia took a step forward—and six hands of six high-level students twitched upon the grips of six weapons.

"Listen to me," Tia said, "I appreciate that you take issue with our actions over the last few hours. But what we have to tell you is more important than any matter of discipline."

Krieg raised one hand and made a gesture with her fingertips to the older students that said, *no need for that*. Or maybe Durren was only seeing what he wanted to, and the signal was better interpreted as, *no need until I tell you so.*

"As Head Tutor of Shadow Mountain," Krieg said, "I beg to differ. Now, you'll remove your armaments—one at a time, please, from right to left. Take them off and pile them in front of me."

Durren expected Tia to argue. Yet she stepped back into place. Her face was stonily impassive.

Hule was at the rightmost end of the line. He casually unbuckled his sword and laid it, along with his buckler, at Krieg's feet. He didn't seem overly concerned to be surrendering it—perhaps in part because his training made him nearly as dangerous with hands and feet.

Arein went next, and was more obviously distressed. Durren knew that, to a wizard, a staff was not a weapon but a tool. Indeed, as the channel for her magic, which in turn was an essential element of her, it was practically an extra limb. Still, she deposited it beside Hule's sword.

Caille appeared barely less uncomfortable to be giving up his own staff—and after that came Durren's turn. He had no especial attachment to his current bow; the one he'd crafted himself had been destroyed in their first fight with Tulpek all those weeks ago, and the replacement he'd been given was not its match. Regardless, a ranger wasn't a ranger without their bow. Placing it at Krieg's feet felt wrong on a level deeper than he could explain.

By comparison, joining it with his knife and short sword was a mere afterthought. Remembering that his arrows were probably classified as a weapon as well, and that there was no way to remove the quiver from his pack, he pulled them out in a handful and added them to the heap.

That left Tia. Durren was half convinced she'd make a break for the exit; he judged that she could outmaneuver six high-level students if she set her mind to the task. Instead, she paced to stand before Krieg, and refused to lower her gaze. Though the Head Tutor was tall, so was Tia. They stood eye to eye as she unbuckled the bandolier of knives she wore beneath her cloak. Rather than kneel, she dropped it onto the pile, with a clink that made Durren wince.

"And the rest," Krieg said.

Tia hesitated. Then she undid her belt. She dropped that also, and Durren could see the many pouches and scabbards that stood out upon its surface. She turned to rejoin the line.

Krieg reached and placed a firm hand on her arm. Again, Durren flinched. Most people knew better than to touch an angry rogue; doing so was a sure way to lose fingers. Yet Tia stopped and turned back.

Krieg nodded towards the pile at her feet.

With a muted sigh, Tia slid off her cloak. The noise with which it met the stone floor was one fabric alone had no right to make; evidently the garment had more than its share of hidden pockets. Without it, Tia was a strange sight. That cloak was to her what Durren's bow or Arein's staff was to them, and wearing only trousers and a tunic, she seemed underdressed and somehow smaller.

Yet still Krieg signaled with a tilt of the head that she wasn't done. Shrugging with resignation, Tia delved inside the waistband of her trousers and drew out three lethal-looking stars of metal and a vial of dark glass as long as the tip of her thumb. Carefully, she placed those with her other items.

"Oh, for goodness' sake." Krieg waved to one of the high-level students. "Just search her, will you?"

The girl she'd picked, a dark-haired and hard-faced paladin, did as she'd been told—and did so thoroughly. Her hands roved unapologetically over Tia, starting at the soles of her boots and ending at the collar of her tunic. After that, she went through her pack, removing and inspecting each item, checking the lining, and then putting Tia's belongings back one by one. By the time she was done, the pile had grown further still: with more pouches and knives, a worryingly fine length of wire, and a greater number of lockpicks than any one person could conceivably need.

The older student held up her hands, as though to say, *That's really everything.*

Krieg did not look wholly convinced. Nonetheless, she motioned Tia back into line.

Durren stared at the mound at Krieg's feet. It represented so much about the five of them, their chosen identities and their entire existence at both Black River and Shadow Mountain. Now those parts were gone, perhaps never to return—and at the thought, his heart sank, like a plumb descending through his body.

They were in trouble. They were genuinely in trouble. And

he didn't know if they'd be able to argue their way out this time.

Arein, at least, was going to try: he recognized that stubborn look of hers, the one that said she'd marshaled her courage and was willing to fight against the most impossible odds.

All the same, she managed to sound meek as she said, "The thing is, Head Tutor, what Tia told you is true. We traced where the dead people have ended up, we found where the shapeshifters are hiding, and we have good reason to think they're preparing to attempt something…maybe something awful. So, we're sorry we didn't quite follow our quest and that we didn't come back when we were supposed to, but you really do need to listen to us. And you need to send as many high-level students to our observer's location as you can."

Krieg took a step nearer, careful to avoid the perilous heap of implements in front of her. She stopped just out of Arein's reach, as though her new status as criminal made her threatening in a way she'd never been before.

"What's to be done and when," Krieg said, "are matters for me to decide. You need concern yourselves with them no longer—if only because you will have absolutely no influence."

"Yes, but…"

Arein's sentence went nowhere. Durren could guess what she'd been going to say, and what had stilled her tongue: she'd wanted to plead that Tia's mother was in danger, and had remembered just in time that no-one except them was meant to know about the estimable Kyra Locke.

Fortunately, all Krieg saw was a timid dwarf girl unable to spit her words out. "Could it be that you didn't hear me? There are no buts. Despite what you may think, none of you are in positions of authority in this academy. You don't determine the nature or duration of your quests, and you certainly don't dictate when and how academy resources are allocated."

She was already turning away when Tia's softly spoken words called for her attention. "Are you one of them?"

"Am I one of *what?*" Krieg snapped.

"A shapeshifter," Tia said. Now she was speaking clearly, as if intent that the students accompanying Krieg should hear. "Are you a shapeshifter? Are you on their side?"

Krieg's slap was so sharp and so sudden that it should have carried Tia off her feet. Instead, she merely staggered.

Tia wiped at the corner of her mouth, where a bright runnel of blood stood out upon the dark gray of her skin. "Because," she said, "if you are then I promise we'll stop you."

Durren felt numb with horror. There was such tension between the two of them that the air seemed to sizzle, and yet neither moved, not the faintest of trembles, as though self-control was the weapon with which they fought.

Krieg broke away first. Perhaps she'd realized that getting into what amounted to a staring contest with a student was beneath her dignity. Or maybe Tia was right, and a third shapeshifter was running the only place that had a hope of stopping the other two—in which case, whatever Tia's opinions to the contrary, they really were doomed.

Krieg turned to the higher level students. "Get them out of here. You know where you're going. Ensure that there are no delays or diversions on the way—especially as regards *that* one." And she indicated Tia.

The older students split into two groups with easy efficiency. Three went to the front of their line and the remainder to the back. None of them said a word, but when they started walking it was evident that Durren and the others, caught between, were expected to keep pace.

Durren, having no wish to be trampled, was glad when Hule and Arein started moving in concert with their escorts— and particularly so when Tia complied, since he'd been preparing himself for another act of rebellion on her part.

However, it was someone else who disrupted their forced march towards the entrance. As they trooped past Krieg, who was watching with chilly contempt, Caille slowed. "What about me?"

The look Krieg gave him denied the slightest interest. "What about you?"

"I mean—this isn't my party. It's not fair for me to be punished for going along with something I had no say in."

Durren was surprised at how disappointed he felt. He had been beginning both to like and to trust the cleric, and here he was, concerned only with saving his own skin. Perhaps that shouldn't have come as a shock, yet it did.

Krieg, at any rate, was eyeing him unsympathetically. "You're saying you were an unwilling accomplice?"

Caille frowned indignantly. "I'm saying, Head Tutor, with all due respect, that I could hardly come back on my own. In any case, a student adventurer is supposed to cooperate with the party they've been assigned to, whether they agree with their companions or not. To do anything else would have been to place their lives and mine in jeopardy."

Krieg did not give the impression of having been moved one iota by Caille's words. Nevertheless, she said, "I accept your point—for the moment. But understand, Cailliper Ancrux, that we will be discussing this matter at greater length in the not-too-distant future. Meanwhile, you'll confine yourself to your dormitory. Regard your time there as a prolog to further discipline. Unwillingness is not the same as innocence."

Caille bowed his head. "Thank you, Head Tutor." He stepped hastily out of line, as though if he didn't she might change her mind.

The part of Durren that was weary and despairing at his fate wanted to spit some rebuke at Caille as he passed. The rest of him was aware that the cleric could scarcely be blamed. In fact, everything he'd said was true, and it was only right that he should be exempt from punishment, when all along he'd been a stubborn voice of reason. Still, Durren couldn't resist averting his eyes as he went by.

Then they were through the door and into the corridor beyond. As Krieg had intimated, the older students had obviously been told in advance where they'd be going. They led the way down passage after passage. Durren, who knew less than half of the academy, was soon utterly lost. In the meantime, their guards seemed fidgety and uncomfortable: it must be troubling to be put in this position of treating fellow students as criminals.

Yet again, Durren thought, they'd managed to make themselves the talk of an academy. In all likelihood, stories of the four exchange students whose term at Shadow Mountain had gone so disastrously wrong that they'd ended up being incarcerated would reverberate from these walls for years.

When their route brought them to a flight of downwards-leading stairs, Durren began to expect the worst: perhaps a dungeon like the one where he and Tia had found the shapeshifter. He soon discovered that, rather, the lower level housed the service areas of the academy, the storerooms, cellars, laundries, and forges that kept the place running from behind the scenes. Sure enough, the door at which they finally arrived wasn't that of a cell. While it was plainly sturdy, there was no barred window and no bolts, though there was a keyhole.

One of the older students dragged the door open and waved inside. Still none of them had spoken. Durren wondered what they'd been told, and if they really believed that he, Tia, Arein, and Hule were dangerous reprobates. Was that why they'd shown such a lack of sympathy?

He'd run out of time to speculate, for Hule and Arein were already inside and he was next. Glancing back, he was once more surprised when Tia followed meekly behind him. Then again, he hadn't failed to notice how their guardians were watching her with special attention; her extraordinary collection of weapons and tools must have made quite an impression.

The door slammed at Tia's back. It sounded weighty and impenetrable. Durren heard the rattle of a key turning in a lock. They were prisoners.

But the room he found himself in was, as he'd anticipated, not exactly a cell. Most likely Shadow Mountain lacked the dungeons that Black River had and Krieg was having to make do. For what the space did resemble was a storage room hurriedly—if not thoroughly—cleared out. Shelves lined two walls, and on them were stains of grease and powder, amid circular marks made by bottles or jars. On the floor were further dark blotches, square ones no doubt produced by crates and the more irregular outlines of sacks. Durren's naive first thought was gratitude that Krieg had tried to make the room habitable, and only afterward did he realize she'd just been ensuring that nothing was left that they could use to make their escape.

In fairness, Krieg's precautions were sensible—for Tia was already searching. She began in one corner and moved round methodically, investigating everything. There remained a couple of flaccid sacks, which looked empty at a glance; she turned them inside out anyway. She tapped upon the walls and floor and, once she was sure the shelves would bear her weight, clambered effortlessly to perch on the highest and test the boards of the ceiling. She rigorously inspected a knot in one beam, and teased at a gap between planks with the tips of her fingers.

Apparently not satisfied, she dropped back to the floor and crossed to the door. She put one ear to the wood and listened, for so long that Durren started to wonder if she meant to spend the rest of the day there. When she did stir, it was only to examine the planks as she had the room's other surfaces. She worked meticulously from top to bottom, though Durren could tell from a distance that the door was unassailably solid.

Then Tia turned away and began again.

The first time she'd seemed composed—almost mechanically so. This time, she was ever so slightly wild. Her movements were too fast, particularly the way that her gaze danced over the surfaces she was checking, as if there was always some potentially crucial detail on the edge of her vision that she was afraid of missing.

Yet she retraced her steps precisely, from walls to floor to shelves to door—and it was clear to Durren, even if it wasn't to her, that there couldn't be anything she'd overlooked.

By the third time Tia went around the room, she was frantic.

Her every motion was too rapid and too violent, as though when she rapped on the stones of the wall or the planks of the floor she was secretly hoping her fist might pass straight through. Durren could see that her knuckles were already grazed. If she kept this up much longer, she was going to really hurt herself.

She was scaring him. He knew the threat she posed she was when she was under control, and this was much worse; she hardly seemed aware of the rest of them. Yet she was his friend, and, now more than ever, she needed him. So he swallowed his fear and paced up to her and, as gently as he could while still restraining her, caught her wrist before she could lash out at one plank identical to the others.

"Tia," he said, "you have to calm down."

She tore free of his grip, and turned on him with such abruptness that he'd have sworn his hair fluttered in the sudden breeze. Her clenched right hand came up and shuddered to a halt a finger's breadth from his chin.

"Don't tell me to calm down, Durren." Tia's voice barely sounded like her voice at all; it belonged to someone older, who had seen and suffered more than she possibly could have. "If Krieg doesn't send help—and she has no intention of sending help—then my mother's going to go into that place alone. And then she's going to die."

Durren wanted to tell her that Kyra could look after herself. And of course that was true; from what Durren had witnessed, she was far more capable even than her daughter. Yet the odds she faced were impossible. The truth was that Tia had every reason to be afraid.

"I understand," he said. "Honestly, I do. But we're locked in this room and nothing you do is going to change that—especially not losing control."

For a moment, the fist stayed bunched beneath his chin. Then Tia dropped her hand. "Don't you think I know that?"

"Yes, I do. So why don't we try and consider this

rationally?"

She turned aside. "What's to consider? We're trapped. And in a few hours, my mother's going to realize no help is coming. I don't see how the four of us sitting around and discussing will alter any of that."

"Perhaps Krieg will think better of locking us up," Arein proposed timidly. "Even if she doesn't, she's sure to send students to the ruins sooner or later. With Pootle there, she has proof that we're not lying. There's a good chance, Tia, really there is."

Tia's expression didn't change: there remained the same mix of rage and fear and the steely self-discipline with which she was keeping both contained. "Fine," she said. "But as long as we're locked in here, we have no way to know."

"Maybe she'll let us out once that happens," Durren suggested. "I mean, most likely she'll cool down soon and see that, on the whole, we did what we had to. She's just thrown us in here to make a point."

Only, he wasn't convinced that was true. Were it not for their hiding Pootle and the mystery of Kyra's identity, he'd have been more optimistic; as it was, Krieg might actually believe that they'd gone against the interests of the academy, and if that were the case, who could predict what lay in store for them?

At least Tia had a hold of herself. And now that she was calm, she could no longer deny the reality of their situation. With their fate entirely in Krieg's hands, there was nothing to do besides wait.

After the initial frustration of captivity had worn off, and after his impatience had been ground away to lassitude, Durren came to an obvious realization: being imprisoned was boring.

In theory, being imprisoned with three other people should have been less boring. In practice, since no-one was in the mood for conversation, Hule, Arein, and Tia's company only soured his mood further.

What made matters worse was that there wasn't the slightest clue by which to measure the passing of time. Wherever they were, he wasn't even able to hear the clanging of the bells that divided up the day. Any break from the tedium would have been a relief, and Durren almost began to hope that Krieg would come and interrogate them. That would have been the rational thing for her to do; but was Krieg interested in being rational? Apparently she wasn't.

Eventually he noticed that his stomach was rumbling. Recalling that he still possessed his pack, Durren opened it and hunted in its depths. He had three biscuits left and half a flask of water. He settled for eating one of the former and taking a couple of sips from the latter. If Krieg wanted them to suffer for their crimes, and if she genuinely wasn't concerned about getting to the bottom of what those crimes involved, who could say how long they'd be in here? Again Durren found himself longing for any respite from this agony of not knowing and not doing.

Then he remembered his lute.

Maybe he'd been forgetting the instrument deliberately. Its presence, in place of his sword and bow, felt like a cruel joke. Yet he really was bored, and he really did need a distraction. Sitting here not speaking for however many hours—or days—it took Krieg to decide what she was going to do with them was hardly an appealing option.

He crossed his legs, placed the lute in his lap, and tested the strings. Not for the first time, the infernal device had slipped out of tune. Durren spent a minute tweaking pegs, until he was satisfied that it sounded approximately as it was meant to. He could feel the others' eyes on him, and refused to look up. If he did, he'd never go through with this, and then he'd be back to misery and silence.

Durren wondered what to play. Nothing too complicated, nor anything so simple that a child could manage it. For that matter, he'd do better to avoid the bawdier songs he'd picked up while listening to other students practicing in the bard's dormitory. After some contemplation and random plucking, he opted for "The Stargazer's Shoes", which had the benefits of easily remembered lyrics and of sounding more sophisticated than it actually was.

He made a clumsy start, conscious of the unaccustomed presence of an audience. By the chorus, his assurance was growing; even so, he sang as quietly as he could without losing his fragile grasp upon the tune.

As he was drawing to a close, he heard movement. He looked round to see that Arein had sat beside him. "That wasn't entirely bad," she said.

Durren was willing to take that as a compliment—at least, all the compliment he deserved. "I'm not so good with the high notes," he said. "Or the low notes either. The ones in between I'm getting the hang of."

Arein laughed. "I noticed that. Still, I've heard worse."

"Thanks." This was the first time anyone had been remotely positive about Durren's abilities as a musician, and Arein's morsel of praise had cheered him more than he could have imagined.

"Do you know any dwarf songs?" she asked.

Durren shook his head. "If you sing one, I could try and

play along," he offered, and immediately regretted the words; he had enough trouble keeping to music he was familiar with.

It was too late: Arein was already singing. The melody, thankfully, was straightforward. The lyrics were in Central rather than Dwarfish and concerned two young lovers doomed by their parents' feuding to always be apart. Arein's voice was soft but lilting, and she shut her eyes as she sang.

Two verses in and she stopped abruptly. "Aren't you going to play?"

"Um…sorry, that wasn't what I was expecting. I thought all dwarf songs were about digging for gold."

Arein scowled. "That's discriminatory, Durren. Dwarf songs are about all sorts of things. Probably less than half of them involve mining or precious metals."

"I'm sorry," Durren repeated quickly. He strummed a few experimental chords to mask his awkwardness. "Why don't you start again?"

Arein did so, and Durren was shocked to discover that, aside from the odd stumble, he managed to accompany her well enough. By the second chorus, he even found the confidence to join in. Just as the song was approaching its end, a third voice, deep and yet mellow, added itself to theirs: Hule had sat down next to Arein.

When they finished, the fighter said, "Now who's for a proper song? One with a little blood and guts."

Hule's alternative turned out be called "The Berserker's Bride", which he claimed was an ancient Durkhaanian ballad. Durren was unsurprised when the titular bride proved to be a battle-ax, and Hule hadn't been joking about the blood and guts. But the lyrics were silly and raucous, and grew all the more so with the three of them caroling together in ill-timed harmony.

Out of the blue, Durren remembered the instruction Reille Crovek had given him on the one occasion when they'd met: *A bard's role is to be the heart and the soul of his party*, he'd said. And what else? *A bard must be ready at all times to raise his companions' spirits.*

The Head Bard's teachings hadn't registered back then, and only now did Durren see that perhaps they should have. Maybe there was more to being a ranger than the ability to shoot arrows straight. Maybe, in its way, what he was doing at this moment was every bit as important.

He wished he had some means to distract Tia as well. She hadn't, of course, joined in. But what could he or any of them say to her? She had good reason to be afraid, and good reason to worry about her mother.

Durren searched his memory for another tune he was tolerably competent at and began once more to play. If this was all he could do, it was better than letting himself be crushed by the reality of their situation. For the truth was that the day was nearing its end and still they were confined here, while deep in the heart of the Dolorwood, the shapeshifters' plans drew towards their unimaginable conclusion.

Chapter 18

Durren felt that he was beginning to come to terms with their circumstances. Having reached a point where strumming his lute was occupying only a portion of his concentration, he had used the remainder to go over and over the events of the last two days. At some juncture he'd decided, deep in his heart, that the choices the four of them had made were the right ones. That was a small comfort, but a comfort nevertheless: at least, when they were returned to Black River in shame or forced to endure whatever punishment Krieg settled upon, he wouldn't find himself looking back with regret.

The sound of knocking from outside the door threw his newly calmed thoughts into fresh chaos. He couldn't resist the sudden flood of questions cascading through his mind. Were they about to be interrogated? Were they being freed? Had Krieg seen sense or was there worse in store for them?

A voice, somewhat muffled by the heavy door, called, "Keep back!"

Did the speaker really expect to be attacked? Then again, Durren couldn't anticipate what Tia might do. For that matter, Hule's limited attention span wasn't holding up well under the pressure of imprisonment; perhaps he'd start a fight just to relieve his boredom.

Luckily, both of them were closer to the rear wall than to the entrance. The portal swung inward with an ominous creak, to reveal three students. One had been tasked with door-opening duties while the other two were carrying wooden trays, on each of which were two bowls. These they carried inside and set carefully on the floor, before retreating.

"You should eat that," the first student said. "You might not want to, but you definitely should."

And with that cryptic announcement, he slammed the door shut.

"Well, that was strange," Arein said.

"Strange or not, I'm hungry." Hule lurched to his feet and stomped over to claim one of the trays. He put it back down within reach of the rest of them and took a bowl for himself.

The contents were the usual brown-gray pulp that the canteen tended to serve, though a glance was enough to assure Durren that their portions had been scraped from what was left at the bottom of the pots when every other student had had their fill. Durren could see why someone might suppose they'd need encouragement to try and stomach such mush.

They hadn't counted on Hule or Hule's appetite. Despite the fact that he'd devoured the last of the hard biscuits from his pack only minutes earlier, he was tucking into the slop with relish.

With a mumbled "Ow!" Hule choked out a mouthful. "What the…"

To Durren's disgust, he began to root around in the stew. He drew something out and swiped away the remaining gobs of half-chewed food. Durren assumed at first that he'd discovered a bone; such culinary mishaps were hardly unknown at Shadow Mountain. But once Hule was done with his cleaning, Durren saw that, rather, what he was looking at was a canister made apparently of leather.

He was almost as surprised by how familiar the object was as by its presence in Hule's dinner. Then he remembered: the night at Black River when Tia had summoned him with a message protected in just such a fashion. Was this in some bizarre way her doing? Yet her face said that she was no less startled than he was.

"Open it," Arein murmured, breathless with excitement.

Hule did as instructed. From within he plucked a tightly wound scroll, which he carefully unrolled, having dropped the two halves of the canister back into his bowl.

"It says…I don't know what it says." His brow scrunched. "It's not even words."

Fortunately, Arein was already on her feet and reading from behind his shoulder. "Oh! Give it to me."

Hule handed over the rectangle of paper.

Reading hurriedly, Arein blurted out, "This is a spell! A spell scroll. The paper is enchanted and the incantation sets the magic loose."

"What does it do?" Durren asked.

"Well, it's hard to be certain…" She muttered a few syllables beneath her breath, as if struggling to interpret particular symbols. "Some sort of obfuscation. I think—smoke, maybe? I don't imagine it's dangerous, at any rate."

"That's all well and good," Hule said, "but it doesn't help

us much, does it? What use is smoke?" Then he registered the expressions everyone else was wearing, and comprehension dawned.

In a flash, Arein had plunged a hand into the second bowl Hule had brought over, while Tia and Durren raced for the tray left by the door. Moments later and the four of them were puzzling over the spoils of their search.

"Mine is just more paper covered with arrows and crosses," Arein complained.

This time it was Hule's turn to interpret. "That's a map. The short arrows are turnings and the long arrows mean to go straight. The crosses are junctions you're supposed to ignore."

"Oh." Arein squinted. "Right. I see that." She looked up. "What about you two?"

"Lockpicks," Tia said—though she spoke the words with faint puzzlement. She turned the two rods of metal in her fingers, and considered the door and its heavy lock.

Durren, meanwhile, was rolling the two delicate globes nestled in his palm, watching how the murky green substance within shifted and lapped against the glass—until Tia snatched them from him. "Best let me have those, too," she declared.

"What are they?"

She offered him a thin smile. "You'll see."

That sounded ominous. "Wait a minute," he said, "don't we need to discuss this?"

Her smile vanished in an instant. "What's to discuss? We want to get out. Someone else wants us out too. We won't get another chance."

"What if this is a trap? For all we know, Krieg sent these items to test us."

"Durren, that's absurd. If she wants our heads, she has as

much evidence as she could possibly need. I don't know who gave us these gifts and I don't care. I'm going, with or without you."

She meant it; of course she did. And his choice was precisely as straightforward as she'd made out: go along with her or stay here.

"All right," Durren said. "Only, at least let's decide on a plan."

Tia worked the lock in perfect silence. Durren was close by her, and not once did he hear the chink of metal upon metal. To take his mind off what they were about to do, he counted. He'd reached forty-three when Tia's hands went still and she signaled with a nod that she was done.

Now it was Arein's turn—though her task was easier. She'd explained that only someone with an affinity with magic would be able to make the scroll function, but that, for anyone who had, success was simply a case of avoiding any mispronunciation that might cause the spell to backfire.

She read under her breath, so that Durren caught no more than the impression of outlandish syllables. She stood just before the door, approximately where Tia had been—since that was where the crude plan they'd cobbled together required her to be.

What they'd realized was that a basket in the corner contained a few spoonfuls of sawdust; presumably logs had been stored there in the past. Given that the basket itself was also flammable, and that the shelves were made of wood, they had everything they needed to start a good-sized fire. If they were desperate enough and stupid enough, they might even do so as part of some misjudged escape attempt—after all, the door was wooden too.

In any event, they only needed whoever was on guard to believe that.

The roiling wall of greasy, gray-black smoke that poured abruptly from Arein's hands should do the job nicely. As the cloud engulfed her, the last Durren saw was her urgently fanning with the hem of her cloak, seeking to drive the greatest possible portion through the cracks and into the corridor beyond.

The goal was twofold: first disorientation and then a literal smokescreen. But there was always the chance that those outside would run for help, and that meant that improvisation was a crucial element too. Which, if Durren was really truthful, made this less a plan and more a loosely strung together series of half-baked ideas.

He could see almost nothing. Arein hadn't been able to guess at the spell's potency; apparently the answer was *very potent indeed*. Durren could barely see his own hand in front of his face, and he certainly couldn't make out the door or Arein—let alone Tia, who'd been waiting with her back pressed against the jamb. The smoke was so dense and oily that he felt he should be able to touch it; it moved queasily, like the luminous jellyfish that swam in the warm coves of the Middlesea.

Durren heard the door scrape. He couldn't tell whether it had opened from within or without. He braced for sounds of a struggle—and remembered who he was dealing with.

Sure enough, a second later, Tia's voice called from inside the cloud: "All right, come on."

By that point, the fog was beginning to dissipate; being magical, it melted away with startling suddenness. Durren hurried through the open door, with Hule beside him. Bodies were slumped beyond, one to either side, and Durren recalled the pair as two of the older students who'd escorted them here. He saw no signs of injuries, but then he wouldn't have expected to—for it struck him that the tiny glass globes had likely been the same as the one Tia had used against the guard back at Black River. He remembered her curious reaction to the lockpicks: could it be that she'd identified them as her own? Had whoever had decided to help them done so in part by pillaging from their gear?

Such questions would have to wait. Their benefactor hadn't led them astray up to now, and maybe that was a reason to assume their intentions were good. Anyhow, wouldn't there be answers at the end of this? All they had to do was make it that far.

Durren didn't suppose that Krieg would have announced their imprisonment, not with the shapeshifter situation unresolved. On the other hand, the four of them stood out sufficiently that any Shadow Mountain students would recognize them straight away as the party from Black River, and that was hardly in their favor. Luckily, they made it out of the cellars without seeing anyone, though once or twice they heard the echo of distant footsteps. Tia led the way at a swift trot, fast enough to cover ground quickly but not so much so that at a glance they mightn't look like four students hastening to lectures or about to set out on a quest.

As they climbed a flight of stairs into the academy proper, she slowed a little. At the first corner, she checked their course by the miniature scroll of directions. Durren could tell from where she'd marked their progress with her thumbnail that they were two-thirds of the way through the list of arrows.

"I know where this is leading," Tia said softly. "We're

heading back towards the transportation chamber."

Durren scanned the remainder of the list, envisaging each turning—and found that she was right. However, the route planned for them was a roundabout one, carefully judged to avoid the busiest areas. They could probably get where they were going in half the time, but only by passing the dining hall and library.

"Do we keep on?" Hule asked. "We're out now; we can do what we like."

"I think we need to know what's happening," Arein suggested. "Someone's tried to help us. There must be a reason why."

Tia nodded—though more as if responding to her own thoughts than to Hule and Arein's remarks. "We keep to the directions," she said.

Barely a minute had passed before Durren was doubting whether she'd made the correct decision—as, rounding a corner, they practically collided with two Shadow Mountain students.

The boy and girl both wore gray, ankle-length robes that marked them out for clerics, and that was enough to make Durren wonder, even as the girl said, "You're the party from Black River?"

Given that Arein was the sole dwarf at Shadow Mountain and Tia the sole dun-elf, there was no use in denying it. Anyway, by then the male cleric was motioning to a door that stood open a crack behind them and ordering, "In here."

Again Durren considered that this might be a trap. Again he came to the conclusion that someone would be going to an awful lot of trouble to prove what they already knew, that the four of them had an unfortunate tendency towards breaking the rules. At any rate, the others were trailing after the male cleric, while his companion stayed in the passage, glancing warily in either direction. She looked every bit as nervous as Durren felt, and that alone implied that, whatever these two were up to, they weren't acting on Krieg's behalf. Hurriedly he followed Arein through the doorway.

The room beyond was small and mostly empty, except for a dusty table pressed against one wall and a pair of crude chairs. On the table, piled neatly, was all of their equipment.

The female cleric had slipped in behind them. "We didn't want to move it too far in case anybody saw," she offered by way of explanation.

Arein picked up her staff and hugged it. "I missed you," she announced to the slender rod of wood.

Durren would have liked to do much the same with his bow. The moment he took the weapon in his hand, he felt that a crucial part of him was restored. Yet he settled for slinging it over his shoulder, cramming his arrows back into the quiver on his pack, and reclaiming his sword and knife.

Meanwhile, though Hule had his scabbard strapped onto his belt, Tia was taking longer, as befitted the daunting array of blades and implements in front of her. Durren found himself speculating how long it must have taken her to sew that many hidden pockets; or did clothes for rogues just come like that? He couldn't even have kept track of them all.

But a minute later and she was ready. Seeing, the two clerics led the way back outside and, without hesitation, started up the passage. Their only choice was to follow—especially since, according to the scroll of directions, they were headed that way anyhow.

This time, their pace wasn't far off a run. There'd be no

accounting for the fact that they were dashing through the corridors of the academy, fully armed and equipped, at so late an hour. Fortunately, they didn't have much farther to go, and the route had been well planned out: they passed no-one, and the closest they came was to hear muffled voices from somewhere below. Soon the two clerics were opening the door to the transportation chamber and leading the way inside.

By then, Durren was already certain of who'd be waiting within; the class of the students sent to meet them had been a definite giveaway. Caille stood towards the middle of the room, and looked as though his nerves were approaching their limits. His relief at seeing them was obvious and immense. "I wasn't sure you'd get this far," he said.

Durren suffered a pang of guilt at how badly he'd misjudged the cleric. "Thanks to you we did. But—how did you manage this? Weren't you supposed to be confined to your dormitory?"

"With help from my friends, that's the short answer." Caille waved towards the two students who'd escorted them. "Look— we stand by our head tutor. All the same, most everybody secretly knows that sometimes she lets strictness get in the way of common sense. When I explained the situation, some of the other clerics felt that supporting you was the right course. Once we'd got our hands on your equipment, that gave us an idea of what to do next."

"Thank you," Arein said earnestly. Hule echoed the sentiment, and even Tia murmured a brief, "Thanks."

Caille appeared uncomfortable at their gratitude. "I honestly don't believe Krieg's intentions are bad," he said. "I mean, maybe they are towards you four, she genuinely doesn't seem to like you. But I think the reason she's delayed sending anyone to investigate the ruins is that—well, she's *afraid*. My party nearly got wiped out. If you hadn't come along when you did, we would have been. That's the closest Shadow Mountain has come to casualties in the entire time Krieg has been Head Tutor. I think that shook her. She doesn't want to send her students into a fight unless she's positive she can win without anyone getting hurt."

"But placing yourself in danger is just part of what being an adventurer is about," Durren said. "Everyone knows that."

Only, despite himself, he felt a twinge of sympathy for Krieg. They had contemplated that she might be a shapeshifter, and somehow missed the possibility that she'd be anxious of putting her students at risk. Perhaps she was preparing at this minute, and merely waiting for the light of a new day before she dared an assault.

Durren's gut instincts told him that tomorrow would be too late to stop whatever the shapeshifters had begun. Nonetheless, he understood her thinking. He'd never paused to imagine the responsibilities a head tutor bore: the young lives in their care, the delicate balancing of the hazards of quests against the obligation to those who relied on their success. Now that he had, he saw that the job was infinitely harder than he'd ever considered.

Still, a wrong decision remained wrong, regardless of the motives.

All the more fortunate, then, that Caille agreed with them. "In the meantime," he continued, "we've been working on a couple of the less conformist tutors. Not everyone in the faculty is blind to how dictatorially Krieg behaves. We've persuaded them, and they're trying to persuade her. Maybe they're even managing, though I doubt there's any quick means to do it."

"And that's why we're here," Hule said.

"Yes. I couldn't think of any other way to help you." Caille turned to Tia. "Realistically, Krieg isn't going to send support in time to stop your mother from going in there alone. This was the best alternative I could come up with. At least the four of you can go back, if that's what you want."

"No," Tia said, "it's...it's good of you, Caille." She glanced at Durren, and then at Arein and Hule, meeting each of their gazes for a moment. "Only, I'm not willing to put all your lives in jeopardy—not even to save my mother. It's one thing for us to return with proper backup, but with the four of us? Against an army of the dead and two shapeshifters?"

Caille cleared his throat. "If it really seems as if Krieg won't act in time, I think I can get a second party together. We'd come after you."

Tia looked startled; the notion that someone she barely knew would risk so much on her behalf appeared to have thrown her completely. "Thank you."

"You're welcome. Anyway, it's not just about you four. We want to stop the shapeshifters before it's too late, and we all want to see the dead back in their graves. This is the worst thing that's happened to Ursvaal in our lifetimes."

Tia nodded. "You're right, this is important. But that doesn't change the risks involved."

"It has to be a vote," Durren proposed. "Either we go now or we wait and talk this through. Maybe there's a better option. Shapeshifters may have some weakness we don't yet know about, one we could make use of."

"They don't," Arein said softly. "Believe me, I've read every book there is to read. They don't have any weaknesses at all."

Durren felt his heart sink at the sureness in her voice.

"What if instead we try and get Tia's mother out of there? A rescue mission rather than an attack?"

"She'd never agree to that," Tia stated with certainty.

"Do you have any more of those little glass globes?" Durren asked her.

Tia checked a pouch. "One."

"Then there's your answer."

To her credit, Tia's response wasn't, *You expect me to knock out my own mother?* She merely nodded, as though acknowledging that Durren had arrived at the one feasible solution.

"So that's the plan?" Arein asked. "We go in and attempt to—" She frowned and corrected, "We go in and we rescue Kyra. Then we come back here and hope Krieg can be convinced to move against the shapeshifters?"

"Or," Durren said, "We don't. Not unless we're all in agreement. And I don't think there should even be a discussion. If one of us doesn't want to do this, it's not fair to persuade them, given what's at stake." He deliberated. "How about we turn around and put a hand out. Make a fist if you're willing to go; hold your palm flat if not. All right?"

Everyone nodded.

Durren turned his back on the others. He didn't have to ponder his decision, though he felt perhaps that he should. Regardless, he knew he'd never be able to live with himself if he didn't do whatever he could to help Tia now. "Ready?"

"Ready," came the chorused reply.

Durren spun on his heel and glanced down. Tia's hand, of course, was a fist. So, nearly as predictably, was Arein's. And he scarcely needed to look at Hule's—

Hule's hand was stretched flat.

"Well, I suppose that settles it," Durren said. He was filled by a mix of shock and relief, and wasn't sure which was greater. "We all agreed."

"I understand, Hule," Tia said—though there was such anguish in her voice that Durren was amazed she'd managed to choke out the words.

Hule stared in puzzlement at the three hands before him. "Wait, I thought…oh." He clenched his fingers, and his cheeks reddened.

Durren barely resisted the urge to laugh. He felt suddenly, curiously light, almost distant from his body, and wondered if this was the sensation someone would experience if they'd been told their hanging had been canceled, only to discover that the good news was a callous joke at their expense.

"What now?" Tia asked Caille—and she was entirely her usual self once more. "Don't tell me you've talked Gallowpall into helping us too?"

Appearing a little uneasy, Caille beckoned the female student who'd met them earlier. "Zulva is fairly certain she knows the transportation spell and that she can home in on your observer," he said.

Inside, Durren flinched. "*Fairly* certain?"

"The thing is," the student named Zulva mumbled apologetically, "it's a very difficult spell…one of the hardest. And I've only been able to test it on inanimate objects; it's against the rules for a student who hasn't graduated to transport anything alive." She brightened. "Even so, the results were definitely more successful than not."

This just got better and better—but there was no backing out. And though he thought about asking what was the worst that could happen, Durren quickly decided he'd rather not know. Perhaps they'd end up on the top of a mountain somewhere in the Wildlands; perhaps he'd look down to find his legs had been magically replaced with Arein's. Really, the joy of magic was that there were no limits to what could go wrong and no way of predicting what might happen when it did.

"Let's go," Hule said, "before I change my mind."

The four of them stepped down together to the sunken area at the center of the room. Zulva had already begun her spell; unlike Hieronymus and Gallowpall, both of whom exuded a confidence close to indifference, her face was scrunched with concentration, and she was mouthing each syllable with the utmost care.

Durren could feel the spell drawing towards its fruition: first in the pit of his stomach, then in the back of his mind, and then as a general tingling that began in his extremities and spread rapidly inward.

This is new, he thought—as the room began to dissolve like dirty slush on a warm winter's day.

Chapter 19

Durren had imagined he was growing used to transportation. Yet this was something else altogether.

To be transported was bound to be disconcerting, not just because you were moving from one location to another without passing through any of the points in-between, but because there was always a period in which you were somehow, impossibly, at start and destination at once. This, though, managed to be worse. Durren's body and mind both recognized that his circumstances were dreadfully wrong and were striving desperately to reorient him—to commit to a single reality.

The visual distortion, too, was more severe than ever. It was as if the chamber and the space they were moving into were two still-wet paintings mashed messily together, and right now the four of them were trapped in-between. Colors ran nauseatingly and changed in an instant, reds to greens to purples to yellows, while at the same time their shapes flowed and reformed. Even sound was broken; Durren's ears were assailed from all sides by a waterfall roar. And that was better than what was going on within his stomach, which threatened to turn inside out at any moment.

Just as he was beginning to believe that whatever remained of their existence would be spent trapped in an amorphous nowhere between places, the scene around them began to resolve itself. Gazing upward, he no longer saw the distorted memory of a stone ceiling but an evening sky studded with early stars.

Durren's head was swirling to match his innards, and he very much wanted to double over and maybe to be sick. Instead, he gritted his teeth and forced himself to look around. They had transported to Pootle's position; the observer was already diving towards them. The problem was that, upon their arrival, Pootle had been over a spot quite close to the ruins—and surrounded on all sides by the dead.

The one slender comfort was that they were in sight of the ruins' entrance. There, a broad staircase cut into the earth, flanked by ancient walls. Skeletons still marched up and down the steps, just as when the four of them had left, descending unencumbered and returning with heavy stone blocks or ragged baskets full of loose masonry.

As yet, none of them had reacted to the party's abrupt appearance. Durren had the same sense as before, that they had no real idea of how to respond to any distraction. No doubt it was as Arein had said, and the spell controlling them had been pared to its simplest form; it wasn't simulating intelligence, merely working lifeless bones as if by puppet strings.

Which was all fine and good, but there were too many of them. Trying to force a path was sure to yield a reaction, and staying where they were would have the same result sooner or later. All they needed was for one of the dead to blunder into them and they'd have a fight on their hands, one that would spread until they were utterly outnumbered.

"I've got this," Arein said. "Everyone—be ready to run."

Durren stared at her. What did that mean? What had she got? Her attempts at using magic against the dead so far had been at best only modestly successful.

Yet she had already begun to mumble and gesticulate, and Durren wasn't about to interrupt a wizard halfway through their spell, especially not one wearing an expression of such intense absorption. Whatever Arein had in mind, he suspected it was going to be dramatic. On the whole, he'd rather she would hurry; more and more, the dead were starting to look their way, in as much as empty eye sockets could be said to look. A few were even taking teetering steps nearer, like small children curious of strangers.

And still Arein muttered, and still the fingers of her free hand curled in the air. *No matter what you're going to do*, Durren thought, *I really wish you'd do it.*

Arein did.

But the spell that crackled from the head of her staff was familiar: she'd used it back in the tannery. Durren sagged with disappointment. Why did she imagine that what had failed to work then would do so now?

Only, the bolt of lightning that shivered through the evening air was subtly distinct. Whereas the previous time it had been a blue so pale as to be almost white, this possessed a subdued and otherworldly green tint that Durren felt certain he recognized. And as he watched, his disenchantment changed to the faint stirrings of hope.

The first skeleton the bolt hit simply exploded.

There was no other word. A skull flew one way, a ribcage another, and arms and legs chose still different directions. Onward the bolt continued, seeming if anything to gather energy from this initial success: a second skeleton was flung sideways, to crash into three more, a third was sliced cleanly in half, and on the zigzag of raw magic leapt, flashing from target to target and leaving devastation in its wake.

Arein sagged. Had Hule not been there to catch her arm, she'd probably have fallen, despite her staff. But after a moment, she'd revived sufficiently to support herself, though her breathing was labored and coils of auburn hair clung to her sweat-soaked brow.

"It's true," she breathed. "The unbalance really *doesn't* like dead people walking around."

So on that occasion in the Dolorwood, when Durren had thought she and Caille were arguing yet again, Arein had in fact listened to what the cleric had to say—as he in turn had relented enough to share his knowledge. Durren was both impressed and surprised; he'd not given either of them credit for being open-minded on a subject about which they felt so strongly.

But as much as she might deserve it, this was hardly the time to be praising Arein. She had promised them a path to the entrance and she'd delivered. Nevertheless, that passage wasn't staying open for long.

"Come on," Tia snapped, and was off before the last syllable had left her lips.

Hule caught her up—not a second too soon. His sword was needed. Arein's bolt had temporarily parted the sea of the dead; like water, they were flooding back to fill the breach. And for all the destruction her attack had wrought, those she'd damaged weren't out of the fight: the loss of a limb here or there did little more than inconvenience them.

Durren hurried to join the fighter, while being careful not to get too close to the blade he was swiping left and right. He was relieved to note that Arein was recovered enough to lope along behind them. Nonetheless, had they had much farther to go, they'd have been in trouble; Durren had no choice except to fend off skeletons with the flat of his sword, and there was no apparent end to their number.

But for once, their magical indoctrination seemed to favor the party; as they reached the steps, the assault receded noticeably, and the nearest dead wavered. Maybe they could only tolerate so much disruption to their routine, and their conduct was more strictly controlled in the region about the entrance.

The dead ascending the stairs stubbornly minded their own business; a good job, because the blocks of stone that most of them carried would have made for fearsome weapons. Those going down showed fractionally greater resistance, though they were easy to dash past and quick to resume their usual behavior. Durren thought of bees around a hive, and how they'd abandon one priority for another according to some imperceptible whim. These skeletons had their orders, and within the ruins those had a more powerful hold on them than ever.

Tia already had her lamp out. Not for the first time, Durren wished it offered normal light rather than that eerie bluish glow. The dead, in particular, looked ghastly: their bones appeared bleached, yet every wizened scrap of flesh or clump of hair still clinging to a scalp stood out in sharp relief. But the radiance also highlighted strange carvings and designs upon the walls, smudged into incomprehensibility by the elements and worse for that—as if they were indecipherable clues to some primeval puzzle.

The stairs descended for a significant distance; so far that, as Durren glanced back from near the bottom, the purple of the night sky was only a slim window high above. At some point, too, the stairwell had tapered, so that the corridor ahead was barely wide enough for the two columns of skeletons to pass each other.

On the positive side, as long as they were left alone, the dead remained content to go about their business. Durren had increasingly needed to hug the rightmost wall, and now skeletal limbs passed within reach and still he was ignored. Too, the ones they'd provoked outside had evidently forgotten their grudge. For the moment, at least, they were safe.

"Arein, do you think you could manage that same spell again?" Tia asked.

Durren understood her reasoning. In the confines of the passageway, Arein's mystical lightning would be calamitous. So he was all the more disappointed when Arein's reply was an apologetic shake of the head. "It might be an hour before I can even try," she said.

"Then we'll keep to the wall," Tia decided. "And if we disturb them, we'll just have to force our way."

Surely she knew as well as Durren did that it wouldn't be much of a fight: once they entered the passage, they'd be hemmed in, and Hule would have no room to swing his sword, let alone Arein her staff. Battling the dead in such close quarters would be a recipe for disaster. She was right, though; there was no other way forward, and no use in starting a fight now to avoid one later.

Anyhow, as usual Tia wasn't inviting a discussion, she was pre-empting one: she'd already slid into the passage, back to the wall and hands tight at her sides. There was ample space between her and the passing row of skeletons, but she had the advantage of being the slenderest of the four of them. When Hule squeezed in after her, the gap was considerably narrower—and Arein, who went third, found herself practically nose to ribcage.

Durren joined the row. Like the others, he stood as upright as the slight curve of the arched passage allowed, and pressed his back as flat as was possible against the cold stone. Then he began to shuffle, one sidestep after another, while trying hard not to think about what he was doing and what might so easily go wrong.

It was a curious, spine-tingling sensation to be this near to the dead. He could see the articulation of joints as they strode past, bones sliding upon bones, all stained by age and decay. He was more conscious than ever that these were the remains of people who had lived in times past—yet here they also seemed entirely inhuman, like a nonsensical new species. They even had their own peculiar smell, the leftover stink of the tannery mingling with what he could only describe as an odor of ancientness.

Durren was looking straight ahead, so that the first he knew of one of them reaching the end of the passage was Hule's deep sigh of relief—closely followed by a still deeper one from Arein. Instants later, Durren was free too, and gratefully breathing air that wasn't choked with the scent of corpses.

He peered around. Skeletons continued to file past distractingly in both directions, but through their ranks he observed that they'd arrived at a shaft—one with no apparent bottom. The tunnel gave onto a walkway of roughly the same width, which curled in a leisurely descending spiral about the outer wall. Glancing up, Durren wondered if perhaps this vast well had once been open to the sky—for though they must be some distance below the earth, they weren't so far down as all that. But he saw only blackness.

Tia had already begun to follow the ledge, and the rest of them stayed near. To do otherwise would have meant being plunged into obscurity, for her lantern remained their one source of light—and the notion that the dead had been working amid total darkness sent a shiver through Durren that went on for longer than it had any right to.

As they progressed, he began to appreciate that the damage here must have been immense: he could see why a veritable army of cadavers had been needed to clear it. In places, the walkway was severely cracked and broken. There were signs that once it had been edged by a balustrade, and in other places that columns had risen. All of that was gone now, leaving the smallest clues to its passing. Durren thought first of an earthquake and then of an explosion. But ultimately there could be no guessing what had happened, centuries or entire ages ago.

Fortunately, as long as they were careful, their route onward was unimpeded—though numerous points had plainly been blocked until recently. There was no keeping pace with the dead, however, who down here were sure-footed as mountain goats. They moved at a trot that was almost comical, until you noticed the rictus grins on fleshless faces.

To divert himself, in what was likely to be the closest to a quiet moment they would get, Durren decided to ask Arein a question that had been bothering him since they'd left the surface. "So you've come round to Caille's way of thinking on the unbalance?" he whispered.

Her indignation was startling, and far louder than he'd have preferred. "Of course not!"

"But...that spell you cast up there looked exactly like his."

"Hardly *exactly like*. All I did was take some of his theories and apply them to my own magic."

"Oh."

"I mean...Caille's not *altogether* wrong. Talking to the unbalance as if it were alive, that's as stupid as anything I've heard. Still, I did realize I was being a touch heavy-handed. You know, shouting when I could be asking."

Doesn't asking imply that the unbalance is *somehow intelligent?* Durren pondered—though he had the sense not to say such a thing to Arein. Clearly her ideas had undergone some modification; maybe more than she herself recognized the scope of. Instead, he said, "Wherever it came from, that was quite the spell. When that first skeleton exploded—"

Arein chuckled, and then looked self-conscious. "Possibly it was a bit too much."

"As far as I'm concerned," Durren said, "it was just too much enough."

He thought she smiled at that, but couldn't be certain, because in that same moment he'd grown aware of another, exceedingly important detail. "The dead...they're no longer coming."

What he was trying to convey was that the inbound stream had dried up. While a few skeletons marched ahead, and those returning towards the stairs were plentiful as ever, a glance back established that no more were entering. What did it mean? Was this change in some way a response to their appearance? As Durren considered the departing line, he perceived that, compared to the burdens of those they'd seen when they arrived, these were carrying mere scraps. All that remained to these stragglers was tidying—and that couldn't be a good sign. No wonder that Tia was picking up her pace.

Durren focused his attention on his footing. Aside from the dead, there was in any case little to distract him. The sole features of note were openings and recesses in the curved wall; some might have been entrances, but were now blocked, and others perhaps had housed statuary or served a purpose beyond his ability to guess. Though at first he'd eyed each nervously, repetition had quickly made the habit futile-seeming.

Thus it was that, when they passed one alcove much like the rest and from the dark within came a ghostly, murmured, "Tia?" Durren was so shocked that he nearly tripped off the edge of the walkway.

His mind leapt straight to the most unlikely conclusions, before he recovered enough to realize that he knew the voice. By then, Tia had dashed to the alcove and was shining her lantern—to reveal Kyra Locke, half sitting and half lying. Her face was gaunter than ever, and her cloak lay open. Despite the fabric's somber shade, Durren could see how a patch of her tunic above her hip glistened wetly.

"Mother," Tia asked, "what happened?"

Kyra tried to hoist herself to her feet, and sank back with a groan. On her second attempt, with Tia's support, she managed to prop herself against the wall.

"I waited until nightfall," she said. "Then I couldn't wait anymore. I had to fight my way through; one of them got a lucky blow in." She took a tortured breath. "My stitches tore. I made it this far and—I stopped to rest a minute." But it was clear she'd been here much longer than a minute.

"I'm so sorry," Tia told her. "Krieg locked us up. We only just managed to escape."

Kyra shook her head. "It's not your fault. I was careless."

Tia looked as if nothing could have injured her more than her mother admitting the slightest weakness. "Can you help her?" she asked Arein, and the urgency in her voice was painful.

"A little," Arein answered. "I'll do what I can."

The two of them set to work, and Durren, feeling useless and intrusive, moved to the far side of the ledge—even though staring into the fathomless blackness made his heart thunder. They'd accomplished what they'd come for; they'd found Tia's mother, and now they just needed to get her to the surface in one piece. But his gaze kept being drawn to the depths. What lay beneath? He knew they'd seen a hint of greater truths, perhaps of secrets forgotten to all memory and record. He had no doubt that this place had been built by the shapeshifters, back when they'd had sufficient numbers to embark on such grand enterprises.

Or had they constructed their architecture in the same fashion they'd cleared its ruins, by employing armies of the dead pillaged from the graveyards of other races? If so, there was yet another reason they'd been despised, to the point of being hounded almost to extinction. Or maybe what Arein had once suggested was true and they'd only contemplated so macabre a solution because all more reasonable options were denied to them. Whatever the case, Durren couldn't resist a pang of awe and sadness to conceive of minds that had devised on such a scale extinguished.

Behind him, Arein sounded distressed as she exclaimed, "Caille's much better at this sort of thing." Moments later, however, she added cautiously, "I think that should help. How do you feel?"

Kyra grunted. "Better." Durren heard the rustle of cloth as

she smoothed her tunic.

He turned around. She certainly looked sturdier than when they'd found her. Dun-elves didn't exactly have color in their cheeks at the best of times, but her skin was less wan and her eyes had lost the worst of their hollowness.

"You have to understand," Arein said, "magical healing isn't a substitute for natural healing. This will hold for a while; you still need to rest and recover. I can't make the wound go away."

"It's not my first," Kyra said, "and it won't be my last. Thank you for what you've done—it's enough."

Durren knew in his heart what was going to happen next, and how they'd deceived themselves in coming here. All the same, someone had to at least try. "Back at Shadow Mountain, Krieg's being persuaded to send a proper force," he told Kyra. "In the meantime, we've come to take you to safety."

Mentally he appended, *We were even willing to knock you out and carry you.* Except, now that the moment had come, he recognized that Tia would never have done any such thing.

Regardless, Kyra didn't so much as look at him. Her attention was only on her daughter. "I have to go on," she said. "To finish what I was sent to do. And, as much as it grieves me to ask, I'd value your help. I wish more than anything that you weren't involved in this, but the choice is out of my hands. We're the ones who are here, and whatever those monsters are doing, it falls on us to stop them. This is what it means to be a dun-elf of Sudra Syn, Tia: we do what's necessary."

To Durren's surprise, Tia frowned. "You don't have to tell me that."

And for the first time in his experience, Kyra actually smiled. "I know."

Tia turned to the rest of them. "This doesn't mean you three have to come."

"Don't be an idiot," Hule said flatly.

To the best of Durren's memory, none of them had ever dared call Tia an idiot. When no sharp objects materialized in the fighter's flesh, he told her, "What Hule said."

Arein nodded her agreement. "We're a party, Tia. We made our decision when we came down here."

"Then," Kyra said, once again all dun-elf professionalism, "we don't have any time to waste."

Keeping track of space was difficult on the winding ledge and amid the deep darkness, which Tia's lantern penetrated perfectly to a point and beyond that failed to touch. However, Durren felt confident that they'd gone through two further revolutions before they reached the end.

There was no saying what might have been here once, though surely something had been. He struggled to accept that any race with the intelligence to build on so vast a scale would also have designed so recklessly. The ledge ended in a broken stub, as if snapped off by a huge hand. There was a low archway in the wall, but the gap was full of rubble and no attempt had been made to clear it.

What had been done instead was more unexpected: on the inner edge of the platform, the summit of a crude wooden tower rose from below. With a little deliberation, Durren ascertained that what he was looking at was a lifting platform driven by a simple mechanism; it was square, and so large that the five of them would fit comfortably.

The apparatus was the first new thing they'd encountered since setting foot beneath the ground. One glance at the timbers was enough to reveal that they'd been cut recently. Had this been constructed by the shapeshifters themselves? Durren couldn't imagine any magic so powerful that it would persuade the reanimated dead to produce such craftsmanship. He had rarely seen better, even in Luntharbor, where generations of shipbuilders had refined their labors to an art form.

"I'm not going on that," Hule said.

"There's no choice," Tia and Kyra both told him in unison.

Hule gave a weary shrug of defeat. "I know. But I don't have to like it."

With no more debate, the five of them stepped aboard. Here at the summit, the mechanism was activated by a wheel. After brief consideration, Kyra turned it one half revolution to the right. Then they were in motion.

The lifting platform might be well built; that wasn't to say it was flawless in its engineering. It rattled and creaked, and generally made noises the opposite of those you wanted to hear from anything that separated you from certain death. The constant vibration made estimating their rate of descent impossible. Durren felt that they were moving alarmingly quickly. Maybe in reality their pace wasn't much above a crawl. Nor was there any judging how far they had to go; Tia's lantern exposed only the curving stone wall, blurred by their motion. Below them was an ink-black lake.

Reaching the bottom, therefore, came as a surprise. One moment they were plunging with the same tooth-rattling motion, the next they'd stopped with a jolt that traveled up through Durren's whole body.

Tia stepped down and began to circle warily about the structure of the lifting platform, lantern held high. To Durren's relief, there were at least no more of the dead down here. What he could see was that a number of arches had once led off the central shaft, and a nub of stone perhaps represented the remains of a staircase, which had done the work that now fell to the tower.

At any rate, the damage was severe: there had been less effort made to remove the debris, and great heaps of shattered stone were pressed against the walls. Of the four exits, three were blocked entirely.

"I suppose we know which way we're going," Hule said.

The open archway was a definite signal of intent: someone had wanted badly to enter one specific area of these ruins and had cared not at all for the others. While Durren had already known the shapeshifters were enacting some long-cherished scheme, that gaping entrance onto blackness declared the fact more clearly than anything had before. They were single-minded—and here was where their determination had led them.

"Dim the lantern," Kyra said softly. "Probably they know we're coming. If there's a chance they don't, let's not announce ourselves."

Dutifully, Tia turned a dial on the top of her lamp until the gap in the shutters was reduced to the narrowest sliver. At first Durren felt that he'd been sunk in pitch: his eyes strained and panic rose in his gullet. He was sure he could feel the weight of the rock and earth above him, and even the pressure of the stagnant air bearing down.

Then he began to pick out shapes amid the dark. Gradually those shapes resolved into figures, and beyond them he discovered that he could make out the walls, though barely.

As he was finally beginning to get his bearings, Kyra commanded, "Come on."

Durren stumbled after. He could just perceive that Kyra and Tia were taking the lead and that Arein was close behind them. When he glanced back, he saw Hule there, hulking amid the gloom. The passage was broad and high and ran on for much farther than he could see. There were occasional openings to either side and some were only partially blocked, but the two rogues at their head saw fit to ignore them. Perhaps there were tracks that Durren's eyes failed to identify. Perhaps Kyra knew more than she was telling them.

In any case, Durren felt a dim sense of familiarity. It had already occurred to him that the ruins they'd unearthed near Black River were of shapeshifter origin. Any last doubt was erased now, for those tunnels and these were very much alike. The clue was in their precision, which, even in so ruined a state, defied that of the finest stonemasons. Whatever the means by which they'd been carved, be it artistry, or magic, or the enslaved hands of the dead, there was a studied perfection to every block and slab that left him impressed despite himself.

He was so absorbed that, when Arein stopped, he nearly bumped into her. Only then did he realize there was light ahead. Tia had fully shut her lantern, and was slipping it back within her pack to free both hands. The glow issuing from the archway before them was the flickering illumination of torches, and Durren found relief in its humble glimmer—until he recalled what its presence here implied.

The dead had needed no light to see by. Perhaps shapeshifters did.

"I'm going on in front," Kyra murmured. "Follow, but keep your distance."

With that, she was gone: one moment there, the next consumed by the shadows. An instant later, Tia mimicked her example, and then there was only the three of them.

Durren resumed walking, picking his steps carefully lest he disobey Kyra's instruction. The passage continued for a considerable way, and the light grew by the slowest degrees. His heart almost stopped the first time a silhouette marred that wavering brightness. The figure was far too large to be Kyra or Tia.

Durren crept closer. He'd never tried to move so soundlessly in his life. Behind him, even Hule was edging forwards with nary a scuff of boot on stone. The end of the passage was readily visible now, as was the disproportionately small arch there, scarcely wide enough for two people to pass through together.

There was still no sign of Kyra or Tia. Durren wished they'd refrained from their vanishing act just this once. What was he supposed to do? Approaching any nearer would mean entering the semicircle of torchlight about the opening. On the other hand, he wasn't convinced he could stay where he was. Given what he could see, he suspected the time for hesitation was past.

Durren could barely discern the second shapeshifter—the one Tulpek had named Apaek and had spoken of with awe and even fear. She was moving around, reducing his glimpses to smears of darkness as she obscured the torches. But Tulpek himself Durren could make out distinctly. He sat on the paved floor in the center of the chamber, cross-legged, forearms resting in his lap, as though he were meditating.

However, in Tulpek's grip was a familiar object, one that currently glowed with its own intense inner radiance: the Petrified Egg, which in human guise he had tricked them into stealing for him. Durren hadn't a magical bone in his body, yet he could feel the raw power rising from it, filling the air like steam from a boiling cauldron.

They'd found the shapeshifters—perhaps too late. Because whatever they'd come here to do, it was already begun.

Chapter 20

The room beyond the entrance was not well lit, though it appeared so from the weighty blackness of the passage outside. Half a dozen torches burned in sconces around the circular wall, dripping sparks that drifted like fat insects; but their light was muted to a dull amber that looked nothing like how fire should. Nevertheless, the room wasn't huge, and the paltry illumination of six torches sufficed to cover its expanse.

So how Tia and Kyra had managed to get close to Tulpek was anybody's guess. Yet they had—and they were going for the Egg. They moved as one, emerging apparently from nowhere and darting with astonishing speed, Tia on Tulpek's left and Kyra on his right.

The second shapeshifter was faster. With a hiss of fury, Apaek crossed the distance between them. Kyra's hands had been very near to closing upon the Petrified Egg, and Tulpek had been unaware, and Durren gritted his teeth as she leaped aside without her prize. At least she *did* leap aside, and Tia too, both of them ducking beneath Apaek's talons.

Durren had been rooted to the spot, though he hadn't known it until then. He felt as if his limbs had been locked in immovably heavy armor that was abruptly vanished. He also felt strangely removed from himself, so that when he began to run—and when he realized he was running towards the danger rather than away—a part of him was left to watch in puzzlement and consternation.

Are you certain about this? it asked. *Are you sure this is a good idea?*

Durren wasn't certain, not at all. Still, his legs carried him, through the archway and into the circular chamber, and he could hear hurrying feet behind him that could only belong to Hule and Arein. However, they had no hope of coming to Tia and Kyra's rescue. They were separated by the width of the room, and by the presence of the two shapeshifters. Really, all they had to offer was a brief distraction.

He had time for a glimpse of the room in its entirety— enough to reveal a detail he'd failed to notice from outside. Towards the edge, spaced evenly, a series of simple columns held the curving roof aloft, and in the gaps between were low pedestals. On each was an object. Durren would have struggled to deduce their nature or function but for the fact that he recognized the nearest. More than that, he had almost been skewered by it on his first encounter with its former owner. The spiraling ivory cone was the unicorn's horn that Tulpek, during his masquerade as their mentor, had manipulated them into helping him acquire.

On that basis, Durren guessed the nature of the remaining objects: a shimmering blue stone, an ornate golden cube, a doll of sorts fashioned from twined bark, and others he couldn't distinguish. Clearly they were items of magical power, and clearly the shapeshifters had no intention of losing them, for each was molded to the pillar on which it sat, as though the stone had obligingly melted.

Durren willingly admitted that he didn't understand much about wizardry. All the same, even he could comprehend that, if you brought plenty of magical things together in one place, what you ended up with was an awful lot of magic. And now he believed he had an inkling of what the Petrified Egg might be. What if this was the purpose for which it had been intended, as a channel and a repository? Durren was unaccountably sure that, with it, Tulpek was drawing upon all the power in the room—and holding it, literally, in his hands.

By then there was no more time for questions. Durren's mind refused to acknowledge anything except the shapeshifter before him, as if the threat she posed made her surroundings faintly unreal. Close up, she was very different from Tulpek, in a way that couldn't be accidental. Apaek had made herself monstrous, sculpting her flesh over the course of centuries into a shape she knew would evoke horror; she'd become terrible, because terror was the reaction she sought.

Having heard their arrival, she turned to face them now, briefly disregarding Tia and Kyra—who seized the opportunity to retreat. She stayed near to Tulpek in a manner that was obviously protective, and she was quick to return her attention to him.

"Begin," she demanded.

"And relinquish control of the dead?" Tulpek's voice was strained.

"Yes. Their usefulness is finished."

"If others should come—"

"There are no others."

Apaek sounded certain, and her certainty was infectious. Even if Krieg had been persuaded into a change of heart, there was no longer any possibility that she'd bring aid in time to make a difference.

Apaek glanced back to the five of them. "This pitiful group is here," she said, "precisely because no-one else dares." The smile she smiled was perhaps the most unnerving thing that Durren had ever seen. "Isn't that right?"

Durren didn't feel the need to confirm or deny her claim. Surely his face had betrayed the answer anyway.

"And what about them?" Tulpek wondered.

"Do you think I can't manage five humans?" Again, there was no doubt in Apaek's voice. Her conviction was more dispiriting than any threat; a threat would have at least conceded that they were worth the waste of words.

Which made it all the worse when Arein blurted out, "Um, I'm a dwarf, not a human."

For the first time, Apaek truly looked at them—and Durren dearly wished she'd stop.

Meanwhile, with the garrulousness of sheer panic, Arein burbled on, "And Tia and her mother are both elves. And, you see, there really isn't any need for us to fight. We just want you to stop whatever it is you're doing."

When Apaek took a step nearer, Arein flinched—but stood her ground. This close, the creature's body was an extraordinary mass of muscle and tendon. Were it not for what Tulpek had said, Durren would never have thought to identify her as female. Both of them were utterly without gender, and indeed without the usual characteristics lumped under the word "identity". As much as her face was grotesque, it was also curiously featureless. Her mouth, made horrifying by those too-many jagged teeth, was at the same time gaping and lipless. Her nose was virtually flat, with nostrils like neat puncture wounds, and her eyes were deep-set but vacuous.

"Believe me," she said, "you'll all amount to the same thing once I'm done. And this won't be any kind of fight."

Then she began to change.

Furled beneath her arms, her wings were futile and unwieldy; in any case, the domed ceiling wasn't high enough to allow for much in the way of flight. In an instant they shriveled, like blackened paper in a fire. Simultaneously, her arms grew broader about the shoulders; her chest and thighs, too, thickened with further ropes of muscle. Her already distorted jaw stretched and protruded, making way for yet more teeth. Her hands distended—as did the claws that lengthened their tips.

Had there been any doubt left, Durren knew then that Arein's theory had been right. This creature wasn't just one of the monsters that had haunted Ursvaal for generations, she was many of them: a different horror for different occasions. Sometimes she'd needed to fly, and so she had sprouted wings. Sometimes she had wanted speed and strength, and so she'd adopted a form like this, which made Durren think of a distorted, elongated wolf. What other nightmarish costumes of flesh might she have? There was no time to wonder—not when this was the shape they had to deal with now.

She moved with inconceivable swiftness. He didn't have an opportunity to consider his bow, or his sword, or anything besides getting out of the way. Hule must have been quicker on the uptake, for Durren heard the clunk of metal striking a resisting surface. An instant later, the fighter was tumbling past, to crash with a grunt against the wall.

Durren found himself nocking an arrow, for all that he knew he should be running. His hands had decided to act on their own accord. He couldn't imagine what they hoped to achieve—he saw that Hule's sword had accomplished exactly nothing—but he seemed incapable of stopping them. Thankfully, his feet showed more sense; they were carrying him backward with rapid strides. Even then, there remained the unfortunate facts that the room wasn't large enough for him to gain much distance and that the shapeshifter was faster than he could ever be.

With Hule still struggling to his feet, Apaek was coming for Durren. She covered the gap between them in a single bound, and he didn't mean to loose his arrow as he flung himself aside, merely failed to keep his grip on the bowstring, so that he felt only bewilderment when the shaft sliced the air towards the bulk of claws and sinew bearing down on him.

It shattered—and that was the last he saw, for by then he was colliding with the flagstones, pain surging into his shoulder. He realized he'd lost his bow, and couldn't bring himself to care. The weapon was useless, as useless as could be. He believed now with absolute certainty something he'd long surmised: they had survived their fights with Tulpek because he'd let them, and for no other reason. Where he had shown a modicum of mercy, his partner had none. She would tear through them without a thought.

And she'd start by tearing through Durren. For unlike with Hule, she had apparently resolved to finish the job she'd begun. She was still pursuing him, following effortlessly, almost as if she understood his movements before he did. And that wouldn't be difficult, given that Durren had no idea of what he was doing. He was stumbling away, at the same time groping to free his sword from its scabbard with fingers grown suddenly bloated and clumsy. And all the while, he wondered how he would possibly dodge the blow that was coming, the one more likely to rip his head clean from his shoulders.

Magic flared. He was aware of a lurid glow from his left, and of a web of light falling, so bright as to appear almost tangible. The spell was Arein's, of course, and a familiar one: she'd used it against the dead with reasonable success. But the dead had been mere puppets to the creature in front of him, and their own magic had been borrowed—whereas Apaek had the stuff coursing through her blood.

Yet, to Durren's surprise, the spell was working. The shapeshifter's motion was noticeably slowed. If all that really meant was that she was restricted to the same speed as he was, at least he could retreat as rapidly as she was advancing. Durren thought to take advantage of the brief reprieve to try once more with an arrow, before recalling he'd dropped his bow. Instead, he managed to calm himself enough to get his sword drawn, and hastily assumed a defensive stance.

Hule was back on his feet. There was a time when he'd have charged in regardless; now he was warier. He circled, eyes hunting a weak spot that Durren suspected didn't exist. Arein too had drawn nearer, though using another powerful spell so soon after her efforts on the surface had evidently left her weakened. For better or worse, here was their chance to make a stand.

Or perhaps not. "Ignore her," Kyra cried, from behind them. "All that matters is stopping the other one."

Durren would have liked to point out that ignoring Apaek was in no way an option—but maybe Kyra already knew that.

Maybe, in fact, she was simply trying to distract the fiend before she eviscerated him.

Indeed, Apaek immediately forgot about him, to leap towards the center of the chamber—and Durren realized that she *did* have a weakness, albeit a trivially small one. Tulpek was sitting perfectly still, his eyes closed, his face more blank and formless than ever. Only his lips were moving. However, the glow from the Petrified Egg had grown painfully intense, and as Durren concentrated he could perceive another change as well.

His thoughts went to the almost-disastrous transportation spell that had brought them here, and at first his conscious mind couldn't make the connection his unconscious had recognized. Then he understood: if he focused on the Egg and its blinding radiance, he experienced a sense of space that couldn't be explained by the dimensions of the room itself. It was as though the Egg was a window opening by degrees, and through it he glimpsed a place distant beyond imagining.

Moreover, he could feel the excess magic pouring from Tulpek. For all Durren's lack of mystical intuition, he'd have had to be a lump of stone to miss it. The air was growing curdled and strange, as if the gathering forces were on the verge of visibility.

It struck Durren that if he, with his magical tone-deafness, was aware of the power accumulating in this subterranean chamber, then Arein must be overwhelmed. Sure enough, when he glanced her way, her expression was ghastly with distress.

"I think I know what they're doing," she gasped. "And we *have* to stop them, right now." She sounded frantic, more so than he'd ever heard her.

"We work together," Kyra said. She'd hardly raised her

voice, and still each word carried clearly. "If one of us gets through, that's enough."

She didn't need to state her implication: that the death of any of them, or even all of them, was a price worth paying. To her, he supposed that was entirely rational; she was an agent of her people, given a job to do that she was determined to complete at any cost. Maybe he was also ready to die today, if his sacrifice saved lives up there in the world they'd left. But Arein? Tia? Hule? The possibility that his friends might never leave this place was an icicle driven into Durren's guts.

Yet he trusted Arein's instincts, and she was right: time was running out. He didn't want to know what dreadful forces would be unleashed when Tulpek finished his spell. With Apaek no longer intent upon him, Durren snatched up his bow from where he'd dropped it, and was reassured to find that it hadn't suffered; he'd half expected it to have been snapped underfoot.

He nocked an arrow. *We work together*, he echoed in his thoughts. The sentiment felt disappointingly empty. Five buzzing gadflies couldn't sting a lion into submission. Their weapons were meaningless against an enemy with unbreakable skin.

But not against the Egg.

Though the conviction came from nowhere, he didn't question it: already he was lining up his shot, and to his relief he didn't need to tell the others what he intended. Hule chose that moment to strike, swinging a low blow towards the shapeshifter's hip, and Tia and Kyra moved in flawless harmony, knives flickering from their fingers.

Hule's sword did nothing except rebound, with a hollow thud that must have numbed the fighter's arms to the elbows. The knives ricocheted, harmless as snowballs. Yet the attack illustrated one vital point: Apaek wasn't invulnerable, and being compelled to defend herself at least focused her attention.

A fleeting distraction would suffice. Durren had his shot readied. A sensation of rightness came over him when his aim was perfect, as though he were no more than a conduit between arrow and target. He loosed, with no doubt. The arrow sailed true—

Into Apaek's cupped palm.

Her hand had darted out with unimaginable speed. She hadn't even been looking his way. Durren nocked another arrow, but the motion was mere habit. In theory, there was no way Apaek could defend Tulpek alone, regardless of how fast she was, regardless of how strong. In practice, he knew now that he could never defeat the sort of reflexes he'd just seen.

He might really have given up, were it not for Kyra. Maybe she sensed the despair among them; maybe she'd simply decided that she couldn't rely on a bunch of students, and her only choice was to act alone. Whatever the case, she too was fast beyond belief.

In the blink of an eye, she'd closed on Apaek. In another, she was ducking under her guard and scraping a blade across her side. It left not the slightest scratch, but by then Kyra was rolling and flinging up her free hand, and by the time Durren had grasped that she'd thrown something, his ears were being buffeted by the resulting explosion.

A bubble of fire popped in the shapeshifter's face. She reared back with a roar that might have sounded fierce if Durren's ears hadn't been ringing from Kyra's assault: a charge of shock dust, he realized, just like the one her daughter had once used.

Kyra wasn't done. With one palm raised to shield her eyes

from the blast, she was sliding beneath the shapeshifter's outstretched arm, and before her Tulpek sat defenseless, seemingly not even aware.

That should have been the end. Surely Apaek was dazed and deafened and in pain at that moment, and surely that should have dulled her response. Yet somehow she turned and lashed out, and though her blow failed to connect, it forced Kyra to back off. The chance was gone, and their opponent wouldn't fall for the same trick twice.

Still, Kyra's example was an inspiration. Durren saw now that all he needed was for a single arrow to get past Apaek, and he had most of a quiver left. He'd been seeking the perfect shot. Rather, what he needed was luck. And luck could be manufactured, with enough rolls of the die.

He loosed an arrow, just as Hule swung for Apaek's wrist and as Tia flicked a knife towards her throat. While she deflected each attack, the motion wasn't as effortless as on previous occasions. Durren was moving without conscious thought, his body become a mechanism to discover the next shot and the next. He sent three arrows flying in rapid succession. Though not one reached their target, he knew a growing confidence: outwitting Apaek's lightning reflexes wasn't impossible. All they had to do was maintain the pressure until that instant when she was a fraction too slow or diverted in precisely the wrong direction.

But he'd overlooked one detail—the most crucial. She had no reason to play by their rules.

Durren had been keeping his distance. Except for Arein, the others hadn't the same luxury. Nonetheless, even Hule, Tia, and Kyra were showing clear caution. They dashed close and then backed into space. Hule, in particular, was well used to dancing around adversaries larger than himself.

That was his undoing. Durren saw the exact moment in which the fighter forgot what he was up against. Kyra and Tia were in retreat, and Durren was readying his next shot, and abruptly Apaek's entire concentration was on Hule. She swiped for him, and instead of ducking, he lifted his buckler to block. He was lucky if the impact didn't shatter every bone in his arm; certainly it must be far greater than he was accustomed to. Hule's shield dipped. And by then her other hand was swooping down—into his chest.

Hule's breastplate might as well have been cut from paper. He gave an astonished grunt, and his sword slipped from his grasp, to land with a clatter. He stared at the fingers penetrating his flesh, as though he couldn't account for their presence. His eyes and mouth were both open very wide. His legs were bowed, as if he'd become suddenly drunk.

Apaek withdrew her hand. It was all that had been holding Hule up. Released, he slid limply to the ground.

Chapter 21

Durren could only watch. He had an arrow ready, but what could one arrow accomplish where the rest had failed? He saw that same doubt on the faces of the others: Hule was about to die, and there was nothing any of them could do.

Apaek was crouched over him. The claws of her right hand glistened wetly. Despite her former urgency, it occurred to Durren that she was savoring this moment. Their blows had glanced off her iron skin; what was to say they hadn't hurt? He sensed her resentment, and her pleasure at Hule's fear.

Without warning, or change in her vacant expression, her hand began to fall. Down her clawed fingers plunged, torchlight glinting from their points and from the still-wet blood there—until they stopped, twitching, like snakes frantic to bury their fangs.

Durren had not seen Tulpek move, hadn't realized he was aware of anything beyond his ritual. Yet somehow he'd crossed the space to Apaek, and now he gripped her wrist.

"This isn't what we do," he growled. "Not killing children."

Apaek's reaction seemed almost unthinking. "Weak," she spat—and with a slap of her free hand, she hurled him from her.

The clout was enough to carry Tulpek through the air, and to smash him down upon one of the low pedestals arranged around the room. His weight was such that the stone splintered, tumbling in jagged shards. Apaek considered him with vague interest, as if not quite able to recall the sequence of events that had left him lying amid shattered rubble, dark ichor already dripping on the flagstones. Maybe she hadn't known her own strength. Maybe in that moment her rage had outbalanced everything, even this plan she'd labored over for months or years or centuries.

At any rate, whether because Tulpek had lowered his guard or because a shapeshifter's defenses didn't extend to their own kind, he was bleeding copiously from five deep gashes. And though he still held the Egg, its light was dimming; again it resembled a mere curio, rather than a window onto some inconceivable other place.

Arein was running towards Tulpek. Durren had no idea what she intended, and he hardly cared—not when Hule was severely injured and at Apaek's mercy. He edged closer, arrow at the ready. Probably the best he could manage would be to buy Hule a few seconds more of life, but he had to at least try.

Yet now Apaek's attention was turned away from the downed fighter. Nor was she looking at Durren, nor at Tulpek, where he lay sprawled and bleeding—though that was the direction of her scrutiny. In spite of himself, Durren couldn't resist following her gaze.

Arein had propped her staff against a column, so as to free

both hands. In her left was the Petrified Egg. In her right was what Durren initially took for a weapon of some sort: a curling spike of lustrous ivory as long as her forearm. Then he understood. The pedestal that Tulpek's fall had fractured was the same one Durren had noted when he'd entered. What Arein wielded was the severed horn of a unicorn.

Did she mean to fight? No, he saw where she was looking—and felt a tightening in his chest. Her eyes were on him. He could read her intention there, as clearly as if she were speaking. He relaxed his bowstring, slipped the arrow into its quiver, and slung his bow over his shoulder.

As Apaek strode towards her, Arein tensed. Durren had never seen her throw, but he was familiar with her habitual clumsiness. He was prepared to dart across to her, even to fling himself in a desperate catch—so that nothing could have astounded him more than Arein pitching the horn straight and true. Fortunately, she also had the sense not to launch it point first. All that was needed was for Durren to snatch it from the air.

No—the crucial part lay before him. He knew what Arein expected him to do. Normal weapons couldn't so much as mar a shapeshifter's skin. Magical weapons might, if they'd had any, or the time and resources for Arein to perform a suitable enchantment. Maybe, though, they had something every bit as good.

Durren took a step nearer. Apaek should have responded to his presence by now—but Arein had thought of that as well. She was holding the Petrified Egg aloft, and of the two objects, that was the one that fascinated Apaek. Perhaps, to her, the fact that she'd gouged her companion's flesh need not necessarily be the end of their partnership. And who was to say she was wrong? Durren doubted such damage meant much to a being that could reshape itself at will.

That made his decision. With the image clear in his mind of Tulpek recovered and tearing the Petrified Egg from Arein's hands, set on finishing what he'd started, Durren dashed after the female shapeshifter—who in turn was closing upon Arein. He clasped the unicorn's horn about its middle and cupped his other hand beneath its severed end, the roughness there a reminder of just what these monsters were willing to do.

They'd mutilated a unicorn. They'd dragged the dead from their graves. They had stolen and lied and manipulated.

Still, Durren felt only dismay as he drove the horn into Apaek's side.

Unlike Hule's sword, unlike his own arrows and Tia's knives, it plunged through her flesh effortlessly. All that prevented the wound from being deeper was that, in the first shock of her pain, Apaek twisted the improvised lance from Durren's grasp. Then he was dodging aside, as her claws slashed above his head, and as she screamed her fury at him. He might have injured her, but she would surely kill him in return.

"Over here," Arein cried.

Her voice was so resolute that there was no choice besides to look: not for Durren and not for the shapeshifter. Arein gripped the Egg in one hand, her staff in the other. Her expression was bleak. And no wonder, Durren thought. She had always been afraid of abusing magic, and now she had access to a level of power most wizards would go their entire lives only dreaming of.

Though Durren could see her lips moving, she made no gestures. Perhaps there wasn't any need when the magic was so close and so potent. Already Apaek was lurching towards her, fangs bared. The horn piercing her side kept her from reaching Arein in a single bound, yet still she'd be on her in a moment.

However, she'd barely covered half the distance before Arein unleashed her spell.

Durren recognized the beginnings of the same magical bolt she'd used twice against the dead. But this was of a different order of magnitude. He felt its crackle from where he was, as if the air itself was becoming charged. He wanted to duck or to hide, even as he knew that neither could possibly guarantee him safety.

The spell formed sparking at the tip of Arein's staff. It was like a wild creature, writhing to be free. Nonetheless, Arein held it there until Durren could no longer believe that so much energy could be contained by anything as paltry as a wizard's determination.

Then she let go.

On past occasions the bolts had been erratic, choosing their course seemingly at random. This one shot straight, as if it were lightning drawn to a rod. Yet the target it sought was not metal but bone: the horn that jutted from the shapeshifter's side.

There, the spell detonated. For an instant, Apaek glowed from within like a paper lantern. Even a body made fluid by magic couldn't hope to absorb such force; the rest dissipated in ragged flashes that arced like shooting stars. Some carved scars in the floor. Others cratered the ceiling. A couple smashed cleanly through supporting columns, which might have been built of fragile pottery rather than of massive, ancient blocks for all the resistance they offered.

The sound of those impacts was so vast that Durren felt it must have been audible far above upon the surface. He imagined the intervening rock vibrating, just as the slabs beneath his feet were. It was as though stone had become water and Arein's spell was a pebble cast into its depths, transmitting ripples that grew and grew.

If that hadn't been enough to shake the chamber to its foundations, Arein flinging the Petrified Egg against the wall certainly was.

They'd never managed to establish precisely what the Egg was. As he watched its destruction, Durren felt he had some idea. A shapeshifter relic, to be sure, something they'd made or found in ages ancient beyond record; a repository of power, kept as insurance for a day when power might be sorely needed. Witnessing its demise, he was suddenly convinced that it had been alive in its own strange way—perhaps even a real egg, once. Yet all it birthed now was dazzling violet light, a screech on the threshold of hearing, and at the last an impression that space itself might buckle, as if the world were flaking parchment and a nail had been hammered into its skin.

The chamber had not stopped shuddering. Durren's senses were nearly useless: he was practically deaf, and blinded by the powdered mortar that rose in clouds and turned the torchlight ruddy. Worse, he was persuaded that the sensation was more than after-tremors. The room really was quivering, as though rattled from outside like a dice cup.

He could just discern Arein through the haze, and that she was backing towards the entrance. He couldn't see Tia or her mother, but then, not being seen was what they did. Anyway, it wasn't them Durren had to find. Frantically he scanned the room, his eyes gritty with dust, his view buffeted as the ground continued to shiver.

And there he was: a prone shape amid the growing gloom. Durren staggered to where Hule lay. A glance revealed that he was in a bad way; the wound in his chest was deep, and there was blood everywhere, in shocking quantities. Under any other circumstances, moving him would have been the worst course imaginable. Right now, it beat leaving him to be buried alive. Durren caught Hule's arm, draped it over his own shoulders and hauled him to his feet, and Hule released an awful, gurgling moan.

Durren ignored him. If he thought about the pain the fighter was enduring, he'd never be able to do what he needed to. "Come on," he muttered between clenched teeth. "I can't carry you, Hule."

He didn't expect a response. But he got one. As Durren took a reeling first step, Hule matched it with an ungainly stumble of his own.

"That's good," Durren encouraged, "keep going."

They passed through the archway. Abruptly, Durren realized that Kyra and Tia were beside him, and Arein was ahead. The passage seemed very long indeed—and very unstable. The dust was equally as thick here, not only billowing from behind but pouring from the ceiling. It was accompanied in places by chips of stone, large enough to be fatal for anyone caught beneath. And the devastation was rapidly worsening, as if these ruins were shaking themselves awake from an ages-long slumber.

Tia caught Hule's other arm and hoisted it onto her shoulders. Hule gasped, without lessening his pace. He was matching Durren step for step, and somehow even coordinating with Tia as well.

They were still being too slow. Close at their heels came a scream of wrath, entirely inhuman, and Durren knew it was Apaek, knew that all that remained to her was revenge on those who'd utterly destroyed her plans. He could hear the thunder of her feet upon the flagstones, and that she drew nearer with each choked breath he took.

As the rest of them sought to hurry, Kyra hesitated. "Whatever you have left," she cried over the clamor of pulverized masonry, "now's the time." By way of example, she threw another small globe, which exploded in a gout of flame before the shapeshifter's face.

But none of them had anything. Durren wasn't about to drop Hule to free his bow, and Arein perhaps wouldn't have used more magic if she could have, while Tia was carrying her lantern in her free hand, its pale light all they had to see by.

Then the ground heaved with fresh violence. Durren faltered; only the fact that he, Hule, and Tia were entangled kept him upright. He felt as if he were trying to walk on waves that swelled with his each clumsy step. The sound that overwhelmed his ears was catastrophic. Nor did it pass, instead subsiding to a bone-rattling rumble.

When he looked back, the passage was gone. There was no separation between walls and roof and floor, just a single, bulging mass of cracked stone and black earth.

And Apaek? Maybe she was beneath those shattered blocks. Maybe she was alive on the other side. Whatever the case, she wouldn't be coming after them. Which meant all they had to do if they wanted to survive was get out of these ruins while they still could. Put that way, it was almost simple.

They made the end of the passage. Any sense of accomplishment died when Durren saw the lifting platform. He had nearly forgotten its existence, and what a huge distance remained between them and safety. Nevertheless, with Tia's help he hoisted Hule aboard. Kyra glanced around to make certain everyone was on the platform and then turned the controlling wheel. The first judder of motion was lost in the turbulence of the earth about them.

As Tia set her lantern next to Hule, all of them crouched around him. Durren saw Arein to his right, her eyes wide and glistening.

"Can you do anything for him?" he asked.

She snuffled away her impending tears and gave a hesitant nod. "I've a scrap of the Egg's magic left."

She bent forward, hovered her hands near to Hule's chest, and began to mumble.

Durren turned his attention to the platform itself. They were rising so slowly, and they had so little time left. Rocks were plummeting from above, and the damage they inflicted only spread, as the walls weakened with each percussion. One clipped the platform's edge, carving a ragged hole large as a barrelhead. Sooner or later, and probably sooner, everything would come tumbling down.

They were perhaps halfway up the shaft now. By the light of Tia's lantern, Durren could dimly make out the summit. He tried to understand the mechanism that was elevating them by such sluggish degrees. Piecing together glimpses of ropes and counterweights and pulleys, his gaze was drawn to one of the three cords that ran beside them, taut with the strain of their ascent.

Not daring to question himself, Durren readied his bow and took aim. He knew the risk he was preparing to take. He also knew that they didn't stand a chance as they were. One impact in the wrong place and this entire tower would be in splinters. None of the others were looking at him, which was for the best, because he couldn't possibly have justified his instincts in words. However, he was reassured to see that Arein was completing her spell, the glow that lit her outstretched hands seeping into Hule's torn flesh. And fortunately they were all already kneeling, close to the center of the platform. That would have to be enough.

"Hang on!" he roared over the surrounding chaos.

Up or down, his thoughts chimed idiotically as his fingers parted, *up or—*

They went up.

They went up *fast*.

Far too late, it occurred to Durren that there might be a reason the platform had been designed to ascend at a steady rate, and that maybe the reason had something to do with not being shaken to pieces. He could hear the timbers straining and splitting even over the wider chorus of destruction.

But he only had a moment to worry. Before the tower could collapse, they had reached its apex, with a lurch and a shudder that threatened to turn his innards to stew. Though Durren could scarcely tell up from down or left from right, he caught hold of Hule, determined to get him off the platform while there remained a platform to get off. Together they reeled onto the spiraling ledge—and nearly crashed into the figure there.

"We found you!" Caille gasped, in a tone that implied he'd long since given up any real hope of doing so.

There were three more students with him, also clerics. They looked harried and scared and greatly relieved that they wouldn't be required to descend any deeper. Durren put aside his curiosity as to who they were and how Caille had persuaded them to place themselves in mortal danger. Introductions were going to have to wait.

He was about to start off again with Hule, though he couldn't imagine how he'd support the fighter's bulk much farther, when Caille nudged him out of the way and slid under Hule's outstretched arm. Following his lead, another of the students took Tia's spot at Hule's other side. A third proffered herself to Kyra, whose expression was set in a stubborn mask that failed to hide the pain beneath. Durren expected her to reject them, and was gratified when she allowed the young cleric to slip an arm around her shoulders.

Then they were moving. Durren almost missed Hule's presence; at least he'd had an excuse to slacken his pace. Alone, he could only press on to the very limits of his endurance. He ran until his legs were numb. He ran until every muscle was filled with fire, which grew hottest at the core of him, where his heart burned and his lungs blazed. He ran until he could hardly remember why he was running, could hardly believe that being crushed by falling masonry would be a worse torment. More than once he tripped over carelessly piled bones, and was aware that these were the last stragglers of the dead, and that they would never be returned to their old graves. They'd be interred here for all eternity—and if he didn't keep going, so would he be.

The slope came to an end with such suddenness that, had it not been for Tia's sharper eyes, Durren might have stumbled off the sheer drop that marked its conclusion. He followed her into the narrow passage, and found that there was barely space for their extended group to cram in together. He didn't care. Because, despite the clouds of dust that poured in from behind them, he could taste the freshness of night air, and nothing could have done more to renew his strength. As he reached the stairs, he no longer felt tired at all; he dashed up them two at a time.

Yet when he finally bounded up the last step, with the sounds of the ruins' destruction pummeling his ears, Durren stopped with a jolt. Around him, the others did the same. Caille and his cleric friends seemed equally startled by the sight before them.

A crowd were gathered in the darkness, spread in a curving line, many of them carrying lanterns and sputtering torches. Durren saw that he was looking at students, Shadow Mountain students: a force consisting predominantly of clerics and paladins to judge by their outfits, and entirely of the most experienced, if the aura of self-assurance they projected was to be believed. Above their heads, a half-dozen observers flitted back and forth.

At the center of the group stood Murta Krieg, staff in hand.

Durren wouldn't have dreamed he could be so pleased to see her. Even if she was too late, even if realistically her being here only meant more trouble, still, he'd taken about as much responsibility as he could bear to take. She could punish him in whatever ways she could devise, as long as he wasn't required to move or to think.

He was almost disappointed to discover that Krieg had different priorities. The first words from her mouth were, "The woman...the dun-elf. I have questions she needs to answer. Make sure she doesn't go anywhere."

The students nearest to her regarded each other hesitantly. Then three of them marched towards Tia, who tensed to stand her ground.

"No," Krieg barked, "the *woman*—"

Belatedly she realized what her students already had. Kyra Locke was gone. Somehow, in the seconds since they'd left the ruins, she'd managed to slip away, break through the encircling line, and vanish into the night.

Durren looked to Tia, expecting to find sorrow or worry for her mother in her face. But Tia only appeared defiant. He wondered if the two had shared any parting words and decided he would probably never know. The Locke family weren't ones to share their secrets.

Krieg had come closer. Her gaze roved across them, noting their dust-caked clothes and settling on Hule's wound. "The shapeshifters?" she inquired—and her tone was, if not gentle, at least not openly admonitory.

"Dead," Arein said. "We think."

"We hope," Durren added.

"We'll stay here," Krieg announced to her retinue—and it was obvious she was planning as she spoke. "We'll wait to make certain nothing crawls out of those ruins, and in the morning we'll begin to bury them. This place will be just another nameless hill by the time we're done."

There was anger in her voice, but Durren couldn't have said where it was aimed; at them, at the shapeshifters or, conceivably, at herself, for letting a task that should have been hers fall to four lowly students.

Then again, maybe Durren was only placing his own thoughts into her head, and Krieg was angry because anger was what came naturally to her. Really, it didn't much matter. "What about us?" he asked. "Whatever you're doing, our friend needs help."

Krieg looked ready to snap the sort of hostile response he was anticipating. At the last she caught herself, waved over two of the clerics, and pointed to Hule. "Do your best," she instructed. "I need him prepared for urgent transportation."

Durren wanted to say, *And show some respect, he nearly gave up his life fighting to protect you and everyone in this miserable backwater.* But he lacked the strength for antagonism, and his concern for Hule was infinitely greater. Anyway, it was clear the clerics Krieg had picked knew their business: barely had they reached the fighter than they'd begun their healing spells. A minute later and, while Hule still looked ghastly, his eyes were no longer so frighteningly glazed and dull.

As they finished up, Tia called to Krieg, who'd spent the meantime arranging her students into a perimeter around what was left of the ruins. "I suppose this is where you arrest us again?"

Krieg turned her way. "You'll go back to Shadow Mountain, yes. And yes, I'll be keeping a close watch on you until I'm satisfied I know each detail of what went on tonight. Perhaps, though, you should view the time as a well-earned rest rather than a punishment."

All Durren had taken from her speech was that one word, *rest*; the remainder was a nonsensical jumble. Glancing about for Pootle, he saw that even the observer was sagging, as if floating was an exertion instead of its natural state.

"Come on, Pootle," he said, "let's get out of here."

Moments had passed before he recalled that transportation spells didn't work that way. To his further shock, he realized he couldn't remember the incantation he'd spoken and heard so very many times now. A black ocean of tiredness filled the space where such vital information had once been.

Fortunately, Tia was more resilient. "Homily, paradigm, lucent," she said.

Only as the night began to dissolve around him did Durren understand that their ordeal was over—and that somehow they'd survived.

Chapter 22

Just as Krieg had said, their treatment at Shadow Mountain proved a great deal better than being locked in an empty storeroom.

Upon their return, they were hurried to the infirmary. Apart from Hule—who'd been rushed on ahead by two burly students bearing a stretcher between them—they were allowed to wash, their worst cuts and bruises were salved and bandaged, and then they were loaned fresh clothes that weren't gray with accumulated dust. Afterward, Durren, Arein, and Tia were escorted to rooms that Durren guessed belonged to one of the tutors; a scout, to judge by the spartan furnishings. Extra beds had been brought in, and in the morning there was a breakfast ready, the quantity sufficient for the tremendous appetite they'd all developed during the night.

Krieg came back late that morning, and their questioning began. However, the first thing she did was assure them that Hule was safe and well. The diagnosis from the infirmary was that he'd suffered no damage that wouldn't heal, though he'd be left with an extraordinary scar. Durren suspected that wouldn't bother the fighter unduly; in fact, he could already hear Hule bragging and embellishing the story of how he'd received it.

Even with that formality out of the way, Krieg's manner was markedly less confrontational than on their previous encounters. Her main interest was in the shapeshifters, and in the ritual they'd attempted to complete. From what Durren could gather, Pootle had only transmitted a few fractured images from the point they'd entered the ruins' lowest level, its perspective no doubt distorted by the unprecedented quantities of magic.

Durren eventually began to appreciate that, beneath all of Krieg's interrogation, a single concern was paramount—one she never quite put it into words. She wanted to know whether the threat that had festered in Ursvaal was truly eradicated. And to that, regrettably, none of them had any honest answer.

"I believe I've learned everything there is to learn here," the Head Tutor declared, perhaps an hour later. "I'm grateful for your candidness, even if I'd rather we needn't had to have this conversation."

She sighed, and for an instant Durren glimpsed the weariness of a woman who'd been up all night, and probably hadn't slept soundly for a good while longer than that.

"You understand, of course, that you won't be able to continue at Shadow Mountain. I've already written to Head Tutor Borgnin advising him to expect you. Your results warrant gratitude, but the number of rules you broke to achieve them would be cause for expulsion a dozen times over."

Durren's thoughts went to Caille and to the other students

who'd helped them. He hoped her harsh judgment didn't extend to them as well.

"Needless to say, you'll be free to stay until your paladin is fit to travel. And you may return to your own dormitories now. I see no use in restricting your movements—if only since, thus far, you've resisted my best efforts to do so. If you wish to attend classes, you can."

With that, Krieg turned towards the door. She hadn't taken a step before Tia's voice rang out. "I have a question of my own," she said.

Krieg tensed, and Durren noticed then that she'd carefully kept away from the subject of Kyra Locke—whose identity, perhaps, she'd begun to guess. "Yes?"

There was a fierce directness in Tia's eyes that Durren had long ago grown familiar with. If he were in Krieg's place, he'd be distinctly nervous—and with that thought, pride coursed through him. One thing was for sure, he was glad Tia was on his side.

Yet what she asked wasn't at all what he might have expected. "Did Head Tutor Borgnin send us here because he knew this was where the shapeshifters would be?" she said.

Krieg remained perfectly still, and her expression revealed nothing. Finally she replied, "I couldn't possibly comment on what my counterpart would or wouldn't do. Our approaches are certainly very different." She paused to consider. "All I can say is that, if such were the case, while I would have to disapprove, I'd also conclude that your Head Tutor has a great deal of faith in the four of you."

After their interview with Krieg, Durren, Tia, and Arein went their separate ways, mumbling goodbyes and promising to meet up later to check on Hule.

Durren wandered back to the bards' dormitory, feeling fuzzy and light-headed. Sleep and food had not done much to dispel the memories of the previous night, and each few steps an image would rear up in his mind, so vivid as to nearly stop him in his tracks: the female shapeshifter as she changed from one monstrous form to another; the otherworldly glimpses the Petrified Egg had produced; the sight of the walls scudding past with obscene speed as the lifting platform shot upward. More than ever before, he felt he'd had enough excitement to last him for a lifetime.

He went to his lectures that afternoon, and was grateful for how dull they were. One was on music, and Durren actually enjoyed that; he concentrated hard on learning the new song he was introduced to, and only afterward understood that his uncharacteristic focus was because he knew Arein would like the tune.

In the dining hall, he tried not to court attention—and was faintly disappointed when he didn't receive any. If this had been Black River, he'd have had to fend off inquiries from every corner. But rumor didn't spread so easily or quickly at Shadow Mountain, and no-one treated him with greater interest than they ever had.

That night in the dormitory, Durren was somewhat more aware of eyes upon him. Then again, maybe they were merely noting the multitude of cuts, abrasions, and bruises that adorned almost the entirety of his body and face. He'd expected to sleep well, for he was no less exhausted than on the night before; instead, he found himself tossing and turning in the darkness, no longer remotely tired. All the turmoil and fear of their hours within the ruins had come back as shapeless panic, and whenever sleep encroached he would find himself remembering, or else misremembering: in his half-formed dreams, they failed to save Hule, failed to break the Petrified Egg, failed to discover a way to defeat the shapeshifters. His unconscious mind tormented him with impossible demands and futile terrors, and he was helpless.

By the afternoon of the next day, he'd realized to his relief that what he'd endured had been like the breaking of a fever. After so long spent running and fighting and worrying and doubting, his mind had needed time to accept that their conflict with the shapeshifters was truly over.

Now that he had, he tried to fixate on his imminent return to Black River. But whenever he looked forward to the day, his thoughts would go back to Tia's question and Krieg's answer, and he began to wonder about matters that were surely better off not pondered. Had Borgnin really sent them here in pursuit of the shapeshifters? If so, why all the secrecy? Had he envisaged the possibility, as they had, that Shadow Mountain might have been infiltrated? Had he also surmised Kyra Locke's identity, and that she'd found her way to Ursvaal? Each time, Durren had to remind himself that these were pointless conundrums: he'd dealt with Borgnin enough to know that answers would probably never be forthcoming.

While they waited for Hule to be released from the infirmary, Durren's life largely went on as normal. Or rather, something more sedate than normal, as—recognizing that he wouldn't be rushing off on any further quests—he started to allow himself to recover. And he enjoyed himself. There was a freedom in knowing his stay at Shadow Mountain was soon to end: he felt he learned more in those few days than in all of the preceding weeks.

Every evening he'd check in on Hule. Despite his apparent good cheer, the fighter was clearly in significant pain, especially for the first day or two. By degrees, Durren came to understand just how close Hule's brush with death had been. Had a claw penetrated even a little farther, he most likely wouldn't be here now. But there was no use in thinking like that; Hule was alive, and steadily he was recuperating.

In the meantime, Durren was conscious that he hadn't seen Caille since their flight from the ruins. He went looking once or twice, hoping to thank him, but the cleric wasn't in his dormitory and no-one seemed certain where he could be found.

Then the day came when Hule was discharged, a message came for them to gather with their equipment outside the transportation chamber—and to Durren's surprise, there was Caille. He appeared as shocked to see them as they were him. In answer to their inquiring looks, he explained, "I was told to wait here."

"Where have you been all this while?" Durren asked.

The cleric scowled. "Where have I been? I've been working, morning, noon, and night."

He wasted no time in filling them in on his misfortunes since their return. If anything, Caille had been reprimanded more harshly than they had. He'd set out minutes before Krieg and her party, without permission and with only an inkling that she would follow, thereby breaking no end of academy rules. For all that, Durren suspected the punishment Krieg had set Caille was more for show than out of genuine malice: for a month he'd be guaranteed double duties on the most unpleasant tasks around the academy, and he was barred from questing until the remainder of his party were fully recovered.

"We're really sorry," Arein said. "We never meant to get

you into trouble."

Caille let out a resigned sigh. "You didn't, I got myself into trouble. And honestly, it's not so bad; a few dirty jobs aren't the end of the world." He smiled. "As for questing, you four have set my expectations too high anyway. From now on, any mission without a brush with death or two is going to be a disappointment."

"Thank you for everything you did," Durren said earnestly. "You took a huge risk for us."

"And," Tia added, "you probably saved my mother's life."

"If you ever need us," Arein put in, "you know where we are. As far as I'm concerned, you'll always be a member of our party."

Did Caille look a little moist-eyed at that? If he did, all he said was, "You'd better get going. Gallowpall hates to be kept waiting."

After the amateurish transfer spell conducted by Caille's fellow cleric, their return to Black River seemed practically ordinary, as though there was nothing at all odd about inhabiting two places at once. Durren knew the instant they'd arrived, as his senses registered a dozen tiny details he could never have knowingly identified, but that belonged uniquely to Black River. There was a certain combination of smells, even a taste to the air and a texture to the flagstones underfoot, that assured him he was home at last.

Durren had thought Borgnin might be there to greet them. Yet in the transportation chamber was only Hieronymus, who gave no impression of being aware that they'd been absent. At any rate, his manner was as indifferent as ever.

However, Durren barely had time to drop off his gear in

the rangers' dormitory—and to bask briefly in the comfort of its familiar surroundings—before a summons to the Head Tutor's office came for him, conveyed by a harried-looking student.

A couple of turns from Borgnin's office, Durren spied Hule ahead. He couldn't fail to note how stiffly the big fighter was moving; he might be back on his feet, but he was a long way from being his old self. As he caught up, Durren noticed something else: Hule's tunic and the design there, a simple, jagged flash cut from gold cloth.

"You're keeping that, then?"

Hule scratched his chin self-consciously. "I thought it would be a reminder...in case I forget that being a fighter can mean more than just hitting and stabbing." Hule's gaze settled on what Durren carried over one shoulder. "And you're keeping *that?*"

Durren realized he'd neglected to leave his lute with the rest of his belongings. "I suppose I've got used to it being there," he said. Vehemently he added, "But I'm definitely not calling myself a bard anymore."

Hule laughed. "I don't blame you."

Tia and Arein were already outside Borgnin's office. The four of them trooped in together, as Durren and Arein exchanged an anxious glance. Only now was it occurring to him that Borgnin might not consider their spell at Ursvaal an unmitigated success—especially since all the details he was likely to have heard would have come from Krieg.

Sure enough, Borgnin's demeanor was serious to the point of severity. "Welcome back to Black River," he addressed them. "I trust your time away was productive?"

You could certainly say that, Durren thought.

It was left to Arein to answer, "We hope so, Head Tutor."

"I'm glad," Borgnin replied, though he didn't particularly sound glad. Distractedly he observed, "Experience is crucial in adventuring. I've no doubt that everything you've learned will have its value."

As usual, Borgnin's desk was busy with books and scrolls. He placed the fingers of his left hand upon one of the latter, unfurled the sheet of paper, and said, "I've been looking over your report from Head Tutor Krieg. My counterpart assures me that the four of you helped resolve a matter of grave consequence, and praises your courage in doing so."

The frown that darkened Borgnin's brows seemed aimed more at the scroll than at them. "Sadly, the remainder of her assessment is less encouraging. There are fronts, in fact, upon which Head Tutor Krieg is positively critical—both in regard to your performance and to the teaching methods of this academy."

No wonder Borgnin wasn't in the best of moods. Durren had already concluded that there was history between him and Krieg, and apparently Krieg had seized on this opportunity to land an easy blow. He felt he should apologize, or explain, or even present their side of the story, and couldn't think of a way to do any of those things that wouldn't sound like making excuses.

In any case, Borgnin was speaking again—and his tone had grown downright melancholy. "Unfortunately, Head Tutor Krieg's report doesn't justify my promoting you to level three, as I'd hoped it might. This is disappointing, as many of your peers have made the transition in your absence. Nonetheless, I'd deem myself remiss to raise you to a level you may be unready for."

Durren found that he was waiting with pent breath. Wasn't this where Borgnin acknowledged that, by saving the day and who knew what else, they'd more than earned the right to be classed as level three students?

"Well," the Head Tutor said, "that will be all. Thank you for your hard work and dedication at Shadow Mountain. I'll expect to see both continue now that you're back here with us."

Was that it? *Thank you for your hard work*? Was that really their reward for everything they'd risked and accomplished? Durren was so stunned that he could only trudge out behind Hule, the entirety of his attention required to put one foot before the other.

Yet by the time he was through the door, it had struck him that he didn't care. What did it matter if he should spend a few more weeks as a level two student? Maybe the truth was that he did have a lot left to learn; maybe doing so would allow him to protect these three people he'd come to regard as his friends, and ensure that none of them ever again had a brush with death to match Hule's. If he'd drawn one lesson from his term at Shadow Mountain, it was that he wanted to be the best ranger he could be—whatever that took.

He realized the four of them were still together, even after they'd passed the junction where Tia and Arein would normally have peeled away to head towards their own regions of the academy. Though they were all wrapped up in their thoughts, there was also a heavy sense of things waiting to be said, like a laden cloud following above them.

Tia was the one to break the silence. "Arein," she said, "there's something I've been meaning to ask you. Down in that ritual chamber, you said you had an idea of what the shapeshifters were attempting."

Durren was startled that he hadn't wondered at the same question himself. Perhaps he'd subconsciously decided that not knowing what would have happened if they'd failed was better than comprehending the weight of responsibility they'd taken upon themselves.

Arein's expression said that the topic was one she'd been both anticipating and fearing. Somberly she answered, "I think they were trying to force open the unbalance. I think maybe they wanted to pass through to the other side."

For the second time in as many minutes, Durren was stunned. While he'd understood the individual words and could piece them together and knew they were important, the actual meaning refused to coalesce in his mind.

"Is that even possible?" Tia asked.

"There are theories," Arein replied hesitantly. "But then, that's magic, there are always a hundred theories about every subject. Certainly some people believe the unbalance is an opening onto a place—a reality—where *everything* is magical. Viewed like that, perhaps the breach could be widened into a door, at least for an instant."

"Why would anyone imagine that was a good idea?" Durren asked, aghast. Yet he already had an inkling of what her answer might be, and so he pre-empted it. "You think they were trying to escape?"

"If I'm right then—yes, that would make sense." Arein paused, a shadow of doubt passing behind her eyes. "In a way, you can't blame them. Magic is such a part of what they are that they belong as much to the unbalance as to our world. And as long as they were here, they'd always be hated and hunted."

"What would have happened if they'd succeeded?" Tia said. Her tone made clear that she was far from being ready to sympathize with the shapeshifters and their plight.

Arein's shrug seemed to extend to her whole body. "I couldn't begin to guess. Maybe everything everywhere would have been destroyed. Maybe there'd just have been a lot more magic floating around for a while. Or maybe nothing much at all. And it's really only a hypothesis. I was sure at the time; but thinking back, it's hard to believe."

"We stopped them," Hule cut in. "What does the rest matter?"

"We stopped them," Arein agreed. "You're right, Hule, probably it doesn't."

Hule looked suspicious. "*Probably?*"

"Well…there's a principle in magic that says that ideas never go away. Once someone's thought of a concept, there's a higher chance somebody else will too. And shapeshifters are hardly the only magical creatures in the world." She brightened. "Most likely that's just me worrying over nothing. Anyway, I should be getting back."

With that and a brisk wave, Arein vanished into an adjoining passage that led towards the wizards' wing.

Hule watched her go. "You know," he said, "sometimes I wish she wouldn't tell us these things." He gave a sigh that said more eloquently than words could, *but then she wouldn't be Arein*, and started in the opposite direction.

That left Durren and Tia. They were closer to the rangers' wing than that of the rogues, and Durren was conscious that Tia should have begun heading for her own section of the academy by now. Since she hadn't, he kept going. Obviously there was something on her mind, but if she meant to come out and say it, she'd have done so already.

As a prompt, he decided to return to the subject that Tia's

question and Arein's explanation had distracted him from. "I'm surprised what Borgnin said didn't bother you more; about us not leveling up, that is. There was a time not so long ago when you'd have been furious."

"I suppose I'm in a good mood." Without slowing, Tia took from a pocket a tight square of paper, which she held up and carefully unfolded.

The letter was brief, and rather than the curving alphabet of Central, the symbols consisted of clusters of dots and short lines. That, along with Tia's evident pleasure, was all the clue he needed to deduce who the sender was.

"Your mother wrote to you," he said.

Tia nodded. "This arrived just before we left Shadow Mountain. It says she's safe, and that she's traveling to Sudra Syn to deliver her report. And that, if I go back, she'll be there waiting."

"And—will you?" Durren tried to keep a tremor from his voice, even as his thoughts assured him that of course she would. Hadn't she only come to Black River hunting her mother's trail, and what could she hope to learn here? Hadn't she only sought advancement to gain access to the resources that higher levels would offer? She was as gifted a rogue as half of her tutors, and quite as capable as those two or three levels above her.

"She also writes," Tia said, "that she thinks I have a lot left to learn."

Staggered by her apparent calm, Durren managed to mumble, "Did she?"

"Yes. She says my skills need refining."

"Perhaps," Durren attempted, "she believes you're better off away from home for the moment? I mean—" But he didn't dare finish his sentence, and suggest that at Black River she could avoid being sucked into the murky waters of dun-elf politics that had so consumed her mother's life.

Then again, Tia's face told him that he wasn't thinking anything she hadn't already contemplated. "I've decided to stay at least a little while longer and weigh my options. After all, I'm not sure how you three would cope without me."

Probably, Durren reflected, there'd be a lot less sneaking into places we weren't meant to sneak into, and attacking people we weren't meant to attack, and generally doing things we'd been specifically instructed not to do. But all he said was, "You might be right."

"Well. Until the next time." Tia turned aside. By the nearest corner, she was matching her steps to the shadows; even in a rare good mood, Tia remained a rogue down to her very bones.

Durren had intended to go straight to the dormitory and unpack. Instead, his feet carried him in an unanticipated direction, up out-of-the-way staircases and down unfamiliar passages. He was driven by an urge he could scarcely explain— except that, now that he was back, he wanted to see Black River properly.

So when he came out on the roofs, he wasn't entirely surprised. More, he knew roughly where he was, a consequence of having spent too much time with Arlo Mainbrow, whose obsession with Black River's labyrinthine architecture was as thorough as it was baffling. From the railed ledge Durren had arrived on, he could see the various wings and towers and steeples, and a glimpse of the yard and walls below.

The air was cool and a biting breeze blew, but after his spell in Ursvaal, Durren barely felt the cold. He found his gaze drifting past the boundaries of the academy, over the forest, towards where rising columns of smoke marked the small trade town of Olgen. In his mind's eye, he saw farther still. Somewhere out there was Luntharbor, city of his birth, and beyond it the Middlesea, and beyond that the southern continent and Sudra Syn, among other distant lands.

Durren realized that the world seemed a great deal bigger than it had only weeks before—bigger and stranger. Given what Arein had told them, it seemed more dangerous too. He'd have liked to suppose that so far they'd just been unlucky, facing dire threats the likes of which they'd never encounter again. Somehow, though, he couldn't persuade himself.

Yet he wasn't afraid, or even particularly worried. Together, the four of them had managed. He had to believe they would again.

A sudden insight occurred to him, like a burst of understanding, as a process that had been dawdling in the back of his mind came unexpectedly to the fore. In that moment of staring at the world, he'd heard a series of notes quite clearly in his head. It was the bridge to "Dance of the Moonflies", which he'd been trying and failing to get right for days. Now he had it: something had clicked.

Durren started towards the rangers' dormitory, lute in hand. If he practiced, really practiced, perhaps he could have the song ready in time for their next quest.

Thank You!

Thank you for reading our book and for supporting stories of fiction in the written form. Please consider leaving a reader review on Amazon and Goodreads, so that others can make an informed reading decision.

Find more exceptional stories, novels, collections, and anthologies on our website at:
digitalfictionpub.com

Join the **Digital Fiction Pub** newsletter for infrequent updates, new release discounts, and more. Subscribe at:
digitalfictionpub.com/blog/newsletter/

See all our exciting fantasy, horror, crime, romance and science fiction books, short stories and anthologies on our **Amazon Author Page** at:
amazon.com/author/digitalfiction

Also by David Tallerman

Patchwerk

The Black River Chronicles
Level One

The Tales of Easie Damasco Trilogy
Giant Thief
Crown Thief
Prince Thief

Collected Short Fiction
The Sign in the Moonlight and Other Stories

About the Author

David Tallerman is the author of the **Tales of Easie Damasco** series - consisting of *Giant Thief*, *Crown Thief* and *Prince Thief* - and the novella **Patchwerk**. His comics work includes the absurdist steampunk graphic novel **Endangered Weapon B: Mechanimal Science** (with Bob Molesworth) and the ongoing miniseries **C21st Gods** (with Anthony Summey).

David's short fiction has appeared in around eighty markets, including Clarkesworld, Nightmare, Alfred Hitchcock Mystery Magazine and Beneath Ceaseless Skies. A number of his best dark fantasy and horror stories were gathered together in his debut collection **The Sign in the Moonlight and Other Stories**.

He can be found online at **davidtallerman.co.uk**.

Copyright

The Black River Chronicles – The Ursvaal Exchange
Written by **David Tallerman**
Executive Editor: Michael A. Wills

DIGITAL FICTION

PUBLISHING CORP

CPSIA information can be obtained
at www.ICGtesting.com
Printed in the USA
LVOW12s1009051217
558599LV00056B/221/P